SO-BFF-366

APR - - 2022

INDIGO HEAVEN

INDIGO HEAVEN

MARK WARREN

THORNDIKE PRESS

A part of Gale, a Cengage Company

Copyright © 2021 by Mark Warren.
Thorndike Press, a part of Gale, a Cengage Company.

ALL RIGHTS RESERVED
This novel is a work of fiction. Names, characters, places, and incidents are either the product of the author's imagination, or, if real, used fictitiously.
The publisher bears no responsibility for the quality of information provided through author or third-party Web sites and does not have any control over, nor assume any responsibility for, information contained in these sites. Providing these sites should not be construed as an endorsement or approval by the publisher of these organizations or of the positions they may take on various issues.

Thorndike Press® Large Print Western.
The text of this Large Print edition is unabridged.
Other aspects of the book may vary from the original edition.
Set in 16 pt. Plantin.

LIBRARY OF CONGRESS CIP DATA ON FILE.
CATALOGUING IN PUBLICATION FOR THIS BOOK
IS AVAILABLE FROM THE LIBRARY OF CONGRESS.

ISBN-13: 978-1-4328-7831-3 (hardcover alk. paper)

Published in 2021 by arrangement with Mark Warren

Printed in Mexico
Print Number: 01   Print Year: 2022

To John Barbour,
my friend

■ ■ ■ ■

SOUTHERN
APPALACHIANS
1860s

■ ■ ■ ■

CHAPTER 1

Even before the war had sucked him into a
life of cruel indifference, young Clayton
Jane had come to understand that the world
held naught but misery. When he was but a
child, the lesson had been made clear not
just by his father but also by the land. Both
were demanding beyond reason and both
fraught with obstacles. Though he had never
met a black man, Clayton understood the
meaning of master and slave. All he lacked
were the manacles and leg-irons.

He was the son of Horace Jane, a Scottish
farmer, who had produced little else but
enemies in his homeland. Upon arriving in
America, Horace took a young, recently
widowed laundress as his wife and plunged
into the still abundant wilderness of the
Blue Ridge in north Georgia. Into this isola-
tion Clayton was born. Raised in a dark and
nameless cove along the Nottely River, the
boy was nine miles from any other home-

stead and fourteen from the village of Hiawassee. Inside the steep walls of these mountains, Clayton might just as well have been stranded in a prison of his father's making.

He seldom saw the faces of outsiders, twice a year if he was lucky. Perhaps a surveyor or a lost peddler. Once it was a sheriff's deputy looking for a man who had killed another over a poker hand in Hiawassee, an idea as abstract to Clayton as the concept of a town.

"Doon't you ever take up the cairds, boy!" Horace Jane decreed after the deputy had left. "There are fifty-two sins in this woorld, and a deck o' cairds holds them all."

The boy squinted at his father, for, whenever the man fell to sermonizing, Horace Jane tightened the knots on his Scottish accent, as if his highlander tongue were better suited for such lessons of morality.

"What are cards?" Clayton asked.

The father removed his briar pipe and spat off the porch. "They're the woork o' the devil, boy. When a man is too lazy to fill his hand with a tool and woork, he picks up the cairds and prays to God for a luck he doon't deserve."

Clayton looked down at his own palms, at the dry skin crisscrossed by dirty crevices

10

and callus. He wondered how those "cairds" would feel in his rough hands. From the time he had been old enough to handle a hoe, he had spent his days working the sloped field, serving his father from sunup to sundown. As he had grown, so had his list of farm chores grown. By the time he had turned eight, his father had strapped him behind the plow mule and inducted him into the rigors of farming meant for someone twice his age.

Now at thirteen, pulling a man's work and then some, Clayton saw the futility of it all. The rocky soil did not willingly yield to plow. The red clay turned over in thick, hefty slabs that had to be sliced again with a shovel. Every buck of the plowshare was like an insult to him, just as it would be to any man who tried to tame the hardscrabble slopes of these mountains.

The farm was perched high on a cruel tilt of land above the coveted black soil of the bottomland, where the rich river silt collected after the spring floods and rendered the soil friable and homogenous. There, only a stone's throw away, the texture of dirt was like something sifted through the velvety fingers of God.

The Jane farm had originally been staked out by a fat, squint-eyed speculator with a specious smile. The survey had included the nutrient-rich floodplain all the way to the river, and there on the low ground Clayton's father had begun to hack out a clearing with a hand axe, as his wife and young child lived in a lean-to. Before he could erect a cabin to finalize his claim on the land, a timber company had somehow won title to the floodplain in a backroom parley in the courthouse at Hiawassee. Unable to hire an attorney, Horace Jane fought for his boundaries with his own Scottish spit and venom, but he was sorely outmatched by the opposing attorney. The judge's decision pushed the Jane family to higher ground and the father into a deeper pit of spite against all men.

The failure in court had not been his only defeat. In that same year, Horace Jane had lost his second son, Clayton's baby brother. The following winter his wife, Clayton's mother, had died.

"A man not boorn into money is created to suffer this woorld."

That was his father's mantra, intoned with a certain melancholy when he worked the field but flung back at God like an unholy curse when he was in his cups. The boy puzzled over the father's devotion to brewing his own whisky. Because he didn't make enough to sell, Horace Jane sealed his own fate and became a drunken martyr who stood alone against the world. As young as he was, Clayton knew his father's drunken stupors were time and energy fatally misdirected.

The boy already understood that his manual labor was penance for all the injustices heaped upon his father. He could have lived off his steady aim with his father's musket rather than the bone-jarring gouge of the plow. If he did wander off and return home with a 'possum or 'coon for the stew pot, his reward was a lashing with a leather strop. Only the mule had it worse.

"You'll lairn soon enow, boy," the besotted father declared one evening from his reeking sty of a bed. "The oonly rewards you reap in this life coom from the sweat o' your oon back. Nae man's gaen' to do your woork for you."

The man seemed born to preach, but now the pedagogical tone meant nothing to Clayton, not on this night when the father had drunk himself into a bleary-eyed torpor. Horace Jane was still an ox of a man with thick nests of black hair matted across his arms, chest, and back, but now he lay sprawled across his rumpled bedding like a fevered child, his only medicine a jug

13

clutched in both hands and balanced on his belly.

"Does that mean you'll be workin' the field alone now?" Clayton dared to say.

Quicker than the boy could have calculated, the father lurched forward and grabbed Clayton by one arm. The man's grip was like iron, and he shook Clayton so violently the boy's bones popped. When he slapped Clayton's face, a mirage floated before the boy's eyes — a flurry of tiny, dark spots moving across his field of vision like charred ash drifting on the air from an open fire.

"You'll doo as I say, by God, and I'll brook nae complaint as loong as you live under me roof!" Horace Jane looked at the jug in his hand as if he had forgotten it was there. Taking a swig, he swallowed and then exhaled in a rush. The stench of the man's breath covered the boy like a foul, damp cloth thrown over his face.

Still trying to recover his vision, Clayton was thrown roughly onto the floor. Tottering like a man crossing a creek on a log, the father struggled for balance as he pointed at the boy.

"You'd be wise to consider your woords about now!"

"I can provide," Clayton replied, his voice

little more than a whisper. "I can! Let me hunt. I can keep meat on the table . . . much as we need."

The man glowered at the boy. "You'll doo as I tell you and woork the fairm."

Clayton's eyes grew moist. "We're gonna die here . . . just like my mother and brother."

The second blow caught him just below the ear and set his skull ringing like a cowbell. Clayton, determined not to give the man the satisfaction of seeing any expression of pain, only glared back at his father's bloodshot eyes.

Horace Jane backed unsteadily toward his bed and lowered himself to the dirty straw mattress. Falling into his former prone position, he perched the jug on his stomach again and closed his eyes.

"I coom to this land to build a fairm, by God," he growled to the ceiling, "and a fairm it will be!"

Of his mother Clayton remembered only the vague visage of a woman with a waterfall of dark-amber hair. If his father was to be believed, she had worshipped her husband until the day she had died. Yet Clayton had to wonder what manner of woman would take up with such a man.

When the war of secession came to the

15

South, Clayton learned the news from a cattle farmer who had contracted with the military. The man was driving his beeves northwest to the stock pens in Chattanooga, and, on the spot, thirteen-year-old Clayton laid down his field tools and hired on as a drover to help manage the herd. Without even a word of parting to his father, he struck out to find a war he barely understood.

CHAPTER 2

He signed on at an enlistment office at the base of Lookout Mountain and buttoned into one of the butternut uniforms salvaged from the dead at Vicksburg. By that time the South wanted *any* of its native sons, no matter his age.

As the recruiter penned the boy's name on his roster, he snorted when Clayton did not lie about his age. "If you can shoulder a musket and march in the footsteps of another man's ghost," the man said with a shrug, "I reckon you'll do juss fine."

At a hundred and six pounds, Clayton was assigned menial tasks: dispensing munitions, caring for livestock, and sometimes carrying a plate of food to an officer's tent. Soon enough, because he showed an affinity for the horses, he came to serve under Forrest and without complaint lived the marauder's life — both deprived and depraved — first tending to the mounts, then,

17

because of his age and size and quiet nature, venturing out as a spy in a costume of rags.

Earning some reputation for his cool demeanor in gaining intelligence amongst the enemy, he gained a soldier's nickname — "Lightfoot," which for him was like a ribbon of honor pinned to his breast. Even Forrest, himself, requested the boy by name for the more pressing forays, when expediency was demanded.

By his final year in the war, Clayton had filled out by some latent miracle of family lineage into a rangy six-footer with broad shoulders and long arms corded with muscle. With this new strength, he became a savage fighter, seeming to take his nourishment from the cannon-scented air, as the men around him thinned to ragged skin and bone on their meager rations.

His spying days behind him, he rode beside men who slashed bloodied sabers and screamed like demons loosed from the gates of hell for the sole purpose of making other men suffer. And as they killed, so did he, too, kill, never acknowledging that the lives he dispatched might eventually become a weight too burdensome to carry. To Clayton that seemed of little importance. He did not expect to survive the war. For that reason, he thought it best to kill as many of the enemy as he could in his allotted time.

His fighting days came to an end at Brice's Crossroads, just seconds after he had committed his most heinous sin against humankind. Charging the enemy by a flanking maneuver with seven other horsemen, Clayton galloped up a low hill in a pasture and routed a unit of infantry, scattering them into a panicked retreat on foot. Riding them down, the cavalrymen hacked down the fleeing enemy one by one.

Approaching one running soldier, Clayton noted how slight the Yankee was. He was just a boy, only half filling his blue coat, its sleeves rolled into thick cuffs at his wrists. A drum was strapped across his shoulder, and it bucked and bobbled on his thighs as he ran. His pant legs made flapping sounds in the tall grass. If only to leave no enemy at his back, Clayton raised his saber, and in that moment the boy looked back, the youth's eyes seeming to ask a question.

The drummer boy was no older than Clayton had been when he had signed up to fight, but that seemed not to matter. The momentum for slaughter was set. The raised arm and the grim blade had its own mind. When the metal flashed and sliced the air with its killing hiss, the boy's head rolled like a melon in the grass and stopped, its eyes staring up into the blue of the sky, as though searching for the angel who would come to take the boy's soul away from all this madness.

Not six yards away a man in blue rose up from a tall stand of cane grass and raised a long musket, its large-bore muzzle like a dark, unblinking eye that had arrived here solely for the purpose of singling Clayton out from all other men on the battlefield. This hatless soldier widened fearful eyes over the sights of his rifle and began screaming in outrage, but the words were lost in the sound of the explosion. A plume of smoke and flame leapt at Clayton as if the door to a furnace had flung open.

The impact of the ball hit him like a sledgehammer, and the muzzle flash temporarily blinded him. Yet Clayton had the presence of mind to accept the moment as an inevitable act of justice. It was all he deserved now, he knew, to be slain just as he had so wantonly slain at every opportunity.

Then all went quiet as he fell from his horse. It was like dropping down a long, dark well. In that moment, he imagined an abyss that had waited for him alone here in this field. His personal entrance to hell. This had been his destiny all along.

As Clayton lay bleeding in the grass, his vision and his hearing slowly came back. The reports of gunfire were distant now. The sky was so clear that its blue color seemed to redefine the boundaries of infinity. The smell of crushed grass mixed with the sharp scent of spent gunpowder. A faint breeze eddied across his face. Time was like a rotted fabric. Somehow it simply ceased to exist.

As he lay weak and semi-conscious, the sensate world around him retreated to a place of insignificance . . . even absurdity. A great sadness washed over him, condemning the meaningless course his life had taken. He was too young to die, he believed, but he was certain that no man deserved it more.

Wanting to check on the welfare of his horse, he managed to roll his head slowly to one side. An arm's-length away, the drummer boy's head still stared into the void above. Clayton tried to speak — just a whisper of apology — but no words would issue from his lips. The two soldiers lay together in the grass, one hopelessly gone and the other waiting in the anteroom of death.

He awoke on a cot draped with stained

sheets. Turning his head on a feather-stuffed pillow, he saw that he was one among many used-up soldiers arranged in long rows inside an infirmary. A nurse told him he was in Murfreesboro, and here he spent the better part of a year trying to recover from the infections that beset his wound.

Though prompted by the officer in charge, not once in those long months did Clayton write his father. He had dispensed of that past. Now that he had somehow skirted death, he had one more past to try to burn out of his memory, but this one proved stubborn. The sins of the war could not be so easily erased. On many a night he awoke to his own voice as he tried to explain the unexplainable to the decapitated head of the young drummer boy.

Two weeks after Appomattox, he mustered out with an ugly, jagged scar indelibly raised across his chest and left shoulder. One of the other wounded near him had told him that it looked like a pink-gray worm pressed flat against the flesh. The wound bothered him — even to walk — but it bothered him less than his separation from his horse. With the fighting over he was told to go home, but, rather than turn south, he looked west.

In Chattanooga he stole a young mare — a

dapple-gray — from a corral outside the same compound where he had made his mark on paper two and a half years earlier to fight for the Confederacy. Now the buildings were filled with coats of blue, and so the leaving was easy. Judging the horse to be a fair trade for the scar that stretched across his chest, he rode bareback across Tennessee, living off the kindnesses of a defeated people who had little to give. That and what game he could bring down with the cavalryman's revolver he had carried in the war.

In Arkansas a toothless weaver woman agreed to cook a stew using a 'possum he had killed. He stayed there two days, long enough to plow her garden bed in return for the meals she had afforded him. On the third morning as he prepared to leave, she approached him outside the sheep shed where he had slept in a pile of hay. Holding a bright orange blanket rolled up under one arm, she dropped a pair of beaded moccasins at his feet.

"A darky soldier trade dese to me for da wool socks I make 'im. He say he take dem off'n a dead chief of da Comanch." It was the longest chain of words the old woman had put together in the short time he had known her. "You take dis, too," she said, pressing on him the rolled up blanket. "It dyed wit' alder bark. Dat keep it from rottin'."

He held the bundle of wool and ran his fingers over its comforting nap. "That's mighty kind o' you, ma'am. Are you right sure you can spare it?"

Her eyes seemed to look through him. "It protect you, too," she prophesied, as if he, like a blanket exposed to the elements, might be subject to some form of natural decay. She placed her hand on his chest, pressing into the scar hidden under his blouse.

"It take care o' you." She smiled. "You gonna see."

As he removed the worn out shoes dispensed to him at the hospital, she bound the rolled blanket with a length of baling twine. Shod in the moccasins, he jackknifed over the back of his horse and then swung a leg to straddle. She handed up the rolled blanket and backed away as though to take in the whole of him with her knowing eyes. For the first time since he had ridden up on her farm, the crone laughed, showing her glistening gums. She raised a bony hand and extended a forefinger toward the blanket.

"You gonna see," she said again. "It take care o' you long as you need."

CHAPTER 3

West of the Missouri he fell in with an outfit of buffalo hunters. They were a dirty lot, no different from soldiers he had known, except that these men had chosen the killing life for the profits they would reap at the nearest trading posts. Clayton took a skinning job with the crew, but the arrangement was destined to fail.

The blood and gore of skinning the dead shaggy beasts brought back his haunting dreams of the war. On many a night he sat straight up from sleep, covered in sweat and trembling as he looked all around him for the source of the voice that had awakened him. On one night the drummer boy's head turned out to be his canteen in the grass. On another, it was the burlap sack he had acquired to carry his pistol and ammunition. When the crew decapitated a bull at the request of a saloon keeper who planned to mount the head over his bar, Clayton pushed on across the beckoning plains.

His father had told him the story of sailing from Scotland, of facing the unknown perils of an ocean to seek a better life. Now Clayton had undertaken his own voyage, thinking less of his future than of discarding his past. Mostly he gave the horse its head in the sea of grass. The dapple-gray was his ship, though he could not think of himself as captain. He was content to drift. One direction seemed as plausible and pointless as any other . . . until he saw the mountains.

For no reason he was ever able to articulate, he took the reins and set his course for the tallest sharp summit. When he reached the foothills he turned north and skirted the jagged peaks, keeping one eye on the ridgetops as though he were appraising each crest for some indefinable allure. Together, man and horse traveled the rolling apron between steep slopes and flat prairie. Always to his right the shimmering expanse of grass swirled in waves, like an angry sea lapping against a rocky shore. On his left, the towering escarpments stood like sentinels keeping watch over the plains.

Crossing the prairie he had learned something that he knew to be a contradiction: that a constant sound — like the slithering of wind-blown grass — can become its own silence. Here at the edge of the mountain ranges another lesson became clear: this dichotomous land had made some claim upon his soul.

The plains seemed to go on forever, the gently rolling land seeming to mirror the endless sky. The vastness of it all gave him his first seed of hope. Here, in this spacious country where a man was constantly dwarfed by the grandeur of his surroundings, he might learn to burn up his past and let the sparks scatter to the stars. Under this broad Western sky there seemed to be more directions, more possibilities . . . not just about what to do with his life . . . but also what kind of man to be.

In the Wyoming Territory, a grizzly bear intruded on his camp and frightened his horse so badly, the mare broke its hobble and ran off. He staved off the bear by waving the orange blanket, leaping about his campfire and flapping the bright wool, the man every bit as wild as the roaming beast.

In the morning Clayton packed his gear inside the blanket and began walking, thinking with every step what the weaver woman had said about the blanket protecting him. He remembered a quiet corporal in the war who had worn a Bible on a cord around his neck, the book lying flat against the soldier's

27

chest. That soldier had never been shot. Yet another man had claimed the same power for an eagle feather he wore in his hat, and he had been shot through the throat by a sniper.

It took him two days to track down the mare. The horse was visibly changed by her experience. At the slightest sound, day or night, her jittery eyes widened and rimmed with stark white, just like the cannon-addled soldiers he had known in the hospital. As he had not named the mare before, now he called her "Skitter."

When he rode up on the Horsetooth Hills, a trapper took him for a Sioux buck and fired off two shots at him before Clayton thought to yell out — the first sounds to issue from his throat in months, aside from a low murmur now and again to the mare. When the man lowered his rifle and waved the boy in, the stranger welcomed Clayton into his dugout for the night.

Inside the crude hovel, the trapper proved to be starved for conversation, but Clayton tolerated the endless prattle as compensation for the strips of pan-fried beaver tail that were freely offered. Long into the night, beside a crackling fire, the mountain man rambled on about the tribulations of a lone trapper setting his wares in the evergreen-sheltered creeks tumbling out of the mountains. His stories were filled with testy encounters with bears, cougars, a rabid skunk, and war parties of Sioux.

At last the trapper seemed to run out of tales to relate, and so he asked about Clayton — his family, his place of origin, and the circumstances that had led him into this wilderness. Dodging every question, Clayton tended to his food, until the man relented and pointed to a space on the floor beside the crackling flames.

"Yuh can lay out y'ur bedroll next to thuh f'ar."

" 'Preciate it," Clayton said, "but I'll pass the night with my horse."

When the boy could eat no more, he joined the picketed mare and, by the starlight, rolled into the orange wool blanket. Curled up with a full belly, he listened to a distant pack of wolves weave their lamenting howls into the night. The soulful notes rose and fell, the sound like a universal anthem for all creatures who had managed to survive another day.

As he prepared to leave in the morning, the trapper called out that breakfast was waiting. More out of courtesy than need, Clayton sat down at the man's fire a second time and felt his hunger awaken at the smell of roasted venison.

"I'm gone make a s'gestion to yuh," the trapper said, frowning with a serious thought. "Yuh'd be wise to shed them long locks b'fore yuh head north."

Clayton chewed a piece of meat into submission and studied the man. "Why's that?" he asked in a flat tone.

The trapper shrugged. "I'm advisin' it," he said and gestured in the direction Skitter waited. "If'n y'ur bound to travel without a saddle an' without a hat" — he glanced at the moccasins lashed ankle-high on the boy's feet — "an' sportin' Injun foot ware . . . yu'd best wear y'ur ha'r like a white man."

They sat by the creek as the trapper sawed at Clayton's long tresses with a skinner's knife, the dark-amber locks falling away in loose ropes and littering the ground like the remains of some creature that had been dismantled by scavengers.

"If'n y'ur dead set on headin' north," the trapper volunteered, "yuh might oughta consider the Lar'mie Plain. It's a place that has always spoke to me. Guess yuh could say it suits my eye, lyin' peaceful and purty like it does twixt two mount'n ranges."

Breaking a stick to use as a drawing implement, the man dropped to his knees and scratched out a map on the sandy beach. After the lines were drawn, he scooped sand in his hands and patted the mounds into parallel chains, forming the mountains.

"This here's the Pennock Pass," he said, pointing with the stick to a gap in the hills. "This's where yu'll get y'ur first look at the Medicine Bows. Take y'ur bearin's off the tallest peak, and yu'll drop down into the purtiest piece o' land this side o' heaven."

The man remained on his knees and looked down at the tiny world he had sculpted. With his head bowed, he might have been a supplicant come to worship before an altar.

"Come sundown there's a color that lifts off that land." He said this so quietly, Clayton had to lean forward to catch the words. The trapper shook his head slowly. "Never seen nothin' else like it in all my rovin'."

Clayton hovered over the rough map and memorized the landmarks. "What might be there for one such as myself?"

The trapper stood and nodded at the horse standing patiently back in the spruces. "Well, I seen yuh ride, and I figure yuh to be a horseman." He swept his hand over the model to indicate the length of the valley. "That's cattle country up there. Maybe yuh

31

can hire on with a crew. That's thuh kind o' work makes a good fit with a horseman."

The trapper walked back to his dugout and returned with a cloth sack. "This here is dried meat, mostly elk . . . and I had some spar' flour I could part with." He laid down the sack at Clayton's feet. "It ain't much, but it oughta see you through to thuh Medicine Bows."

The boy picked up the sack and considered its weight. The provisions were a generous gift, he knew, especially from one so cut off from towns, fort suttlers, and trading posts. Clayton had nothing to offer in return. He lashed the gift to his blanket roll so that it balanced out the weight of his pistol bag.

"I'll cut some wood for you," Clayton said and tied his horse to the tree again.

The trapper pushed a hand at the air, waving away the notion of any debt tendered in the transaction. Embarrassed, he looked down at the ground.

"Hell, son," he grunted. "That ain't required." An odd smile pushed sharp dimples into his broad face. "I don't often git vis'tors."

But Clayton had already moved to the man's cache of long-limbed firewood, where he went to work with an axe, cutting the cumbersome lengths into hearth-sized logs. After two hours he had doubled the size of the supply stacked outside the dugout.

"Yuh always work that hard at y'ur chores, son?"

Clayton narrowed his eyes at the question. " 'Bout all I *do* know is how to work hard." He nodded toward the gift sack hanging by his horse's ribs. "I figure any man who moves on without paying his debts . . . he's less a man than when he arrived."

CHAPTER 4

It was mid-autumn when Clayton Jane nosed his horse onto the grazing lands of the Afton Ranch. He was sixteen years old, one hundred sixty pounds, and his hair a dark amber like the rust-brown spots on a hawk feather. He had followed the Medicine Bow River north and intersected the south pasture of Afton's, where he met five men dressed heavily against the cold. They were bringing cattle up from a draw, and, upon seeing him wrapped in an orange blanket, they approached in a curious but relaxed manner. He knew by the way they rested their hands on their saddle horns that they had not been in the war. Though they spoke friendly enough, these men studied the bright blanket with a question turning in their eyes, but none made mention of it.

One of these cow hands — a Negro with tobacco-brown skin and warm, welcoming eyes — brought up the subject of a job.

Once the topic was part of the general conversation, each man played his part in the typical ribbing of a new hand.

"D'you know cattle, sonny?" one asked. "They're so dumb you might think there's nothin' to know, but you'd be wrong."

"Can ya handle a rope?" said another. "To work for the Rollin' F, you gotta be able to throw a loop under your horse's belly and over a ant'lope at a full gallop."

"Are ya a hard worker?" called the man in front. His earnest query quieted the other men for a time.

"I reckon it's the one thing I am," Clayton said to a question he could finally answer.

The lead man turned in his saddle and smiled. "That's good enough for me."

"I'll work for you," Clayton said, and with that his career as a ranch hand began.

The Negro told him J. J. Afton — a wealthy Englishman — was a fair man to work for. There was no denying they needed more hands. A month past, two of their crew had been killed by Sioux, which was why no less than five men rode together at all times.

The ranch lay hard up against the Snowy Range of the Medicine Bows some seven miles north and west of the Little Laramie River. Across the broad valley to the east lay

35

the Laramie Range. Scattered throughout, he was told, were displaced bands of hostile Sioux, Cheyenne, and Arapaho. Beyond the mountains to the west lay the Wind River country and the Shoshone, a tribe that had shown itself inclined toward peace with the white man. The Arapaho and Cheyenne were pushing on to the south away from conflict, but the Sioux honored no boundaries claimed by the white trespassers.

He learned all this on the ride back to the ranch, yet no man asked Clayton about his past. This deliberate avoidance of his history — and all the misery that had comprised his life — coaxed him into believing he was on the verge of a second chance. Among these men, he experienced his first taste of redemption, because he sensed in each of them a story similar to his own. Though not tainted by the war, these saddlers had climbed out of their own dark pits and somehow found their way to this valley for a better life.

The more Clayton eyed the terrain of this country, the more he could believe in its prophecy. The clear streams sparkled in sunlight even in the shade of century-old cottonwoods, as if the water were privy to some source of internal light that blinked at will on its surface. The lonely rock outcrops, scattered throughout the plain, broke up the grassy expanses like islands dotting the sea of prairie. To the west, the juniper-tufted cliffs rose abruptly, standing like the ramparts of a gigantic fortress that appeared to reach to the sky.

Each of these features was like an individual ingredient taken from an ancient recipe that existed before any man had set foot on this land. As the parts came together in Clayton's mind, he let them simmer in his thoughts, until they afforded him the promise that he needed. Already, as he rode among these men, he began to feel a part of something.

Though, before this day, he had never laid eyes on this verdant valley, he suspected that he had come home. For all his wandering since the war, he had felt light and subservient and aimless, like a windborne seed driven by the fickle wind. Now he was thinking about roots sinking downward into dark, rich earth.

Like the old cottonwoods by the creek a man could grow straight and tall here at the edge of the prairie. By planting his seed here in the Laramie Plain, he silently declared to himself that he had every right to begin his life anew. Maybe this was why God made a world with so many different landscapes, giving a man every indication that redemption lay in the terrain in which he settled. All a person had to do was find the proper setting to begin the transformation. Clayton tried to believe he had found his.

When the sun eased below the crests of the Medicine Bows, any trace of doubt evaporated. There was a change out on the prairie. Around the scrub brush and grasses, all of which was now flooded in the shadow of the mountains, the air showed a faint glow of blue that stretched the width of the valley. He remembered the trapper had mentioned this, but Clayton had not put much stock in the fanciful idea. Now, witnessing it for himself, it was like looking at a scene through colored glass. But more than that, by passing through its eerie tint of light, he felt himself become a part of it. Just as it had spoken to the trapper, this land seemed to whisper in the boy's ear.

By the time the Afton ranch came into view, the alluring color had faded, and the gray details of the terrain darkened with the coming night. Up ahead, the buildings showed the steady burn of lights in several windows. It was like a small town that marked the end of their journey. Of their own will, the horses picked up speed, and Skitter followed their lead. This equine response seemed a confirmation of Clayton's optimism.

"Who's hungry?" one of the men called out.

"Hell, I could eat a cross-eyed mule!" came a reply.

"You know you can catch that, don'tcha, J.T.?"

"What?" J.T. rejoined. "Bein' cross-eyed?"

"Naw, bein' a ass. But I reckon you're too late on that."

Everyone except Clayton laughed. The Negro pulled up alongside him and spoke in his quiet way.

"Dey juss havin' fun. Dey'll be some good hot food waitin' on us at da bunkhouse. You'll see. And we'll hunt you up some proper gear. I gotta extra saddle I ain't usin'. You welcome to it if it suits you."

As they galloped onto the low ground by the creek, Clayton leaned forward to stroke the lunging neck of the dapple-gray. "We're home, girl," he said and reined her in so that she would not take the lead. "Easy now," he whispered. "We got to earn this."

■ ■ ■ ■

LARAMIE PLAIN,
WYOMING
TERRITORY
SPRING, 1876

■ ■ ■ ■

CHAPTER 5

John James Afton walked from the main house across the yard toward the north bunkhouse. He watched the long, squat building's metal flue spew a whip of gray smoke that changed direction like a broken compass. This fickle wind was typical of the long valley of the Laramie Plain at the end of the day. He snapped down his vest over his waist and turned his head to inspect the kingdom he had raised from the raw land.

Seven buildings spoked outward from the main yard — the space Elizabeth Afton referred to as "the courtyard." Around the perimeter she had planted islands of roses and bordered them with rings of ochred rocks. Afton liked less the color than the order it gave the space, but more than that he was gratified that his wife had found some tangible means to lay her claim to this land alongside his own.

Hers was a legacy of English refinement.

His was structure and scope and what that meant toward his standing as an English-born American cattle baron. The barn alone would have marked Afton as a wealthy man. It was, he claimed, the largest building west of Kansas City and east of San Francisco. And it might well have been.

Spreading out from the hub of these buildings was a maze of corrals, paddocks, feedlots, and holding pens for a hundred-twenty horses and mules, forty hogs, and sixteen chickens. Beyond these structures, surrounding the ranch complex like a long rectangular moat, was the only fenced pasture on the property. It was home to the champion breeder bull that Afton had brought from England. After its siring duties last year, Afton was counting on a herd increase of six to eight percent.

Beyond the fencing spread the vast piece of prairie that Afton had claimed for "New Surrey Downs," the official title he had bestowed upon his vast holdings. Fifteen thousand acres sprawling from the Shin Bone Flats and then south across the best water and grasslands in the valley. The jewels in his crown — more than nine thousand cattle — moved through these perimeters like a living symbol of cash flow.

Though Afton had given the ranch a

44

proper English name, it was known throughout the territory as the "Rolling F," as his
crew had dubbed it after the sound of Afton's name. "Surrey Downs" had no fair
chance on the tongues of American cow-
punchers, who coined words with such
facile indifference that they seemed to create a new language complete. Bending the
words "Surrey Downs" to their liking, the
Rolling F cowboys called themselves "the
Sorry-Damn boys" and took pride in the
moniker.

Such was the paradoxical humor of the
self-deprecating American cowboy. Call one
by the wrong handle and a man might earn
himself a busted lip. Give a cowboy a
chance to call *himself* that same name with
a smile, and he might laugh about it over
beer with any man.

By appearances alone, Afton might have
been the wealthiest man in Wyoming. No
one — not even his wife — knew that he
had forfeited ownership to his brother-in-
law, who had settled Afton's failed invest-
ment debts back in England. Still, it had
been easy to disregard this as a mere formal-
ity and to live out his accustomed role as
owner. England had been far away. Until
now. The letter in his pocket fairly burned

against his chest. England was coming to him.

There was still enough light to reflect the high sheen of Afton's hunting boots so that from a distance they flashed in bright blinks of light as though he were splashing through a shallow ford in a stream. Short-Stuff sat on the bench outside the first bunkhouse, waiting to see if the pain in his gut would send him for a third time to the privy. When he saw Afton's purposeful approach, he pulled himself up by the awning post, opened the door, and leaned inside.

"Mr. Aff's comin'!" he announced.

The old dog they called Shank had been lying in the dirt before Short-Stuff, its misshapen rear leg stiff and near useless. The dog pushed itself up and hopped two steps toward the open door, anxious for what might come its way after the evening meal. When the dog saw Afton, it circled back to the dirt, dropped down on its belly, and pricked its ears as the Englishman stepped up on the porch and entered the bunkhouse.

A poker game ran at the end of the long table where the men took their meals. It had been a slow game, and the players were half asleep from the roundup in the north. It was their first night in the bunkhouse in four days.

The work had not been hard but tedious, searching every coulee and stand of brush for strays, and, when finding one, bringing it back to the herd accruing at the flatlands around Shin Bone Creek. Then going back and picking up where they had left off. It was what cowboys did, but it lacked the rhythm and flow and feeling of completeness that would come when they would drive the collected herd south . . . then again north as the spring grasses greened.

Swampy had been clanging dishes and pans in the washbasin. With his hands still in the soapy water he turned his head and watched Afton take his captain's stance beside the woodstove. The men at the table fanned their cards shut. Short-Stuff sidled in and closed the door behind him. The tobacco smoke lifting from the table was the only movement in the room.

"Good evening," Afton said, lifting his elbows and sliding his hands into his coat pockets. He looked around the room and breathed in deeply through his nose. The sharp bite of peppercorns and onions wove into the woodsmoke from the stove, the tobacco, the salt scent of the men, and the stench of their unwashed clothing. It was the smell of a full crew, and that was what Afton needed.

"Where's Clayton?"

"Ain't here, Mr. Aff," Nestor said. "He's with the north herd."

Nestor Purdabaugh, also known as "Purty-Boy," was the youngest of the lot, employed only a month, but in that time had assumed the duty of supplying a voice on Clayt's behalf whenever Clayt was absent. Some of the men looked to him to elaborate on his answer, but it was Short-Stuff who piped up when Afton's gaze settled on him.

"Clayt's out on the flats at the Shin Bone. Gone stay out the night."

Afton frowned and looked at Clayt's bunk. The bed looked naked without Clayt's orange blanket.

"Saw painter tracks down at the creek," Short-Stuff explained, "so he's layin' out with the herd."

"Painter!" Afton said. "Do you mean a cat?"

"A big'n accordin' to Clayt," Short-Stuff said.

Afton pushed his lips out and in, the sure sign that his focus had now turned inward. He kept up the motion as his head turreted to count the faces. Then he frowned.

"Is someone from the other bunkhouse with him?"

"He's by hisself," Nestor volunteered.

Afton's frown tightened, cutting deep lines like incision marks across his forehead. His eyes fixed on Short-Stuff again.

"Ain't nobody with 'im," Short-Stuff confirmed and turned from Afton's gaze to study the blue haze of cigarette smoke drifting across the room. It seemed to trespass through the strained silence like someone skulking away from an unwanted conversation.

"Didn' *want* nobody with 'im," Rascher added, rubbing at the ankle of his boot. The half smile that cut across the big cowhand's broad face could have been interpreted any number of ways, but the dark beads of his eyes danced with self satisfaction. He tipped his chair back against the wall, raised a tin can to his mouth, and let go a dollop of tobacco.

Nestor laid his closed hand of cards facedown on the table. "I offered to stay out with 'im, Mr. Aff. Reckon if he intends on bringin' down that cat, he knows he can do it better by hisself."

"Like ever'thing else," Rascher mumbled.

"What about these Sioux?" Afton probed. "Should he not have someone with him in case he encounters them?"

"We ain't seen the first sign o' them Sioux

up on the Shin Bone," Nestor said. "Clayt says they're likely up in the mountains. Leastwise he ain't worried 'bout 'em out there on the flats tonight." Nestor grinned. "Tell you what though. I wouldn' wanna be that damn painter tonight."

Afton simply nodded, as though approving Clayt's decision. "How many more days will you men need in the north pastures?"

"Prob'ly wrap it up tomorr'," Lou Breakenridge said from his bunk. He laid his open book flat on his chest and threaded his fingers into a hammock behind his head. Breakenridge generally spoke as foreman when Clayt was not there to do it officially.

Afton turned to the white-haired Negro seated near the woodstove. "What's the count up there, Chalky?"

On the axe-hewn bench of cottonwood, Chalky Sullens sat in his long johns, his wrinkled face placid and unassuming. His skin was the golden brown of dried tobacco leaves. His hair looked like tiny coils of silver-white wire pressed flat against his skull. He was the oldest man at the ranch, having built most of it when Afton was just getting started in the territory. Chalky ran a needle and thread through a pair of trousers and kept on with the steady work of his hands even as his liquid, brown eyes came up to Afton.

"I 'magine we gone have 'bout two hun'erd and fo'ty from da Shin Bone," Chalky said, answering the question out of courtesy, while knowing full well that Afton really meant to ask about Clayt's safety. "Clayt be aw'right, Mistah Aff. We be movin' dat herd south tomorr'."

Everyone had known that Breakenridge was right, but now that it had been confirmed by Chalky's quiet voice, it was gospel. Every man nodded his agreement — all but Grady Brooks, who sat alone pushing mink oil into his boots with his bare fingers.

Grady's duties with the forge, the hogs, chickens, and vegetable garden defined the only segregation at the ranch. Even his work with the milk cows did not earn him a place among the fraternity of cowhands. A cowman was a horseman, and that modest elevation from ground level to the throne of a saddle made all the difference in the hierarchy of a working ranch.

Afton turned back to Lou Breakenridge. "What about the northeast pasture? What is our progress there?"

Lou sat up enough to prop on an elbow. "Buck's boys started pushin' his herd south today. We'll join up with 'em by late afternoon, 'less we find the cattle too spread out on t'other side o' the creek. And providin' there ain't too much snow in those ravines running up to Shannonhaus's."

At that name, Afton raised his chin and flared his nostrils. "I want you men to be sure of every animal you drive out of there. If there's a question, you give the benefit to Shannonhaus. Don't touch a brand to anything you're not certain of. I'd rather have a quiet neighbor than an extra calf or two." All this he delivered in a low dirge, like a confiding father embarrassed about his own advice. Then, back to business, he let his voice carry through the room. "How many dead?"

" 'Bout thirty-six, so far," Nestor volunteered and checked Lou's face.

"Thirty-nine," Breakenridge said. "Ain't countin' the stillborns. And ain't no way to know how many the ki-yotes drug off. Not too bad, considerin'." Lou lifted his head to let Afton see his smile of admiration. "Looks like your cross-breed plan is workin' out, Mr. Aff. Yearlin's are carryin' fat to spare, and their coats look good."

"What is the overall standing count up to now?" Afton asked.

"With Buck's count," Lou said, "some'res

'round nine and a half thousand, be my guess."

Nestor nodded at Breakenridge's assessment and carried that nod to Afton. "Clayt says you might can count on nine and a half and then some."

Afton stepped away from the stove so as to better face the knot of men at the table. He glanced at the scattering of coins from the suspended card game, and then he sucked in his cheeks, putting on his authoritative face.

"I have some guests coming in at the end of the month. Family. They'll be staying in the house, of course, but I need to get the old mill shed cleaned out for use as a studio." The room was so still, the occupants might have been posing for a photograph. The flame in the stove made a popping sound. The wind pried a tune out of the gap in the door.

"A what?" Short-Stuff said. Every other face held the same question.

"We have a painter coming to live with us." Afton made a dismissive gesture with his hand. "I'm talking, of course, about the kind that paints . . . not a wild cat."

Nestor's boyish smile widened. "They comin' in from England, Mr. Aff?"

"Yes, from Surrey. My sister and her

husband. And their boy . . . my nephew."

"What's he gone be painting?" Swampy said and looked around at the bare planks of the bunkhouse. "Wouldn' hurt none to have a coat o' somethin' light in here."

"She," Afton corrected. "My sister paints with oils."

"Owls?" Swampy's voice rose and fell with the word.

"She does portraits and landscapes with oil paints. The point is, gentlemen, I need all of the branding finished by the middle of next week." Afton took his pipe from his pocket, and with it he pointed toward the main yard. "Then I want four men on the mill shed. We'll store the saw in the barn. Then get that lumber out of there and store it out back here." He pointed to the back wall of the bunkhouse. "Then clean it up and get it looking presentable."

"The lumber?" Nestor asked, frowning.

Someone threw a balled-up rag that hit Nestor in the chest. Rascher slapped his cards down on the table.

"Which'a us are to be workin' on the shed?"

"I'll leave that for Clayton to decide," Afton said. "How long will he be out?"

"If I know him," Nestor said, "he ain't comin' back till he gits that cat."

54

Breakenridge propped his book upright on his chest and spoke from behind it. "He'll likely be back tomorr'."

Afton nodded. "Well, tell him I want to talk to him. Tell him to come in tomorrow night regardless." He looked at Swampy. "How are your supplies holding?"

The cook considered the coming roundup and studied the closed doors of the larder. He began squeezing his wet hands into the towel that hung from his apron.

"I'll be needin' to take the wagon into Ivinson's come Sa'urday." He held resolute eyes on Afton but let a grin surface enough for the men to appreciate his selection of day.

Afton nodded smartly. "Be sure to check by the house before you go. Cora will have a list for you." He walked to the door and stopped. "What about the mustangs? Any sign of that herd that was on the flats last spring?"

"Not yet," Breakenridge said. "They'll likely be back."

Afton gave them the side of his face and a final nod. "Good night then." The response was a collective murmur that he had learned to acknowledge with a nod.

When Afton's footsteps left the porch, the poker players picked up their cards. Swampy took up the fry pan of leftovers and scraped fat and gristle and beans into the dented pie tin he kept for the dog. He carried it to the door, speaking the dog's name with a musical timbre never squandered on humans. The men inside heard the pan touch down and the low whisper that was Swampy's evening ritual with the crippled cur.

Rascher upended a bag of tobacco into his mouth, wadded the empty package, and tossed it to the woodpile. "Six bits to you, Big-un," he said to G.T. and let the front legs of his chair bang to the floor.

"Reckon Clayt'll git that painter?" G.T. asked. They all knew the question was intended for Lou, who, except for Chalky, had known Clayt the longest. But they knew just as well that Breakenridge did not consider questions he had already answered.

"Man's a fool to go at a big cat like that by hisself," Rascher volunteered and then huffed a quiet laugh through his nose. He shook his head. "And at night."

"I guess you was just dyin' to stand watch with him?" G.T. said, his big melon head holding a poker face on Rascher. Rascher made a show of chewing on his plug.

Nestor, too young to see the danger in it, smiled at Rascher. "If it was you up there with Clayt, prob'ly git yourself shot when you started up your damn snorin'."

Rascher rearranged the order of his cards, all the while working up a look of mock concern. "Well, thank you for 'xplainin' why I weren't chose, Purty-Boy. I'd hate to think it was he didn' like me or some such."

Swampy returned to the sideboard. "I can cook up cat purty damn good if you git it here fresh." Everyone looked at him . . . even Chalky.

Nestor laughed, and there was that tone of youthful wonder in his voice. "Swamp, you ain't never cooked no damn painter."

Swampy picked up the big pan of gray water and carried it to the back door. "Cook any damned thang what's got ha'r on it," he stated flatly. He stood there staring at the latch. "Anybody gone open this goddamn door for me?" There was a beat of silence until G.T. heaved himself up from the table.

"Cooked me up a badger once't," Swampy continued. "Don't matter long as it's got ha'r. Skunk, badger, painter. Long as it's got ha'r."

Swampy flung the water out back, and G.T. lumbered back to his chair. There he fanned open his cards and laughed in the deep well of his chest.

"That might 'xplain tonight's stew. Seems

I remember picking some hairs out o' my teeth."

Short-Stuff cackled, and the boys in the room laughed more at Short's witchy laugh than the thought of hair stew. Swampy walked back inside and ignored them.

"Think I'd pass on skunk, Swamp," Nestor said.

Short-Stuff sobered and pressed his hand to his belly. "Might be too goddamned late on that," he said and slipped out the door for another trip to the privy.

"Long's you boys are bellyachin'," Rascher crowed, "see how these cards go down." He laid down his hand. From his bed, Lou rolled his head to watch Rascher rake in the coins, but his attention was drawn to Nestor. The youngster stacked his forearms on the table and pinched trouble on his face as he glared at Rascher's cards. When Nestor happened to glance up, Lou shook his head once, the movement little more than a twitch. Nestor closed his mouth and looked at Chalky. He was afforded the same advice there.

"You boys oughta git some sleep," Lou said and closed his book. He kept his eyes on Nestor until the boy reluctantly stood and turned from the game.

"Well hell, Purty-Boy," Rascher sang out,

"you cain't walk off after playin' poker like a jackass at a spellin' bee. We're liable to remember you that way. Sit down and restore your reputation, son."

Nestor turned back and waited, but when Rascher would not look up, the boy drained the last of his coffee and spoke into the empty cup.

"Hell, I'm just proud to be the one put that smile on your sour face. Some o' the boys put up bets there weren't room on your face for one." Nestor walked toward his bunk above Breakenridge's. Lou did not look at him, but the subtle grin that Nestor saw was enough to let him know that he'd probably done what Clayt might have done.

CHAPTER 6

The sky blossomed into a haze of lavender, and birdsong from the redwings fluted from the reeds at the creek. As it always did, the sound of the moving water seemed to retreat with the opening of the day. It was Clayt's habit to take a step back at dawn, as if to observe his life from a distance, to mark the turning of the great wheel that moved the world toward another day. Then gradually he came back to the details close at hand, for they were what mattered for the present. He watched it all: the cattle emerging from darkness into fine resolution, the methodical movements of the birds flitting through the trees, and young leaves in the aspens and cottonwoods defining themselves against the growing light in the sky as they fluttered in the cool air that poured down the slopes of the valley.

Sitting by his morning fire, Clayt knotted the old alder-dyed blanket close to his throat and sipped from his coffee cup. The morning was cold but not bitterly so, and there was the promise of seasonal change in the greening of the trees and in the new grass pushing up through the dry winter stubble. The hot coffee in his belly warmed him as he awaited the rising sun.

He loved this time. Loved to be part of the unfolding of a new day. If ever he missed a sunrise, he felt like a man stepping into the chow line for a meal that might run out before he could fill his plate. When the sun peeked over the low bluff that marked the edge of Shannonhaus's land, Clayt set down his empty cup and strapped on his chaps.

He was laying sod and rock over the ashes of his fire when he saw a rider crest the hill to the southeast a half mile away. Watching the lone figure approach, he stood very still, his right hand casually propped on the butt of his pistol, a pragmatic pose he had adopted for moments like this, when two seconds of hesitation could be costly.

Satisfied that the rider was not an Indian, he picked up the coffee pot, swirled what was left in the kettle, and poured the dregs onto the fire pit. Then, at the creek, he splashed water into the pot and rubbed his finger inside the smooth curve of the enamel. As he rolled the blanket into a tight

61

coil, he watched the rider drop behind a scrim of willows at the creek, but already he knew by the way the man sat his horse that it was Lou Breakenridge.

By the time Breakenridge had emerged from the trees and slowed to skirt the cattle, Clayt was mounted, taking his horse at a walk to meet him. They met forty feet away from the big oak, whose creeping sundial shadow the cattle would follow through the warm afternoon, but, like the cattle, these men chose the open sky this early, where the direct rays of the sun would touch the valley within minutes.

Clayt reined the dapple-gray around, and the two men sat their horses facing the cattle, each warming to the other's presence without need of words. Together they watched the livestock and let the dawn spread around them in a flood of pale-yellow light.

The new calves nosed the bulging udders of their mothers, and the cows stood for it, at once indignant and nurturing. The two range hands sat watching the proceedings, each knowing that this kind of bovine behavior was the norm and could never be fully explained. Their flanked horses stood quietly, stirrup to stirrup, eyes heavily lidded as though this rendezvous were the primary purpose of their day. Breakenridge squinted at the brilliant bead of sun breaking free of the low ridge to the east. Behind it the sky had come alive with streaks of pink, purple, and scarlet, wild and without order like an artist's palette.

Then Breakenridge studied the stout walnut stock jutting from Clayt's rifle scabbard, staring at it intently as though it might have a story to tell. "Swampy's countin' on cat meat for supper. Boys are takin bets on the taste."

When Clayt did not answer, Breakenridge turned back to the cattle and watched the dew steam off the grass and rise in serpentine wisps. "Swampy swears he can cook up anythin' fav'rable 'long as it grows hair." Lou chuckled under his breath. "I ain't so sure 'bout that."

"Swampy'd do well to soak some beans today," Clayt said.

Lou looked quickly at Clayt and arched an eyebrow. "So . . . you didn' see the cat?"

"I saw it," Clayt said plainly.

Lou frowned. "You didn' git off a shot?"

Clayt nodded toward the sycamore by the creek where he had laid out for the cat. "I did," he said and cracked the barest of smiles. "Maybe just not the kind you're talkin' 'bout."

Breakenridge raised his chin at the weapon sheathed in Clayt's saddle scabbard. "That G.T.'s shotgun?" He knew it was and did not expect an answer. Any man on the ranch was as recognizable by his weapon as he was by his horse. Or his hat. Lou took off his hat and squinted up into the timber on the higher ground to the west before settling his gaze on Clayt. "So, you saw it? The painter?"

"We had a little talk."

Lou stared at the side of Clayt's face. " 'A little talk,' " he repeated in a flat tone.

Clayt nodded. "I don't reckon he'll be back 'round these parts for a while."

Lou smiled. "You didn' kill him." It wasn't a question.

Clayt made the dry clicking sound with his teeth that usually meant he had a different idea on matters. "Weren't no need," he said. Grinning, he raised his chin to a newborn calf nudging at the belly of a white-faced cow. "That'n there can sing a harsh lullaby most of a night. I considered killin' *it.*"

They watched the calf lock onto the udder, and no sooner had the baby settled in to suck but the cow lowed its protest and stepped forward a few stiff paces, leaving the newborn in wide-eyed confusion.

"Mama must be dry," Lou said.

Clayt shrugged his head to one side. "Or maybe she ain't the mama."

The sun surfaced full above the low ridge, elongating like a burning drop of oil rising upward out of the land. Popping free of its mirrored mirage it hung low in a sky now so clear that the translucent wings of insects brightened like flakes of snow over the creek. Lou twisted at the waist, opened the flap of his saddlebag, and rummaged for a cloth sack.

"Here you go. 'N case you missed Swampy's cookin'."

Clayt opened the sack and unfolded a newspaper-wrapped package. Inside it were two thick biscuits, each soaking up the grease from a slab of pork. The biscuits were cold, but the salt smell of the meat stirred his appetite.

"Thank God Swampy ain't yet figured out how to ruin a biscuit," Clayt said.

Lou smiled. "Give 'im time. He's ruint near to ever'thin' else."

Clayt tore off a bite and chewed as they watched the lost calf raise its head and bleat. A circle of empty space widened around the complainer.

"So, you and this cat," Lou said with a little melody in his voice, "what was it you two talked 'bout?"

Clayt thought about that as he chewed. " 'Bout the difference b'tween Rollin' F stock and a mule deer, I reckon."

Lou nodded to the shotgun. "This like that time you discouraged that wolf in the timber? What is it you pack in those special shells?"

"Mustard seed."

Lou made a snort. "That draw blood?"

Clayt shook his head. "It ain't the impact . . . even comin' outta ten gauge. It's the hot sting o' the mustard he remembers. That and the embarrassment of it."

Breakenridge frowned with his eyes as he smiled. "You're thinkin' a painter gets embarrassed?"

Clayt shrugged. "Pair that with the sting." He finished the biscuit and wiped his mouth with the back of his hand. "I reckon it burns long enough to hold a place in his memory. And he's gotta hate it that it was one o' us done it to him."

"Cain't be much range with the seed so light. How close would a man have to git?"

Clayt stuffed the sack and remaining biscuit into his saddlebag. "Close."

The herd nosed at the scattered pile of day-old hay, which was better than three-quarters gone and most of that left trampled in the mud. Lou surveyed the bluffs across the creek, knowing it was good panther country. He shook his head and laughed quietly.

"There ain't another'n like you in the territory, you know that?"

The pleading calf pushed deeper into the herd, and the animals there began to move upon themselves, their ridged spines catching the early light like the rippling of water.

"We known each other . . . what . . . goin' on nine years?" Lou said. "You ever gonna 'xplain to me how it is you can move up close on a wolf and a cat like that? Chalky teach you that? He never taught me nothin' like that."

"Chalky taught us a hellava lot 'bout this land, Lou."

Lou laughed outright. "You got that right. Hell, he's the only one'd give me the time o' day when I started out. Him and you, I mean." Lou caught himself from reminiscing and studied Clayt sitting his old dapple-gray, thinking how alike the two were. The old mare was content to wait till Christmas for a reason to move. "How'd that edgy girl there take to a night with a painter?"

Clayt plucked a loose pine needle from the mare's mane. " 'Bout like you'd 'xpect. I banked a fire up near the timber and picketed her there."

Lou smiled at the hoary muzzle of the old gray. "You ever think on throwin' your saddle on somethin with a little more juice?"

Clayt leaned down and stroked the long smooth muscle along the mare's neck. Her head turned part way around, and her ears rotated lest he speak.

"She's stuck with me over a lot o' ground," Clayt said, his quiet voice carrying the timbre of appreciation. "Reckon I'll stick with her."

Lou tried for a wry smile and studied the horizon. "For a man who sometimes gits into ticklish situations, you sure picked yourself a skittish horse. How're you thinkin' she'll do around some o' them damned Sioux — them a-whoopin' and a-screamin', their faces painted up for killin' *you* and stealin' *her*? Might be good to know you could outdistance old Chatka and his band did they show up."

Clayt gave the horse another pat and straightened in his saddle. "She's still got 'er legs."

Lou looked over the field and imagined the flats at night: Clayt stalking the painter, an intense focus on his face . . . that and patience. Lou had witnessed it before whenever Clayt took over saddling a stubborn mustang that the other boys had given up on.

"You hunt with Ind'ans back in Georgia?" Lou asked.

Clayt shook his head. "Cherokees was mostly gone. If there *was* any out there in them woods a-watchin' me push a mule and a plow cross the side o' that mountain —" He shook his head and left the point hanging.

The lone calf wailed. Its plaintive cry rose above the sound of the creek and grated the ears with the intrusion of a rusted hinge. The rest of the herd was motionless. Its passivity seemed less a conspiracy of indifference than a condition of life. This was the acceptance of what was true and immutable. Their white and red and spotted faces appeared placid in the yellow glow of the cool morning.

"Reckon her mama is one o' them dead we found up the ravine?" Clayt said.

Lou considered the calf. "Could be they just got separated when we drove 'em in."

Clayt pursed his lips and watched the lost animal bawl. "That ain't likely. Not with the Sorry-Damn crew."

Lou shrugged. "Rascher might a split 'em up just to keep it wailin' all night for you."

The calf stood splay-legged with a string

of mucous dangling from its muzzle. "Rascher's a cowboy," Clayt said. "Ain't much with people, but he knows cattle." He looked off to the ravines running into the creek from the bluff. "Think I'll send Rascher up toward Shannonhaus's today. Finish clearin' out them canyons."

"You think Rascher and Shannonhaus can have a civil conversation 'bout who owns what calf?"

"I figure those two are the ones not likely to git into it. They're both sour as a green chokecherry. I figure one don't wanna start talk with the other."

Lou grinned. "We're a Sorry-Damn bunch, ain't we?"

Clayt huffed a quiet laugh through his nose. "I've heard that."

Clayt nodded toward the calf as it wobbled on knobby legs toward the creek. Lou turned his mount and Clayt "chick-chicked" from the side of his mouth. They nudged their horses forward at a walk, and the calf's head came around at their approach. The calf moved off a little faster toward the cottonwoods, and Lou wheeled his horse in a gentle arc to turn the calf back to the herd.

"Hey-up, dogie," he sang out. "Let's git on back to mama."

When the calf merged with the other

animals, Lou pulled alongside Clayt again. "Mr. Aff's wantin' us to git the herd to the south pastures today. Wants the brandin' finished by mid-week. Some o' his kin comin' in. He wants the old mill shed cleared out. Wants it changed over to a studio."

"A studio," Clayt said. His eyes took on an amused look.

"He wants four men on that next week. We'll need to take out the whole saw assembly, clear out the dust and lumber, and fix it up proper."

"When're they comin' in . . . this kin?"

"End o' the month or there 'bout," Lou said. "Comin' in from England."

They were quiet for a time, each man watching the morning settle into the flats. The murmur of the creek wrapped around them and seemed to Clayt the song of eternity, both past and future, the sound of it pulling him in both directions.

The dark and convoluted gorges of Appalachia had been full of streams, although, in his memory, the tone had been different. Clayt wondered if it was the moss that had grown in those dark Georgia coves, softening the roar of the water. Or maybe it was the stone itself. He remembered how a Georgia rock removed from water would sweat for days. Out here, a piece of shale could look dry sitting on the bottom of a creek.

"Buck's boys already got the east herd down to the south pastures. Some of his boys'll join up with us 'round mid-afternoon, help us move these here." Lou nodded toward the cattle nosing at the new grass. "Then Buck and his crew are gonna set up a night camp and stay with the herd. Give us another night under a roof."

Clayt pulled up the collar of his coat against the lingering morning cold. "I reckon I'll stay out with 'em, too."

"Nope," Lou announced. "That'll be me. Mr. Aff's wantin' you back at the ranch."

Clayt nodded, but his eyes were fixed on the hill to southeast. His stillness and focus drew Lou's eyes to that direction. A group of horsemen crested the rise. The sheen on their horses' rumps caught the rays of the sun from behind and glinted whitely as they came on at a trot in a loose group. There was already enough heat radiating off the ridge to distort them into a wavering image, as if a slow curtain of water were rising up before them.

"What kinda studio we talkin' 'bout, Lou?"

"Mr. Aff's sister is a paintin' artist. Said

she paints with oil." Lou turned his frown on Clayt. "You ever hear o' anybody paintin' with oil?"

The distant riders dropped below the bright edge of light that illuminated the hill. As a group they fell into grisaille shadow and soon melted into the dark of the willows. When they emerged from the trees a hundred yards away, the quiet of the morning hung around Clayt and Lou for a final few moments before the work would begin. Breakenridge leaned forward, both hands pressed on the pommel, and he watched Clayt pluck more grass awns from Skitter's mane. Even when moving, there was a certain stillness about Clayt. It was as though he made not even the most trivial of efforts without first thinking it through.

"So, you gonna tell me? How it is you learnt to git up close to a painter like that?"

Clayt continued to stroke the coarse strands of his horse's mane, but his eyes drifted to some distant place. "I learnt some things 'bout that in the war."

73

CHAPTER 7

Lou's forehead creased like a freshly plowed
garden. "The war?" With his mouth hanging open, he stared at Clayt. "You never said
nothin' 'bout the damn war. Hell, you
weren't hardly old enough, were you?"

Clayt kept up the grooming, pursed his
lips, and glanced at Lou just long enough to
telegraph the message that he was not
comfortable with the direction the conversation was taking. But it was a hopeless
gesture, he knew. When Lou had hold of
something by the tail, he was known to keep
pulling.

"That how you got that scar on your
chest?"

Clayt turned a burr in his fingers as
though to inspect it. When he tossed it aside
he turned his attention toward the cattle.
He could feel Lou's questioning eyes on the
side of his face like heat radiating off a
branding iron.

"Part o' what I did for the army took me over to the other side," Clayt said quietly. "Among the enemy, I learnt 'bout not bein' noticed."

The silence that crystallized between them hushed Lou's voice to a whisper. "You're sayin' you was a spy?" He leaned forward, the better to see Clayt's face. "You and me are 'bout the same in years, ain't we?"

Clayt looked at him but only for a moment. "You can grow up right quick in a war, Lou."

"Well, hell," Lou fairly sang, "how come you was to sign up so young?"

Clayt took in a deep breath and eased it out. "Guess I just didn' know no better." He turned to study the approaching riders. "I reckon taking up the fight weren't much diff'rent than the war aw-ready goin' b'tween my father an' me."

Lou realized he had stopped breathing, lest he miss one of the soft-spoken words Clayt let slip. When the quiet stretched out, Lou cleared his throat and forced a laugh.

"Well, I reckon if you were spyin' you didn' have to kill nobody, did you?"

Still forty yards out, the group of cowhands slowed on their approach to the herd. Some of the cattle raised their heads. Others, the ones closest to the approaching

75

party, began to fold back into the herd, searching for sanctuary inside the numbers. Clayt watched it all — the reaction of the animals, the way the men sat their horses, the widening gulf of light bringing into sharp resolution the familiar details of the valley. Even with all these images occupying his vision, another picture formed in his mind. He saw the head of a young boy lying in a cushion of grass, its eyes staring upward into the firmament.

"We all killed," Clayt explained.

Lou's astonished face froze like a mask. "Well, how many did you have to kill?"

Clayt shook his head. "Didn' keep count." He grew very still. "Sometimes, though . . . at night . . . the dead faces seem to line up for me. Like each man is expectin' some kind of explanation from me." He looked at Lou. "More'n a dozen, I'd say." His voice tapered off to nothing, as though he had intended his reply to be lost on the wind.

Lou looked down at the butt of Clayt's Colt's revolver. He remembered when Clayt had purchased it at Ivinson's. It had cost the better part of a month's wages. In all these years he couldn't remember seeing Clayt pull his gun except to signal someone at a distance. The holster was one Chalky had made, premium leather softened by a decade of rubbing with saddle soap.

The incoming riders parted around the herd — five going one way and six the other — the division a tacit one defined by the nature of the men and their self-imposed social order. Nestor, with an open smile splitting his face, spurred his mount past G.T. and Chalky. His teeth shone white beneath the fledgling moustache he was tendering.

"You kill it?" Nestor called out. The boy's head jerked around in search of a carcass. Then he focused intently on Clayt. "Where is it? You kilt the painter, didn' ya?"

Clayt feathered the reins through his fingers and offered half a smile for Nestor's disappointments. "Nope."

Nestor's smile snapped like a length of taut twine. His lips closed over his teeth, and the blue of his eyes deepened. So full of bewilderment, he could find no words.

Clayt slid the shotgun from his scabbard. When he tapped his heels lightly and "chick-chicked" out the side of his mouth, the dapple-gray moved forward. By the time he reined up next to G.T.'s gelding, G.T. had Clayt's Henry rifle out. They exchanged weapons, and each man tamped his own weapon deep into its proper scabbard.

" 'Preciate the loan," Clayt said. "I'll clean

it for you tonight."

G.T. frowned at the offer. "Hell, Clayt, it was due a oilin' a month ago. I'll do it."

Nestor's excitement built all over again. "So you did git off a shot at it?"

Short-Stuff eased his horse into the parley. Rascher and the others reined up at the fringe. They all nodded to Clayt, except Rascher, who bit off a chew of tobacco and worked his jaws in a lazy rhythm as he stared off into the distance at nothing. The lost calf started up its mewling again, and everyone turned to it.

"Short," Clayt said, "how 'bout you throw'n a rope over that whiner. Walk it through the herd. See can you find the mama."

Scowling at the animal, Short-Stuff nodded and ran his tongue around the inside of his mouth as though preparing to answer the miserable creature. He turned and gave Clayt the same expression he had afforded the calf. Playing out a loop in his lariat he reined his horse around, calling for one of the men to follow.

Clayt looked the men over, pairing them up for the jobs that lay ahead in the day. It was a ritual the men knew well, based not only on each man's abilities but also on the current disagreements between them that made for friction. These seasoned cowhands awaited their assignments like schoolboys acquiescing to the wisdom of a trusted teacher. Rascher's jaws attacked his tobacco as though he were working on a tough piece of steak.

"Rascher, you cover the canyons up to Shannonhaus's bound'ry. Nestor and Short will go with you." Clayt turned to face Breakenridge. "Lou, you and G.T. cover the willows on t'other side o' the creek. See what you can flush outta there. The rest o' you can stay here to receive what the others drive in. Keep the herd settled. Chalk, the two o' us will drive down any from the timber." He waited to see if any man might have reason to protest. When he looked directly at Rascher, the older man would only give Clayt the side of his face.

"G.T.," Clayt continued, "we're gonna need some more hay from the barn. If you and Lou git back here ahead o' me and Chalk, go ahead and eat your meal, then head back to the ranch for a wagonload. If you can git back in time, might be we can let the whole herd follow you and the hay down to the south pastures come late afternoon."

No one made a move to leave yet, but there was a palpable energy gathering in the

79

group. The horses sensed it, raising their heads and blowing. The creak of saddle leather and the jingle of bits was a language unto itself, and each man readied for the day in his own particular fashion, habits that few of them could have named but were as familiar to them as morning birdsong. G.T. hunching his rounded shoulders and rolling his head to stretch the kinks from his neck. Lou biting his lip as he sorted the coils of his rope. Chalky pulling down on the brim of his hat, the movement like a solitary ripple of water quietly rising from the bottom of a deep pool. Only Nestor appeared not to change. His flame was always burning.

"Let's give it a good go today," Clayt said. "Might can git to the brandin' tomorr'."

"Is any-damn-body gone tell me what happened 'bout the damned cat?" Nestor complained.

"Don't you worry none 'bout that painter, kid," Lou said. "Clayt peppered it with some mustard seed, and it's prob'ly lit out for Canada."

Nestor, his mouth agape, looked from Breakenridge to Clayt. "Mustard seed?"

Rascher leaned and spat. Pretending to look off to the bluffs, he tightened his mouth into a curl of disgust and shook his head.

"Ain't always gotta kill somethin'," Clayt reminded the boy. "There's other agreements can be reached."

Nestor wrinkled his brow as if Clayt had spoken in the choppy tongue of the Sioux. He checked each man's face for a conspiracy. It wouldn't be the first time he was the brunt of a joke.

Rascher spat tobacco and spoke loud enough for every man to hear. "Just so you know, I ain't workin on no damn *stu*-di-o." With the others now turned to him, he let some challenge show in his face. "I hired on to work from a horse." His gaze lingered on Clayt for a moment. Then he turned away and spat again.

"I'll let you know on that," Clayt said evenly, "once I sort it out."

Rascher's head came around quickly. "I told you I ain't doin' it." He pushed his chin toward Nestor. "You can git this greenhorn moon-calf to clean it up."

Clayt smiled at Chalky. "Reckon you can teach Rascher to drive a nail, Chalk?"

"I know how to drive a goddamn nail," Rascher growled.

Ignoring Rascher, Chalky smiled at Clayt. "Yas-suh," he replied in his typical singsong

81

manner. "I reckon dat shed gonna take some work aw-right."

Rascher slapped the rump of Nestor's roan, and the horse crow-hopped. "Let's go, Purty-boy," Rascher said. "We got cattle to drive in." Rascher moved off toward the creek, his broad back shifting with the rhythm of his horse's gait.

When Clayt spoke again, his voice was low and contained as he singled out Nestor. "If you boys see Shannonhaus today, tell 'im we got two o' his steers. See can he come down to the flats b'fore mid-afternoon and collect 'em, else we can square up in a day or two in the south pasture."

Nestor took off his hat and scratched the back of his head. "Anything p'ticular we oughta do should we come across a mad-as-hell painter with hot mustard up his ass?"

Lou leaned forward on his pommel and held a poker face. "Well, now . . . that all d'pends on which Sorry-Damn cowboy the cat jumps." Then he winked at the boy. "If he starts chewin' on Rascher, come and git me. I'd like to watch that."

Short and Nestor kicked their horses into a trot to catch up with Rascher. Lou and G.T. paired off and forded the creek. Clayt watched the rest of the crew fan out among the herd, and then he looked up to check the position of the sun.

"Ready, Chalk?"

"Yas-suh. I always ready."

Chapter 8

After pushing their horses to the summit, Clayt and Chalky weaved down the timbered hill, stitching through the aspen and lodge pole pine at a slow walk. Using only hand signals each moved along the contours close enough to keep the other in sight through the blinks of light between the tree trunks. Then crisscrossing down the knob they checked every ravine and boulder field for strays, carcasses, or any sign of Sioux.

By early afternoon they had driven down seventeen head. When more boys trickled in from the willows and then from the rough country up by Shannonhaus's spread, the count of recovered livestock tallied up at thirty-one.

They had not taken a break for a mid-day meal, so G.T. shooed cattle from the shadow of the oak and built a fire to heat water for coffee. They hobbled their horses near the creek and sat among the roots of the oak, each man carrying his own food wrapped in newspaper. The cattle dozed under the high sun.

Clayt filled his cup and sat with Chalky, Short, and Nestor. Stretching out his legs and crossing them at the ankles, he leaned back into the tree trunk and gazed at the bluff.

"What you reckon's keepin' Rascher?" Clayt said, directing his question to Short-Stuff. Short shrugged and squinted across the creek. Clayt sipped coffee and dusted biscuit crumbs from his chaps. "You boys see anythin' o' Shannonhaus?"

Short was tearing at a strip of dried beef with his teeth. He let off on the struggle long enough to shake his head.

"Didn' see nobody," Nestor reported. "Didn' see no cat neither." He turned his gaze to the herd, and then his face turned pensive. "You think we'll make the count, Clayt?"

Clayt held his cup steady and considered the numbers. He liked it that Nestor brought his thoughts back to the running of the ranch. The boy might make a good foreman one day.

Clayt nodded. "We oughta pick up a dozen out o' the bottoms when we drive 'em south. Maybe the same from up on the slopes."

G.T. had four biscuits laid out before him on his slicker. He sawed through one with his belt knife, the tip of his tongue arched to his upper lip, and then he unscrewed the lid off a glass jar. He wiped the blade on his pant leg, tilted the jar, and dipped the knife into a lumpy mire of gelled condiment the color of pine sap. Breakenridge stared as G.T. spread the amber paste, closed the biscuit, and stuffed it whole into his mouth.

"Damn, Big-un," Lou said. "You eat all that . . . you might wanna shore up the wagon with new springs b'fore climbin' on. How much're you weighin' these days, any-way?"

" 'Bout two o' you," G.T. said, his voice clotted with jam and dough.

Breakenridge cocked his head, playing for remorse. "Now there's some bad luck." He looked toward the horizon and shook his head. "Twice as big . . . only half as purty."

G.T. was ready for this. "Don't seem to bother Tessa and them other girls down at Sorohan's." He layered a second biscuit with a single stroke of his knife, closed the two halves, and stuffed it into his mouth. The bulge in his cheek served to widen his smile. "They say I'm twice the lovin'. Least

Tessa did."

"What the hell's that mean?" Nestor said, frowning. " 'Twice the lovin'.' "

G.T. shrugged. "Don't know for certain, but I liked the way she looked when she said it." His smile turned impish. "I reckon some girls just like saddlin' up to a bull."

Lou laughed. "That lil' pea-shooter o' your'n ain't what I see hangin' off no bull."

G.T. laughed to show he could take a joke. When the chuckles from the boys died down, he turned an over-earnest face to Breakenridge.

"Son, you ain't never seen that pea-shooter riled up to size."

"Well, thank the good Lord for that," Short-Stuff mumbled.

"G.T.," Nestor challenged, "you ain't never bedded Tessa, and you know it."

"Hell, I know that, but the other'ns told 'er 'bout me. Hell, you ain't been with her neither." When he saw Breakenridge shaking his head and laughing, G.T. held up another biscuit and pointed at him. "And I bet you ain't neither, Lou."

Breakenridge shrugged. "That's for me to know and you to wonder 'bout."

G.T. licked his fingers and shook his head with conviction. "Nope . . . if you'd been with Tessa . . . you sure as hell would'a let

87

us know 'bout it."

"What about Sa'urday, Clayt?" Nestor said. "Swampy's goin' in for supplies. We gonna git to go into town?"

Clayt stood, poured himself more coffee, and walked to the edge of the shadow pooled under the oak. "I figure twelve men to stay with the herd. Nine from Buck's crew, and we'll add three. The south pasture's too damn easy to let slip a few into the coulees. I reckon a few young Sioux lookin' to make a name for themselves could cut out a few head and disappear back into the canyons in the time a sorry damn night-herder might light up his cigarette."

"Which o' us will be stayin' out with the herd?" G.T. asked.

"Well, I figure Chalky and Lou for the mill shed carpentry." He turned to them to make it official with a nod. "I'll find out what Mr. Aff is needin' in there. G.T. and Rascher can do the heavy work haulin' out the saw, the lumber, and such. I'll put Chalk in charge of all that." He raised his cup to Chalky, who always showed his consent with a certain relaxed stillness. "Git that studio up to snuff, and then you boys can go into town. That'll leave Short and Nestor and Harry," Clayt said. "Two o' you can stay out with me. Shy of a fistfight, I'll leave it to you to work it out."

Short-Stuff eyed Harry, who raised up on an elbow from his nap and pushed his hat brim out of his eyes. Each seemed to be waiting for the other to speak.

"I'll stay out with you, Clayt," Nestor volunteered.

"Good by me," Clayt said and looked over his cup at Harry and Short. "You boys wanna flip for it?"

"Shi-it," Short-Stuff groaned, "I'll lose a damn coin toss ever' time."

"Well, that's settled then," Harry said and lay back down.

Short-Stuff's face darkened. "Aw, hell. Go ahead and throw the damn coin then."

Clayt dug into his pocket and came out with the spent shotgun shell. He held it up for approval and indicated a bare spot in the dirt.

"I'll toss. Whoever is closest to bein' pointed at by the business end o' this cartridge spends Sa'urday night with the cattle."

When Harry and Short leaned in for a better look, Clayt flipped the shell end over end. It thumped to the dirt with a hollow ring and came to rest like an accusatory finger pointing right at Harry. Short-Stuff's face went slack.

"I'll be goddamn," Short breathed. He looked in wonderment at Clayt. "I won."

Harry lay back down and covered his face with his hat. Short-Stuff stared at him with his mouth open. He examined the shotgun shell again, then exhaled heavily.

"Aw, hell," he said. "I'll stay out with the damn animals. I don' wanna haff to hear him cryin' 'bout it for a week." Short-Stuff crushed the newspaper wrapping of his finished meal. "Ain't nobody down at Tessa's wanna see me comin' no how."

G.T. laughed. "Well, hell, Short. You think them girls are pinin' away for Harry?"

"Hey, slacker!" Nestor said, nudging Harry's boot with his own. "Short's givin' you his side o' the bed at Tessa's."

"Damn, Short," Lou said, "you're choosin' a heifer over one o' Tessa's girls?"

Short-Stuff tossed a stick at the fire and curled his upper lip. "Only one they ever gimme down there is that little fat piccaninny." Short's head turned quickly to Chalky. "No offense, Chalk."

Chalky kept watch on the horses by the creek, his expression unchanged. Short looked back at Clayt, checking to see if more apology was due.

"Where'd you last see Rascher?" Clayt

said, changing the direction of the conversation.

Short looked toward the ravines across the creek, but Nestor was quick to fill the gap. "Rascher left us and went up that draw below Shannonhaus's land. I covered that same ground yesterday. Weren't nothin' up there, but he went on anyway. Said if we didn' meet up by a hour b'fore noon in the main canyon that we was to bring on in what stragglers we had. So that's what we done. We even waited a extra quarter hour in the canyon." Nestor pursed his lips and shook his head. "No Rascher."

Clayt threw the dregs of his coffee into the grass and walked down to the bend in the creek, where the water broke over the small shoal. Kneeling, he dipped his cup in the stream and let the current flush it clean. It was the warmest day of the spring so far, and the water was running gray from snowmelt. When he stood, his eyes fixed on the mouth of the canyon that led to the west end of Shannonhaus's holdings.

Back at the oak the men lounged in the shade and finished up their meal. Watching Clayt down at the creek, Nestor threw out a quiet question for anyone who would listen.

"How come Clayt don't wear no spurs?"

"Don't need 'em," Lou said. "You seen

him ride. He can purty much control a horse with just his knees and neck-reinin'."

Nestor lay back and propped on both elbows. Lifting a leg, he turned one boot in profile and spun the rowel with the toe of his other boot.

"Hell, I like the way it sounds when I walk."

Lou stood and brushed off his trousers. "He don't need that neither."

Nestor frowned with a word half formed on his mouth, but Breakenridge was watching the approach of horsemen to the south. Nestor saw them, too, and started to yell out to Clayt, but Clayt was already leading his horse back toward the oak, his attention fixed on the incoming riders.

CHAPTER 9

"That'll be Buck comin' in," Clayt announced. "Let's git goin'." He booted into the stirrup and mounted with an easy swing of his leg. "I'm ridin' up to Shannonhaus's and see what's b'come o' Rascher. You boys keep your eyes open." He met Lou's eyes, and Lou nodded — their tacit contract for Breakenridge taking over in Clayt's absence.

"You're goin' up there alone?" Nestor said.

"Won't be alone once I find Rascher," Clayt replied. Seeing the disappointment in Nestor's face, he added, "I need you here with the cattle. I don' wanna lose any beef to Chatka and his bunch. Keep a lookout for sign, but don't go off into the timber to follow anythin'. Sioux will do that . . . leave you some sign to bait you away from the others. You hear me?"

Nestor's nostrils flared, and the tendons in his jaws bulged like marbles. His eyes burned with the fervor of a disciple. He nodded in short, stiff jerks.

"Short," Clayt said, "you boys find the mama for that bawlin' calf?"

"Nope. Dragged it all through the herd. Didn' none of 'em want that lil' beggar."

Clayt tightened the ties on his saddlebag. "G.T., better bring back a jar o' milk and a rag. Tell Swampy I need it for a orphan calf. And bring a little scrap section o' that rubber hose we used on the windmill repair."

The incoming riders slowed to a walk as they neared the herd in the clearing. Buck was out front, and it was easy to see that he had something on his mind.

"You boys havin' you a Sunday picnic out here in the shade?"

Lou was ready with a retort. "We're celebratin' 'bout us sleepin' in the bunkhouse again tonight. There's a rumor you boys'll be freezing your asses off in the rain."

That got a sour look from the men on horseback, and they looked up at the sky as if reading signs for the fickle weather in the valley. Their doubled bedrolls and slickers were lashed down behind their cantles. Every one of them knew that a night out in the wet of a spring thaw was worse than a dry hard freeze in January.

"Before we git started," Nestor yowled

through a yawn, "we was wonderin' if any o' you boys needed a little help on identifyin' the fore end of a cow from its ass. Just so you remember how to get 'em off on the right foot."

"Oh, we got that down," Whit said. "We just look for the end that looks like your grinnin' face, and then we point the other end to where we're headed."

G.T. dangled the end of a rope over the crown of Nestor's hat so that it hung in front of the boy's face. Then he mewled like the motherless calf. Nestor swatted at the rope, and the laughter mingled together from both groups as the line dividing the two bunkhouse crews blurred. They were all Sorry-Damn cowboys, and every one of them had gritted his teeth through his share of bone cold nights over the last weeks.

"Lou's in charge," Clayt said. "I'll join up with you boys in a coupla hours, after I round up Rascher."

"Where'd that ol' snake crawl off to?" Buck asked.

As an answer Clayt nodded toward the mouth of the ravine across the creek. His eyes ran across the new arrivals and stopped on Whit.

"Where's your pistol?"

The cowboy looked down at his waist and

shrugged. "In my bedroll."

"Wear it on your belt where you can git at it. You might not git a chance to slide out that Winchester when Chatka comes callin'."

Clayt twisted in his saddle to face Lou. "Once you git started, keep the herd away from water till right before you bed 'em down. Then let 'em drink their fill. Any questions, you ask Chalk."

Breakenridge flicked a two-fingered salute from his hat brim. Clayt reined around and took his horse at a walk to the creek, across the rocky shallows, and up the sandy beach that rose to the willows. Beyond the trees he picked up the trail of Nestor, Short, and Rascher — three sets of hoof prints moving in single file. When the tracks split, one set headed south along the base of the bluff. These were the largest prints that Clayt knew were made by Rascher's big paint.

Around the first big fold in the bluff he found a fresh camp set back near a small spring that seeped out of the rock. The rivulet of water trickled in a winding course over the shelf of rock to a sandy cavity that had been dug out in the shape of a bowl. Nearby in the dry sand, a ring of stones was filled with gray ash and the stubs of un-burned sticks and charred cigarette butts.

Cattle tracks gouged the sand everywhere, and among them were lines of boot prints that stitched back and forth across the clearing. Rascher's horse had laid down tracks on top of them. Another horse had been here, leaving its prints near a stand of chokecherry bushes where it had been picketed. Next to the tracks of Rascher's big paint, he found a wet spot of brown glistening on a slab of rock. Clayt dismounted, dabbed a finger, and smelled. It was tobacco.

A half-mile into the canyon, the cattle prints thinned out sufficiently that Clayt could easily follow the tracks of Rascher's paint. Climbing deeper into the defile, he encountered patches of still frozen snow in the shadows. After another quarter mile the canyon narrowed, and the floor gave way to bedrock, where Rascher's trail was reduced to subtle scrapes and scratches in the stone. Resigned now to go clear to Shannonhaus's land, Clayt climbed the stair-step shelves of stone slabs.

He had ridden this canyon many times before and a year past — from the rim — had seen it in flood, cataracts of foaming brown water roaring like sustained cannon fire. In that spring freshet, he remembered how the air had been thick with the smell of silt, like the breath of an ancient, musty beast let loose from the belly of the earth. Now the air was cool and pure, and the narrow rooms clicked with the rhythm of Skitter's hooves. The sounds echoed off the walls like the turning cogs of a windmill all around him.

One side of the canyon opened into a familiar twilit room as spacious as the loft of Afton's barn. Here the walls arched to a domed ceiling over a circular pool of blue-green water, whose surface lay so still and placid as to look like ice. He dismounted and led his horse deeper into the room through a maze of barrel-sized rocks. Stopping at the edge of the water, he listened. A drip of water from above smacked wetly on a dark slab of stone on the far side of the pool. The rhythm was slow and steady, like a clock that had defected from the outside world's passage of time. Cool air lifted off the water and touched his skin like the swabs of alcohol he remembered from the hospital in the war.

At its apex the ceiling was thirty feet high, low enough to darken the room to a perpetual crepuscular blue. The mare lowered her head to drink, but Clayt pulled her up.

"Too rich, girl. No good for drinkin'." His voice swam around the shadowed room, and the horse's head jerked up, her ears pricking at the blur of echoes. "Come on now, Skitter. You seen this place before."

Skirting the pool he returned to the sunlight in the main bed of the canyon and, on foot, climbed to the next level, where veins of snow streaked the walls, filling the cracks between rocks like mortar pressed by a mason's trowel. He filled half the crown of his hat from his canteen and held it for the horse, and as he did he spotted another brown stain of tobacco spattered on dry rock.

When the canyon floor gave way to sand and dirt, the tracks of Rascher's paint again gouged the soft earth with clean crescent shapes. Then the walls tapered lower, and Clayt emerged in a long draw bordered by shallow slopes of sandstone and loose shale. Here the snow was missing altogether, but the ground was dark from recent melt.

Following the paint's tracks he climbed to the rim and saw two men sitting their horses a quarter mile across the ridge. Neither horse was a paint. So intent were the riders in conversation that, at first, they did not see him. When both men finally looked his way Clayt raised a hand in greeting. Neither rider reciprocated.

When he had closed the distance to a

hundred yards, he recognized Shannonhaus by the girth of his body and the maimed left arm hanging useless by his side. The other man was a stranger. When Clayt reined up a few yards away, he saw that Shannonhaus's jaw was set into the familiar, inhospitable clamp of teeth that he afforded all visitors.

"Mornin', Mr. Shannonhaus," Clayt said and touched the brim of his hat. "Clayton Jane with the Afton ranch."

"I know who you are," the old man snapped, his eyes fixed on Clayt like dull nail heads. His natural strength — denied its rightful outlet through two good arms — always found compensation in the scowl fixed upon his face. Clayt had never seen the man with any other expression.

The thin stranger next to Shannonhaus was dressed in a dove-gray suit as ill-suited for the prairie as his pale skin. The man kept his face unreadable, his slate eyes studying Clayt from under the short brim of a bowler hat. His hair was almost white, fine as a woman's where it curled over his ears. He would not last half a day under the sun, Clayt estimated. The light mane of the man's palomino was a perfect match, and Clayt could not help but wonder if the man had chosen the horse like a piece of apparel.

With his hands fingering the reins, the stranger sat off to one side, as if favoring a saddle sore.

A third man on a buckskin rode up from the line shack. Clayt recognized Shannonhaus's son, Leland, a leaner version of the father but, like the elder Shannonhaus, quick to show anger. Leland was a year or two older than Clayt, but the snap in his eyes and the sharp edge to his words made him seem a younger man too ready to fight over trivial issues.

"Lookin' for one o' my men," Clayt said. "Wonderin' did you see him up this way?"

Leland kicked his horse forward and spoke up before his father could answer. "What the hell would any o' yours be doin' up here on Shannonhaus land?"

Keeping his face neutral, Clayt held his eyes on Leland's. "Reckon I'll ask 'im that when I catch up with 'im." Clayt cocked his head a fraction. "Could be he got lost."

"That draw only runs two ways," Old Man Shannonhaus said, his words clipped by his tight jaws. "Anybody who knows this piddling spring knows it runs southwest to the creek."

"Cain't argue that," Clayt said congenially. "Only thing is . . . one o' my men's missing, and I aim to find 'im."

"Well, he ain't here," Leland announced.

Clayt took off his hat and wiped his forehead with his sleeve. Using his arm as a shield to hide his eyes, he studied the ground. The paint's tracks were unmistakable. Next to the hoofprints, molded in the soft, dry dust as a skewed triangle, were three concave splotches of brown where tobacco had soaked into the dirt. Six feet away lay a smoldering cigarette butt. Hoof tracks overlapped, showing where several horses had stood, shifting their weights while standing for their riders. Clayt checked the sun, replaced his hat, and directed his words to the father.

"We got a coupla head belong to you down on the Shin Bone. You might wanna send someb'dy over before we drive the herd south today."

"How many?" Leland demanded, as if he had not heard.

Clayt looked at him again and reached into his reserves for courtesy. "Couple."

"We're missing a hellava lot more than that," Leland snapped.

Clayt nodded and looked away, trading Leland's disagreeable face for the dry windswept chaparral crowding the rock shelves and boulders. On this end of Shannonhaus's land the grass grew only in sparse pockets. It was a bad place to run cattle, worse in high summer when the grass grew high enough to tickle the belly on the beeves, for it would hide the crevices. There were just too many damned places for an animal to break a leg. Clayt gave Leland the side of his face and addressed the father.

"I reckon all o' us are missin' more'n we'd like."

"I don't see how Afton can mind losing a few," Shannonhaus growled. "What's your count up to now?"

Clayt forced himself to apply his employer's code of civility with his neighbors. The best he could do on that score was to offer a shallow smile.

"Reckon you can ask Mr. Afton 'bout that." Clayt turned his smile to the dandy on the palomino as the man brushed at something on his trousers and then examined his hands. There was not a callus visible. "Any o' you boys got a chew?" Clayt asked friendly enough. "I'm fresh out o' tobacco." He kept his eyes on the stranger.

"I don't use it, I'm afraid," the stranger said, flashing a meaningless smile. The Scottish timbre of his words surprised Clayt, taking him back to a time he seldom revisited. The Scotsman's eyes angled to the signs in the dirt, and when he looked back at Clayt, the two men stared at one another as if they each had a hold on different ends of the same secret.

"What about your strays, Mr. Shannonhaus?" Clayt asked.

"Leland," the old man ordered without turning, "send some boys down there to get 'em. While they're down there, have them look through the rest of Afton's herd." He reined his horse as though to leave but stopped. "You can tell Afton that his hired help can learn my boundaries. I don't like trespassers."

"Well," Clayt said, as if he had heard an amusing tale. "I can tell 'im."

The talking was done. The elder Shannonhaus kicked his spurs into his horse's flanks and started off down the hill toward the line shack. Leland followed, jerking the reins so that the buckskin snorted and chewed at the bit. The white-haired man produced a silver case from his coat pocket and opened it, revealing a collection of dull red paper packages twisted at both ends. The man opened one and placed a lozenge on his tongue.

"For my stomach," he said and shrugged. "Bad gut," he added. Rolling the paper into a tight ball, he cocked his arm and casually tossed the wrapping to the ground. When he kept staring at it, Clayt turned his head to see that it had landed squarely inside the triangle of tobacco pockmarks.

"So you're Jane with the Afton outfit, are you? Well, sir, I'll be paying you gentlemen a visit soon."

"That so?" Clayt said.

"Aye," he said. "The name's Dunne . . . Wallace Dunne." Tipping the front of his useless hat, he leaned in the saddle and offered his hand. Clayt took it, surprised at the man's strength. "Good luck finding your man, Mr. Jane," he said. Reining his horse around, he let the palomino choose its way through the rough scree.

Clayt looked down again at the wadded red paper lying in the dust next to the three small depressions made by brown spittle. The Scotsman had practically scratched a message in the dirt for Clayt, pointing out the fresh tobacco. Rascher had been here. Clayt knew it, and Dunne knew it. And now Clayt knew that Dunne held no particular allegiance to Shannonhaus.

Clayt watched them ride off, the three men spread out as if they had reached a tacit agreement not to communicate among themselves. Clayt leaned and stroked Skitter's neck.

"We'll git back to the flats, girl. I believe

we got more friends there."

Clayt crossed over the high ground and began retracing his path, descending the bluff along the canyon's stair-step passage that had been carved out by eons of flash floods. He would rather have followed Rascher's tracks to see where they might lead, but Afton had warned against riling his neighbors. Clayt would have to be content with questioning Rascher later. And taking his word for it.

He arrived at the creek in time to see the herd moving south behind G.T. in the hay wagon. Along the left flank, Rascher was slumped in his saddle, walking his paint at an easy gait with the cattle, swinging his quirt in lazy circles, working his jaw on the lump of tobacco bulging his cheek.

CHAPTER 10

Because the orphaned calf would not tolerate the wagon bed or a lead rope, it was after dark when Clayt reined up at the barn with the heifer slung over his thighs behind the pommel. Balancing the calf in the bow of the saddle he dismounted, lifted down the animal, and held it weightless until it got its legs. With a grip on the scruff of its neck, he led it into an empty stall inside the barn and closed the gate on its pitiful braying.

Walking Skitter toward the main house, Clayt looked up at the stars as he unbuckled his gun belt. Of all the images his eye could have conjured from that night sky, it was the stranger with pale hair that came to mind. The man had spoken only a handful of words, but the Scottish twang had been like a lucifer flame touched to Clayt's skin.

When he stopped at the front steps, he looped his gun belt over the pommel and stared for a time at the pistol jutting from its holster. The stench of war crept into him like a red stain spreading across gray wool, reminding him that he could judge no man who had visited the hell of the war years. Old Man Shannonhaus had been at Petersburg with an artillery unit out of Indiana. The story went that he had been close to a munitions explosion and had suffered not only the use of his arm but lost his mind for a time. His crew had been killed in horrible fashion, and the ambulance officer had thought him dead for all the bloodied body parts piled over him. That was the story that circulated among the hands working for Shannonhaus.

Clayt plucked a piece of dried grass from the orange blanket rolled behind his saddle. Then he ran his hand across the smooth nap of the worn wool. He thought of the way men sometimes protected themselves by wearing a false mantle of hostility. Or, for that matter, blind congeniality — like the Scotsman, Dunne. He wondered if one was any worse than the other.

The crippled dog limped across the yard and sniffed his boots. Clayt knelt, scratched the cur behind one ear and then the other. Then he ran his hand along the stove-up leg in back. The dog raised a suppliant face, and Clayt thought about how alike they were — he and this dog — both damaged in some way and both holding on to this ranch like it was a lone buoy that had somehow floated within reach in this sea of prairie.

After removing his chaps and dusting off his trousers, he climbed to the porch, where he stood before the hand-carved, oaken door that Afton had brought from England. Knocking three times, he listened and then stepped back. Through the front window he saw Cora, the housekeeper, approach. He took off his hat. As soon as the door opened he heard the clink of silverware.

"Miss Cora," Clayt said, and she made the little curtsey that always made him feel that she had mistaken him for someone else. "Mr. Afton havin' his supper?"

"He is expecting you, Mr. Jane," she announced. Her Surrey-bred voice curled and twisted words as if hers was another language entire. Yet she spoke as quietly as the tinkle of glass. Her hair was gathered into a dark knot at the back of her head. Even with her meaty arms, full bosom, and ample hips, she appeared fragile — her skin the color of milk, her eyes permanently slanted with some unnamed worry. "They're just finishing." Frowning past Clayt, she opened the door wider and stepped onto the porch toward the dog. "Shoo! There's nothing for you here! Go away!"

Clayt turned and watched old Shank limp toward the north bunkhouse. When he turned back to the housekeeper, she patted the back of her hair as if the confrontation with the dog had somehow disheveled her.

"Please come in," she said, regaining her composure.

The exotic pronunciations of her English accent always made his step across the threshold seem a passage over an unexpected boundary. She left him standing in the dusky hallway with the rows of cased daguerreotypes hanging above the wainscoting. It was his ritual to study them as he waited, as it was too many eyes staring out at him not to take notice.

He supposed them all to be Afton's family — or, perhaps, Mrs. Afton's — and, by the manner of their poses and clothing, people of high standing. He had never asked about them, just as he would want no man to ask about his family. The faces in the pictures appeared old, as did the copper plates bearing their images. Clayt allowed that these people were probably dead. Photography and death wove together like a prophecy in his memory. In the war he had seen boys pose for portraits meant to be sent home . . . to be remembered by. Each soldier had assiduously printed a mailing address on the back of the plate. Clayt, who had never sat for a photograph, sometimes wondered if this was what had saved him in battle.

The monotonous ticks of a clock measured out the silence in this part of the house, its rhythm bringing to mind the steady drip of mineralized water in the canyon room. Both places were dark and cool and divided by audible intervals of time, but the hallway felt nothing like the canyon room — not at its heart — and he decided that this had something to do with the permanence of one over the photographic reminder of mortality in the other.

Cora returned and waved him into the main room of the house, where a just-lit fire was working its way up through a stack of split cottonwood in the hearth.

"Mr. Afton says to please come in and have a seat by the fire. May I take your hat?" Clayt shook his head and remained standing in the center of the room. Cora made her little bow but hesitated. "Is Mr. Taylor out with the livestock tonight?"

Clayt cocked one ear forward. "Ma'am? Oh, you mean G.T.? He oughta be at the bunkhouse. I came straight here, so I don't

111

know for certain."

Her face flushed, and her gaze angled to the fire crackling in the hearth. "Well, please tell him that he can return the jar when he would like some more preserves for your crew." She hesitated again, studying his expression. "How did you like the peach preserves today?"

Clayt turned his hat in his hand. He gave her as stoic a look as he could muster.

"Miss Cora, I reckon there's some things too good to be figurin' on handin' out in shares. Guess you'll have to ask G.T. 'bout them preserves." He lowered his voice to the timbre of a secret. "But if I had to say, I'd wager it was the finest part o' his day."

Her smile spread upward into her eyes, and she blushed pink from chin to forehead. John Afton walked into the room with a cloth napkin in his hand. Both his smile and silky, brown moustache curled upward at the ends. His teeth shone in bright contrast.

"Clayton, come join us for some of Cora's pie. Cora, would you set another place?"

Clayt raised his hat and gently fanned the air between them. "I can come back when you're done eatin'. I've not sat down to my own supper yet."

Afton put a hand on Clayt's elbow and turned him toward the dining room. "It's buttermilk pie, isn't it, Cora?" Without waiting for an answer Afton stopped abruptly. "There's word from the fort that Chatka made a raid over on the headwaters of the Platte. Killed three men." He leaned forward and lowered his voice. "I don't want Mrs. Afton hearing about such matters." He nodded toward the dining room. "We'll want to hear how the roundup is proceeding."

Stepping into the dining room, Clayt felt as out of place as a dog that had strayed into a Sunday service. The candles lighting the table gave a regal glow to the linen, gilded porcelain plates, and brightly polished silverware. A large mirror on the wall gave the impression of more candles burning in an adjoining room. Another fire struggled in the smaller hearth. Elizabeth Afton's face shone like alabaster when she smiled.

"Clayton, come tell us of the hinterlands. Are there any wildflowers in bloom yet?"

Afton sat down at the head of the table. Inside his house, he appeared a taller man than he was — even sitting. His movements were precise and flowing so that a man could temporarily overlook Afton's stiff manner on a horse. Clayt looked down at the chair offered him and considered the state of his trousers after days in the saddle.

Elizabeth patted the tablecloth and produced a mock frown.

"Sit," she insisted. "I want a full report." Then she smiled the smile that reduced any ranch hand to a model of obedience.

Clayt lowered himself into the chair like a man easing through a stand of briars. He set his hat on the floor. When he looked at Mrs. Afton, he saw the same high forehead captured in one of the photographs in the hall. Her eyes shone with anticipation.

"Well, up in one o' the seeps by the flats . . . I seen some orchids. And there's some paintbrush and shootin' star 'bout to open up in the meadows."

Sitting forward, Elizabeth Ashton widened her eyes. "Which orchids?" She threaded her fingers into a shelf under her chin as though she expected a long story.

"It's what we call 'chatterbox.' " He glanced at Mr. Afton before going on. "It's got a little piece o' the flower that waggles like a tongue when the wind hits it just right."

Elizabeth smiled, sat upright, and brought her hands together in a single celebratory clap. "John, I believe I will have to go out and see this orchid." She looked back quickly to Clayt and began nodding enthusiastically, enlisting his support in this matter.

"Lizzie," Afton groaned, "you've got more flowers right here at the ranch than you know what to do with. It's not safe that far out." He propped his elbows on the table. "What about this mountain lion, Clayton? What the men call a 'painter'?"

"Didn' amount to much. You ain't gotta worry 'bout that."

"Did you kill a mountain lion?" Elizabeth asked. Clayt liked the way she allowed herself to be surprised. Sometimes he thought her reactions were meant to represent both herself and her husband, as he seldom broke out of his business demeanor.

"No, ma'am."

Afton studied Clayt. "But there *was* one out there at the flats?"

"Was," Clayt said.

Cora served slices of pie on small white plates trimmed in blue. Before Clayt she placed a folded napkin and a shining fork with a raised design on the handle.

"You won't find better pie in the best restaurants of London, Clayton," Afton said. He cut off a wedge, chewed, and closed his eyes. Cora waited. Afton exhaled through his nose. "Cora, you are the best kept secret in Wyoming."

115

Her eyes darted to Clayt's and held for a moment, telegraphing a message to which he did not know how to respond. He knew it had something to do with G.T. Maybe she expected him to say something more about the pie — something meant to be repeated in the bunkhouse. He forked up a bite, chewed, and nodded.

"Reckon we'll need to keep that secret goin'. If the boys catch wind o' this . . . me eatin' Miss Cora's pie . . . and them gnawin' on Swampy's fry bread —" Clayt shook his head in mock gravity and forked off another piece. Smiling, Cora returned to the kitchen.

"Will we top nine thousand?" Afton asked.

Clayt nodded. "Closer to nine and a half."

"What about Shannonhaus? Are any of those his?"

"He sent down two o' his men and got what was his. There was only three."

"Any trouble?"

Clayt finished the last of the pie, looked into his plate, and conjured the image of the Scotsman in his city clothes. Clayt wiped his mouth with his napkin.

"No trouble. Not as I could see."

"Good. Let's keep things that way. This is not a good time for confrontation."

Clayt laid the napkin beside his plate.

116

"Anything I oughta know 'bout that?"

Afton sat back in his chair. "We are having some illustrious guests coming our way."

"Lou told me 'bout your family comin' from England."

Afton smiled and arched an eyebrow. "I'm talking about the president of the United States. And Hayes, the new nominee the Republicans hope to take his place."

"They're comin' here to the ranch?"

"Well," Afton said, flipping one hand palm up. "Not for certain. I will extend an invitation, of course. President Grant will no doubt lodge at Fort Sanders. Still, we might coax him out here for a meal." Afton leaned forward on his elbows and spoke in a conspiratorial whisper. "I'm hoping to arrange his portrait . . . done by my sister."

"Oh, John," Elizabeth purred. "You're putting the cart before the horse. You've not even approached her about this, not to mention the president."

"Well," he said, knitting his eyebrows low over his eyes, "her visit will coincide with the president's. If *he* agrees, I really don't see how she could refuse." He sat back in his chair but held on to his discontent. "The point is . . . I don't want trouble with Shannonhaus right now."

"He is a most disagreeable man," Elizabeth Afton said, conjuring up a puckered frown. "Small minded and rude."

Taking up his fork Afton pushed a flake of crust across his plate and conceded his wife's point with a cant of his head. "Perhaps he is not so small minded that extending some of that free-range pasturage on to *my* land is in his plans."

Clayt stared down at his plate and let the quiet draw out. "Mr. Afton," he said, "I reckon I know how the boys would react if they found Shannonhaus's men grazin' cattle on Rollin F grass. It's likely to cause a scrape."

Afton frowned. "How do you mean? With guns?"

"Hard to say. You cain't never really predict that. Sometimes words are enough. Other times it can slide right down into a shootin' exchange."

Afton glared into the fire, the skin across his forehead tightening. Then his eyes snapped back quickly to Clayt.

"Are you asking me to tell you how to handle it, if such a situation arises?"

"Nos'r. I'm just tellin' you what to be ready for."

Afton shook his head. "A few acres of land is not worth a man's life."

"Nos'r. Not to you. But maybe to Shannonhaus. He ain't got the water sources you got."

Afton tapered one end of his moustache with his fingers. "This is not the time for a range war, Clayt. Or for trekking off to the courts in Cheyenne." With his elbow resting on the table Afton tapped his closed fist against his mouth. "Do you really think it could come to that? Shooting, I mean?"

"The old man is mostly cantankerous, but I never knowed him to jerk a gun on a man. But there's men on both sides o' this can git mean right fast. Shannonhaus's son is one."

"And who on our crew?" Afton asked.

"Given the right circumstance, could be anyb'dy. Like I said, you cain't predict it."

"You're talking about Rascher, aren't you?"

Clayt shook his head. "It ain't just him. He's a lot o' sour vinegar and wind, but anybody might say just the wrong thing to spark it off. Any o' the boys could. Don't none of 'em much care for Shannonhaus . . . or a man that'd choose to work for 'im."

Elizabeth Afton set down her fork, her pie half eaten. "What would you do, Clayton, if you found Shannonhaus's cattle on our land?"

"Well . . . depends. If it's just cattle . . .

run 'em back up to Shannonhaus's. If there's drovers with 'em . . . tell 'em to move on and take their herd with 'em."

"And if they refuse?"

Clayt smoothed a crease in the tablecloth with his fingertips. Then he let his hands rest idly on each side of his plate as he looked squarely into Mrs. Afton's probing eyes.

"They ain't likely to do that."

She studied his jade-green eyes and thought them oddly opaque, his face unreadable. She nodded slowly before glancing at her husband. The quiet became heavy, and Clayt could see there were more questions stirring inside both Aftons.

"You reckon Chatka talked like this 'bout us a few years back?" Clayt said with a chuckle. "Him wonderin' what he oughta do should more of us move into the valley?"

"Have you seen any signs of Indians around the flats?" Afton asked.

"Nos'r. I reckon they're up in the hills out west of the south pastures." Clayt pursed his lips and nodded. "But they'll make a run at the cattle b'fore too long." His eyes fixed on Afton and took on a thoughtful glaze. "Was prob'ly a hard winter for Chatka and his band."

"Are the men prepared for him? Do they

take these Sioux seriously?"

"They'll make a good showin' when the time comes."

"How is the boy working out? Purdabaugh?"

"Nestor? He'll do just fine."

Cora came in and began collecting dishes. Clayt picked up his plate and handed it to her.

"Mighty good, Miss Cora."

She smiled with a flutter of her eyelashes. "Shall I serve tea now, Mr. Afton?"

Afton pushed back his chair and stood. "Yes, we'll move into the study."

Elizabeth Afton stood, removed a white sweater from her chair back, and draped it over her shoulders. "I'll leave you men to your business. I have letters to write. Good night, Clayton."

Clayt scooped up his hat and stood. "G'night, ma'am."

Afton led the way to the next room, stood before the fireplace, and picked up a curved pipe from the mantle. After opening a ceramic jar, he tamped tobacco into the pipe bowl with his slender thumb.

"Do you expect those mustangs to return this spring, Clayton?"

Clayt took his place at the middle of the room, spread his boots, and held his hat with both hands before his thighs. "Hard to say, Mr. Afton. Depends some on the movement of these Sioux. That and the weather. But animals follow habits purty much like we do. We'll prob'ly git a go at 'em b'fore too long."

Afton sat in the leather chair closest to the fire, leaned to one side, and adjusted his jacket. Once he got the pipe burning to his satisfaction, he hooked one knee over the other. His polished boots picked up the reflections from the fire like mirrors.

"These bloody Sioux," Afton said through clamped teeth, "this Chatka . . . he bothers me." He removed the pipe and pointed with it to the furniture. "Sit down, Clayton."

It was the chair regularly offered — a red cushioned upright with gold embroidery. Clayt had never sat in it.

"I'll just perch here and stretch my legs, if you don' care. I been in the saddle most the day." As was his ritual, he set his hat upside down in the chair.

Afton turned to the fire, took a long draw on the pipe, and let the smoke seep from his mouth like thoughts slow to form. The smoke smelled rich and sweet and reminded Clayt of his father's curing shed. Cora entered with a tray and walked first to Clayt, turning the tray to put the cup with

122

coffee directly within his reach. It was a tacit transaction they had practiced for years, ever since Clayt had returned those first English teas barely touched. Afton took his tea and waited for Cora to leave.

"This Chatka is a mad dog who needs to be shot." Afton held the saucer and cup steady, his face a mix of anger and vulnerability. "Isabella's world is not like this."

"Sir?"

"My sister, Isabella. I cannot . . . I *will* not . . . allow anything to happen to her. Or to her family." Afton rotated his cup by the handle and paused. "Do you understand?"

"Yes'r, reckon I do."

Afton drank and set the cup and saucer aside. "On the other hand, I can't keep them here at the house all the time. They'll want to see the country." He laughed ruefully. "Isabella will want to paint it. All of it." He snorted. "I think she would paint Chatka if he would sit for her."

Clayt tried the coffee. It was too sweet. He wondered if Cora was trying to balance out his deficit of peach preserves. He held the saucer before him and balanced the cup on it as he looked at the fire. The dark andirons stood erect inside the twist of the flames. Under Chalky's tutelage, Clayt himself had pounded out the irons at the forge in that first year of his training, before Grady Brooks had taken over the blacksmithing full time.

"I reckon they'll need to be part of a strong party whenever they ride out from the ranch," Clayt said. "Say four or five of the boys if you can spare 'em."

Afton laughed like a man who had an answer for everything. "I can, and I will." He picked up his tea again, sipped, and set down cup and saucer with the certainty of a man who had thought out his options. "I want someone riding out ahead of them . . . a scout . . . who knows everything breathing within a mile radius."

"That'd be Chalky. He can read sign good as any Ind'an."

Afton nodded and pinned Clayt with a peremptory stare. "All right. And you're to be with Isabella. If she is at the river, you are at the river. If she wants to ride the canyon country, you are to be there beside her. The same is true for her husband, but I doubt that he will be as difficult. He is —" Afton circled his head as he searched for the words. "He is like me, a businessman."

The flames were like snakes' tongues flicking at the logs. Red coals pulsed beneath the iron grate. The mortared stone threw back a wave of heat that now felt oppressive. Clayt moved to the hearth and set the cup and saucer on the mantle. Backstepping, he returned to the center of the room. Keeping his eyes on the flames, he evened his voice.

"This mean you're takin' me off foreman?"

Afton waved that off. "I'm elevating you to a new position." He waited for Clayt to meet his eyes. "I want you to ensure the welfare of my sister."

Clayt had never seen such resolute authority in the Englishman's face. He knew that Afton would stare like this until Clayt gave a proper reply.

"I'll do whatever it is you need me to do, Mr. Afton. You know that."

Afton clamped the pipe in his mouth and struck another lucifer. "Who would be best to take over your responsibilities for the time that my sister is here?"

"That'd be Lou."

"Breakenridge?"

"Yes'r."

"All right then. You tell him. And tell the others. I want this shift of responsibilities to take place without problems. And let Chalky know that he is to report directly to you. I'll leave it to you to choose the other men you will need for the escort party."

"When is it 'xactly you'll be 'xpectin' your kin?"

"They arrived in Boston a few days ago. The trip by rail should take five days. They should be under way now. They will keep me informed by wire."

Clayt found himself looking at the paintings hanging above the mantle. He had admired them before, but now he studied them, wondering if they were the work of Afton's sister. He took note of the extreme dark and light in each composition. That was the one common likeness connecting all of them. Sunlight cutting into deep forest. Sky-glow gilding the edge of an old man's face as he worked by a window. A candle held by a child in a dark room. The renderings of light appeared to be real, as though a lantern was burning behind each canvas.

"Those were done by Isabella," Afton said, unasked.

Clayt continued to study them. There weren't many different colors in any one painting, but the chosen colors baffled him. He did not think that the sky could be such a visceral purple or that shadows truly contained the blues and golds rendered here. Still, he recognized the images for what they were.

"Reckon havin' that escort is gonna leave us short handed," Clayt said. "You given any thought to taking on some new hands?"

"How many do you need?"

Clayt tilted his head. "Well, three anyway. Wouldn' mind four."

"Do you know anyone who would be dependable?"

"There's a few boys in town oughta tote the load. They might consider it."

"I'll go on your judgment about that. When can you talk to them?"

"Best time to snare these boys is at night . . . down at Sorohan's. I could go into town tomorr' night."

"All right. You can offer them the going pay. It will most likely be for just the month."

Clayt looked down at his boots. "If it's all the same to you . . . I'd rather offer somethin' less. Our boys here might not take to part-time saddlers pullin' in top pay."

Afton frowned and pursed his lips. "All right, you decide, Clayton."

Clayt nodded and looked again at the paintings. He tried to imagine them without those ill-conceived colors and was surprised to admit their function in the end result. Perhaps the intention, he thought, was to stretch a man's credulous hold on the world.

"Wonderful, aren't they?" Afton remarked.

Clayt's eyes explored the paintings. "They keep you lookin' at 'em."

Afton smiled knowingly. "She can create a likeness like a photograph when she wants to. This goes deeper."

Clayt examined the portrait of the old man, wondering if such tints lay buried like ore beneath the surface of a man's skin. Perhaps only an artist could mine it out.

"What is it your sister'll be wantin' in this studio, Mr. Aff?"

"Clean. That's the first thing. No dust. It gets in the paint. The shelves and table should work for her once they are scrubbed. More than that, I don't know exactly. I suppose we ought to make an easel. Could you make that?"

"Just a tripod with a lil' shelf, ain't it?"

Afton nodded. "I suppose it will need to be collapsible. She'll want to take it out into the prairie."

"I reckon we can come up with a easel."

"Well . . ." Afton gripped his pipe with his teeth and slapped his thighs as he stood. "Go have some supper, Clayton."

Clayt picked up his hat, and they walked to the entrance hall. He let himself out with a goodnight, but Afton surprised him by stepping out onto the porch.

"Keep an eye out for those mustangs, Clayton. I've got a buyer at Cheyenne for sixty of our equine stock. We'll want to replace them."

"Yes'r," Clayt said and walked down the steps.

"Good night, Clayton," Afton said and went inside, closing the door behind him.

Clayt rubbed Skitter's neck and checked the sky. He stared at the stars for a time, trying to divine a color he might have missed between the points of light, but there was nothing there that could not be called "black." He wondered what paint Afton's sister might choose for this night sky. He relaxed his gaze to stare at the whole sea of silent stars and only then realized the calf in the barn had quieted. Skitter turned and nickered.

"I bet you're thinkin' you're due some sweet grain 'bout now, ain't you, girl?"

He led the mare in a half circle to start for the barn but stopped short when he heard the door to the house open again. Cora's broad silhouette hurried down the steps.

"Mr. Jane," she called quietly. In her hands she held something that caught glints of light from the window behind her. "Would you take this to Mr. Taylor for me?"

He could not see her face, but her voice trembled like a child's. Clayt felt a jar pushed into his hands, and already she was backing away.

"I was wonderin', Miss Cora, if you wouldn' mind makin' up some warm milk for a maverick I got in the barn." She stood for a moment without speaking. Then she looked toward the barn. "I'm thinkin' her mama died on 'er," he added.

"All right," she said. She wet her lips with her tongue. "How do I feed it?"

"I reckon I'll need to send somebody over to show you."

The sudden silence was like a curtain falling around them, creating an unexpected intimacy. When she got her voice, it was fearful but charged with hope.

"When should I take the warm milk in there?"

"Better give me 'bout ten minutes. I'll see can I git someb'dy over there and help you." He handed back the jar. "You might wanna give this to 'im yourself . . . seein' as how he's keepin' it private and all."

CHAPTER 11

It was a full day of branding in the south
pasture, and the boys switched off on their
duties — sometimes standing guard over
the herd, other times cutting out calves, rop-
ing and wrestling them to the ground to be
seared by red-hot metal. G.T. kept a healthy
bed of hot coals for the stamp irons by running Nestor and Short-Stuff to the edge of
the hills for downed hardwood. There was a
rhythm to the work that satisfied all, save
the cattle. In typical fashion they balked at
the rough handling. When enough of the
herd was gathered in the field, Swampy set
up the chow wagon for meals and kept coffee brewing.

It was early when Clayt rode back to the
ranch. He cleaned up, put on his best shirt,
and rode off for town before the others had
returned. On the hunch that he might
encounter the mustangs, he took the lesser-
used trail that skirted an old buffalo wallow.

Though he saw none, he did see their signs. The unshod hoofprints whispered to him like a benediction to the natural cycles of the prairie, and he took satisfaction in knowing that the animals still ran free.

The twilight coaxed from the prairie grass a faint blue. It was not something you could point your finger at but a glow that seemed to leach into the night air like the seepage of a subtle fluorescent gas. He had seen it many times, but now he wondered how an artist might capture that blue-tinged air that hung over the land at early evening. Chalky called it "God's last breath, blowing out da candle flame of da day." And just as daybreak allowed Clayt his rightful ownership of the coming day, this parting color was like an elegiac entry in a ledger that recorded what a man had accomplished on that given day. That was what mattered, Clayt knew. *What* you did. And *how* you had done it. It was important, because it was something larger than any one man. The thread of small deeds performed by each Sorry-Damn cowboy stitched together to make the fabric of a working ranch. It was that fabric, Clayt knew, that defined who he was.

By the time he hooked up with the main road, the colors had muted. When he spotted the silhouette of the penitentiary's peaked roof spearing upward out of the scrub, the stars had spread across the sky like tiny flecks of mica suspended in black water. Pulled by the smell of the river, Skitter picked up her gait.

At the bridge Clayt dismounted and walked his horse down the bank to drink her fill, and as she drank he watched the lights from town push up a dull halo above the prairie. He mounted, clopped across the bridge, and crested the rise beyond the river.

The town was spread out in silent dots of light. In just eight years the settlement had grown to a size no one would have anticipated before the railroad had come. In daylight Laramie seemed an intrusion on the land, but he liked this nocturnal view. It was like a placid lake reflecting the map of the stars. With the susurrus of water behind him and the incessant sweep of wind in his ears, Laramie bared its soul to him from the confessional of distance and darkness.

By the time he was close enough to hear the notes of a tinkling piano, he felt his defenses begin to sharpen. The notion of a town as a thing of beauty was now unexplainably behind him, like something he had accidentally dropped out in the emptiness of the grasslands. He passed the outlying abodes that marked the edge of town, wondering how a complete life could be had in such a small space. The homes were built of rough-sawn pine but dressed out with enough ornate carpentry work and coats of paint to elevate their status above the plain outbuildings standing behind them. Smoke streamed from metal flues. Lights glowed through curtains of yellow and blue and fancy white lace, every window like the cover of a book. There was, he knew, a story spelled out behind each one of them, and, just as the marks made in books eluded him, so did these colorful blurs of light hide the lives of those within.

There was a paradox to it. Four walls might look a lot like a box to him, but a house could fairly define peace and solitude — that is, if a man lived inside those walls alone. A cabin might not be so bad somewhere down the line. He had imagined such a life up on the flats at Shin Bone. It was something to consider.

He crossed the Union Pacific tracks and turned onto Grand Avenue, where the larger houses of brick and quarried stone flaunted their owners' wealth. There was a riddle to mansions, too. A man could probably get lost in one of those houses with so many rooms that the variety of furniture pieces seemed endless. But, as he had learned, the size of such a house could mark a certain smallness for the people inside its walls. Along with the money these citizens had amassed, there often came a certain haughtiness attached to it.

Clayt pulled up in the light spilling out from Sorohan's. The piano was lively, but he could hear by its unchallenged clarity that a crowd had not gathered. He slid his rifle from its scabbard, walked inside, and propped the rifle behind the bar. The gray-haired bartender in stovepipe hat closed the cover on a book and watched Clayt walk the length of the bar.

Two poker games were in session, and a few of the town regulars perched around the periphery hoping for a big spender to buy drinks. That wasn't going to happen tonight — not with this crowd — but the beggars seemed ever-optimistic. A group of businessmen smoked cigars at a table in back. Their glasses were empty.

The "companion women" had not come down from upstairs, which explained the unusual quiet in the room. The piano player closed his song with a flourish and turned in his seat to assess his audience. Taking a cigar from a tin can, he walked out the back door.

"Well," the bartender said, "all them cattle must be tucked away in bed somewhere. Haven't seen you in a month." His whiskered cheeks were webbed with broken blood vessels, and his moist eyes loomed unnaturally large behind thick spectacles. Clayt reached across the polished bar to take the palsied hand offered to him. It felt weightless.

"Emmett. Not much doin' tonight."

Emmett surveyed the room. "Aw, it's early yet." He bent beneath the bar and came up with a yellow envelope. "A boy ran this over yesterday evening, figurin' one of you Sorry-Damn boys would come by tonight."

Clayt took the envelope, seeing by its color it was a Western Union telegraph. He turned it over twice and looked up at Emmett.

"For Mr. Afton," Emmett said. "From Ogallala."

Clayt tucked the letter into his shirt and nodded toward the book lying on the bar. "What're you plowin' through now?"

"Still wading through Mr. Shakespeare. You'd like this one."

"Only if I could read it," Clayt said.

Emmett tapped the book's cover. "This'n here's King Henry taking his soldiers over the channel to fight the Frenchies." Emmett opened the book and flipped back through the pages, not reading but shaking his head. "He's outnumbered somethin' terrible, but old Henry's the kind could convince you to go in a grizzly's den if he done made up his mind it's the right thing to do. He's a talker. Damned if he don't get my blood to boiling."

"How's it play out?"

"Don't know yet. Tell you this though. If old Henry makes it out a this'n, I might have to buy your English Mr. Afton a drink next time he comes in."

Clayt leaned into the bar and scanned the room. "Seen Johnny Waites 'round?"

"He was in the other night."

Clayt turned and watched the game where three cow hands played for small change. "Is he workin'?"

"Johnny? I couldn't say."

"Wouldn' know where he's stayin', would ya?"

Emmett puffed air from his mouth, and, as he did, his lips fluttered like a sheet hung out in a stiff wind. "I can tell you what a man drinks and which whore he's best suited for and that's about it."

Clayt dug coins out of his pocket and counted them on the bar top. "Gimme a coupla cold beers, Emmett." While Emmet tapped the barrel, Clayt turned around the open book and let his eyes rove over the rows of neat tracks etched across the pages. They always brought to mind the little plover, whose sharp little toes stitched arrow-straight lines on the sandy shorelines of rivers and lakes. It seemed a miracle to him that a man could pull a polished sentence from such marks as these. When both mugs were set on the bar, he picked one up and tapped the rim of the other.

"That'n there's for King Henry. What you say we drink one to him."

Emmett performed a small bow from the waist. "King Henry accepts and thanks you for your kindness." He lifted the beer and buried his bushy moustache into the foam.

Clayt studied the three cowboys seated at the table again. Their game was sluggish and, by the looks of the pot, more sport than profit or loss. One man — a tall one with a red kerchief — Clayt had seen out on the range with Johnny Waites.

"You heard about the president coming to Laramie?" Emmett said. "Grant and this Hayes they want to see follow 'im into the White House. You ever see a president before?"

Clayt sipped his beer, keeping watch on the trio of cowboys at the table. A thick-shouldered man with a broad face slapped down his cards, closed his eyes, and pinched the bridge of his thick nose. Clayt set down his mug and felt the coolness of the drink spread agreeably through his chest.

"I reckon he'll look purty much like any other man out stumpin' for a vote."

When the tall cowboy raked in the menial pot, Clayt took off his hat and left it on the bar. Carrying his beer mug, he ambled within a few paces of the table. Sipping his drink he waited for one of the men to take notice. It was the dealer who looked up.

"Don't mean to intrude on your privacy, boys," Clayt said.

"Come on and sit down," the dealer invited. "Your money's good here."

Clayt shook his head. "I'd like to talk with Johnny Waites." He nodded toward the tall one. "Thought you might know where I could find 'im."

The man was a Texan, Clayt remembered, a saddler who had taken up with Johnny in Amarillo. The Texan ran his hand over his mouth, stroking the drooping tails of his moustache as he studied Clayt.

"You're the foreman out at Afton's."

"Clayton Jane," Clayt said and sipped from his mug.

"You looking for someone to hire on out

139

there?" the Texan asked.

Clayt squinted one eye. "I'm lookin for Johnny," he said friendly enough.

The dealer shuffled and sailed cards to his friends with deft flicks of his wrist. The tall Texan picked up his cards and opened them into a tight fan. He kept his eyes on his hand and said, "I reckon you can find Waites up at Shannonhaus's spread."

"That right?" Clayt said. "Shannonhaus is hirin' now?"

The man's mouth twisted to a crooked smile. "If you can pass his goddamn test."

Clayt took another sip from his mug. One of the girls appeared at the upstairs handrail and stood there tying something in her hair. She wore a dull-yellow dress and hoops of jewelry on her wrists. Clayt watched her inventory the room. When her eyes stopped on him, her mouth twitched as if she might smile, but she didn't. She turned and disappeared down the dark hallway.

"What kinda test we talkin' 'bout?" Clayt probed.

The lanky drover hissed air through his teeth and tossed two cards into the deadwood. "Think you could level a rifle and hit one o' these at eighty paces?" He picked up a shot glass and grunted a sarcastic laugh. "Shit. I didn't come out here to join up with a damn circus."

"And I didn' come to work no damn brickyard," the dealer said, "but it might come to that." He raised his chin to Clayt. "So, you hirin' up there at Afton's or ain't ya? Bud and me's gotta find some kind o' tolerable work . . . and soon."

Clayt nodded. "I'll keep that in mind. You boys have a good evenin'."

When he stepped back to the bar he finished off his beer and saw Tessa standing on the landing above him. Leaning on the rail with both hands, she hunched her shoulders around the dark curls of her hair and smiled. Her dress was a purplish shade of blue, a darker, shinier version of the prairie's glow at dusk. Clayt raised his empty mug to her, and her smile widened.

"Better give me another, Emmett, and some o' that Irish whiskey that Tessa favors."

She was waiting for him at a table in the back corner, her smile now pushed lopsided under one cheekbone, her eyes boring into him as though she could read the story of his life and tell him about every turn where he had gone wrong. He sat down and admired her. The potency of her perfume was as portentous as the smell of coming rain.

"You've been spending more time with

141

cows than you have with me," she said.

Clayt pushed the shot glass to her. "That's my job," he said and tried to read her face for hurt or amusement. He decided on the latter. She traded the smile for a contrived look of astuteness and began nodding slowly.

"I guess that's why they call you 'cowboys.' "

Her skin was darker than most women's, but when asked about it her eyes danced with private humor, and her tight-lipped smile turned impish. The whites of her eyes were startling and her hair as black and shining as obsidian. Tessa would never admit to mixed blood, not because she was ashamed, but because she put no stock in such prejudices. She was who she was because of something inside her . . . not due to the shade of her skin. She pushed her mischievous smile to the other side of her face and tilted her head back as though to see the whole of Clayt.

"Wouldn't do to be called a 'Tessa-boy,' I guess," she quipped.

Clayt smiled into his drink. "Don't have quite the ring to it, I guess."

"Doesn't have a *ring* at all," she teased, wiggling her bare ring finger. "Not without two magic words."

Clayt worked on his beer and tried to catch up to her thoughts. She was always saying clever things, some he did not pick up on until a day later.

Clayt narrowed one eye. "I thought it was *three* magic words a girl wants to hear."

Tessa frowned and smiled at the same time. "Honey," she said in her most jaded voice, "we hear those three words all the time. They're easy to come by. I'm talking about 'I' and 'do.' " Raising her eyebrows, she smiled at his blank stare.

With the lift of one hand he gestured vaguely at the room. "There's plenty o' boys like a go at that with you, Tessa."

"There's more than plenty would like a *go* at me," she laughed. "I let my girls handle them." She tapped the toe of her shoe against his boot. "Most of them."

Clayt studied her for a time. "You're sayin' you wanna settle down?"

Her smile was now devilish. "With the right man," she said, and by the way she said it, he could guess on a dozen meanings for it.

Clayt looked at the merchants in deep discussion two tables away. A haze of cigar smoke wrapped around them as though they had created a separate room for themselves.

"I reckon the right man will come along some time," he said, giving her an honest smile. Admiring the lines of her face, he could imagine no sane man turning her down.

"Oh, sure . . . they come along," she agreed. "But they're usually too blind to see what they got."

Clayt swirled the remains of his beer and watched it settle. Clearing his throat he nodded thoughtfully before looking up.

"This you and me we're talkin' 'bout here?" Clayt asked quietly.

Tessa gave him a hard smile. "Who else shares my bed?"

He didn't have an answer to that, but he knew not to take it any farther. The piano started up again, but it was distant now, incapable of filling the silence between them.

"Do you think you might recognize love if it came your way, Foreman Jane?" she finally said and grinned.

"Don't reckon I know much 'bout all that, Tessa."

"Well, who do you suppose is going to teach it to you . . . if it isn't me?"

He leaned forward on his elbows and lowered his voice to a hoarse whisper. "You're the finest lookin' woman I know,

Tessa. Smart, too. Way ahead o' me."

"But you wouldn't say it, would you?" She smiled at the way he could keep a question from showing on his face. " 'I do'?" she explained, reminding him. She reached across the table and slid a hand over his, her fingernails digging in like they did when she lost herself with him in carnal heat. "If you can't say it now, I'll be satisfied for what we have for the present." She squeezed his hand tighter. "Want to come upstairs?"

The piano player's fingers jumped all over the keyboard, the upbeat song wholly inappropriate to their conversation.

"I do," Clayt said.

Smiling, she rose to lead the way but stopped and looked back at him when his choice of words caught up to her. Her eyes danced with impish reproof.

"Cute," she said in a flat tone.

Clayt pushed back his chair. "Let me go see to my horse first."

CHAPTER 12

The room was dark but for the thin incision of light under the door. The piano had stopped, but the voices from the saloon downstairs remained a constant river of guttural male sounds and the occasional high, cascading laugh of a woman. Clayt sat up in bed and let his feet lightly touch the floor. Behind him Tessa's soft, even breathing made the room seem a refuge from the noise in the saloon below.

The aroma of her bath oils and perfume made him think of Mrs. Aff's rose bushes. He raised a forearm to his nose, checking to see if he now carried such a scent. There was no way to tell. Everything in Tessa's room seemed steeped in the concoction.

He felt his way to the box of lucifers by the oil lamp, scratched a stick into a flame, and lighted the wick. As he stepped into the bottom of his long johns, he stared at the items carefully laid out on the dresser.

146

Tessa's little blue snap purse from which he had once seen her draw a one-hundred dollar note. Next to it stood the small ornate clock that she said was from France. It read ten minutes after four. Instead of numbers there were jewels inlaid along its dark wooden face, and he smiled when he thought of the day she had told him that he knew how to read time in French.

Beside an opened envelope lay a folded letter. He leaned closer and took note of the way Tessa's name looked. At least he assumed it was her name. Next to it was a hairbrush. On it he saw the same long strands of black that he sometimes plucked from his coat and vest after visiting her room. There were rows of green, brown, and purple bottles, and he had no idea what these things contained or what purposes they served, beyond the notion that they fell into the province of female applications. Clayt reasoned that — at least for the women at Sorohan's — such dedicated attention to appearance might be compared to a ranch hand oiling his gun or soaping his saddle.

He sat down on the bed to pull on his socks. Looking around the room, he wondered how many other men knew the sanctity of this chamber. Or if any other man

147

did. As far as he knew, Tessa had never lied to him. He trusted her as he trusted few men. She had said that only Clayt won her favors, and he had no reason to doubt her. She had never asked him if he practiced a reciprocal loyalty to her. Tonight was the closest she had come to talking about where they stood as a man and a woman. It had made him feel less uncomfortable than uncertain.

"When are you going to tell me how you got that?" Tessa whispered. He turned to her and found her eyes fixed on the scar puckering the left side of his chest.

"You don' wanna hear 'bout that," he assured her.

She directed her regal gaze to his eyes. "But I do. It's part of you, isn't it?"

He stared at her for a time. "Not no more. I've put it away to the past."

Tessa offered the sweetest of smiles. "You can tell me anything, Clayt."

He tried to ignore her by pushing his arms through the sleeves of the long johns, but she reached out and stilled his hands on the first button. Easing down to the mattress, he propped on an elbow and faced her.

"I reckon I can talk to you 'bout most ever'thin'." He raised a hand and almost touched his scar. "But not this."

She reached out and gently stroked the dead, hardened skin. "It's a bullet wound, isn't it?"

Clayt nodded and looked down at the contrast of her smooth fingers against the rough terrain of the old wound. The scar never made him think of the man who had fired the musket. Being shot had been his due. Instead, the image that formed in his mind was the isolated head of the young drummer boy as it lay silent in the grass.

"I cain't talk 'bout it, Tessa," he whispered. "Don't ask me to."

Tessa slithered across the blanket and wrapped her arms around him. Resting her cheek on the scar she spoke with a tenderness he had heard only a few times in the years he had known her.

"I won't ask again. I'm just glad you lived through it. I'm glad you are here."

When he made no response, she began slowly stroking his back. "It's who you are now that matters, Clayt." She curled around him so he could see her smile. "You're a Sorry-Damn cowboy whose roof is the sky and whose boundaries reach across the prairie. You're the foreman for the largest cattle outfit in the Territory, and, from what I hear, you are damned good at it. Most every man who knows you, respects you."

He frowned at her. "Don't think too highly of me, Tessa. It don't fit me."

She lay back in the bed, yawned, and covered herself with the blanket. "It fits you just fine, Clayton Jane. And somewhere inside that complicated head of yours, you know it." Yawning again, she closed her eyes, and within a minute her breathing took on the rhythm of peaceful sleep.

Clayt finished dressing, picked up his boots, and lifted his gun belt from the chair. Quietly, he stepped out into the hallway, where the conversations from the barroom rose up to him like the rumble of machinery. After pulling on the boots and buckling the belt across his hips, he walked the dark hallway to the top of the stairs and studied the faces in the bustling crowd below. The saloon was as busy as he had ever seen it. Every table hosted a game: faro, keno, monte, and freehanded poker. The bar was lined with miners, timber men, brickyard laborers, and the few cowhands who had either no inclination or no money for gambling.

At a table near the front window, Johnny Waites studied a tight fan of cards held under his chin. When the piano started up, Clayt descended the stairs and walked the length of the bar, where Emmett twisted a rag inside a glass.

"That old Ind'n woman still sell baskets of flowers down on the corner some mornin's?" Clayt asked.

Emmett frowned and looked toward the door. "Believe she does."

Clayt laid two pieces of silver on the counter. "If you'd buy one o' those little baskets and give it to Tessa for me" — he dug out another two coins — "and keep this for your trouble . . . I'd be obliged."

Emmett made a quick earnest nod. "You got it, Clayt." With nimble fingers, he snatched up the four coins off the bar top.

Clayt turned to see Johnny Waites standing now, stooped over his table, sweeping coins into his hat. Waites laughed as his attention was divided between his winnings and Clayt. When he got to the bar he inverted the hat, and coins rattled down on the countertop like a spilled toolbox.

"Hey, you Sorry-Damn cowboy. I got more money than a feller oughta be allowed to carry 'round." He straightened and eyed the array of whiskey bottles lined up across Emmett's shelves. "Maybe you and me oughta use some o' this to see how much trouble we can git into." Johnny's smooth drawl was near musical, as Southern as Clayt's. He raised the emptied hat above the pile of coins and perched it atop his head. His trademark smile widened.

"You done with your game?" Clayt asked.

"Hell, yeah, and glad to git done." Johnny laughed and nodded back at the table he had vacated. "One o' them boys is slicker'n a bull snake in a greased fry pan, if you follow my way o' sayin' it. Have a drink with me?"

Clayt nodded once. "I could use some coffee."

Johnny slapped the counter twice with the flat of his hand. "Professor! Set us up down here, will you? Some o' that fire-in-the-gut for me and a coffee for my pard here."

When Johnny started counting coins, Clayt faced the bar and lowered his voice. "I hear you might'a got a job with Shannonhaus. That right?"

Johnny kept counting as he shook his head. "Me and Bud and another fella went up there when we heard he was hirin'. Hell, they even fed us a meal." Abandoning the coin tally he leaned his forearms on the bar and quieted his voice. "They got a damn Cajun darky from Loosanna can fry up chicken and taters that'd make you wanna go back home to your mama." He stuffed the coins in his pocket but for three he left on the counter. Johnny frowned and shook his head. "Didn' take the job. Didn' none o' us take it. Didn' none o' us *want* it, if you follow my way o' sayin it." Johnny shrugged and patted his bulging pocket. "Well, no matter. This oughta hold me for a spell."

Emmett set down a steaming cup in front of Clayt and then poured a shot glass and stoppered the bottle cork with the heel of his hand. Johnny picked up one of the coins and, with a flick of his thumb, spun it. The piece of silver hopped onto the counter in a twirling blur and hummed in a tight spiral on the polished wood. Johnny settled his hands lightly on the edge of the bar, the ends of his fingers just touching the wood like a piano player about to commence a performance.

"There you go, Professor," Johnny said, nodding toward the two dormant coins. "The one a-spinnin' is for you if you can grab it b'fore I do." Johnny's eyes sparked with the challenge. The tip of his tongue curled to his upper lip. "I'll give you first move."

Emmett stared at Waites without expression. Without warning he tossed the whiskey bottle toward the cowboy in an arc that topped out just above Johnny's hat. Johnny's smile broke, his eyes fixed on the airborne bottle, and his hands reached instinctively for the catch. He fumbled with the bottle before cradling it in his arms, but Emmett had already slapped the spinning coin flat on the bar, picked it up, and then snapped up the other coins. Without a word he took the bottle from Johnny's hands, winked at Clayt, and walked away.

Johnny raised his eyebrows and stared at the empty space on the bar. "He ain't as slow as he looks, is he?" Then he broke out in a grin that made it seem as though his day had started anew.

Clayt leaned an elbow on the bar. "What's this I hear about Shannonhaus runnin' a shootin' match for his hirin'?"

Waites sipped the top off the glass, then raised it like a piece of evidence in a court trial. "Hell, he sets up a little damn piece o' rock 'bout the size o' this glass here." He looked out through the door. "He walks us back, say, from here down to Ivinson's store. Hell, we just shot to see if we could hit the damn thing. Least we could do for all the fried chicken we damaged."

He downed the rest of his drink with a toss of his head and exhaled. "He only give us the one shot each and didn' none o' us hit it 'xcept me." Waites shrugged. "Just a lucky shot, prob'ly." He pursed his lips and shook his head. "But hell, I didn' like the sonovabitch. Didn' none o' us like 'im. Cain't see workin' for a man who don' know how to talk to another man without it soundin' like the goddamn bark of a dog, if you follow my way o' sayin' it."

Clayt looked into his coffee. "They say the war 'bout give 'im all a man could handle."

Johnny Waites looked at the side of Clayt's face. "I ain't talkin 'bout the old man. Hell, he weren't even there. I'm talkin' about that sour apple son o' his — *Lee*-land." Waites hissed through his teeth. "That boy asks a hellava lotta questions of a man. Wanted to know what side o' the war I fought on." He laughed. "Hell, I weren't even o' age, so then he wants to know 'bout my daddy . . . 'bout which side *he* fought on."

"You tell 'im?"

"Reckon I had to give him somethin' for the meal. Told 'im I was from old Ala-bam. But, hell, that ain't no news. Anybody within earshot o' me knows I'm from ol' Dixie. Told him my daddy's affairs was none o' his goddamn business, but it shouldn' be hard to figure out considerin' where we come from."

"And how'd he like your answer?"

Waites's eyes widened. "That's when he

started talkin' serious 'bout hirin' me."

"This before or after shootin' at the rock?"

"After."

Clayt swirled the dregs of his coffee, then pushed the cup away. "We could use you boys at the Rollin' F. Can only offer you a month or two. You interested?"

Johnny smiled broadly. "Hell, yeah. You boys startin' your roundup?"

" 'Bout done with that. We need more men on the herd. We got the same concerns as ever'body 'bout Chatka, and some o' the boys'll be out on special jobs some o' the time. You reckon your friends'll go along?"

"Hell, yeah. We gotta pass any more damn tests?"

Clayt shook his head, put his back to the bar, and scanned the room. "When you were up at Shannonhaus's, you meet a fella with real light hair, fancy clothes?"

Johnny's lips pushed out again. "Reckon I knew ever' man out there. Least the ones I saw."

Clayt stepped behind the bar and picked up his Henry rifle. "Well, you boys come on out Sunday evenin' in time for supper and git set up. Pay's eighty cents a day. We'll replace any ammunition you use on the job. That sound 'bout right?"

"Swampy still scorchin' your victuals for you?"

"He is. That a problem?"

Johnny shrugged. "Well, hell, we'll show up anyway." When Clayt started to leave, Johnny put a hand on his sleeve. "That fella you's askin' about. He have a accent?"

Clayt moved back to the bar and stared into Waites's eyes. "Scottish."

Johnny nodded once to the back of the room. "Wouldn' be him right over there, would it?"

At the back table in the shadow of the upstairs landing, the pale Scotsman was sharing a laugh with a local merchant. Still smiling he stood, put on his banker's hat, and wedged a black book under his arm.

"It would," Clayt said.

"Says he works for a minin' comp'ny some'eres back East," Johnny said. "Talk to 'im for five minutes and you and him are bosom buddies from way back, if you follow my way o' sayin' it." Johnny's eyebrows floated upward, and his mouth slanted to a crooked smile. "But I reckon you're 'bout to find that out for yourself."

"Mr. Waites," the Scotsman said happily as he approached the bar. His Scottish tongue curled around the two words with a flourish. He wore the smile of an old friend.

"And Mr. Jane, I believe. We met briefly up at Shannonhaus's." He nodded in a courtly manner and offered his left hand. "Wallace Dunne. A pleasure again, sir."

Clayt hesitated for a moment, and then, seeing a fresh bandage on the man's right-hand fingers, Clayt extended his left hand. Dunne gave a firm handshake and laid his book on the bar.

"Can I buy you gentlemen a drink?"

Johnny Waites held up his flattened palm as an answer. Then he slapped the hand lightly against Clayt's upper arm and started backing away.

"I gotta appointment with the privy out back. See you Sunday."

After nodding to Johnny, Clayt turned back to the Scotsman. "I was just on my way out. Maybe another time."

"Of course," Dunne said and raised a finger as though recalling something that had slipped his mind. "If I could just ask a favor. I plan to call on your Mr. Afton soon and wondered if you might give me directions to his ranch."

Clayt studied the man's face. There was not a man in Laramie who could not direct a visitor to the Rolling F. With his rifle, Clayt pointed west down the street.

"You just head across the river by the

prison, then when the road forks —"

"Excuse me," Dunne interrupted. "Is there a sign there? At the fork?"

"Nope, just a fork. Left one takes you down to Chimney Rock. You take the right. That trail will take you northwest. Then it forks again at a old windmill. There's a old stone house all caved in there. You take the right fork again, and you'll be headin' due north. You'll cross the Little Laramie inside a hour. After that —"

Wallace Dunne was chuckling as he raised his good hand to stop Clayt. "I'm sorry, sir. This thick skull of mine won't take in too much at any one time." He opened his book and with his unbandaged hand extracted a sheet of clean newsprint. From his jacket pocket he produced a pencil. "Would you be kind enough to draw a map?" Dunne laughed sheepishly. "It's a big country. I've been lost out here once already." He pushed the paper and pencil before Clayt. "You'd be doing me a great service, sir."

Clayt looked at the little man appraisingly, wondering how he had ever found the Shannonhaus line shack above the Shin Bone. Leaning, he propped the rifle against the bar, straightened, and took the pencil. Beginning with a slow sinuous line, he drew the course of the river. Then he bisected that with an east-west line that forked into a Y.

"This here's the Laramie River, and, right here, this is the Lil' Laramie." He added the tributary. "The town's right here." East of the river he made an X. "Here's the prison." He made another X and then extended a plodding line from the north fork of the Y. He lifted the pencil and spoke to the paper. "I'll see can I draw you a windmill."

"No, don't bother. Just write it in there, if you would. And label the prison, too, Mr. Jane . . . just so I can keep it all straight."

Clayt looked at the paper, drew in a lot of air, and exhaled. He made a stab at rendering the blades of a windmill, but it looked like a warped wagon wheel in need of a rim. Beneath this he extended two support legs and exed in the braces. At the top of the paper he started etching a jagged line. "This here is the bluffs up at Shin Bone. There's a little creek running out 'bout here." Clayt tapped the pencil to his map.

"If you could just write that in, please," Dunne said.

Clayt clinched his jaws and stared at the paper, determined to be done with the map. After attempting a circle the size of a silver eagle, he laid the pencil down on the paper

160

and slid the crude drawing to Dunne.

"That circle there, that's the ranch," he explained and tapped his finger to the spot. "If you want words in there, I reckon you'll need to write 'em in yourself."

Smiling his apology, Dunne held up his right hand showing the first two fingers bandaged together in white gauze. "I'm afraid I've injured my hand, Mr. Jane."

Clayt considered the map for a time. "Well, Mr. Dunne," he began and looked up at the Scotsman. "I cain't write none either, but I cain't blame it on my hand. I just never learnt how."

For one instant, the affable light in Dunne's face extinguished. "Well, I'm sure I can find Afton's. After all, it is the largest ranch in the county, isn't it?"

" 'Xactly what is your business with Mr. Afton? So I can let 'im know."

With his good hand, Dunne reached into the inside pocket of his coat and framed a business card with his slender fingers. When Clayt only glanced at it with dull eyes, Dunne looked at it himself and cleared his throat.

"Oh, of course. I guess if you don't write —" He laid the card on the bar and assumed the tone of a businessman. "I represent an extraction company based in Philadelphia — Pennsylvania Consolidated Coal and Mining. We're looking into coal deposits."

"Thought all the coal was over in Carbon County," Clayt said.

Dunne pulled in his lips and nodded as if he were hearing good advice. "My company is hoping to tap into another big deposit here. We'd like to acquire mineral rights and provide the means to extract it." He smiled. "Believe me, Mr. Jane, it's a proposition that would be profitable for all concerned."

"Reckon I wouldn' know much 'bout that, Mr. Dunne."

"Well, don't you see? It would be a joint venture."

Clayt tried to look out at the night through the window, but the glass reflected the interior of the saloon like a mirror. The room was like a cage now, and the sound of the voices filling it hummed like insects worrying his ears. He thought of the quiet prairie and the long stretch of trail under the moonlight.

"Reckon that'll be up to Mr. Afton," Clayt said and choked up on his rifle. "Might be, I'll see you out there," he said and nodded to the bar, "if you can follow that map."

Dunne cocked his head and bobbed a finger at Clayt. "I'm fairly good with a man's speech patterns. Is it Georgia?"

When Clayt nodded, Dunne smiled with satisfaction. "And I'm betting you fought in the war. Am I right?" His right hand lay on the bar and idly rolled the pencil back and forth, the bandaged fingers bending nimbly. When Dunne saw Clayt looking at it, he stopped the motion.

"Take care o' that hand now," Clayt said. He picked up the card and walked out.

CHAPTER 13

The pounding of Chalky's hammer rang out
from the mill shed, resurrecting the sounds
of those earliest days on the Rolling F, when
Clayt had signed on as one more hand in
the growing outfit. In those days the buildings and fences had risen like the beginnings of a new town out on the grassland,
and the wide valley had become irrevocably
centered by its ballast. Now the Afton holdings were a kingdom, and, except for
Chalky, Clayt was the hired hand to claim
the longest history at the ranch.

In the yard Lou Breakenridge ran a file
across the teeth of a handsaw — the rasping
sound clean and repetitive. G.T. and Rascher had coupled two wagons gate to gate
to accommodate the long, rough-sawn
boards they hauled from the building; and
when Rascher drove the lead wagon off
behind the big, heavy-hooved Morgan, G.T.
lifted the tongue of the reversed wagon off

164

the ground and navigated from the rear.

Clayt sat his horse and watched the double-wagon rig trundle off toward the barn. Then he dismounted and stepped up on the porch of the mill shed. Chalky stretched a measuring line across a rotting baseboard inside the room.

"Nine'y-fo'," Chalk called out. There was a melody to his voice when he worked with wood, not unlike his soft singing to the cattle when he night-herded.

Behind Clayt, the grating of the file quieted. "Where the hell *you* been?" Lou said to his back. "You git caught in a rainstorm?"

Clayt turned to see Lou staring at his wet hair. "Bathed in the river," Clayt replied. To preclude any questions about his ablutions, he pointed to the floor beside the lumber piled against the wall. There lay the headless body of a prairie rattler still writhing upon itself. It was bright with color, like a trade belt made of yellow and brown beads. At the decapitated neck, a wet stain darkened the dusty floorboards.

"Who found that'n?" Clayt said.

Lou stepped inside holding the saw down by his leg. "G.T. 'bout got hisself bit. Then Rascher took the axe to it." Lou squinted at Clayt and cocked his head to one side. "You been into town?"

Clayt nodded as he studied the dusty room. His gaze settled on the snake again.

"You reckon they got rattlers in England?" Clayt said, throwing out the question for either man. The three men looked blankly at the snake.

"Well," Lou said, "whether they do or they don't, I reckon Mr. Aff's sister ain't gonna be happy to hear 'bout this'n."

"Or any da others we likely find in dis here woodpile," Chalky said. "Rattlers . . . dey usually den up, ya know."

Lou checked the floor around his boots and then stepped back outside. The grating rhythm of the file picked up where it had left off. Clayt sized up the walls for new windows and tried to imagine an easel set up here, gathering light for an artist's work.

"Mighty dark in here, ain't it?" Clayt said.

"We gone fix dat," Chalky said, his melodic voice full of the confidence of what his hands could do. Clayt turned in the doorway so that both men could hear him.

"Mustangs are runnin' up by the old waller. 'Bout forty growed ones . . . then I'd say eight or ten colts and fillies."

"You see horses or tracks?" Lou said, holding off on the file.

"Saw the herd this mornin. It's the same bunch. Got 'em two dark stallions that cain't decide who's in charge."

Lou was a statue, the file frozen in mid-stroke on the saw's teeth. His eyes narrowed to the northeast as if he might catch sight of horses from that distance.

"We goin' after 'em?" Lou said.

Clayt nodded back to the woodpile. "Ever this studio gits done."

Chalky laughed. "Ever Lou git done sharpnin' dat saw."

Clayt rolled up his sleeves and stepped down from the porch. He loosened a tie thong on the back of his saddle and carried a bundle of sun-bleached planks into the shed, where he laid them out on the table.

"Mind if I dip into your toolbox, Chalk?"

"Naw-s'r. He'p yo-se'f." Chalky's hammer remained silent. "Where you find dem?"

"Braces and lattice off that windmill out to the old Pender place."

"Mm hmm." Chalky's humming reply was like the quiet beginning of a hymn. He drove a nail into a board with two clean strokes. Then he straightened and spoke out the door. "Old Lou . . . he t'ink he already out bustin' some wild mustangs. Oughta be t'inkin' 'bout sawin' one o' dem planks nine'y-fo' inches."

Clayt stepped down to where Lou was still

167

staring out at the horizon. "You 'bout finished up sharpenin' that?"

Lou looked down at the saw as if to remind himself what tool he was holding. "Huh? Yeah, I'm done."

"We got time on those mustangs," Clayt said. "We need to git this studio finished up in a coupla days." He took the saw from Lou's hand and held it up at eye level. The teeth burned with a bright silver edge. "Nice job."

"We gonna run 'em into that corral we started up on the Shin Bone?"

"Be my plan," Clayt said. "Drive 'em down the coulee and through the willows."

Lost in the thought of the mustangs, Lou frowned down at the dirt and began nodding. "That oughta work."

Clayt returned to the workbench inside and began sawing the rough end off one tip of a stick of lattice. Lou kept staring into the distance until the grind of the saw sank in. He stepped up on the porch and leaned against the doorjamb.

"Guess I'm s'posed to git out another saw and sharpen the damn thing. That about right?"

Chalky was laughing outright now — the sound a congestive rasp in his chest. Lou's next words trailed off as he turned to the sound of a distant horse coming up fast from the south. Clayt stepped to the edge of the porch, and Chalky followed. Every man in the yard stood motionless, each focused on the rider.

"That's Nestor!" G.T. called out. "Tryin' to kill his damn horse with his spurs."

Clayt stepped down from the porch and mounted his horse in one continuous motion. Moving out at a trot, he rode toward the gate and reined up when Nestor began calling on his horse to slow. The horse was worked up to a white froth, snorting and sucking in deep breaths of air, its roan coat dark with sweat. Nestor circled Clayt once before he got his mount under control. The boy's face glowed with heat, his hat pulled down to his ears.

"Sioux came outta the draw and run off 'bout a dozen head. They shot Short clean through." He poked a finger below his collarbone. "Hit one o' Buck's boys, too."

"How bad is the other'n?" Clayt asked.

"It ain't too bad. Nicked his ear. It's bleedin' some, but it ain't too bad."

"How many Sioux?" Clayt said.

"Ain't sure. Short's bedded down in the trees. The rest're with the herd. 'Xcept Buck. Him and a few others are trailin' the stole cattle. Tol' me to come fetch you."

169

"Come on," Clayt said and wheeled his horse around. Chalky and Lou were walking toward them but stopped when the two horsemen approached. When Clayt and Nestor reined up, Lou was still holding the file and Chalky his hammer.

"Git ever'body out here," Clayt said and pointed to the center of the yard. "Sioux hit the herd."

Lou started at a run for the bunkhouse. Clayt turned in his saddle.

"Nestor, go rub down your horse, and then I want you up in the windmill to keep a lookout. This could be a trick to pull us outta here an' git the horses at the ranch."

Clayt gave Chalky a sober look. "Better git some bandages and sulfa. Looks like we got two men hit."

The triangle clanged in staggered notes of three. When the door to the main house opened, Cora stepped out onto the porch, and then Afton followed in his shirtsleeves. He paused for a moment, then hurried down the steps. Grady Brooks came jogging from the hog pen with a manure shovel in his hand. Behind him was Swampy, his long gloves glistening red with blood and pasted with tufts of white feathers. Everyone converged on Clayt in the yard.

"We got Ind'an trouble in the south

pasture." Clayt pivoted his head to include all the men. It was so quiet that the sudden wing flap of chickens could be heard from the coop at the east end of the compound. Afton's face was hard set, his mouth clamped into a firm line. "Some o' us are goin' out there, and the rest will keep a lid on here. Could be this is all 'bout our remuda." Clayt nodded toward the corral, then looked up into the windmill. Nestor was perched just below the blades, staring slit eyed to the south. The boy had fashioned a sling of rope for his rifle.

"Chalk, G.T., and Rascher . . . git your bedrolls and plenty o' ammunition. Swampy, pack us somethin' to eat. Ain't no tellin how long we'll be out." He waited until the four named started for the bunkhouse. "I want the rest o' you boys to listen to Lou. You're to stay here and position yourselves around the buildings. Listen careful to where he tells you to set up." Clayt looked at Lou, and Lou nodded. "Nestor'll be in the windmill to keep an eye out. Nestor!" Clayt called out, "you see anythin', you pull off two shots back to back . . . real quick. That's the signal. Then git the hell down from there and take up whatever position Lou tells you."

Clayt took the time to establish eye contact with each man in the crowd. "Expect the worst. Don't slack off on stayin' alert. Keep plenty o' cartridges with you. If they come, you might be holdin' your particular ground for a long time. Don't expose yourself. Switch off on shootin' from a standin' position, kneelin', and lyin' down. Don't let 'em predict you so good they can pick you off." Clayt turned to Afton. "Mr. Aff, this might be a good time to git the women to stock up food and water in the root cellar."

"What about sending someone to the fort?" Afton said.

Clayt shook his head. "Take too long. We'll handle this like we always done."

"All right, but send someone back to fill us in as soon as you can. If I don't hear something by noon I'm coming out there myself."

"We'll send word back. Just stay put here, Mr. Afton." Clayt reached inside his coat and handed Afton the telegram. "This come for you day before yesterday."

The men went into motion around Afton, who opened the envelope and read the telegram. His eyebrows lowered over his eyes, giving him the look of a man in pain. He let his hand fall so that the yellow paper slapped against his leg.

"Bloody hell," he hissed and walked to the bunkhouse where Clayt was carrying out boxes of ammunition to his saddlebags. "My sister will be here in two days." He raised the paper and shook it. "By God, I'll pay a month's wages to the man who kills Chatka."

Clayt glanced over his horse at the barn where G.T. and Rascher strapped gear behind their saddles. "I'd just as soon you keep that b'tween us, Mr. Aff. I don't want nobody takin' chances like that. Not for money."

Clayt knotted the tie-downs, mounted, and waited for a reply. Afton's mouth pushed out and in as he stared south toward his unseen problem. After a time, he nodded. Clayt reined his horse around and led out toward the gate, Chalky, G.T., and Rascher following behind him.

When they reached the trees that bordered the little creek south of the ranch, they turned southwest into the hill country. Keeping to the low ground between swells they wound through a series of shallow, twisting coulees that opened into a grassy basin below a slope of timber. Clayt nosed Skitter uphill into the pines and slowed the party to a walk.

Rascher called from the back, "Why the hell're we goin' this — ?"

Clayt turned so quickly that Rascher left his complaint unfinished. Clayt made a short chop with a hand before his mouth — his signal for quiet. Rascher exhaled heavily through his teeth and looked away. Chalky kicked his horse alongside Rascher's.

"If dey after Mr. Aff's hosses," Chalk whispered, "dey be comin' dis same way."

Rascher spat and looked off into the trees. "Shit," he growled. "I don't like it. It's too hemmed in. And we're losing time."

Clayt turned his horse and moved downhill beside Rascher, so close that each man's leg pressed into the other's horse. Clayt's face was taut as a clenched fist. Unable to look at Clayt for more than a glance, Rascher glowered at the trees.

"You wanna try a diff'rent way," Clayt began in a hard whisper, "go an' try it! You wanna stay with us, you're gonna have to keep your mouth shut. I wanna hear Chatka b'fore he hears me. You understand that?"

Rascher scowled and pulled his rifle from its scabbard. Clayt sidled Skitter even closer until Rascher's mount nickered and sidestepped. Rascher's head came around.

"I heard you," the older man snapped in his own raspy whisper, but still loud enough to be heard beyond the timbers.

They followed the contours of the hills for two miles, then dropped down along a cascade of water and kept to the braid of trees that bordered the creek through the grasslands. Where the creek turned hard south, they turned east and moved into open country toward the gnarled dead oak that marked the high ground of the south pasture.

Beyond the rise, the cattle milled about as if nothing had happened. Riding herd on that side was Harry Sims, sitting his sway-back mare. His rifle butt was propped on his thigh, the barrel pointed skyward. It was a good minute before he saw the approaching group, and when he did he pulled back on his reins and lifted the gun where it might better swing to his shoulder. Clayt raised his hand, and Harry lowered the rifle to his leg.

"Where's Buck?" Clayt asked.

Harry shook his head. "Ain't seen him git back. Went after the stole cattle."

"Who'd he leave in charge?"

Harry looked toward the trees on the low ground. "Hell, I don' know. Me, maybe." He pointed. "Coupla the boys are down yonder at the creek with Short."

"Chalk," Clayt called, and Chalky eased

his horse forward. "Better go down to the creek and see 'bout Short." Clayt turned back to Sims. "Who was it got shot'n the ear?"

"Aw, that weren't nothin'. Turns out he snagged it on a tree limb. He's aw-right."

Clayt watched the rider on the far side moving along the edge of the herd. "G.T., tell that flanker to git over to that rise on the other side of the creek where he can see down toward the Chimney Rock Road. He sees anything, he's to let go with two rounds back to back and then git back into the trees."

"Whatta ya want me to do, Clayt?" Sims asked.

"G.T.'ll come back and take your spot to keep the herd settled. I want you to ride to the ranch and tell Mr. Afton everthin's under control. I'll find Buck."

Harry glanced at the sun and back. "Hell, they been gone over a hour now."

"Well, the ones done the stealin' cain't travel any faster than the cattle. Keep your eyes open, Harry. We damn near rode up on you ourselves."

Skirting the herd, Clayt and Rascher rode south and picked up the tracks of the horses and stolen cattle. Right away they found a half-naked body face down in the grass. On the bronze skin of his back, a hoof mark had daubed him with a semicircle of dirt. A bright gaping hole in his neck had tapped a wellspring of blood. Around the Indian's head the blades of grass glistened with deep red, all of it buzzing with flies.

"What!" Rascher said. "Ain't you never seen a dead Ind'an b'fore?" He leaned and spat a brown dollop of tobacco beside the dead man's head. "Right there's one that'll never run off with a man's livestock again."

From his saddle Clayt inventoried the dead man's accoutrements: a few ragged skins tied around his torso with crude thongs; a white man's butcher knife sheathed in a deerskin scabbard looped to an empty cartridge belt; a single raven feather tied to his hair by threads of sinew. The warrior's dark skin seemed to be wrapped around a collection of bones. His arms and legs were like sticks. There was no thick flesh to be seen on any part of him. Though his body appeared weathered, Clayt judged by his face that this one could not be much older than a boy.

Baring his teeth, Rascher sneered down at the corpse. When he looked back at Clayt he coughed up a single laugh.

"You'll git used to it." He laughed again from deep in his chest. "This here is just a trial run for you." Rascher leaned in for effect. "See your first dead white man . . . an' you'll likely lose your breakfast." Rascher's mouth stretched into a garish smile.

Saying nothing, Clayt nudged Skitter forward, and Rascher followed. At the first dry creek bed they reined up and inspected two more dead Indians sprawled in the sand behind a scattering of boulders. Their attire was similar to that of the first corpse, except that one wore two feathers in his hair. The other wore a bone.

"They're Cheyenne, ain't they?" Rascher asked.

Clayt shook his head. "Sioux. Just boys really. Looks like they ain't had nothin' to eat for a spell."

Rascher looked around at the boulders. "Poor place to set up for ambush," he said. "Ignorant bastards." He pointed to the open ground behind the rocks. "They'd'a had to git across all that if they planned on savin' their own skins."

Clayt counted the cartridge shells strewn across the sand and examined an empty ammunition belt coiled beneath a limp arm. Each dead Indian gripped a rifle in one hand as though he intended to carry it with him into the afterlife.

"They didn'," Clayt said.

Rascher frowned. " 'Didn' ' what?"

"Plan on gittin' away," Clayt explained. "They sacrificed themselves as a rear guard. Let the others make up some time with the cattle."

Clayt dismounted and knelt beside the bodies. All the loops in their cartridge belts were empty. He picked up the closest boy's rifle — an old single-shot.

"Breechloaders," Clayt said. "This is the Springfield the army issued after the war. Prob'ly took 'em off o' dead soldiers." He studied the dark bronze of the metal. The trapdoors were open. "Shell's jammed in the breech," Clayt said. He picked up a slender length of metal tied to the dead man's waist thong like a talisman. One end was hammered to a crude flat point.

"What the hell's that?" Rascher said.

"Looks like a piece o' old ramrod. Prob'ly for pryin' out jammed cartridges." Clayt stood and took in the lay of the land. "This ain't like what we hear 'bout Chatka. These people here are starvin' an' desperate." He mounted, turned in his saddle, and looked back toward the pasture. "Yeah, these two were tryin' to buy some time." Clayt shook his head. "Pretty near suicide with these Springfields up against our repeaters."

They followed the tracks up the long slope

and down another to the broad plain around the river. As they approached a ravine, Clayt reined up.

"We'd best spread out and hit this gully up yonder in diff'rent places."

Rascher made his rough laugh. "You're thinkin' them Sioux are down in there?"

"I ain't predictin'. I'm allowin' for what could be."

They separated and had been apart only a few minutes when Rascher whistled. Clayt checked his end of the ravine, then rode down to where Rascher was staring into the ditch. Two steers stood trapped at the bottom. Both issued deep mewling complaints and tried to gain some purchase on the wall of the ravine, but each time they tumbled back to the bottom.

"They'll keep till we come back," Clayt said.

After a half mile the tracks swung west into the mountains. Up in the shadow of a bluff a string of cattle moved toward them through the mouth of a canyon. Pushing them were three men wearing wide-brimmed hats.

"There we go," Rascher said. "That's our boys."

Buck was out front, his eyes blazing with the intensity of a predator. Without words these three met and turned their horses to watch the cattle stream by.

Rascher broke the silence. "Well, what the hell happened?"

Buck seemed in no mood to answer. He just shook his head.

"You boys all right?" Clayt said.

Buck scowled and kept shaking his head. "We're all in one piece. 'Xcept for Short." He turned to Clayt. "He gonna be awright?"

Clayt nodded. "Looks like."

The cattle passed, and Buck's big jaws flexed with the regularity of a clock. The man riding drag swung a coil of rope, prodding a yearling that favored a front leg.

"That'n there come up lame in the chase," Buck said. "Damn Sioux don' know shit about runnin' cattle. They run 'em hard into a ravine back there. Left two of 'em stranded."

"We saw 'em," Clayt said. "Any more hurt besides this'n?"

Buck leaned and spat. "Not as I can see. We lose just that'n, we'll come out awright."

Rascher stood in his stirrups. "Where the hell'd the damn Ind'ans run off to?"

Buck looked over his shoulder into the canyon. "Some'eres. Hell, I cain't see 'em.

They're up on the side o' that hill in all those rocks." When Rascher kept glowering at the shale slopes, Buck added, "You wanna go after 'em . . . be my guest."

"Tell me 'bout what happened," Clayt said.

Buck leaned forward on his pommel and set his face hard. "We was just about finished up with breakfast when a piece o' the herd started breakin' off at the south end. I thought it might just be a rattler or a badger or somethin'. When they crossed over that dry wash, I sent Short and Whit down to drive 'em back. Next thing I know a pistol's barkin', and Short is yellin' from hell to breakfast how he kilt a Ind'an. By the time some o' us got mounted and got over there, them som'bitches was emptyin' their rifles from the rocks. I saw Short git knocked off his horse. We dragged 'im outta there and got 'im back to the trees. Then Harry and the others come up and poured lead into the rocks till it got quiet. We waited a while, then finally I had to just ride in there from 'round back. They was two of 'em, and they was deader'n' hell." Buck jabbed a thumb toward the canyon. "Tracked the rest of 'em to here, opened up on 'em, and they scattered like jackrabbits up the slope." He pointed up the boulder-strewn hill.

Clayt studied the many hiding places on the slope. "How many would you say?"

"Seemed like five'r six movin' the cattle." He poked the thumb again. "Back there I counted a dozen. I guess some was waitin' in there. But they didn' make a stand. I don't think a shot was fired but what weren't ours."

"We won't git another chance like this," Rascher said, slapping the forestock of his rifle. "We got a fresh trail. They got single-shot carbines that jam. Let's go rid the country of the damn thievin' sonzabitches."

Clayt untied his lariat from the saddle and played out a length through the hondo to make a sizable loop. "There's twelve o' them . . . and five o' us. Those're bad odds to go in an' flush 'em outta where they already dug in. And you don't know how many might be back there waitin' in reserve. You go ridin' in there, and you're gonna fill the sights of a Springfield, sure as hell."

"Hell, they prob'ly ain't even got cartridges. You heard Buck."

Clayt shook out the lariat to his right. "I ain't willin' to gamble my men on that."

Rascher faced the canyon but held his horse in check. He propped his rifle butt on his hip and chewed aggressively on his tobacco, contempt boiling off his face.

Clayt nodded toward the lame animal that struggled to keep up with the others. "Buck, let's cut that'n out."

Buck kicked his horse into a quick start and worked his way ahead of the animal, where he spun his horse to face it. Each way the yearling started to move, Buck leaned that way in the saddle and laid the reins over in a graceful arc. His horse pivoted hard off its hind legs, changing directions at Buck's will. Approaching the flustered steer from behind, Clayt dropped the loop over its head, and the crippled animal began to bawl. The other cattle shuffled on, heedless of the sound.

Clayt dallied the rope around the pommel, spoke to Skitter, and dismounted. At his approach, the frightened steer stretched the rope taut, but Skitter stood her ground. Clayt knelt and felt along the animal's foreleg. When he brought his hand away, it was smeared with blood.

"Been shot. Right up here by the shoulder."

"Hell, it was prob'ly us done that," Buck whined. "I told the boys not to shoot into the herd, but —" He shook his head. "We're a Sorry-Damn bunch, ain't we?"

Clayt scrubbed his hands with dust and

stood. "Hand me my spancel from my saddle." Buck handed down the short hobbling rope, and Clayt dropped a new loop over the wounded creature's head. He loosened the lariat and handed it to Buck. "Ride with me a minute, will you?"

When Clayt mounted and started leading the limping steer back toward the canyon, the skin around Buck's eyes bunched, and his open mouth formed a small circle. "Where the hell're you goin'?" Buck kicked his horse into a walk, and Rascher followed. The three riders passed through the mouth of the canyon and entered the flat-bottomed bowl where the cattle had been abandoned. Clayt climbed down and walked the steer to a lone limber pine and tied it off to the trunk.

"What in the blue blazin' hell are you doin'?" Buck whispered.

Rascher worked the lever on his rifle, the ratcheting sound crisp and clear as it spread out to the slopes.

"Lay off on that," Clayt ordered sharply. "There ain't nothin' to shoot."

"Let's git the hell outta here," Buck urged. The young steer bellowed, and the rising moan of complaint that careened through the canyon was a lonely sound. "Clayt?" Buck said a little louder.

Clayt walked back to his horse and mounted and left the canyon at a walk. Buck backed his horse a few steps, then wheeled around to catch up. Rascher set the stock of his Winchester against his shoulder and swept the barrel across the hillside.

"Put that away!" Clayt commanded, the iron in his voice turning Rascher's head.

"Well at least shoot the goddamn animal!" Rascher barked.

"Leave it!" Clayt snapped. The order left no room for argument. When Rascher eased down the hammer on his rifle, Clayt turned to follow the herd.

"You think it was Chatka?" Buck said, catching up to Clayt.

"If it was . . . he sure as hell could'a killed the lot o' you." Clayt gave Buck a look. "You boys could be lyin' face down in your breakfast plates 'bout now . . . without your hair. And we'd be outta a hellava lot more'n one yearlin'."

"Why do you reckon he didn' make a run at us at night? We'd a played hell tryin' to take after 'im in the dark."

Clayt shook his head. "Ever' part o' this points to these people just bein' damned hungry . . . ready to do whatever they got to do to git some food in their bellies."

186

"Why'n't they follow the buffler like they used to," Buck complained. "Hell, they could'a gone south and found all the meat they wanted."

Ahead of them the prairie unrolled over a series of low hills that ran uninterrupted to the Laramie Plain a few miles distant. Beyond that was the ridgeline of the Horsetooths. From there the plains ran clear to Mexico.

"This land ain't as big as it used to be," Clayt said, his voice so quiet he might have been talking to himself. "Was a time the Sioux and Cheyenne had the run o' this country. I wager there's more white hide-hunters on the whole of the southern plains right now than there are Sioux warriors in the territory."

They held their horses to a walk and did not speak for a time. The wind was in their faces, and a meadowlark sang out in the prairie. The trampled new grass carried a faint scent of anise. The rhythm of the hooves became a soothing sound, and Buck began to slump in the saddle as was his habit. He coiled Clayt's lariat and handed it to him.

"How come you was to leave that steer back there, Clayt?"

Clayt shrugged. "Seemed like the sensible

thing to do. It didn' have much of a future, and those people are damned hungry. You ever been that hungry?"

Buck slapped his belly and adjusted the fit of his cartridge belt. "Hell, I'm always hungry."

Clayt gave Buck a sideways glance, but he said no more.

CHAPTER 14

In the late afternoon Harry Sims returned to the south pasture in the buckboard, his mare still saddled and tied to the tailgate. Nestor rode beside the wagon on his roan. The bed was loaded with hay and partially covered by a lashed-down tarpaulin of canvas. Blankets, a sack of cured ham, and boxes of cartridges were piled in the boot.

After the bulk of the feed was spread for the cattle, they padded the wagon bed with six inches of loose hay and threw the sheet of canvas on top of it. G.T. and Buck transferred Short-Stuff into the makeshift ambulance, Short cursing the rough handling by these two as vehemently as the "sonovabitchin' Sioux" who had shot a hole through him. Clean white bandages — Chalky's work — were sculpted to Short's pale chest and shoulders, all of this in stark contrast to his sun-browned face, neck, and hands.

"Damn, Short," G.T. ribbed, "you look like the turtle that lost his damn shell in a poker game."

In no mood for humor, Short-Stuff put on his sour face. "Least I was skinny enough to let the bullet pass through. If it was you, they'd be a-diggin' a post hole into your chest and minin' for lead till they struck a lode."

Whit climbed up to the driver's seat, and, with two of Buck's boys as escort, the wagon turned and bumped across the grass due north with Short's string of complaints rising above the rattle of the axle. While the herd was occupied with fresh hay, Clayt called the men together under the shade of the cottonwoods by the creek. They were ten strong and renewed in vigilance, their pockets bulging with ammunition. Most lay down on the cool earth and leaned on an elbow. Others squatted, their rifles across their knees.

"I'll make this quick," Clayt said. "It ain't likely that bunch is comin' back, but we're gonna play it like they might. I want six men on the herd at all times. Keep the herd bunched up so no man is far enough from another he cain't hear him should he call out. Anybody thinks he's got company, call it out . . . and quick. Don't give 'em a

190

chance to cut you down quiet-like. Every other man here is countin' on you." Clayt met each pair of eyes to drive home the point. "Buck, which o' the boys was last on night-herd?"

Buck raised his chin. "That was me, Whit, and Short and them other two that rode back with the wagon."

Clayt glanced at the distant wagon bouncing over the prairie. "Buck, why don't you git some sleep. The rest o' your boys can take watch right up to dark."

"Hell," Buck said and pushed his hat brim up to show a determined face. "I cain't no more sleep than I can sing a opera. I'd rather stay in the saddle."

Clayt nodded. "Come dusk you boys git something to eat, and then git some sleep. My boys'll night-herd it from there till 'bout time the moon's been up a hour. We switch off then and then again at dawn. We ain't gittin' caught with our britches down no more."

Buck had been kneeling by the creek, cupping water in his hand to rub across the back of his neck. Exhaling heavily, he picked up a rock and stood. After shaking the stone in his hand like a pair of dice, he flung it across the creek.

"Could'a happened to any o' us, Buck,"

Clayt said. "Let it go. If ever'thing stays quiet, your boys can ride back to the ranch tomorrow at midday. Then you can spell us for the night." Clayt looked around the crew. "Any questions?"

Rascher leaned against a ghost-white sycamore and thumbed his knife shut. "Yeah," he said, "I got a question. If a god-damn Ind'an shows up, are we s'posed to shoot 'im or let 'im pick out a damn animal for his breakfast?"

Several heads turned to Rascher, but most watched Clayt. Clayt's face showed nothing, and his hands worked smoothly on the tie-down he was tightening on his saddle-bag. Rascher stuffed the knife in his trouser pocket and used the moment to insert a wood sliver into his sneering mouth. The light breeze moving through the trees joined with the lap of water in the creek to make up a sound unnaturally magnified around them.

"Buck, you and your boys go ahead and mount up," Clayt instructed. "The rest o' you oughta think on gittin' some sleep. Gonna be a long night."

No one moved. Clayt fixed his eyes on Rascher.

"Let's you and me have a little talk."

"I aw-ready heard enough talk," Rascher

192

said, still leaning against the trunk.

"No . . . you ain't," Clayt said, his words wound tightly now, his voice quieter.

The others began to stir now, taking care that their movements were not intrusive on the moment. No one spoke as they vacated the area, even if just to recline again a dozen paces away. The men cleared napping spots or checked the cinches of their saddles, but each man found his opportunity to cut his eyes toward Clayt and Rascher.

Clayt walked to Rascher and stopped. "Step across the creek with me."

"What the hell for?"

Clayt smelled the man's tobacco breath and saw the brown stains stenciled around his teeth. To the men looking on, Clayt appeared only half as thick as the older cowboy, but his deliberate quiet and stillness was like a raised flag signaling danger.

"Step across with me, or I'll put you over there."

Rascher continued to lean against the tree. While, before, his posture had defined defiance, now it served as an immunity. He smiled and looked at the boys bedding down.

"Don't look at them," Clayt said into his face. "Look at me. I'm talkin' to you."

Rascher sneered and removed the wood

sliver from his mouth. "Go to hell, Jane."

Quick as a snake, Clayt grabbed a fistful of the cowboy's collar with one hand and his cartridge belt by the other. Hauling the bigger man with surprising speed to the sandy beach, Clayt heaved him forward over the shoal. Rascher stumbled, splashing through the shallow water, and crashed against the far bank on hands and knees.

By the time Rascher got to his feet, Clayt was right behind him, thrusting him again toward the scrub brush, where Rascher tripped and fell face down into the dirt.

"You goddamned sonovabitch," he rasped between breaths, one hand pulling at his bandana. When he got to his hands and knees, he coughed up phlegm, spat, and worked his jaws as if assessing for damage to his throat. When he stood and glared at Clayt, his heaving lungs gradually settled. His eyes burned white and vicious against the heat reddening his face.

When Rascher's hand moved toward his hip, Clayt clasped the butt of his own Colt's, his thumb cocking the hammer of the gun in the same movement. It had happened as quick as the snap of a stick. So still and tense and focused was Clayt that he seemed possessed of a spirit altogether alien to these men.

"Make sure you wanna do that." Clayt's words were barely a whisper, but their effect was paralytic. The men watching from the other side of the creek lay still as a graveyard, each man frozen in whatever pose afforded him a view of the altercation. For several seconds nothing happened. Then Rascher brought his hand back to his throat, coughed, and spat into the dirt.

"Goddamn you," Rascher rasped and scowled down at his wet boots and trousers. "Why the hell'd you drag me through that water?"

"Over here you ain't got your audience."

Rascher squinted as though wanting to ask a question, but he just tugged on the bandana again. "You ain't nothin', Jane. You ain't got no right to —"

"I ain't nothin' but part o' the Sorry-Damn crew just like you," Clayt interrupted. " 'Xcept I'm the foreman. Long as I am, I give the orders. That's the way it works. Foreman decides how things git done. Then we do it. You decide right now where you fit into that. I'm sick o' your bellyachin'."

Rascher spat again. "I been working ranches longer'n since b'fore you were pissin' in your own bed. It's me oughta be foreman here."

"Time don't earn you nothin but a back-ache and poor eyesight," Clayt said, his voice an even purr. "You got to prove yourself to git to somethin' better. You can do that right now." Clayt lowered the hammer on his revolver, unbuckled his gun belt, and laid the rig aside on a barkless log of cottonwood. Then he slipped off his coat and draped it beside the Colt's.

Rascher's face darkened. "I ain't gotta prove nothin' to you!" he snapped.

Clayt pointed at Rascher. "You want my job?" Clayt said quietly and beckoned the man forward with a curl of his fingers. "Come here and take it from me."

Rascher crossed his arms over his chest and hissed through his teeth. "Afton wouldn' keep me on for another minute if I bloodied up his favorite little tin soldier."

For three heartbeats only the sound of the creek marked the passage of time. "That all you're gonna do . . . is talk?" Clayt said evenly.

Rascher stood for a moment looking down, fingering his cartridge belt as though he might unclasp the buckle, but it was a feint. Head down he charged like a bull, his momentum building and a savage growl rising from deep in his chest. Clayt waited until the last instant and sidestepped to hammer Rascher with a bare-knuckled blow to the back of the skull. The big cowboy went down like a sack of grain.

Clayt's arms and back tingled with a dark and sharp-edged energy — like the hissing slither of a saber sliding from its sheath. The old fever of war, he discovered, lay just beneath the surface of his skin and threatened to erupt like a boil. He knew he could kill again. He even wanted to. But now with this fever came the conscionable weight of what killing wrought. Especially here on the Laramie Plain — this stretch of wild prairie and mountains that had taken him in and offered another chance. He took a step back, trying to give himself time and the perspective that was part and parcel of being a foreman. But what he saw before him made the blood in his veins turn to ice.

The grass glistened wetly as though someone had emptied a vat of crimson paint on the ground. All the world seemed to smolder through a lens of red. Staring back at him from the blood-soaked grass was a boy's head, disembodied and yet fully sentient, smiling with curiosity, watching Clayt to see what he would do next.

Trying to purge the image from his mind, Clayt sucked in a lungful of air. When he exhaled, the curtain of memory rose to expose the present.

Rising, Rascher scooped sand and dirt with both hands and flung it as he charged again. Clayt jerked his head away, side-stepped, and took a glancing blow beneath the right ear. His vision was blurred, but he struck out repeatedly at the silhouette before him. Again and again he lashed out, venting his fury. Each blow seemed to feed the demon that was rising from his core. His knuckles were smeared with blood — whose blood, Clayt neither knew nor cared. Someone called him from a distance, but he gave the sound no credence.

Rascher lay on his back, his face bloodied, one eye fluttering like the crimson wing of a moth. When the man rolled toward one side and fumbled for his pistol, Clayt closed the distance and wrested the gun away, bending it back against the wrist until Rascher squealed at the wrenching of his finger caught in the trigger guard. Clayt jerked the pistol free and cocked his arm high, ready to slam the barrel into Rascher's head.

"Clayt?" a voice said. "Easy now, Clayt. It's me . . . Nestor."

Not three strides away Nestor stood behind the cottonwood log, his boots beaded with water and his lower trouser legs dark. His eyes were unduly wide. Squeezing his hands together like a man washing his hands, he shifted his weight from one leg to the other.

"He's all done in, Clayt," Nestor said softly. "You whipped him."

Clayt slowly straightened from his fighting crouch, and right away the heat of violence drained from him, leaving him cold and spent. The gun dropped from his hand into the sand. He looked down at the beaten cowboy. Moaning, Rascher cradled his right hand with his left against his chest. His face was raw and torn. A crescent of dark tissue opened and closed like a second mouth cut into the flesh beneath his left eye.

"You aw-right, Clayt?" Nestor said climbing over the log, his movements fluid and careful, like a man approaching the uncertainties of a wounded animal.

"I'm aw-right," Clayt said.

Rascher dragged himself to the log and tested his right hand, closing it to a fist and opening it, each time baring his teeth at the pain. Glaring at Clayt, he said nothing.

"Is this settled?" Clayt said, his face now hard and angular.

Rascher would not look at him. Clayt stepped forward and kicked the sole of the cowboy's boot. Rascher's eyes fixed on the foreman, but he would not reply.

"This ends right here one o' two ways," Clayt said. "Either ride with us or ride out. Ain't gonna be no more halfway. Can you take orders from me?"

Rascher spat to one side. "Who can take orders from a man that gives his beef away to the goddamned savages that shoot up his crew?"

"It ain't yours to figure. You either do what I say or you clear out. Which is it?"

Rascher rolled to his knees and stood. He studied his swollen finger as he spoke. "I'm a damned good hand at workin' with cattle. Better'n most out here."

"I ain't never questioned that. That ain't what we're talkin' 'bout here."

Rascher tried to hide the surprise on his face. "I cain't be givin' up no good-payin' job like this," he admitted, his voice surly and yet uncharacteristically ingenuous.

"Maybe you can work for Shannonhaus," Clayt said. "Seems you and him are friendly enough."

Rascher angled his head away and gave Clayt a sidewise look of doubt. "Like hell."

"I followed your tracks up that draw that runs to his line camp on the south end. You wanna tell me that was somebody else on your paint?"

Assessing his injuries, Rascher bared his

200

teeth and touched a finger to his gum. The finger came away streaked in blood.

"I had some words with the younger Shannonhaus . . . Leland."

"What about?"

"Nothing to speak of. Told him to come and git his strays."

Clayt waited for more, but Rascher busied himself by probing at the gash on his cheek. Clayt stuffed his shirttails deeper into his trousers, turned, and buckled on his gun belt. Then he picked up Rascher's gun.

"Go to the bunkhouse, git your things, and clear out. I'll have the pay you're due sent to Sorohan's." He raised the gun, holding it around the frame. "You can pick this up there, too," he added, stuffing the gun in his belt.

"You're firin' me?" Rascher said and watched Clayt make for the creek. "Well, wait a minute, damnit," he said, his voice rising in need.

Clayt knelt at the water's edge and washed the blood off his knuckles. Paying no attention to Rascher, he walked through the water to the far bank.

"Wait a minute, will ya?" Rascher called out. "I reckon I can work for you."

Clayt turned and waited. Rascher moved to the edge of the creek, propped his hands on his hips and looked down at his boots. He took in a lot of air and expelled it.

"I can work for you." He sucked in his cheeks and nodded. "I can."

They stood that way for a time, the sound of the water coursing between them, holding Rascher's words afloat and testing their worth. Rascher's face was pained, but he held his eyes on Clayt's. Clayt slipped the gun from his waistband and threw it in an easy arc over the water. With his left hand, Rascher caught it against his chest.

"Clean yourself up and go git Chalky to close that cut," Clayt said quietly. He walked through the maze of reclining cowboys, mounted Skitter, and started for the herd.

CHAPTER 15

Johnny Waites and his two friends rode through the Rolling F gate as the sun touched down on the crest of the Medicine Bows. In their company but slightly behind came Wallace Dunne in his gray suit and Eastern hat. Dunne fought the jarring gait of his mount as it slowed from a trot.

Clayt stepped from the bunkhouse door and watched the riders approach. Across the yard the calf bawled in the barn where G.T. and Cora were feeding warm milk to it through the rubber-hose teat. Chalky's hammer pounded a steady cadence in the mill shed, then it stopped, and Clayt could hear Chalky's patient voice explaining something to Nestor. Lou looked up from the window frame he was mitering.

"Hey, you Sorry-Damn cowboys," Johnny Waites called out. He reined up his big blue roan and crossed his wrists on his pommel. He wore his habitual smile and a new shirt, blue as the summer sky. "We in time for some supper?"

Swampy marched out the door and leaned into his bandy-legged walk to the last awning post, where he banged an old railroad spike around the sides of the iron triangle. Clayt walked out into the yard, shook hands with Johnny, and tipped his head toward the door where Swampy stood frowning at them with his hands on his hips.

"Just in time," Clayt said. "You can throw your gear in the other bunkhouse. Three beds waitin' on you in there." He nodded toward the tall Texan named Bud and then waited to be introduced to the third man.

"That there's Lonny Stiles," Johnny said.

Clayt stepped forward and offered his hand to Stiles, the broad-faced man he had seen losing at poker. "Met you at Sorohan's," Clayt said. They shook hands.

"I was givin' away my money then," Stiles said. "Hopin' to make some here."

Clayt pointed to the barn. "Find you a rack for your saddles and throw some feed in the stalls for your horses. After supper you can let 'em out in the corral out back."

"I reckon you 'member Mr. Dunne," Johnny Waites said.

The Scotsman had hung back as a matter of courtesy, but now he coaxed his horse closer. "Mr. Jane," the Scotsman said formally and touched the brim of his hat. There were no bandages on his fingers.

Clayt squinted at the man and splayed his hands on his hips above his cartridge belt. "Mr. Afton know you're comin', Mr. Dunne?"

"I sent word for him to expect me. I met your cook in town last night."

Clayt nodded and let his eyes drift toward the bunkhouse, where the serving of supper had begun. " 'Xcuse me a minute."

Swampy ladled from the cook-pot and at the same time presided over the quota of biscuits each man selected from a tin tray. Clayt walked behind the serving line and spoke quietly beneath the banter of men as they questioned the color of the hash.

"Swamp, did you take a message to Mr. Aff from a man named Dunne?"

"Who?"

"Wallace Dunne . . . a Scotsman. He just rode in. Says you're s'posed to 'a brought in a message."

Swampy's eyes narrowed, and his upper lip pushed to his nose. The cowboys standing in line stopped their shuffling and looked on as though some natural order of the world had been interrupted.

"Aw, hell," Swampy groaned and slapped

down a serving. The copper ladle rang against the plate, and the cowboy receiving it backed his boots away in the event of overflow. "I couldn' hardly understand the feller no how," Swampy complained. "What the hell was it I was s'posed to tell Mr. Aff?"

"Mr. Dunne's 'xpectin' Mr. Aff to be 'xpectin' him . . . tonight."

Swampy served two men in silence, banging the ladle on their plates and glaring fish-mouthed at nothing. Clayt exchanged glances with the men as they tried to hide the amusement on their faces.

"You can figure on one more, Swamp. That's on top o' the three I aw-ready told you 'bout." Clayt knew he would get no response, so he turned and walked to the door.

"Hell in a hail storm," Swampy grumbled. "I ain't the Western Union Telegraph Company. I'm s'posed to be the damned cook."

Lou Breakenridge stepped up to be served, waited until his allotted portion was deposited, and then let his jaw drop in mock surprise. "*You're* s'posed to be a *cook*? Well, I'll be damned. I been wonderin' 'bout that."

Swampy dabbed with his ladle, trying to retrieve some of the hash he had doled out to Lou, but Lou was too quick. The laughter that rippled through the room returned Swampy to his natural state of indignant aloofness.

When Clayt walked back outside, Johnny Waites and his friends were in the barn. As a model of patience, Wallace Dunne sat his horse and gazed around at the buildings.

"Mr. Dunne, why don't you join us for a meal with the boys first."

Dunne looked toward the main house, smiled, and rested a hand on his thigh, the elbow cocked up. "Am I to understand your cook did nae relay my message?"

"I'll go have a talk with Mr. Afton. See can he give you a little time once he's finished up with his meal." Clayt gestured toward the bunkhouse. "Just rest up in here for a spell and eat your fill. I figure we owe you that."

Returned from the house, Clayt was the last man to be served. Swampy said nothing as he dumped a generous ladle of hash onto Clayt's plate. Instead of two biscuits, three. Clayt set his plate on the table where Dunne, G.T., and Chalky had settled. Someone had taken down the lantern from the nearby post and set it on the table, making long shadows behind the coffee pot and cups. With his head tilted, Dunne examined his plate. Then he watched G.T. spoon up a mouthful and chew.

"Mr. Dunne," Clayt said, "we can go up to the house soon's we're done eatin'. Then when you'n Mr. Afton are done talkin', you can stay the night if you're of a mind. Not a good time to be on the trail alone . . . 'specially at night." Clayt shrugged his head to one side. "We're full up in the bunks, but I can give you some blankets and set you up in the barn. Or . . . you got the wood-stove in here, and you're welcome to it, but the hay loft is a sight better'n this floor."

"That's very kind of you," Dunne said and spooned up a first try at the hash. As he chewed he stared intently at his plate, his empty spoon leveled before him. He stopped chewing, watched Swampy at the cookstove for a time, and then closed his eyes as he swallowed. When he took a breath again, he spoke to no one in particular.

"Interesting. What is it?"

G.T. leaned forward and presented a sober face to Dunne. "Mountain oysters, be my guess." G.T. made a sawing motion in the air with his spoon. "See, part of a roundup is castratin' the males that ain't cut out to be bulls." He smiled. "We don' waste nothin'."

Dunne checked the faces around him, smiled, and nodded as he spooned up more.

208

A dozen conversations wove together in the room — each carrying a low business-like tone that worked around the industrious rhythm of the cowboys' style of eating. When someone laughed, it was short-lived and contained, never dominating the room like the laughter in a saloon. Each man seemed both private and accessible at once.

Clayt ate in his typical quiet fashion, but his focus was expanded and peripheral, taking in everything. Chalky's report on the status of the studio. Lou's plan to corral the wild mustangs. Nestor explaining the night-hawk shifts to Johnny Waites and his friends. The words skipped around the room like stones skimming on water, making complicated patterns of growing rings that ran together into the common fabric of a working ranch. If pressed, Clayt might have repeated it all, nearly word for word. He had developed this skill when he had gathered information for Forrest in the war. Employing it tonight, he knew, had something to do with Wallace Dunne's presence.

The Scotsman's eyes locked on the far end of the table, where Short-Stuff bent low over his plate, managing a spoon with his left hand when he was not worrying with the sling yoked around his neck. Beside him, Rascher wore a white bandage on a cheek.

"I understand you had trouble with some Indians," Dunne said.

G.T. nodded and spoke through a mouthful of biscuit. "Made a run at the cattle." He pointed with his spoon toward Short-Stuff. "Shot ol' Short." G.T. poked a thumb at his own shoulder. "Missed the collarbone by shy of a inch."

"Is it bad?" Dunne said, peering down the table at the wounded man.

"He's so skinny, went clean through. Prob'ly be his old self in a coupla weeks."

Whit snorted but kept his eyes on his plate. "Well, we can all sure as hell look forward to that now, cain't we?"

"Looks like you had more than one man hurt," Dunne said.

"Naw, just Short," G.T. reported. "The other'n got poked with a tree limb."

Dunne pointed his spoon toward Rascher. "Must have been quite a limb."

G.T. glanced at Clayt, said nothing, and then busied himself with his meal.

The Scotsman pressed on. "Tell me about this Chatka? What does that mean . . . 'Chatka'?"

G.T. stopped chewing and frowned at Chalky. "That got a meanin', Chalk?"

Chalky nodded. "Chat-ka Wash-tay. It mean 'Good Left Hand.' Dey say he use one arm good as da other."

"Is this Chatka a constant menace to you men out here?" Dunne said.

The men looked to Clayt, deferring to him for this broader question concerning the ranch as a whole. Clayt set down his cup and wiped his mouth.

"Ever' time a Ind'an passes by on the horizon, people are gonna swear it's Chatka. Ever' raid is Chatka. Ever' butchered carcass is his work. Ever' string o' smoke risin' off the hills is his camp. Fact is, nobody can really say what he looks like."

"So he's a specter, of sorts," Dunne said.

G.T. smiled. "I reckon he inspects the cattle purty good, if that's what you mean."

Clayt looked down into his coffee and gently swirled the contents. "Chatka's just a man. Might be good with both hands. But, still, he's just a man . . . prob'ly doin' the best he can to scrape out a livin'. Purty much the same as we're doin' only his kind's been at it a lot longer in this valley."

Dunne propped his elbows on the table and leaned forward. "It sounds like you might be sympathetic to the red man, Mr. Jane. I suppose being a Southerner you understand what it means to be invaded.

211

And dispossessed."

Clayt took paper and tobacco from his pocket and began rolling a cigarette. "Don't reckon I ever figured it that way, Mr. Dunne." He ran the paper along his tongue and sealed it. "In a few more years, I reckon I'll be more Wyomin' than I am Southern. That oughta suit me just fine."

"As I hear it," Dunne said, "you rode with Nathan Bedford Forrest's cavalry." He paused, but Clayt just stared at his cigarette with empty green eyes. "I've not met a Southerner yet who fought in the war and could forget it." Dunne let his eyebrows arch. "A man can hold a grudge for a long time."

"Holdin' a grudge and holdin' a memory might be two different things," Clayt said and gave the Scotsman a look that suggested he was trespassing into a territory too personal to reduce to words.

As G.T. studied Clayt and Dunne, trying to grasp their conversation, Nestor stopped eating and turned on the bench to face Clayt. "You was in the war, Clayt?"

Clayt leaned forward, lifted the oil lamp, and raised its shield. Everyone at the table watched him light his cigarette. The silence spread through the room and brought up every man's head. Taking a deep draw on the cigarette, Clayt exhaled a long stream of smoke that wafted toward the rafters, and then he propped both elbows on the table.

"When we all went off to fight, Mr. Dunne, we left our homes behind. We pushed all the way out to Arkansas once. And I seem to remember that Gettysburg is some'eres up in Pennsylvania. Seems to me it was as much us pushin' as the Yankees."

"That's a very generous point of view from someone who embraced a lost cause," Dunne said. His voice was like a rusty blade prying at an old wound. "Now if it was me coming from the South and seeing what the Yankees did to my home, I don't know that I could be so forgiving." He took a handkerchief from his coat pocket and began wiping his fingers one at a time. "A man worth his salt might never put that to rest." Dunne stopped the motion with his hands. "Hard to turn off that kind of hate."

Clayt said nothing. In the lamplight Nestor's taut skin took on the sheen of candle wax. He cleared his throat and tempered his voice to a respectful whisper.

"You never told us you fought in the war, Clayt."

Clayt touched the backs of his fingers to the side of the coffee pot. Standing, he lifted the pot, carried it to the woodstove, and set it on top. Then he walked back to the table, and sat down. It wasn't just Nestor waiting. Every man in the room seemed to expect a story.

"I was just a kid," Clayt said quietly, but his voice carried through the room. Even Swampy stood motionless in the kitchen. "Didn' know the half o' what I was gittin' into," Clayt continued. "Or why." He glanced at Dunne. "Sure as hell didn' know much o' anythin' 'bout a cause." He glanced at Chalky. "And I damn sure weren't fightin' to keep a man a slave." Then more quietly he added, "B'fore the war, I was damned near to bein' one myself."

"Damn, Clayt," Nestor said, "What were you . . . 'bout fifteen?"

"Closer to thirteen, I reckon."

Chalky laid out paper for a cigarette, and Clayt tossed him his tobacco pouch. Chalky's long fingers doled out the proper dose with a gentle dexterity that belied the latent power invested in his hands. He rolled the paper into a tight and even symmetry and pulled the lamp closer, raised the shield, and leaned to light his smoke.

"Reckon dat was Chatka makin' off wit da cattle, Clayt?" Chalky said, turning the direction of the conversation. He tossed back the tobacco pouch, and Clayt caught it.

Clayt shrugged with his eyebrows. "If it was, I'd wager his band ain't farin' any too well up in the hills. Those three that was kilt . . . you could count ever' rib on 'em."

"We left 'em a steer to butcher," Nestor announced to Dunne. Right away he dropped his smile. "Well . . . Clayt did."

With his elbows propped on the table, Dunne wove his fingers together into a double fist and rested his chin on the pads of his thumbs. "Left them a steer?"

"Dat an'mal was sufferin' and was gone die fo' sho'," Chalky said. "No sense to wastin' it."

The room was quiet. Clayt got up, walked to the stove, and refilled his cup.

"You surprise me, Mr. Jane," Dunne said. "Is this recompense for the blood you spilled in the war?"

Clayt sat again and looked at the side of his cigarette as though considering its burn. Then he laid it on his plate and stared at Dunne over his cup as he sipped coffee. Breaking the tension, Swampy approached from the oven and slapped down a platter of fry bread at the center of the table.

"They's two for each o' ya, so fight amongst yourself all you damn wont, but

215

don't none o' ya come cryin' to me. There ain't no more once you destroy this batch." He bumped Nestor on the shoulder with the back of his hand. "Climb up yonder and git down a jug o' molasses from the shelf so I can pour out portions."

G.T. was first to fork two steaming pieces of bread off the platter. Clayt carried his plate to the sideboard. From the supply cupboard he took down two blankets, set them by the door, and settled his hat on his head. G.T. squinted at him, waiting.

"You ain't havin' no fry bread, Clayt?" G.T. asked.

Clayt shook his head and watched the visitor pass the platter without taking a share. "You 'bout ready to go up to the house, Mr. Dunne?"

"Aye, I am, sir," the Scotsman said and rose. As he left the room with Clayt, G.T. was overseeing the division of surplus bread among all who remained.

It was a clear night. The howl of a wolf carried from the Snowy Range, the far off sound as distinct as the scuff of Dunne's shoes in the dirt. They walked to the barn, where Clayt laid down the blankets and checked the fuel in a lantern.

"This's where you can sleep. Lucifers are in that jar. Best not to carry this lantern up to where we got the hay stored." Clayt pointed to the stall with the maverick calf. "If that'n starts up on you, you're in for a long night."

"What's wrong with it?" Dunne asked.

Clayt looked into the dark stall where the animal waited. "Orphaned."

They crossed the yard without speaking. With the light spilling from the house, the leaves of the rose bushes shone like curved slivers of ice beneath the windows.

"You're a hard man to get riled, Mr. Jane," Dunne said as they reached the steps. "I can't tell if you're really as collected as you appear . . . or learned to cover it up."

Clayt stopped and faced him. "Cover what up?"

Dunne touched the top button of Clayt's jacket. "That old fire burning just inside there." Dunne lifted his eyebrows and slipped his hands into his trouser pockets.

"Mr. Dunne, you been talkin' out the side o' your mouth since I met you. Sayin' one thing and meanin' another. A man could get wore out tryin' to figure which one o' you to answer to. Maybe you oughta just save the act for somebody else. I don' know what it is you're after, but, whatever it is, I wish you'd just git to it."

Dunne's smile slowly widened. "So . . .

217

the fire emerges." He laughed quietly through his nose, and his head bounced once. "I never met a rebel yet who could let go of the war. Your lost cause went down hard, didn't it, Corporal 'Lightfoot' Jane?"

Clayt kept his voice even. "You seem to know a lot 'bout things that ain't your business, Mr. Dunne. I'm gonna tell you this, 'cause you're a man who don't seem to know when to quit. If I'd had a better grip on the whole story, I ain't so sure I'd a joined up for the war. And if I did, I cain't say for sure which side it would'a been. But as I see it, none o' that matters now. It's in the past. There ain't nothin gonna change the past."

Putting a grin on his face, the Scotsman rocked back on his heels and gripped the lapels of his open coat. His eyes studied Clayt as if from behind a mask. When the visitor said nothing more, Clayt turned, walked up the stairs, and knocked on the door. Dunne followed and stopped slightly behind Clayt on the porch. The door opened, and Afton, himself, greeted them. Clayt made introductions and stood for a moment, listening to the two men assign, each to the other, the place names connected to their accents — a slew of Scottish and English towns and shires. Clayt began backing toward the steps until Afton beckoned with his fingers.

"Clayton, come in and sit with us. I'd like to have a talk with you after Mr. Dunne and I are finished."

"Actually, Mr. Afton," Dunne said, removing his hat, "what I have to discuss with you is of a personal nature. I was hoping we could have a private meeting."

Afton made a dismissive turn of his hand. "I have no secrets from Clayton. And he may be of help with this talk of mining. He knows this land better than I do."

Dunne offered a weak smile and followed Clayt inside.

CHAPTER 16

They settled in front of the fire with tea and coffee. Clayt, for once, lowered himself into the chair that was routinely offered and refused. He set his hat on the floor. Afton tamped tobacco into the bowl of his pipe, scratched a lucifer, and held it before him as he sucked the flame inverted into the bowl. With his tobacco smoldering, he sat and crossed his legs as he watched Dunne nod with approval at the furnishings in the room.

"You've done very well for yourself, Mr. Afton. Very well indeed."

Afton removed his pipe. "I understand you want to talk about mineral rights."

Dunne smiled and laid his hat on the table. "I have a letter I'd like you to read." He fanned open the left lapel of his coat, and under his arm a holstered revolver flashed from the firelight. He tore open a seam in the coat's lining, the threads popping like a chain of distant small-caliber gunshots. From the lining he produced two envelopes. Tapping them in his hand, he looked at Clayt before handing an envelope to Afton.

"What's this?" Afton searched his pockets for his spectacles, and Dunne, still holding the second envelope, folded his arms across his chest. Clayt remained quiet, watching Afton open the paper and then narrow his eyes as he scanned the letter. The crackle of firewood and the tick of the clock marked time as Clayt waited. He felt the sense of remoteness he always experienced when words were being read in silence. When Afton lowered the paper his mouth was set in a firm straight line.

"The senator has a very high regard for you, Mr. Afton," Dunne remarked in his affable way. "Do you think we might have that private conversation now?"

When Afton frowned at the letter again, Clayt picked up his hat and stood. "I need to git some work done on that easel," he explained and began to make his exit.

Afton pointed his pipe stem at the chair. "Sit down, Clayton." He gave Dunne a resigned look. "Mr. Dunne, I don't know you," he said bluntly and held up the letter and shook it, ". . . except through this piece of paper." He waved the pipe through the air, leaving a thin arc of smoke hanging between them. "I knew the senator when he was a businessman in Cheyenne, and, though I appreciate his faith in me, I can't say that I can reciprocate. To tell you the truth, I wouldn't vote for the man."

Clayt was still standing, hat in hand. While Afton waited for an answer from the Scotsman, Clayt lowered himself again onto the expensive upholstery.

"On the other hand," Afton continued, "I've known Clayton for a decade. He was just a boy when he came to us, but there is no man I count on more. I entrust him with the business of running my ranch, my cattle, the horses. He supervises my employees and makes decisions on everything. Whatever you have to say to me, you can say in his presence. If you require his discretion about this conversation, you need only ask him. He will tell you if he will honor that or if he will not. But, whatever he says, you can rely upon it." Afton leaned forward to return the letter.

Dunne opened the second letter. "This one," he said, pushing it toward Afton, "is a wee bit more" — Dunne smiled and waggled his head from side to side — ". . . shall we say 'persuasive'?" They exchanged letters.

Clayt watched his employer's eyebrows push low until they touched the frame of the spectacles. When Afton had finished reading, his gaze returned to the top of the page, and he brought the paper closer to his face. This time when he lowered the letter, his lips parted with an unspoken word. Dunne reached for the letter, and Afton surrendered it automatically. "Do you understand now, sir, why I must insist that our conversation be a private one?"

"I understand why you ask, Mr. Dunne. But what you must understand is that talking to me is the same as talking to Clayton. He needs to know everything that bears on New Surrey Downs. Whatever you relate to me, I will simply pass on to Clayton, so we can save ourselves some time by conferring together now . . . the three of us." He sat back again, whipped off his spectacles, and waited for compliance.

Dunne pushed out his lips and studied Clayt as though he were a stubborn knot that refused to be untied. "No man tells the truth all the time," Dunne said. "That man would be a fool."

Clayt looked down into his hat and ran his finger around the sweatband. When his head came up, his eyes fixed on the visitor.

"I reckon you'd know more 'bout that than me, Mr. Dunne."

Unblinking, Dunne returned Clayt's stare. The sound of the clock seemed to grow louder as time stretched out. Closing his eyes, the Scotsman let out a long sigh.

"I suppose so, Mr. Jane." His wrinkled mouth seemed a concession to all the things a man could not change about his life. He offered one of the letters, but Clayt made no move to accept it. Dunne's serious expression broke with a self-deprecating laugh. "Sorry, I forgot." He turned to Afton. "Your foreman doesn't read, does he?"

"Clayton has not had the advantages of a formal education," Afton replied stiffly.

Folding the letters, Dunne nodded. "Have you ever seen him write?"

"I think you would have to concede, Mr. Dunne," Afton replied, "that a man who does not read does not write."

Dunne considered the folded papers, ballooned air in his cheeks, and exhaled. He stood and walked to the hearth and set the letters on the smoldering logs. The three men watched the papers curl and char to brown, then burst into yellow flame. Silhouetted against the firelight, Wallace Dunne's stark-white hair caught flecks of light that added years to his age. He looked more suited to tallying up numbers behind a desk than riding the range at night with covert letters.

"All right," he agreed, shaking his head. "There are few guarantees in my work. Sometimes you have to run on your instincts. I suppose this is one of those times." He returned to his chair, sat, and slapped his forearms on the armrests. Cocking his head to stare at Clayt, he allowed a faint grin. "I suppose I'd made up my mind about you that day we met at Shannonhaus's line shack. Most of that being what I heard from a few men after you'd left. They say you're a man of your woord."

"You're a Pinkerton, ain't you?" Clayt said.

Dunne's reluctant smile was answer enough. Afton took his pipe from his mouth.

"You knew he was a detective, Clayton?"

Clayt nodded at Dunne's right hand. "He's a fast healer," he said and then met the Scotsman's eyes. "Started addin' up when he pulled those papers from his coat linin'."

" 'A fast healer'?" Afton said, frowning.

Dunne offered a wry smile as he held up his hand and flexed the fingers twice. "I had to run a shill on your foreman here, Mr. Afton." He shrugged and glanced at Clayt. Spreading his hands, he made a sheepish look. "One of the necessities of my trade."

When neither Afton nor Clayt replied, Dunne leaned forward quickly and propped his forearms on his knees, as if he had made up his mind about something. "Look . . . the mining prospect is just a cover for my being here," he said, his voice low now, as if someone in the next room might be listening. "The Pinkertons are more than just detectives, gentlemen. In the war we were agents on special assignment. Our job was to cross over to the other side to compile information about the enemy." He nodded the side of his head toward Clayt. "Your man here ought to know a wee bit about that."

Afton frowned and turned to Clayt, but Clayt held his gaze on the Scotsman.

"During the war the Pinkertons worked closely with the president," Dunne continued. "We still do."

Afton raised his chin. "Has this something to do with the president's pending visit to Laramie?"

"Aye, sir. Indeed it does. And throughout that visit, we are responsible for his welfare and safety."

Afton nodded. "And how does that involve us?"

Dunne inched forward in his chair and steepled his fingers before him. His voice became a low hum that was barely audible inside the triangle of men.

"The president has received letters . . . seven of them . . . each threatening assassination. All the letters were posted from Laramie." His fingertips bounced lightly off his mouth as he studied Clayt. "Do you see now . . . there is a reason I kept pushing you to write woords on that map? I wanted to see your handwriting." Dunne shook his head. "I've been trying to get samples from all over the county. Primarily from ex-Confederates." He spread his hands. "All we have are letters from a man with a grudge. He says he will kill President Grant if he sets foot in Albany County. The threat includes Governor Hayes as well."

"Who?" Clayt asked.

"The new Republican candidate. From Ohio."

Afton set down his pipe on the side table. "How can we help?" he said.

Dunne settled back in his chair and turned one hand palm up. "I'm a new face around here. I can't get into all the social circles I would like to. I'm going to need help with that. I can gain an audience with the land-owners to talk about mineral rights, but there are only so many men holding property. There are plenty working for them." He pointed toward the main yard. "You've got two bunkhouses full of laborers. There's a limit to what one man with a Scottish accent can do."

Afton's face closed down. "You suspect someone here at New Surrey Downs?"

Dunne shrugged. "I have to suspect every-body, even if the threat is false. It's my job to take the threat seriously and to consider any man capable of the act."

"What are you asking of us?" Afton said. "I mean, I want to help. I want the president to know that he can count on us. But what do we do?"

"He wants us to do his spyin' for him here at the Rollin' F," Clayt said. "That 'bout right, Mr. Dunne?"

Dunne shrugged. "Yes, I do need your help, gentlemen."

"Surely you are not the only agent that was sent out here?" Afton said.

"For the moment I'm all there is. There will be more, of course. Sometimes one man going in early can gather more information than an army could."

Dunne glanced at Clayt, and in that brief

and silent exchange, both men knew that each understood something about being behind enemy lines.

"I can 'preciate your problem," Clayt said. "You got no choice but to consider the threat a real one, even if it ain't." He shook his head. "It's always stacked ag'in' you when you're on that end of it. A man wantin' to kill another'n — even the president — has got a big edge on the ones tryin' to stop 'im." Clayt began shaking his head. "But I got a particular problem with this. I cain't be spyin' on men and 'xpectin' 'em to trust me at the same time. I lose that trust . . . I'd just as well try runnin' this herd by myself."

"I'm nae asking either of you to betray anyone. Personally, I doon't believe it is possible to be disloyal to a traitor and a murderer. I simply need to see samples of every man's handwriting so I can compare them to the letters that have threatened the president. No man who is innocent has reason to be insulted."

"Seems unlikely a man would use his own style o' writin' for such a letter," Clayt ventured. "There's plenty o' ways he could git 'round that."

"Aye, we know that, Mr. Jane. Believe me, these letters have been analyzed by experts.

The writing is childlike, but the form is consistent. Someone may be modifying his natural style."

"Or maybe it's someone new to writin'," Clayt said.

"Aye, it could be," Dunne agreed. "Or perhaps it could be a man who uses someone else — like, say, a child — to get the words down on paper."

"What is it you have in mind?" Afton said. "Do you want us to line up the hands and have them all sign their names on a piece of paper?"

Dunne shook his head. "No, sir. That would be too transparent. I plan to enlist Mr. Ivinson's help in this . . . at his store. With his connections with the Union Pacific, he has, like you, a reputation that puts him above suspicion."

Afton clamped his pipe in his teeth and frowned. "What can Ivinson do?"

Dunne pushed out his lower lip. "Well . . . he can start asking each man who picks up supplies at his store to sign for the goods. Then, you could, in turn, send each of your men into town to pick up something."

"And you're doing this with all the landowners? Shannonhaus and the others?"

"Right now, it's just the three of us who know about this. Even Ivinson will not know

I am a Pinkerton. Nor the county sheriff. I'll have to work out other methods with the other landowners, but I have no plans to take them into my confidence as I have with you. The fewer who know about this, the better. Can I count on both of you to honor that?"

Afton glanced at Clayt and then spoke for both of them. "You may, sir."

Dunne turned squarely to Clayt. "I need to hear that from you, too, Mr. Jane."

For a time Clayt merely stared back at the Scotsman. Then, turning to Afton, he spoke as if they were the only two in the room.

"Them papers," he began and hitched a thumb toward the fireplace. "They were enough to convince you this man is who he says he is?"

Afton closed his eyes and nodded once. When he opened his eyes again, Clayt could see that his employer was dead set on assisting their visitor in every way.

Clayt nodded to Dunne. "Long as Mr. Afton tells me to, I'll be quiet 'bout it."

They sat in silence, listening to the hiss of the logs in the hearth. Afton sucked on his pipe, but it had gone cold, so he set it on the table again.

"We never signed for nothin' at Ivinson's before," Clayt said.

Dunne smiled. "At my suggestion, I think Mr. Ivinson will initiate a new stoore policy. Everyone who purchases on credit will sign."

"All right," Afton said, "you talk to Ivinson, and we'll rotate the crews. Every man will have his turn to ride in for supplies. But if you're not going to reveal your identity to the other ranchers, how will you convince them to do the same?"

"That is something I will have to woork out, sir . . . ranch by ranch. Now remember, as far as anyone knows, you and I have talked about mineral rights tonight, but nothing has been decided. You're going to need time to think about it." Dunne stood and buttoned his coat. "I appreciate this, Mr. Afton. I want to stress again how vital it is that nothing about our conversation be mentioned to anyone. No offense meant to you, sir, but . . . not even to your wife."

Afton rose. "I understand. You need not worry about that."

Dunne waited for Clayt to stand. "As to our relationship, Mr. Jane, it's best to maintain an air of acrimony. It could help me get closer to certain men."

Afton laughed. "Clayton has no enemies in this valley."

Dunne could not suppress a smile. "Every

232

man worth his salt has enemies, Mr. Afton. Yourself included."

Afton frowned but did not argue. "Clayton, have you made sleeping arrangements for Mr. Dunne?"

"Yes'r. He'll be in the barn loft."

Afton frowned again. "Nonsense! We have an extra room here in the house."

Dunne appraised the décor of the room. "Oh, but it *is* tempting. Thank you, sir, but I prefer the cruder accommodations." His eyes turned wistful. "Woord does get around, you know. I'll have a better chance of talking to the woorking class in this valley if I don't defect over to the upper crust." He smiled and shook hands with Afton.

"We have a party leaving for Laramie in the morning," Afton said. "You can return to town in our company."

"I'll do that. Noo, I'll find my way oot and let you two talk." He turned to Clayt and extended his hand. "A fresh start, Mr. Jane. I've always believed in them."

Clayt shook the Scotsman's hand. "Reckon I learnt to do that, too, Mr. Dunne."

When Dunne had closed the door, they listened to him scrape down the front steps and march out into the yard. Afton moved to the hearth, clasped his hands behind him, and stared into the flames. The firelight flickered silver on his face.

"It irks me to think of someone in this valley threatening the president. If Grant were shot here . . . what would the country think of us?" He paced across the room, his hands still joined at his lower back. "And my sister. She'll be here. It is worrisome enough to think of her in the countryside with Chatka on the loose. And now this threat!"

"Could be that's all it is, Mr. Afton . . . just a threat. Somebody wantin' to let the president know not ever'body likes 'im. And, even if it is true, I 'xpect there'll be a mess o' soldiers 'round Grant wherever he goes." Clayt gazed into the fire, crossed his arms over his chest, and cradled his chin in the cup of one hand. His fingers slowly stroked the three-day-old whiskers on his cheeks. After a time he began shaking his head. "It don't make much sense for a man to write his intentions 'bout killin' the pres'dent." He turned to look at Afton. "Why would he do that?"

Afton propped one boot on the hearth. "I don't know. But it has to be taken seriously, and we'll help however we can. But Isabella remains my primary concern." He clasped his bent knee with both hands and leaned on stiffened arms. "She and her family are coming in tomorrow on the two o'clock train. Whom have you chosen for the escort?"

"Chalky, Nestor, Whit Densmore, and Harry Sims. I'll ask Johnny Waites to handle the wagon. He's one o' the new boys an' handy with a rifle. On the return trip to the ranch, we'll send Chalk out ahead and Nestor with 'im for relayin' messages. That'll give us two other men on horseback with the wagon. Three countin' you. And Johnny in the wagon. Whit and Harry will ride out to the flanks to keep a lookout there but close enough to join the wagon if need be."

"What about you?" Afton said, frowning. "Anytime we are out on the prairie, I want you wherever Isabella is."

"I'll be ridin' drag, keepin' a eye on the trail behind us."

Afton listened, but his eyes seemed distant. He picked up his pipe from the side table and tamped the charred tobacco with his thumb. He turned the pipe in a circle as he worked it from every angle, but instead of relighting it he set the pipe back on the table.

"Mr. Dunne seems to know something about you. What did he mean about your understanding his work as a detective?"

Clayt moved to his chair and picked up his hat. Turning it in a slow revolution, he shaped the brim to his liking.

"Guess they gotta military record on me some'ere," he conceded.

Afton narrowed his eyes with an unasked question.

"From the war," Clayt explained. Lowering the hat by his leg, he met Afton's eyes. "You know ever'thin' 'bout me since I come to this valley. If you got a question 'bout before that . . . 'bout my war years . . . I reckon you'll need to be askin' it."

Afton's eyebrows slanted to a peak over the bridge of his nose. "But how could you have been part of the war, Clayton? You were just a boy when you came here."

"I might'a looked like one, Mr. Aff. But whate'er there was o' the boy in me . . . I reckon I left that back in Georgia a long time b'fore I signed up for the war."

Afton tightened his gaze. "And you fought for which side, the South, I presume?"

Clayt hitched his head and stared at the fire. "Didn' know much 'bout sides and causes back then. I just did like ever'body else 'round me. We thought we were protectin' somethin'. We just didn' really know what it was."

As he studied Clayt's face, Afton looked like a man trying to recognize an unfamiliar shape in a semi-dark room. Then his expression relaxed, and he began to shake his head with decisiveness.

"I won't ask you anything about the war, Clayton. If ever you want to talk to me about it, I will be here to listen. But I think I know who you are. A man proves himself by his day-to-day actions. Nothing about your past can change that."

Afton turned to the fire, and the tendon in his jaw flexed with a steady rhythm. Clayt watched him for a few moments and then fitted his hat to his head.

"Reckon I'll go finish up that easel. Come mornin' we'll hitch a team to the spring wagon and be ready to pull out after breakfast." Clayt walked to the foyer alone and opened the door. With the night air touching his face he stopped at the threshold and looked across the yard at the dark outline of the blacksmith shop attached to the dairy barn. Farther down the yard, eight rectangles of dull yellow light marked the two bunkhouses. The big barn was black and massive against the star-studded sky, and the horses out back clustered in dappled shadow.

Clayt felt his years at the Rolling F pull

taut inside him — like a glue holding together the muscle, sinew, and bone of his body. Tonight it had been held up to a light and tested and found not to be wanting. He stepped back to the room where he had left Afton and saw the man still staring into the fire. His back was rigid and his chin buried in the folds of his ascot. A captain at the helm. Afton did not turn. Clayt watched him for a time, then turned, walked outside, and quietly pulled the door until it latched.

Stopping on his way to the mill shed, he leaned against the top rail of the corral. From the black knot of horses bunched there, Skitter detached, walked to him, raised her head over the rail, and blew a flutter of air through her nostrils.

"We come a long way, ain't we, old girl? And it ain't been half bad a go."

At the sound of his voice, some of the other horses lifted their heads his way and pricked their ears. From her soft nostrils Skitter breathed out a long rush of air that ran like warm goose down along Clayt's neck. He stroked the flat plate of muscle along the horse's upper jaw and kneaded the tendons around the base of her ears. When he stopped she nickered softly, bobbed her head back inside the fence and trotted back to the herd. The other horses parted for her and then settled, as though each animal were filling some appointed slot in their communal arrangement of cohabitation. Clayt watched them in their stillness and listened to the wind tease the windmill blades with false starts.

A coyote yammered from out in the night, and Clayt turned toward the sound. As a salute to a life scratched out of the hardscrabble prairie, he lifted his chin to the animal. When the coyote called again, he believed he heard the vocalization for what it was meant to be — a simple statement of being . . . a declaration of another day survived. And now another night. All of it fought for and hard won. All you could do was choose the way you moved along the playing field in the time allotted you. And wherever possible, prolong it with a measure of grace. Choose the way you react to the unexpected. Believe in yourself enough to know that the promises you make to yourself might be more important than the promises you make to another man. It was what Afton had meant, Clayt knew, when he had talked about a man going about his day-to-day work.

Noting the position of the stars, Clayt estimated how much time had passed since supper. He figured he would put in two more hours on the easel, then he would need some sleep.

CHAPTER 17

The steady huff of the engine and the grinding grate of the wheels filled the depot's landing platform with a sustained roar. As the train slowed to a stop, its brake lines released spreading plumes of steam around the legs of the bystanders on the siding. The white vapor swirled in a gossamer tide and then came apart in wispy shreds. From the tall smokestack perched on the engine, cinders and black smoke poured across the sky, tainting the air and scorching the throats of all foolish enough to stand downwind of it.

The group of people gathered seemed both awed and excited, as if they had assembled here to see some enormous mythical beast coaxed in from the prairie. Then, just as it seemed the train might settle, the cars banged at their couplings, telegraphing along the line in a long, thunderous chain of metallic clanks.

The great bulk of the locomotive seemed out of place here among the buildings of Laramie. The dark plume of smoke that had just moments ago billowed from the stack and trailed windborne over the prairie now swept down, dirty and biting, burning the eyes of everyone. The few women outside the depot retreated inside the telegraph office with handkerchiefs cupped over their noses and mouths. The men turned their heads and clamped their jaws to wait out the acrid assault.

With the long line of cars at rest, the engine shut down and let off a shrill whistle. With this one long blast the engineer re-announced the coming of the age of the railroad. The town never tired of it. Spectators still flocked to the station to see the monstrosity of galloping iron and the new faces that would emerge from it. With the train put to rest, the blur of conversation and the shuffle of footsteps on the landing became vivid and startling — like the sounds of the world heard after emerging from deep water. John Afton raised an arm and waved, stepping forward with a bounce that caused Nestor to turn on his heel and grin at the boys waiting under the station awning. They watched Afton cup his hands to his mouth and call out to the first car.

A heavy man on the coupling platform slipped long fingers into shining, black gloves. His high forehead was crowned by a derby hat, his movements exacting, eyes darting. His mouth was lost in the shadow of a full moustache, each tip waxed to a curled point. Beneath his black overcoat he appeared full of ballast — like a bowling pin. Spotting Afton he made a perfunctory flourish with one finger from the hat brim and casually stepped down to the boards.

The two men shook hands, and another spray of steam escaped from the brakes, forcing Afton to lean forward to be heard. Then he began searching the windows of the car while the taller man turned his head by increments, as though cataloguing the layout of the town. Turned in profile, the skin on his face was as smooth as a child's, the cheeks so colored that they might have been smudged with women's rouge.

A porter clomped down the metal steps, then turned back to offer a hand to the woman who had appeared behind him. With a brush of his hand the mustachioed man instructed the porter aside and then spoke to the woman, but her eyes were on Afton.

Clayt had lipped a freshly rolled cigarette. He lowered the unstruck lucifer from his belt buckle and stared at the woman on the coupling platform. Beneath her soft-brimmed hat she was etched in hard shadow and light, and he could not help but think that she resembled her own paintings that hung in Afton's study. He studied her much the way he had the paintings, seeing the whole of her as something carefully composed and beyond the realm of what was expected in day-to-day life.

Snapping the lucifer to a flame he kept his eyes on the Rolling F boys as he lit up. Each man was still, lost in private thought, soaking up the vision of this woman as if they were watching through a crack in a door. In their faces was the unspoken sadness that was part of being a cowboy, something few men wanted to acknowledge, there being too much of the "what-if" and "what-won't-be" buried inside it. But he also knew that there was a need to see such a woman, even if from a distance, to remind them of dreams that might still hold a place in their unformed plans.

Her walnut-brown hair was pulled back from her temples and gathered in back, where the woven pattern threw off glints of rust-red and gold from the mass of deeper brown. She was trim and angular in the way that all women were who laced themselves up in the confining accoutrements of the day's fashion, but her movements were natural, unaffected. She smiled at Afton and wrapped a shawl about her shoulders, and the movement of her arm brought to mind the smooth and flawless cast of a riata from a seasoned hand.

The smile transformed her face, but it stopped just short of joy, for the intensity in her eyes did not abate. From that distance her eyes appeared amber to Clayt. He had never before seen eyes that could command a moment so thoroughly. It was as though the world had stopped for her so that she could plumb her emotions to their fullest in this moment of reunion. He imagined her painting this way, lost in deep concentration as she dabbed at the colors she mixed, those amber eyes burning as though the heat from her stare fixed the pigment to the canvas. She swung her hands together in front of her dress, where she loosely clasped them. Then she simply stared at Afton. The passenger standing behind her — a short, thick man in a brown suit — waited without complaint. He was like a child pausing before a rare and edifying curiosity.

Before she could detrain, a round-cheeked, dark-haired boy wriggled around her and clambered down the steps. He dodged the grasp of his father and ran out to face Afton.

"Are you my Uncle John?"

Afton cocked his head and laughed. "I am indeed . . . if you are Thomas Walsh."

"Tom," the boy corrected.

Afton bent at the waist and touched a finger to the boy's chest. "The last time I saw you . . . you were wearing a diaper."

The boy made a face and let his arms drop by his sides. Afton laughed again and looked over the boy's head at the mother descending the steps. Straightening, he stepped toward her, putting a hand on the boy's head and tousling his hair lightly as he passed.

Father and son watched Afton enfold his sister. She swept off her hat and returned the embrace so vigorously that Afton began to laugh and look behind him with apologetic eyes, until she stepped back to arm's length.

"You've changed," she said.

"Well, what did you expect? It's been . . . what . . . nine, ten years." He shook his head appraisingly. "And you are even more lovely, if that is possible." Afton turned and made a gesture to include all three of his guests. "Henry, Thomas, Isabella . . . welcome to Wyoming." He delivered the words with uncommon melody, then lost his ebullience, and refocused on his sister. "Isabella," he breathed, shaking his head again. When he bent to kiss her, Nestor leaned back into the shade of the awning, raised his eyebrows, and with the rest of the boys found anything else to look at.

Clayt watched the boy named Tom start toward them — something in the dead earnest expression of this boy reminding Clayt of himself at that age, which he took to be ten or eleven. Yet there was some quality in the boy that Clayt could not claim. It had to do with the boy's fluid ease, the freedom to follow his every curiosity. His eyes moved studiously over Clayt's attire and stopped at the buckle of his cartridge belt.

"Do you work for my uncle?"

Clayt had to catch the words and listen to them echo again through his ears. The words proved familiar enough — with a little listening — but cinched up by the boy's English tongue. Clayt took a last draw on the cigarette, dropped it on the boards, and covered it with his boot.

"I do. Name's Clayt." He offered his hand. The boy looked at it for a moment, then checked Clayt's face. Apparently he saw what he needed and shook hands.

"I'm Tom Walsh." As soon as he had said

it, his gaze returned to Clayt's cartridge belt. "Is that for a six-shooter?"

Clayt nodded, and the boy stared at the place on Clayt's hip where he judged the gun to rest beneath his coat. "Can I see it?"

Clayt checked the loading dock. Afton and his sister were deep in conversation. The boy's father dug coins out of his vest pocket as the porters lined up luggage on the platform. Clayt pulled back his coat to expose the gun. The walnut grips and blued back-strap of the butt gleamed darkly against the leather of the scabbard. The boy's eyes widened, two vertical wrinkles creasing the skin above the bridge of his nose.

"You don't have ivory handles," the boy said, but he threw off his disappointment for a pleading tilt of the head. "Can't you take it out so I can see it?"

The cowboys lounging next to Clayt were watching him, their stillness as absolute as when the woman had stepped from the car. Few had seen Clayt's Colt's in the hands of its owner. Clayt let the coat fall back to cover his weapon, hooked his thumbs behind his belt, and waited for the boy's eyes to meet his.

"Reckon I better tell you somethin' 'bout Wyomin', Tom." Clayt knelt and lowered his voice for privacy. "It might be a shade different where you come from, but out here it's considered bad policy to pull your gun amongst other folk. It could be took the wrong way. You understand?"

Tom Walsh looked pained, but it seemed impossible to suppress his curiosity for too long. "Wild Bill has ivory handles. Do you know Wild Bill?"

Clayt's eyes slanted to a question, and Tom's forehead creased with lines again.

"You have heard of Wild Bill Hickok, haven't you?" the boy pressed.

Clayt grinned. "Hickok? Sure. Just never had the pleasure o' meetin' 'im."

"*I* met him," Nestor spoke up.

Every head turned at that. The Rolling F crew stood slack-jawed, staring at Nestor. They were still frozen like that when Afton approached with his party.

"Let's get this luggage packed into the wagon, Clayton. We're going to walk down the street to the restaurant for a little refreshment before we start back."

Afton's sister stepped abreast of him and eyed the ranch hands with the same intensity she had afforded her brother. "I'd like to meet your employees, John." Her voice was clear and melodic, her accent even more pronounced than her brother's.

"It's just a small part of the crew," Afton explained with a dismissive wave of his hand. "This is my foreman, Clayton Jane." He swept the hand toward Clayt.

She stepped forward and offered her hand. Her eyes were honey-gold, each backlit by an internal light. Clayt had never seen anything like them, and, by an unexpected whimsical logic, he wondered if the uncommon colors in her paintings were due to her unique eyes.

"Mr. Jane, John has written me about you. I've been curious to see the man to whom he entrusts the running of the farm. I am Isabella Walsh."

Clayt's hat was in his hand though he did not remember removing it. "Well, it's mostly a ranch, ma'am. I cain't take no credit for farmin' it. We got a man named Grady Brooks handles that part." Clayt smiled, but she did not return the gesture. Under her inspection he felt as though a lamp had been lit and held up close to his face. He thought about that blue-violet light rising off the evening prairie and wondered if, to a painter, some kind of color might rise off a man at certain times, according to that man's nature.

Afton cleared his throat. "Clayton, would

you make the introductions for me with the men?"

The Sorry-Damn boys straightened, shuffled their boots on the boards, and held their hats with both hands. They were as quiet as the dead when the introductions began. One by one, Clayt named each man and gave that man time to mumble his greeting, if he so chose. Isabella Walsh stepped toward each of the cowboys in turn and shook his hand. Her husband stood with his hands in his trouser pockets tumbling unseen coins and keys, turning his head up and down the loading dock, watching the crowd.

When Isabella engaged Chalky she remarked how impressed she was that he had overseen the construction at New Surrey Downs and how she looked forward to seeing the buildings. Chalky was ever quiet but smiling. In the presence of her straightforward manner, Whit and Harry were without words, but Nestor rose to the occasion.

"We're right pleased you folks could visit," Nestor announced. "Anythin' you might need, you just let us know." While the other ranch hands watched wide eyed, Nestor made a little bow from the waist and swept his hat out to his side.

"He knows Wild Bill, Mother," Tom said, staring unabashedly at Nestor.

She smiled and laid her hand on the boy's shoulder. "Thomas is quite taken with the rough edge of your frontier. He reads about it all the time. The dime novels."

"When he *ought* to be addressing his lessons," Henry Walsh intoned.

That was when Clayt put his finger on the wide gulf between young Tom Walsh and the farm boy that Clayt had once been. This English boy had a mother. Her touch on his shoulder gave the boy a sense of proportion and potential, as though that touch was a lasting provision that might be carried out into the world to serve him in ways that Clayt could not fathom.

"It occurs to me that you must have taken the boy out of school," Afton said.

"Only four weeks," Tom said and wrinkled his face. "To make up for it, Mother gives me lessons every day."

"Good for you, Isabella," Afton said. "Let's walk over to the restaurant and have some tea. Clayton, if you and the men would bring the wagon to the Laramie House."

Each cowboy picked up a bag and walked silently to the wagon, where Johnny Waites was slumped in the driver's seat, asleep with his mouth open and his chin on his chest.

"Hey, Johnny," Harry yelled, heaving a trunk into the bed. "Wake up so you can meet old Wild Nestor Purty Boy. Damn, that's got a ring to it, don't it?"

"It's Purdabaugh!" Nestor complained. "And I did meet Wild Bill!"

After loading the luggage, they took the horses and wagon down Grand Avenue, ribbing Nestor all the way. When they tethered their animals across the street from the restaurant, Harry and Johnny were still smiling at Nestor's expense.

"Hey, Purty Boy!" Harry poked. "How long did you ride with Wild Bill?"

"I tol' you I only met 'im," Nestor murmured sullenly. "It was in Kansas. He come into a store where I was waitin' on a friend o' mine, and we just got to talkin'." Nestor looked to Clayt for support, but Clayt was untying the water bucket behind the driver's box.

"Well, what the hell did the two o' you find to talk 'bout?" Harry said.

"It was on account o' his sister. I knew 'er back in Illinois, and damned if he didn' remember me. We mostly talked 'bout *her*."

Harry went very still, and his face sobered. "You ain't yarnin' us?" His voice was hushed with awe. "Well, what's he like?"

253

Nestor lowered the tailgate on the wagon and sat in the bed to think about his answer. "Well, I guess I started up the conversation. He didn' have much to say to the likes o' me. Kinda distant-like and . . . I don' know . . . like he was too busy sortin' through brands of cigars to talk to a feller. Kinda showy, too, if you wanna know. But he could damn look straight through you. Like a little light turnin' on in his eyes."

"I hear he can shoot the cork through a damn whiskey bottle at thirty feet without scarrin' the neck," Whit said.

"All I seen 'im do with pistols was wear 'em at his sides like a coupla rattlesnakes ready to strike," Nestor admitted. "Like I said . . . kinda showy. Ivory handles." Then he frowned. "I bought the damn cigar for 'im. I still ain't sure how he finagled that."

The boys laughed. Clayt walked from the trough across the street and held the bucket for the draft horses to drink, rationing as he moved from one animal to the next.

"Way I hear it," Whit said, "he's fast to kill a man."

Harry pointed his finger at Whit. "Tell you what *I* heard. Drover over in Cheyenne told me Hickok, on a five dollar bet, could snatch a coin outta the flat o' your hand b'fore you could close your fingers over it."

Like an actor on a stage, Harry carried his stare of conviction to Nestor. "Ever try that, young'n?" He dug into his trouser pocket as he spoke. "Here you go, Purty Boy, show us what Wild Bill learnt ya."

Harry flipped a coin with his thumb and then snatched it out of the air with a downward swat. When his fingers uncurled, a dollar shone in his palm. When Nestor slipped off the wagon, everyone gathered around to witness the contest. Clayt finished watering the last horse, retied the bucket, and leaned against the side of the wagon to watch. Nestor, wiping his hands on his trousers, stared at the coin.

"Whatta I gotta do 'xactly?"

Harry dangled his free hand a foot above the coin lying on his other palm. "Just start 'bout here and see can you grab it. I won't close up till I see you move."

"Can *you* do it?" Nestor challenged.

"Hell, yeah," Harry said, "if I'm playin with a blind man."

Everyone laughed except Nestor, who rocked side to side from one leg to the other. He stilled himself as he raised his hand to the appointed height. Staring at the coin, he ran his tongue across his lips. Harry's grin tightened, his eyes bright with amusement.

"I just go when I want to?" Nestor asked.

Harry's grin dissolved. "That's the point, Purty Boy. You try an' outfox me and out-quick me, all at the same time."

"And what if I grab it?" Nestor said. "Do I keep it?"

Harry hesitated. "Hell . . . I guess you can if you can snatch it."

The men around them focused on the coin as if it might move of its own accord. For a long moment the space around the wagon seemed severed from the rest of the town. Clayt could see the tension growing in Nestor's eyes, telegraphing right into the hand he held above the coin, and Clayt predicted to the split-second when that hand went into motion. When it did, Harry's hand balled into a fist, trapping one of Nestor's fingers, and everyone standing there heard the knuckle joint pop. It sounded like the muffled snap of a twig beneath a blanket. Nestor backed away slinging his hand from the wrist.

"Goddamn, Harry! You didn' say you was gonna tear my finger halfway off."

Whit and the other boys made no effort to restrain their delight, but Harry was do-ing a good job of holding a poker face. "Well, hell, Purty Boy, how're you gonna ride with Wild Bill if you ain't quick enough

256

to pick up a damn dollar?"

The other Sorry-Damn boys burst out in a chorus of laughter that drew the attention of passersby on the boardwalk. Nestor's face darkened as he glared at Harry.

"Ain't no way a man can git his fingers 'round a coin that fast. Hell, you cain't do it neither."

Harry cocked his head and let his eyebrows float upward. "Might could on a bet."

"The hell you say," Nestor huffed, still nursing his finger.

Harry gazed at the storefronts as if he were in the midst of a serious calculation. "What would you say to five dollars?" He smirked and gave Nestor a one-eyed dare.

Nestor stared back at him, then looked at the other boys, and last at Clayt, who turned his attention across the street to the restaurant. The boy, Tom, stepped out of the door and spotted the men around the wagon. When his mother came through the door she bent to him, and they talked face to face, Tom constantly pointing toward the wagon. She straightened and looked across the street. Even at that distance, Clayt could see she was looking right at him. He nodded and waved the boy over. Still holding Clayt's eyes, she said something that released the boy like a jackrabbit from a failed snare.

By the time Tom had joined the crew at the wagon, Nestor was poised liked a man about to jump off a bluff into a river, both his legs bent, his back hunched forward as he held the coin on his stiffened palm. The tendons in his wrist were tight as fence wire.

Harry raised his hand and let it hover above like a spider dangling from a strand of silk. Tom edged through the knot of men to watch.

The smack of Harry's hand was like a dry stick of wood popping in a fire. It took everyone a moment to realize it had been his other hand, flashing up from below to slap Nestor's from beneath. The coin jumped up and Harry snatched it out of the air with the hand that had waited above the coin. Nestor looked as startled as if he had been slapped across the cheek. To Harry's innocence, Nestor's face was a portrait of indignation.

"You didn' say nothin' 'bout usin' your other hand."

Harry's eyebrows floated up. "Didn' say nothin' *ag'in'* it. Just said to grab the damn coin and that's what I done."

Nestor looked at the few gathered around. They were grinning like monkeys and

258

watching to see what Nestor would do next. Nestor squared his shoulders to Harry.

"That ain't fair, and you know it."

"All I know, Purty Boy, is what ever' man here knows. You owe me five dollars." Harry held out his empty hand.

With creases etched into his forehead again, Tom walked to Clayt. "Are they angry at one another?" Clayt cracked half a grin and shook his head. But when the argument built at the rear of the wagon, Tom looked nervous and sidled closer to Clayt.

"Sorta like a game, I reckon," Clayt said, laying out a blanket on the makeshift seat he had fashioned in the wagon bed, where the boy and his family would sit. "Don't reckon anybody likes losin', but somebody's always got to."

Tom watched Nestor count out five bills to Harry. "It doesn't look like a game."

Clayt leaned on the wagon and watched the transaction. "Yeah," he said, "I reckon you're right." He took in a deep breath and let it out slowly. "Reckon this'll stick in Nestor's craw for a month o' Sundays." He motioned for Tom to follow and walked to the wagon gate, where Harry pocketed his winnings.

"How 'bout I give it a go?" Clayt said and stood before Harry.

Harry's smile relaxed. "What . . . you mean on a bet?"

Clayt dug into his pockets for coins and studied the sum of what was in his hand. "I got seven dollars says I can take that coin off you fair and square. One hand only."

Without taking his eyes off Clayt, Harry pivoted his head a few degrees away. "Seven dollars?" Now it was Harry's turn to check the others' faces, as though the Rolling F boys might know something about Clayt he didn't.

Chalky pushed away from the hitching rail, where he had quietly witnessed the bet and banter. His dark hand stretched into the center of the wager and added three more coins to Clayt's cupped hand.

"Make dat ten," Chalky said and returned to the rail.

Harry forced a laugh. "Hell, Clayt, I don't wanna take your money."

Clayt almost smiled. "My money's good as Nestor's. You game or ain't you?"

Harry mustered a grin now, but everyone could see it was manufactured out of embarrassment. He shook his head ruefully, as if he had no choice.

"Well, Lord knows I can use the money." Now he laughed outright. "I ain't never made fifteen dollars in the same day."

260

Clayt moved to the wagon and laid all but one of the coins on the gate. This last coin he flipped to Harry, who reacted quickly and snatched it out of the air. All the while that Harry positioned the coin, Clayt kept his eyes fixed on Harry's. His disqualified left hand went behind him, as his right came up slowly to hang above the prize, fingertips down. Tom shuffled into the crowd, vying for a better view.

"You ready?" Clayt said. His voice had that same calm as when he explained the day's job to his crew while the dew still clung to the grass.

Harry swallowed. "Hell, yeah, I'm ready," he crowed, mustering some bravado.

Clayt was in no hurry. As the time stretched out, Harry's face tightened like the mouth of a bag cinched up by a drawstring. Each time Harry blinked, he did so quickly and then widened his eyes unnaturally, trying to clear his vision.

Suddenly Clayt struck. His hand was a blur, moving straight down and returning to the place it had been hovering at the start. It had happened so quickly that no one showed a reaction. The picture was changed only by the fact that both men's hands were now balled into fists. There had been no slap, just a dull thump. The two men stood perfectly still, their clenched fists frozen between them, one over the other. No one in the crowd moved or spoke, not even the boy. The scene could have been a photograph.

Slowly Harry let his fist down to his side. The movement drew every eye, but he did not need to open his hand. They knew from his expression that he no longer held the coin. Clayt pivoted his fist and opened his hand palm up. The coin lay shining against his calloused skin like a talisman that had materialized out of the air.

"God . . . damn," Whit said, then quickly frowned and looked at Afton's nephew. "I mean . . . God-a-mighty."

Johnny Waites smiled from his perch on the wagon box and winked at the boy. "Better check for fang marks, Harry. That looked like a rattler to me."

Harry was quiet as he counted out money from his pockets. "I ain't got but eight, Clayt. I'll have to owe you till we get back to the ranch."

Clayt nodded. "You're good for it," he said and doled out coins to Chalky and then to Nestor. "Looks like we make a purty good team," he said to Nestor, just loud enough for the others to hear. Nestor's mouth hung open, and his eyes fixed on the coins.

"Guess we do," he said, trying to match the confidence in Clayt's voice.

Clayt raised the tailgate, latched both sides, and turned to lean his back into the wagon. Everyone was watching him as Tom approached and stared at Clayt.

"Can you teach me how to do that?"

Nestor joined them, looking as serious as Clayt had ever seen him. "Yeah, can you show me, too?"

Before Clayt could reply, the Afton party came out of the restaurant. Mr. Afton and his brother-in-law were in animated conversation with Sheriff Teague. The sister walked behind them lifting the front of her dress from the dusty tread boards. A step behind her was Teague's middle-aged deputy, Frank Maschinot, hurrying his pace to keep up. As the group approached, Walsh did all the talking, bending the ear of the sheriff, who nodded but held an appraising gaze on the men clustered at the wagon.

"Boys," the sheriff purred as a greeting. The Rolling F crew mumbled salutations and quieted. "Well," Teague said, inserting a toothpick and clamping it with his back teeth, "you boys comin' into town to see the pres'dent?"

No one answered. It was the longest string of words the sheriff had ever put together for their sake. And it was a first time for social amenities.

"I hope to have the president out to the ranch to dine with us," Afton announced and glanced at his brother-in-law for a reaction.

The sheriff lifted his eyebrows and patted his round belly. "Well, Mr. Afton, I can put together an escort for that." He winked at Clayt. "Head it up, myself."

Afton did not appear amused. "Clayt can put together an army if it's needed."

Teague thrust his hands into his coat pockets and studied Clayt with an amused grin. "Heard about your little parley with Chatka." The sheriff feigned an all-business face. "Runnin' any more specials on free beef up there at the Rolling F?"

"Don't know for certain it was Chatka," Clayt said, ignoring the question. "Just a ragtag bunch 'bout half starved."

"You plannin' on feedin' ever' Ind'an what's half starved?" Teague said, tainting his good-natured teasing with a hint of ridicule.

Only the sheriff laughed. Deputy Maschinot bowed his head and closed his eyes to cover his embarrassment. Clayt met Teague's self-absorbed stare but said nothing.

"I doubt we got a steer out there big enough for you, Sheriff," Johnny Waites said. The boys laughed modestly at this. Teague smiled, conceding the point.

Afton made a show of checking his pocketwatch. "Well, we'd best be off for New Surrey Downs."

Clayt walked to his dapple-gray, and Maschinot turned with him, walking out of earshot from the others. "The sheriff ain't got the first notion o' what 'hungry' is," he mumbled. "How's Short doin', Clayt?"

"He'll be aw-right," Clayt said. "Stove up for maybe coupla weeks."

"Listen," Maschinot said, tugging up on his cartridge belt against the swell of his belly. "I hear this minin' man name o' Dunne and you had a run-in."

Clayt stopped and untied Skitter's reins. "Didn' amount to much."

"Well, I just thought you oughta know. He was askin 'bout you 'round town."

"He just likes to know a little 'bout any man he's dealin' with, that's all." Clayt mounted and nodded to the deputy. " 'Preciate you lettin' me know, Frank."

The Rolling F entourage made its way west along Grand Avenue, where Afton pointed out the businesses along the main thoroughfare. Just as they approached Ivinson's, Tessa and two of her girls stepped out of the store onto the boardwalk, where the young black boy who worked for Ivinson swept plumes of dust into the street with a stiff broom. One of the girls smiled broadly at Nestor, who pretended not to see her. Her straw-colored hair was tied up beneath a fancy hat, and her typically rouged cheeks were pale and ordinary in the daylight.

"Hey, Mistah Clayt!" the boy called out. "Mistah Chalky!"

Clayt and Chalky each raised a hand. "Ezra," Chalky greeted the boy.

Inspired by the boy's salutations, the blonde whore sang out in a high, bird-like voice. "Hey, Mistah Nes-tah."

Nestor turned but could not decide upon a proper response. The back of his neck flushed with color. Everyone looked to the boardwalk in time to see the girl make a curtsy. Her friend giggled into a gloved hand as she waved with the other. Tessa stood behind the two girls clasping the black ledger in which she recorded her business accounts. Her smile was aimed at Clayt, who touched his hat brim and nodded.

The girl who had called to Nestor stepped to the edge of the boards, propped her fists on her sides and wiggled her hips. "Bye-bye now, you Sorry-Damn cowboys."

266

Clayt turned in his saddle in time to see Tessa leaning in, talking to the girl, their noses just an inch apart. The black boy had stopped sweeping to watch the reprimand. Behind them, Old Man Shannonhaus appeared in Ivinson's doorway and watched the Afton party pass. Leland emerged from the store, and together father and son turned and crossed the street for the livery.

As the wagon trundled toward the west end of town, Whit spurred his horse closer to Nestor's, leaned out from his saddle, and softened his voice. "Hey, Mistah Nes-tah," he sang, using the same melody as the whore's. He dodged Nestor's backhanded blow and at a glance from Clayt dropped back to the rear.

The party departed Laramie with four hours of light left to the day. The sun hung over the mountains like a beacon to set their course. At the river Chalky and Nestor rode out ahead at a gallop, their horses' hooves rumbling on the bridge like a sudden clap of thunder.

In the wagon bed, Tom rose up on one knee to watch the riders depart. Then he turned to Clayt, who rode a few yards back from the wagon.

"Where are they going?" Tom asked.

Afton's sister glanced at Clayt. In that

brief exchange, he understood that Afton had apprised them of Chatka and the dangers of the open prairie. They held one another's gaze long enough to forge a tacit contract that would ensure the well-being of a young boy's expectations of the world around him. Clayt nosed Skitter closer to the wagon.

"Reckon we oughta let Mrs. Afton know when to 'xpect us, don't you?"

The boy seemed not to hear him. "Will you show me the trick with the coin?"

Clayt narrowed his eyes and glanced around him, playing the part of someone checking for an eavesdropper. "Maybe tomorrow," he said quietly and leaned low enough to prop his forearm on the pommel. "We got to keep this b'tween the two o' us. I cain't be showing these boys my secrets. 'Specially ones that turn a profit." Clayt straightened and dug into his pocket. "But you might as well go ahead and start practicin'." He tossed a coin, and the boy caught it in his lap.

Isabella Walsh looked at Clayt over her son's head. "John says you will be our guide when we venture out into the countryside."

Tom's head came up at that. "Which horse will I ride?"

"Well, that's a two-way bargain, Tom. The

horse's got a say in it, you know."

When Tom looked to his mother as if to verify this was so, Clayt reined Skitter out to the flank and began to drop back behind his party. He kept his eyes sharp, scouring every rise and fall in the land, but his mind was on the boy and the woman. He realized he was indulging in one of those "what ifs" that a cowboy tries to steer wide of. Yet it seemed harmless enough to wonder what it might have meant to have had such a woman for a mother.

CHAPTER 18

The sun rose like a hot copper coin from behind the Laramie Range. Then right away a long bank of clouds above the mountains swallowed the burning disk, and it was gone. Above it a streak of purple-red — that color found in the heartwood of juniper — lay across the early morning horizon like a distant lake tainted with blood, and in time the sun rose again from this. A double dawn.

The air tasted clean. The horses in the paddock stirred at the sound of Clayt in the feed room. The crippled dog had followed him from the bunkhouse, and now it lay down in the loose hay to watch him.

"Shank," Clayt said, "when you gonna tell me the story 'bout that leg?" He gave the dog a moment, as the old hound looked back at him with alert eyes. Clayt shook his head and chuckled. "You're right. That's your business . . . and none o' mine."

When he emerged from the barn with two

buckets of sweet grain, the horses snorted, bobbed their heads, and vied for a spot at the fence. He opened the gate, went in, closed the gate with his boot, and latched it with his elbow. When he moved toward the feeding troughs, the horses swung their heads free of the fence and pushed their way toward the wooden boxes along the corral fence. One-handedly Clayt spread the bucket-loads without breaking stride, sluicing rows of pungent grain into the long troughs.

After the second trip he swung the empty buckets, clacking them together to back away the animals that had taken their share. Chalky sidestepped through the fence and with broad arcs of his hat took up the task with him, shooing away the pushy dun mare.

"One man feedin' all deez hosses," Chalky said in his soft, melodic voice. "Mmm mm." He watched Clayt climb into the loft and begin forking down fresh hay. "An' all dem boys back in da bunkhouse juss now pullin' deyselves outta da bed. You da boss, Clayt. You s'posed to sit back a little, watch da other'ns work."

Clayt threw down two more loads, leaned on the pitchfork, and looked down at the animals nosing through the hay. "I like spendin' the mornin' with the horses."

271

"Den how come you hurryin' 'round like you's late fo' yo' own weddin'?"

"I got a coupla screw holes I need to drill out b'fore I finish up that easel this mornin'." He straightened and looked toward the house. The stovepipe from the kitchen threw out a steady stream of smoke, but Clayt could hear no activity inside. "I got no idea what it is we're s'posed to do today . . . or when we're s'posed to do it."

"I finish up here," Chalky said. "You go on an' drill dem holes."

Buck and his crew saddled up and left for the south pastures while Clayt turned the final screw into place. Old Shank got up from beneath the workbench and limped onto the porch to watch the cattle crew ride out from the yard. Clayt gazed through the open door until the riders disappeared behind the trees at the creek. A flock of crows lifted from the branches and wove through the trees like black rags carried along by a gust of wind. He tried the legs of the easel, swinging them out to their appointed triangular stance. Then he set the braces and tightened the thumbscrews.

"I reckon she'll do," he said and stepped back to appraise the construction. He imagined Afton's sister standing in front of it, applying paint to a canvas propped on its adjustable shelf. He judged it to be the perfect height for Isabella Walsh.

The crippled dog limped closer and fixed doleful eyes on him, its useless leg held inches off the ground and hanging like a dead tree limb. The limp tail began a tentative arc, like the swing of a faulty pendulum. Whenever the dog looked at him this way, it seemed to be asking a question.

"I ain't got no more answers 'bout anythin' than you do," Clayt said quietly and leaned to scratch the scruffy coat of fur on the nape of the dog's neck.

A pair of boots scuffed in the doorway behind him, and Clayt turned to see Johnny Waites sipping from a coffee cup. When Johnny raised his cup as a morning salute, Clayt straightened, raised his chin as a greeting, and then loosened the thumb-screws on the easel. Shank settled under the bench.

"That old three-legged cur ever say anythin' back to you, Clayt?"

Clayt smiled, folded the long wooden legs, and secured them with the leather ties he had sliced off a pair of old chaps. "Not so you could hear," Clayt said, "but I ain't give up on 'im yet. He'll come through with a word or two one day."

Johnny drank from his cup again and gestured out into the yard. "Ain't never been paid to sit around a ranch b'fore." He started to sip more coffee but stopped the movement with the cup an inch in front of his chin. "Would you look at that," Johnny breathed, his eyes fixed somewhere beyond the yard to the north.

Clayt stepped beside him and gazed out into the prairie beyond the corral. Rays of light lanced through the breaks in the clouds, and each place the beams touched the grass, the earth glowed like a white flame. Together they watched the play of light without words, each knowing that such an interplay between heaven and earth passed all too soon. Dew steamed up in gossamer swirls like spirits awakened from the land. When the prairie faded back to gray, Clayt propped the easel against the wall and swiped the dust from his sleeves with his hands.

"That for surveyin'?" Johnny asked.

Clayt shook his head. "Paintin'."

Johnny drank from the cup again, and then he lowered it, a question working in his eyes. " 'Paintin'," he repeated.

Clayt hung the drill on its peg and lifted Chalky's toolbox to the floor. "Like a picture you hang on a wall. That kind o' paintin'." He nodded at the easel. "A artist uses it to hold up the canvas he's paintin' a picture on."

"You gone *ar-tist* on us, Clayt?"

Clayt shook his head. "Mr. Afton's sister."

Johnny supplied a humorless smile and looked out the door toward the house. "Reckon she's likely paintin' that husband o' hers 'bout now. With a bucket o' hot tar."

Clayt stepped out onto the porch and divided his attention between rolling a cigarette and studying the house. The smoke from the flue was clearer now. Cora's stove would be settled for cooking. The horses were quiet, resigned to their quota of feed. The hay was better than half gone. The dog limped onto the porch, lowered itself to the boards by degrees, and sighed.

"That right?" Clayt said, letting Johnny understand he wanted to know more.

Waites stepped beside him and tossed the dregs of his coffee into the dirt. "I was out to the chicken house this mornin' gittin' Swampy some eggs," Johnny said quietly. "Heard someb'dy cussin' up a blue streak, sounded like. When I passed the house, it was comin' outta that front corner room. It was that Mr. Walsh. I figured him to be lightin' in on the boy 'bout somethin', but I listened for a while and damned if it weren't the wife he was puttin' through the wringer. She said somethin' quiet-like — I couldn' hardly make out the words — and he comes back like a damn bull with a burr up his ass, if you follow my way o' sayin' it. I never heard a man talk like that to a woman, 'xceptin' it was a drunk a-yellin' at a whore."

Clayt had been rolling a cigarette during the explanation. Now he turned his back on the house, struck a lucifer against the awning post, and cupped his hand around the flame. He took the first draw on the smoke and looked beyond the front gate to the creek. One by one the crows were returning to their roost. A few last spokes of light fanned out from the low clouds, dimmed, and disappeared altogether.

Johnny gestured with his cup toward a buckskin gelding that ate alongside Clayt's mare. "Them thick-skulled horses git 'long better'n most people," Johnny philosophized.

Clayt kept his focus on the hills rolling beyond the trees. He raised the cigarette halfway to his mouth, broke the ashes with a flick of his thumb, and lowered the arm.

"That'd be a close call. Your mare tried chewin' a hole in the neck o' that sway-backed sorrel when I parceled out the grain."

Johnny laughed. "Well, I sure as hell wouldn' chew no hole in a woman like *that,* would you? I mean, she kind o' seems above all that, if you follow my way o' sayin' it."

Clayt nodded. "Yeah, I reckon I do." He looked at the house again. "You figure they're done with breakfast yet?"

Johnny shrugged. "I wouldn' mind if that damn windbag husband o' hers stayed inside all day if it meant the difference in hearin 'im lay into his wife like he done. I don't know as I can hold my tongue if he gits that goin' again."

"Holdin' your tongue might mean holdin' on to your job. You'd best git that settled in your head right now." Clayt studied his half-burned cigarette and threw it into the yard. "I better go an' find out how this day's gonna run. You wanna finish fillin' the water troughs?"

He crossed the yard and climbed to the front porch of the main house. Pausing, he listened, thinking about what Waites had overheard. Before he could knock, the door swung open, and Tom looked up, his eyes ablaze.

"Uncle John said I can pick out my own horse to ride today."

Clayt nodded and looked past him into the dark hallway. "Well, might be good if we do that pickin' together." He heard the clink of cup and saucer in the dining room. "Ever'body in there done with their breakfast?"

"I ate a long time ago. May I go choose my horse now?"

Clayt listened for another sound from the house, but the rooms seemed unnaturally quiet. "I better check with your uncle, Tom." He stepped inside, and the boy followed, closing the door behind him. "Reckon can you go and fetch him for me?"

"Then may we go choose my horse?"

Isabella Walsh appeared at the study entrance. Clayt had not heard her approach. With her face lowered she stepped behind her son and placed her hands lightly upon his shoulders. She managed what might have been a modest smile, but in the dim lighting Clayt had to bend down to see her. Her face turned reflexively to one side.

"Good morning, Mr. Jane," she said, her voice subdued and without the warmth she had spread among the crew yesterday.

"Ma'am," Clayt said and removed his hat. "I come by to see what you folks might be plannin' on doin' today. Will you be wantin' to ride out from the ranch?"

Henry Walsh appeared at the study entrance, closed a black ledger, and held it down by his side. With his eyes fixed on the back of his wife's head, he stilled altogether, as though curious to hear her answer. When Clayt met his eyes, Walsh looked down at his vest to brush at the fabric with his fingertips.

"No," she said. "I don't think so. I won't be getting out today."

"Mo-ther," Tom pleaded. "Uncle John said I could ride a horse today, and Clayt said —"

"Thomas!" the boy's father interrupted. "Address Mr. James properly."

The boy lowered his head and backed to the wall, pressing his spine into the pine paneling beneath the gallery of portraits. Clayt turned his hat in his hand and worked the band closer to the base of the crown. The clock in the next room ticked like a rope stretched taut, testing its limits.

Clayt smiled friendly enough and spoke to Walsh in the same tone he had used with the horses. "It's 'Jane' . . . Clayton Jane . . . but my friends all call me 'Clayt.' "

Walsh stepped into the hallway and stiffened his mouth to a tight *V*-shaped smile, but his eyes continued to drive home his point. "All the same, Mr. Jane, he will address you as he has been taught to address his elders."

The boy's eyes remained dedicated to the floor. Clayt nodded to no one in particular and turned to the boy's mother. She was staring at Tom with her chin up, her eyes trying to deliver some message redemptive to the moment, but the boy would not look up. With her head turned in such an unguarded way, Clayt saw a dark crescent of puffy tissue high on her cheek. A lattice of capillaries spanned the corner of the eye like a tiny, red spider's web.

"So, no ridin' today?" Clayt asked, looking from the husband to the wife.

"She's not feeling well," Henry Walsh said, forcing dry laughter into this unsolicited assessment of his wife. "She will want to get out and see the country at some point. That's all she's talked about for months. But do take Thomas with you. Perhaps he can learn something about managing a ranch . . . that sort of thing."

Tom's head came up at that, but his mother showed no sign that she had even heard. Walsh sniffed sharply, pulled a pipe from his trouser pocket, and clamped it in his teeth, making a garish smile that showed an uneven row of teeth beneath his moustache. He leaned back on his heels and engaged the photographs lined up on the wall.

"May I, Mother?" the boy begged.

Isabella Walsh frowned at her husband but made no reply.

"Just not too far out," the boy's father instructed. "What with these . . . uncertainties about." He removed the pipe from his mouth and jabbed the stem toward Clayt. "I think it best you not lose sight of the buildings. Wouldn't you agree?"

Afton's sister held her quiet gaze on her husband. Without waiting for an answer, Henry Walsh clenched the pipe in his jaw, turned smartly, and walked back into the interior of the house.

"Mr. Jane," Isabella Walsh said formally. "I've decided Tom and I *will* ride. Anywhere you would like to take us. Thank you for asking."

Tom came off the wall and threw his arms around her waist. The woman's eyes softened as the boy's joy spilled out.

"Clayton!" Afton said congenially as he entered the hallway. "Good morning. Have you three talked about a plan for the day?" He smiled at Tom's unbridled excitement. "You must have promised this one the best horse in the herd."

Clayt waved his hat toward the mother and son. "We were just gittin' down to some details."

281

Afton stopped and clasped his hands behind his back. "Where will you go?"

Clayt glanced at the woman before answering. "I was thinkin' up to the Snowy Range. Up there by Looking Glass and then on past there up to the salt lick on the ridge."

Afton made an embarrassed laugh, as though an unknowing miscalculation had been tendered. "Well, wait now. Perhaps they should see the ranch before trekking off into the mountains."

"Well, sir," Clayt reasoned aloud, "it's only 'bout six miles out. And once we're up on that ridge, they'll git to see the whole of the Laramie Plain."

Afton pushed his lips out, then in, as he considered this. His eyes cut to Tom, who once again hung in a state of suspended anticipation. Clayt could see by the angle of Afton's head that the man would reject the idea out of hand.

"That is an excellent plan," Isabella said, walking past her brother into the study. "We'll be ready in ten minutes. Come, Thomas."

Tom checked his uncle's face for confirmation, and, seeing no dissent, he smiled up at Clayt. "I'm ready right now."

When he got the final nod from Afton,

Clayt opened the door and turned back to Tom. "Johnny Waites is down at the barn. Why'n't you go on down there and see what horse he thinks will be a good fit for you."

The boy was out of the house like a convict making good his escape. Clayt looked at his employer again, to hear any last instruction.

"Take as many men as you need to keep them safe, Clayton." Afton raised an index finger. "That is your number one job right now. Keep . . . them . . . safe." After driving home his point with his best commanding pose, he pulled a piece of paper from his shirt pocket and opened it. Leaning in closer to Clayt, he lowered his voice. "This is a short supply list from Cora for Ivinson's. We'll start sending in a man each day to accommodate Mr. Dunne's project."

Clayt nodded toward the paper. "What's on it?"

Afton frowned at the list. "Lard . . . flour . . . and salt."

Clayt nodded. "Does it say how much of each?"

Afton shrugged. "Yes . . . small amounts, really. We're only doing this for Dunne, you know. And for the president, of course." He snapped down his vest and seemed to stand a little taller, taking visible pride in the idea of serving such an esteemed official. Then he reached out and patted Clayt's upper arm. "Be careful out there today." Turning on his heel he strode back down the hall and disappeared into the study.

Clayt stopped by the bunkhouse and rousted Nestor, Whit, and Harry from the card game they had chosen to kill time while waiting for orders. Swampy laid out the necessary victuals for the excursion — some salt pork, a dozen biscuits, and three jars of stewed apples. G.T. had his saddlebags laid out on a table and was packing extra food for himself when Clayt approached him with the abbreviated supply list.

"Need you to go into town to git some things at Ivinson's. It's all wrote down here in Cora's hand." G.T. frowned at the proffered note, then carried that frown to Clayt. "And be sure and sign for it," Clayt said. "New policy."

Short-Stuff drank coffee at the long table in his stockinged feet, his left arm idle in its sling. He set down his cup and grunted deep in his chest.

"Take a long damn pencil with you, son," Short suggested. "I made that run for Cora yesterday. Ivinson was wantin' me to scratch out my life story, and I cain't write a lick." He snorted. "He ended up signin' the damn thing for me."

"Take Grady with you," Clayt said. "Git him to sign, too." Clayt worked the buttons of his coat, ignoring G.T.'s puzzled expression. "New policy," he said again.

By the time Mrs. Walsh arrived at the barn, the escort party was saddled up and ready to ride. Tom was ecstatic, trying to take in everything at once. At the corral his eyes jumped from horse to horse and then to the saddles and the men dressed out in their worn-to-comfort work clothes. In contrast the woman moved into the barn like a shadow, her face lowered, her presence cautious and contained.

On her head was the fawn-colored, soft-brimmed hat pulled low over her face, her hair tucked under it but for a few long wisps that fell over her collar. She wore a man's trousers and a plain, blue, gingham shirt. Her light jacket was the only garment that fit her well. On her feet were lace-up boots dotted with multi-hued drops of paint.

When Tom kept trying to squirm out of a stiff waistcoat he did not want to wear, the woman frowned and relented. Then the boy saw Clayt in his buckskin riding coat. On the spot, Tom reassessed his own garment and casually slipped his arms back into the sleeves as he dodged into a stall.

285

"Is that there goin' along with us, ma'am?" Johnny Waites said, nodding to the willow basket she carried.

When she looked up at Johnny, Clayt saw that the welt beneath her eye was now well defined — blue-green and curved like the foot of a rocking chair. It took nothing away from the inherent beauty of her face, but her eyes were listless and flat, wholly lacking the gold sheen that had burned in her irises at the depot. The cowboys glanced at her obliquely from various poses of deference. She smiled apologetically at the basket.

"Cora put together some food for Thomas and me." She raised her eyebrows. "I suppose she thinks we cannot eat the same food you men do."

"Swampy's done allowed for your noon meal, ma'am," Johnny said, "but it'd be a shame to waste what you got."

"I don't care what I eat," Tom announced.

Johnny leveled a finger at the boy. "You and Swampy are gone git along just fine."

Chalky rode out from the barn at a walk, and Nestor followed behind him. They booted their horses into a trot at the gate and turned west and moved soundlessly up the slope of the first hill into a ray of sunlight. Soon they crested the rise and disappeared like two candle flames submerging in their own pool of wax.

"Where are they going?" Tom said.

"Scoutin' the trail," Clayt said and faced the boy squarely. "Did you and Johnny pick out a good mount for you?"

"Not yet," Tom said. "I was waiting for you."

Clayt jerked a thumb at the corral. "Let's go out back and match you and your mother up with a coupla smart cow ponies."

When Clayt and Tom walked into the paddock, Mrs. Walsh stood by the gate, her lackluster gaze now somewhat piqued for the selection of horses.

"If one strikes your fancy, let me know," Clayt said looking over the animals. He nodded to Johnny Waites, who scissored through the fence and made his way toward the horses bunching at the far side of the paddock. "Think on one o' those two that Johnny's headin' for . . . that lil' chestnut with the high socks . . . and that black'n there."

"The black one," Tom declared without hesitation.

Johnny lifted the rope off the snubbing post and began separating the coils in his hands. When he looked back, Clayt pointed. With an easy toss, Johnny laid the loop over the head of the black mare and led the animal toward them.

"Will she be gentle?" Mrs. Walsh called out. "He's not ridden a horse."

"She ain't been rode for a while, but she's a sweet'n," Clayt said. "Be like warm molasses once we git her away from the barn. Don't none of 'em like to leave the others."

She watched the mare toss its head, testing the hold of the rope. "Did you train her yourself, Mr. Jane? John says you are the one who best trains the horses."

"No, ma'am," he called back. "Not this'n."

Her face closed down. "Perhaps he should take one that you have trained."

"Ma'am," Johnny said walking toward her with a twinkle in his eye. "It's the easy ones that Clayt don't have to git introduced to, if you follow my way o' sayin' it."

Clayt stroked the pony's neck and soothed it with a soft hum. "This'n's steady, Tom, and she'll do good by you if she can have her say in the bargain."

Tom wrinkled his nose. "What do you mean?"

Clayt lifted the horse's forefoot, checked the hoof, and eased it back to the ground. "Come on over here and let 'er git to know you a little."

Tom checked his mother's face, then

shuffled within an arm's reach of the horse and gazed into its dark, liquid eyes. "How do I know if he likes me?"

"Well, first off," Clayt said. "She ain't a 'he,' so don't insult her. Be about like someb'dy callin' you by a girl's name." Using the backs of his fingers, he tapped the boy's shoulder to show he was having some fun. Tom twisted his mouth to one side to hold back a laugh. "As for that likin' part," Clayt continued, "we can stack the deck a mite on that count." He reached into his coat pocket and held out his fist. "Cup your hands under mine."

Tom made a bowl with his palms, and Clayt trickled a small pile of grain into his hands. The smell was sweet and rich, like Afton's pipe tobacco before it was lighted.

"Don't tempt her with your fingers. You know how to hold your hand so she cain't bite you?" Clayt showed the boy with the specks of grain still clinging to his palm, letting the mare nuzzle at the meager offering. Then Clayt stood back, wiping his hand on his coat. The black mare blew through her nostrils and turned to Tom, who took note of the animal's rising interest in his hands. "Go ahead," Clayt said. "Then let her smell you. A horse can tell a lot by a man's smell."

"If you're afraid of her," Johnny Waites

said, "she'll sense it."

"I'm not afraid!" Tom shot back, his face wrinkled with defiance.

Johnny laughed. "We ain't the one you need to convince on that score."

Tom offered up the gift, arching his hands backward and pushing the grain against the mare's mouth just as Clayt had done. The soft lips plucked delicately at his skin until every speck of the feed was gone.

"Do you think she likes me yet?" Tom asked.

"That'll take some time," Clayt said. "She's got to know you better."

Tom's face fell. "How long will that take?"

Clayt shook his head. "It's one o' those things cain't be rushed, Tom. But I'll tell you this. A man and his horse can form a tight partnership . . . sometimes to where they're thinkin' the same thoughts. It gets to where it's hard to imagine one existing without t'other." He gestured toward the mare. "Blow into her nose, gentle-like."

Tom did as he was told. The horse nickered and stepped closer, blowing warm air that stirred the hair on the boy's forehead. Tom smiled at his mother. When she returned the smile, some of the amber light came back into her eyes.

"She's wantin' to git to know you a little,"

Clayt coaxed. "Give 'er time for that. Let 'er curiosity make all the introductions. You two are gonna do just fine together."

Clayt walked into the tack room and brought out a stiff brush. "First thing you do is get 'er clean for the saddle. That way there won't be no dirt and grit pushed down into the skin." He made a series of short strokes on the mare's back, each pass ending with a quick snap of his wrist that whisked away a little cloud of dust. "You just brush the way the hair's growin'." He looked at the boy. "I'll do the top. You do the sides."

Thomas held out his hand for the brush. "I can reach the top!"

Clayt stepped back by the woman, and together they watched the boy stand on his tiptoes to groom the horse. The mother's face relaxed, and Johnny winked at Clayt before turning to the sound of horses at the gate. Lou Breakenridge and his night crew filed into the yard and reined up outside the barn.

"How 'bout I cut out that chestnut with the purty socks for the lady?" Johnny said.

Clayt looked back at the wagon where he had loaded the new easel. He was about to ask the woman about her preference for a saddle or a buckboard seat.

"That will do just fine," she said. She watched with interest as Johnny swung the rope in a lazy circle to isolate the chestnut from the others.

"I was wonderin'," Clayt said, "if we oughta hitch up a team to the wagon."

Her eyes slanted with a question. "The wagon?"

"Yes, ma'am. I weren't sure how much gear you might be wantin' to carry 'long."

She frowned at the willow basket. "Can't we just pack it into a pannier?"

Clayt looked toward the mill shed, wondering if he should tell her about the easel. "I was meanin' the things you might be needin' for your paintin'."

The little bit of light that had come into her face from watching the boy now snuffed out. "I don't paint, Mr. Jane. Not anymore." Now the smooth skin on her face appeared hard as alabaster.

Johnny had roped the chestnut and was leading it toward them, but checking Clayt's face he tied the horse to the fence and moved off to help the boy throw blanket and saddle over the mare.

"Well, ma'am," Clayt said and nodded toward the chestnut, "that'n there is a good horse. I 'xpect you'll sit her fine." He touched his hat brim. " 'Xcuse me." He walked to the barn, where the night-herd crew rubbed down their horses.

"I wanna take one more man with me," Clayt said to Lou. "You reckon we can pull someb'dy off o' Buck's crew?"

"I ain't tired. I can go." It was Rascher, speaking from one of the stalls.

Clayt studied him, appraising him for alertness. "You been out all night."

"I pulled the first watch. I been sleepin' since midnight. I'm rested up enough."

Clayt kept steady eyes on him for a time. Then he nodded.

"Throw your saddle on a fresh mount and pack extra ammunition. I want you behind us coverin' our backs."

Rascher picked up saddle and blanket, and Clayt and Lou watched him march back into the corral. Lou stepped beside Clayt and cracked a grin.

"You reckon next he'll be askin' to help out Swampy with the cookin'?"

Clayt watched Rascher single out a big sorrel and slip a bridle over its head. "Long as he does his job, I got no complaints."

"Well, if he does start to cookin'," Lou said, "whattaya say the two o' us start takin' our meals in town?"

CHAPTER 19

They took the high ground across the west pastures, following the fresh trail laid down by Chalky and Nestor. Harry and Whit rode flank on the left, Lonny Stiles and the Texan named Bud Townsend on the right, each a good one hundred yards from the main party, which consisted of Clayt and Johnny Waites, the boy, and the mother. Rascher lagged behind, keeping watch on the back trail.

In the hour it took them to reach Looking Glass, Clayt had not spoken to the woman — allowing for the privacy she had established for herself ten yards out from the boy. They paused on the rise above the lake and looked across the water at the snow-peaked mountains and at their perfect image inverted on the mirror of the water's surface. The woman sat her horse and took it all in, tracing the smooth curve of the shoreline with her eyes, following it to the escarpment that surged abruptly upward like a castle wall, its crenulations broken into a jagged skyline.

The boy remained in motion, eager to put into practice every riding suggestion offered by Johnny Waites. When the horses nickered at the smell of water, Clayt instructed the woman and the boy to restrain their mounts, explaining how the mining had tainted the water.

"There's good water up at the foot of the mountains," he promised.

When they arrived at the ruins of the line shack that had burned one winter past, Clayt sat his horse and noted the crisscross trail left by Chalky as he had scoured through the spruces, trying to cut fresh signs. Clayt dismounted and held Skitter back from the spring that welled up from the mossy roots of the massive sycamore.

"Any o' you want water fresher'n what you got in your canteen, there you go," Clayt said and pointed to the clear pool. He knelt and ladled water with his hand as the boy and his mother watched.

"You *drink* that?" Tom asked, wrinkling his nose again.

As the boy watched, Clayt drank from his cupped hand, made the quick exhale of a quenched thirst, and then cooled the back of his neck with his wet hand.

"It's sweet comin' up out o' this ol' sycamore," Johnny said, smiling to reassure the boy. Then Waites put on his poker face. "Almost good as sars'parilla."

Tom's forehead wrinkled, and his eyes narrowed. "What's that?"

"That, my young friend," Johnny declared, "is what passes for a real drink 'round these parts . . . till you git to be a full-growed man." Johnny squinted one eye and pointed at Tom. "Which, in your case, I figure to be just a few more years."

Johnny dismounted and collected the chestnut's reins as the mother stepped down. Tom scissored a leg over the cantle and slid down from his saddle on his own. Getting his legs, he stared at the crystal-clear, rocky bottom of the pool.

"What does it taste like?" Tom asked.

"Ain't any water to match it in the valley," Johnny assured him and gathered up the reins of the boy's mare. Johnny pointed to the line shack, now a shell of scorched planks. A section of blackened stovepipe jutted upward from the charred ruins like the barrel of a paper-thin cannon angled at the sky. "It's how come this line shack was to burn down. The feller stayin' out here flat refused to waste the sweet water on a grease fire. Least that was his version of it. That about right, Clayt?" Johnny winked and scooped a handful of water.

Isabella Walsh knelt next to Waites and dipped one hand into the spring, replicating the technique used by the men. The boy, needing no more inspiration than the sight of his mother drinking from this new land like a wild animal, went to his knees, frowned at his soiled hands, and lowered his face to sip off the water's smooth surface. When mother and son had taken their fill, Clayt wet a clean bandana in the cool water.

"I named my horse 'Black Knight'," Tom announced. He stood and offered the mare a leaky bowl made with his hands. Water dribbled down his arms and bled into his sleeves. When the animal pushed by him, Tom wiped his hands on his trousers and watched the mare stretch her neck forward and siphon up water with supple lips.

"Good name for 'er," Johnny said. "She's dark as a starless night."

Tom spun around. "Not that kind of night! Like a knight in a castle!"

Clayt took both sets of reins from Johnny and handed them to the boy. "Can you make a good knot?"

Tom frowned at the leather straps. "Every-body knows how to tie a knot."

Clayt nodded. "Okay, you're in charge of these two horses, Tom. Let 'em drink a coupla minutes, then tie 'em up over there by the trees in that sunny spot." Clayt nodded to a sunlit opening. "That way they won't cool down too fast."

Rascher trailed in, and Clayt pointed to a gap in the boulders that gave a view to the south. Rascher reined his horse through the opening, and Clayt watched him slip his rifle from its scabbard just before disappearing behind the rocks.

The woman had moved out from the trees to stand nearer the rolling plain they had just crossed. A low quilt of checkered clouds held fast in the east, and the sun gilded their upper edges with incandescent lines that stacked row upon row, like the petals of a yellow rose. Much like the stark contrast of light and dark in the paintings in Afton's study. The woman stood very still, looking out over the valley.

Clayt watched her bear witness to this incarnation of the sky, and he tried to see the colors of the clouds as she might, and wondering if, like him, she was able to see the prairie as a window that afforded a grander scale of things. Like the frail possibility of a God who still watched over the land and the people who moved across it.

When he was fresh out of the war and had first seen the painted sky of the evening plains, Clayt believed he had met with the knowledge that the gates of heaven might open to most any man. But not to himself. The image of the beheaded drummer boy clung to him like a festering scar. For him there could be no absolution.

"If there is such a thing as heaven," he had once told Chalky at the end of a workday, "I reckon for me it'll have to be Wyomin'."

Clayt wrung out the wet bandana and walked it to the woman, who turned at the sound of his boots in the rocks. "This'll help keep the swellin' down on your eye." Lowering her gaze she took the folded cloth and covered the bruise. Clayt busied himself inspecting the clouds. "Might be some rain come tomorr' mornin'. Snow if this wind keeps up from Canada." They stood for a time, her head bent to the compress, his face raised to the sky.

"I want to apologize for my appearance," she said. "And my behavior."

Clayt held his gaze on the distance, seeing neither clouds nor sky nor the Laramie Range to the east. "No call for that, ma'am."

"I'm unaccustomed to John's house. I fell

in the dark and hit a chair. I must look atrocious."

Not wanting to see her face caught in a lie, he kept his eyes on the horizon, and the world sharpened into crystalline focus again. "No, ma'am. You look just fine."

The gold nimbus etched upon the clouds faded until drab shades of gray robbed the sky of its spectacle. They were quiet as the wind carved a path around them, and the silence seemed to deliver them from the fantasy she had manufactured. When the sun broke free of the cloud bank, the blue of the sky was born. The grasses in the valley pulsed with light — a tide of silver-green water rippling across the land. Within minutes the heat rising from the prairie blurred the details of the grass, and to Clayt it appeared as a shallow river. A constant motion, green upon green.

"You've been working for John a long time," she said, her voice little more than a whisper. "He speaks very highly of you."

Clayt took off his hat, pinched the crease in the crown, and pursed his lips. The cool air touched his damp scalp, making him feel unduly exposed in the woman's presence. Settling the hat back on his head, he spoke out to the grasslands.

"He's a fair man . . . the kind most men

would wanna work for."

"You started very young. You're from one of the Southern states, aren't you?"

"Georgia," he said.

Her eyes fixed on the far side of the valley, and he wondered if she knew they were gazing east toward his forgotten homeland. And hers. He did not ordinarily attribute a grasp of directions to women, even with the morning sun blatantly announcing the east.

"You're a long way from home, Mr. Jane," she said, her voice detached, dreamy.

"No, ma'am. I'm home now. Just took me some time to find it."

She smiled at his words. "Yes," she said. "What a beautiful slice of irony." She caught herself and let her voice go soft with apology. "Do you know what I mean by that? 'Irony'?" She watched him smile at himself, then shake his head. "Well," she began, "it's when a thing seems the opposite of what should make sense." She tilted her head to one side in a shrug. "And yet it does."

Clayt thought about that and decided he liked the idea. "I like a fifty-cent word now an' then. Just don't git much chance to use one out here."

They were facing the prairie, their shoulders a foot apart, their lives so removed one from the other that the long silence that followed seemed a natural disposition, marking their claims to separate corners of the Earth. He could smell some scent to her that he guessed to be an herb from her homeland. Something clean and antiseptic, not unlike the fragrant resin of the spruces behind them or the sage down in the valley. In his mind he tried to transpose this same scent onto Tessa, but the fit was wrong. Tessa's rich perfumes were too much a part of her. Denying her that scent would be like stealing the bright feathers off a meadowlark and expecting to recognize it still.

"If you're rested up, ma'am, we can head on up the slope now . . . to the salt lick. You can see the whole o' the plain from there."

"All right," she said and offered her first generous smile since leaving the ranch.

After signaling Rascher, Clayt led the way through the spruces and began the climb on a narrow trail that snaked through a garden of house-sized boulders. They passed through in single file, letting the horses set the pace. With the limitations imposed by the slope, the flankers split up with two going in front and two behind. Throughout the climb Clayt took note of the small stacks of rock left by Chalky at the base of three separate trees — a trail mark telegraphing that the old scout had cut no new signs.

Before an hour had passed they broke out from the trees under open sky on a broad rock ledge. Here on this shelf an exposed vein of mineral salts streaked across the stone like a petroglyph of lightning. It was a place that felt ancient. Clayt knew that people had perched here from the beginning of time to look off across these plains. He knew it as surely as he knew the lay of the land surrounding the Rolling F. Above them the sun hung isolated like a burning ship sailing across a deep, blue sea. The clouds continued to checker the eastern sky as the wind held steady from the north.

Clayt dismounted and scanned the ridgeline above him. Nestor stood on an outcrop of rock and waved his hat in a high arc overhead — a semaphore that all was well. Even higher on the slope, Chalky sat in profile against the sky, his head pivoting slowly as he scanned the country. The steady motion of his head was signal enough for Clayt. Stiles and the Texan set up downslope fifty yards. Johnny, Whit, and Harry, still sitting their horses, awaited instructions.

"You boys head back down the trail we just come up," Clayt instructed the trio. "I want one o' you to set up at the burnt line shack and keep your eyes open. Another'n

303

go down only 'bout halfway. Johnny, you git set up on a ledge down there where you can see 'em both. Any o' you sees trouble, pull off two shots quick-like, and the lot o' you hightail it back up here. Don't go gittin' yourself cornered so you cain't git back to us."

Whit and Harry exchanged glances. Johnny pulled his Winchester from its scabbard and wheeled his horse around. Harry hesitated, looking at the willow basket sitting on the rock.

"You boys got somethin' in your bags for a midday meal?" Clayt said.

Harry curled his lip. "Yeah, we got *somethin'*. Ain't sure what to call it." He pulled his package of food from his open saddlebag and smelled it through the newspaper wrapping. "Chatka shows up, I'll just kill 'im with this," he said and hefted the package in a weighing motion. He turned to join Whit, and together they started back down the trail, passing Rascher, who reined up and bit off a plug from his tobacco.

Clayt pointed south to the edge of the clearing. "Rascher, set up over where that deer trail skirts 'round the mountain." Clayt swept his finger down the slope. "From there you can see anyone comin' straight up the mountain."

Rascher twisted in his saddle and rose up in his stirrups, the leather creaking and popping like an old door hinge. Peering down the slope he pulled at his chin, his meaty fingers scraping dryly across a rough stubble of whiskers.

"I figured Afton to join up on this jaunt . . . coverin' the country with his kin." When Clayt said nothing, Rascher eyed the basket. "We cookin' up some grub here?"

Clayt shook his head. "Dry camp. We're eatin' cold. You brought your own?"

Rascher's face compressed. "Nobody tol' me," he carped.

Clayt twisted in the saddle and dug into his saddlebag for the parcel of food Swampy had packed for him. "There you go," he said and tossed the package to Rascher.

Rascher caught it and raised it to his nose. "What the hell is it?"

"Go take up your post. You can eat there. Two shots from below means we got trouble. You do the same. Two shots. Then git back here, understand?"

Frowning, Rascher looked around the clearing and watched the woman dismount. "What're we doin? Havin' a picnic?" He worked his jaws on the tobacco.

Clayt's jade eyes hardened on the sneering cowboy. "You might wanna remember,

305

you asked to come on this."

Without a rejoinder, Rascher leaned, spat, and reined around his horse to start for his appointed place.

The boy stood behind Clayt, waiting. "Should I tie up the horses again?"

Clayt unlashed his coil of rope and pointed to the jagged pale line that sparkled in the rock. "Take this an' tie 'em where they can reach that salt vein. They'll like that."

The woman stood near the edge of the plateau, gazing out into the empty space that yawned above the valley. Seeing her take in this view made Clayt want to look from there, too. He knew this had something to do with her paintings . . . that she saw things in a way that was different from other people. He wondered if she could see things in this country that he might have missed. After untying his bedroll, he whipped it out as a tablecloth on the rock and began laying out the food from Cora's basket. The boy, finishing his task with the horses, ran to him and watched.

"Tom, why don't you pull that blanket off the back o' your horse and fold it so you and your mother gotta place to sit. How's that sound?"

"Would you show me how to do the trick with the coin? You said you would."

Clayt nodded. "I ain't forgot. How 'bout after we eat?" Cupping his hand to his mouth he started to call to the woman, but, seeing her standing in such stillness, he walked to her and stopped, scuffing his boot when she did not turn. Her eyes were intent on the land spread out below the escarpment. From this height the spring grass was transformed into a shade of green richer than what they had seen at the spring. The grass rolled in the wake of the winds sweeping out of the north. Like a river of grain. Verdant and fluid, the river of grass rose over the swells in the land and then fell into the swales until breaking against a boulder field where it disappeared around the curve of the Medicine Bows. The rush of the high country wind filled their ears as a surrogate sound for the shoals he imagined below.

Quietly, he stepped beside her, as though they had now established a precedent for guest and guide to measure each vista by the sum of their eyes. The great volume of space that opened before them made their niche on the cliff seem hidden, intimate — just as it did on those occasions when he and Skitter came here alone.

Her head turned slowly, her eyes soaking up the view as though committing it to memory. He found himself waiting, listening for the lilt of her accent, wanting to hear her assessment of the plain.

"Which direction is the ranch?" she asked and pointed. "Is that it?"

"No, ma'am, thos're boulders." When he pointed just east of due south, her eyes followed. As she frowned, two little lines appeared above the bridge of her nose, just as they had with her son. "See where that line o' trees runs north and south? That's the creek. And just off to the right there . . . that's the roof o' the barn makin' them angles."

The wind gusted, folding the soft brim of her hat against the side of her face, and she pressed down the crown to anchor it. Turning, she looked at him the way Tessa sometimes did, seeing the things that lay deeper than the surface. But this woman's inspection did not include the half smile that Tessa used to tease him.

"What made you decide to bring us here, Mr. Jane . . . to this place?"

Clayt took in a long, slow breath and then eased it out. "I come up here sometimes . . . when I wanna see things set to their proper size."

She kept looking at him, the question lingering in her eyes. Then she turned back to the valley, took off her hat, closed her eyes, and inhaled deeply through her nose. Her eyes were closed for so long, he was afraid she might be crying.

"Thank you," she said, her voice little more than a whisper.

While her eyes were shut, he studied her, trying to imagine how a man could strike such a woman. Her arms came up behind her head, and she pulled the pins from her hair. The wind loosened her hair and whipped it across her face in flashes of color, like light bending through a dark prism of glass. Walnut darkened to black, and then sudden ribbons of gold caught fire from the sun. The chaos of her hair seemed balanced by the constancy of her face, where a smile of contentment softened her features.

He thought to ask her if she would like to eat, but held the question on his tongue, thinking the smile more nourishing to her than the food. He looked back at the boy, practicing with the coin, trying to snatch it off the blanket. Clayt chose his steps carefully and left Isabella Walsh perched above the Laramie Plain.

CHAPTER 20

"You 'bout got it?" Clayt said, rolling a cigarette.

The boy made a face. "Not really."

Clayt lipped the dry cigarette, squatted on his heels, and folded the blanket several times until it showed a loft of several inches. Then he laid the coin on top.

"Don't think 'bout pickin' up the coin," he instructed. "Think 'bout punching that blanket down so fast with your fingertips, the coin don't have time to go with it. Then just wrap your fingers 'round that dollar purty as you please."

Tom frowned, but Clayt could see he was thinking about it. The boy lifted his hand above the coin and at the same time touched the tip of his tongue to his upper lip.

"Hit it hard, now," Clayt said.

When Tom struck the blanket, his thin fingers folded, and the coin jumped to one side, where it tinkled over the rock. He wrinkled his nose and looked at Clayt, who fingered a match for his cigarette. The boy watched with interest as Clayt lit up.

"Mother said I can never smoke because it's not healthy. What does it taste like?"

Clayt held the cigarette at eye level and considered it. "I guess 'bout like suckin' air outta burnt-out boot." He smiled at the boy, wet his fingers on his tongue, and pinched the coal between thumb and forefinger. He pocketed the smoke, fluffed up the blanket, and laid the coin on top. "You wanna make your fingers into a stiff cage. And that coin there is a grasshopper you wanna catch. Knock down his perch, and, before he can jump, close the cage on him. Keep your fingers stiff till you feel the coin jump up and touch your palm. Let it come to you."

The boy readied himself again. This time his teeth were set and his eyes blazing.

"Hit it hard, Tom," Clayt prodded.

The boy made a quick stab downward, and then his body froze as his expression blossomed into wonderment. Opening his hand, he beamed at the coin.

"I did it!" he yelled and started running toward his mother. "I grabbed the coin, Mother!"

Smiling, Isabella walked toward them, her arms folded against her stomach and her hat gripped at one side. "Let me see," she said.

Tom ran back and set the coin on the blanket, but Clayt picked it up straight away. "Whatta you say we give 'er a go with somethin' a little quicker'n a blanket."

Tom looked suddenly hurt. "With you?"

Clayt held out his flat hand. The coin caught the light from the sun and seemed to float above the web of lines running across his palm.

"Just like you done with the blanket, Tom. Think o' knocking my hand down so hard the coin ain't gonna have time to drop. All you gotta do is git my hand outta the way so you can close your fingers 'round the prize." Clayt's face went solemn. "You grab it, and it's yours for keeps."

Tom assumed his pose, and Clayt watched his eyes. When the move came, it was tentative. The coin slipped from both their grasps and clinked on the stone. Tom sagged with disappointment.

"Try 'er again," Clayt encouraged. "This time I want you to punch your fingers so hard that you knock my hand down to my knee."

"Won't it hurt?"

"If it don't, I'll be disappointed. It'll mean you ain't strong enough to git this trick to work for you."

"I *am* strong."

"Maybe so . . . in your arm. But you gotta match that with your thinkin'. Man's gotta be strong of will, too."

Tom set up again, his lower jaw thrust forward and his narrowed eyes burning into the coin. Clayt was still as the rock on which they stood, his hand like a steel trap that had been set and now radiated a latent energy.

When the boy's hand struck, the moment seemed frozen in time. The blur of action had come and gone, leaving their fists poised one above the other. Clayt opened his first and smiled. Tom turned his fist around and revealed his prize. Letting out a short chirp of a laugh, he turned to show his mother. She smiled and nodded her approval.

"That's yours now," Clayt said. "Fair and square."

"You didn't let me win?"

Clayt gave the coin a hard look. "That there represents almost a day's work, Tom. A ranch hand don't let go o' his wages so easy."

Tom turned the coin in his hand, his face mirroring its bright sheen. "I thought you had to be delicate with your fingers to pick it up. I never would have figured out you have to hit so hard."

Clayt nodded. "Reckon that'd be some irony," he said and checked the woman's face. Isabella Walsh smiled. Clayt looked back at the boy. "Our secret, all right?" He nodded toward the hands working at their lunch among the rocks. "We cain't be lettin' all these boys in on the trick if we're to use it on 'em."

"Yeah!" the boy said excitedly.

"Yes, sir," Isabella corrected quietly.

Tom lowered contrite eyes. "Yes, sir," he whispered.

When the boy and his mother sat to eat, Clayt walked back to the edge of the cliff and scanned the plain for movement. Perched on the edge of the prairie, he felt the gratitude toward the valley that he always experienced. From this cliff he had always grasped the larger picture of his life, seeing all the way back to his beginnings but always securing his own definition of who he was now. Today his appreciation for this grand view expanded as he wondered how it might affect a woman beaten by her husband.

He now saw the land as common ground for the two of them, but within that commonality they came at it from different directions. He knew more about the land's component parts and their applications, but he was fairly certain that she drew from its composition a form and totality of colors to which he was not privy.

Putting his back to the slanting boulder that fit him so well, he sat. The sun had warmed the rock, and he removed his hat to let his head settle back against the stone. Because the rock faced east, and because the view from there seemed endless, he could never help but wonder what had become of that far end of the continent, where he had once charged through murderous gunfire and killed the men who dispensed it. It was still easy to imagine that those hills remained denuded, trampled and muddy, and shrouded in the smoke of artillery fire. Meadows with names that would be remembered for the corpses that had piled high on impromptu battlefields.

As he relit his cigarette the phantom herd of mustangs appeared on a distant rise in the southeast and moved across the sloped plain in ghostly silence. He could make out the two stallions in the lead, one nipping at the other on the run.

"They're like water."

Clayt sat up straight and turned. Isabella Walsh stood next to the boulder and squinted, following the progress of the horses as they banked along a camber of earth in near single file. Clayt stood, holding the cigarette down by his leg.

"They follow the land just as would a river, if one flowed here." Her words were tinged with admiration. He watched with her as the powerful creatures twisted and turned as a unit, snaking down the folds in the terrain just as runoff would race down the tilt of the land in a flash flood. He felt a sense of pride that, like her, he had seen the landscape in terms of a river. But where he had divined a current in the flow of the grasses, she had found it in the horses. The two ideas were wholly different but at the same time connected. It was the grass that sustained the horses.

"We aim to round up them mustangs and bring 'em in to the Rollin' F herd."

" 'The Rolling F'?"

Clayt lowered his head and grinned. "We mostly call your brother 'Mr. Aff' . . . when it's just us boys talkin'. That's where we git the 'F.' And t'other part is 'bout the lay o' the land . . . the way it rolls with all these little hills." He hitched his head to one side. "We use that for our brand on the cattle."

The woman narrowed her eyes. "How do you mean?"

Clayt considered the folly of trying to draw a picture for an accomplished artist, but the woman's expression was earnest and true. He walked to the nearest spruce and broke off a dead branch. Returning to the boulder, he knelt and scratched out the letter *F* in the sand. Beneath that he made the sinuous line of a snake in motion. Then he stood and let the symbol speak for itself.

"And the Sorry-Damn boys," she said. "That must derive from Surrey Downs?"

He scraped at the sand with the side of his boot and laughed quietly through his nose. "Yes, ma'am. I reckon it suits us." Only then did he see the slice of loaf bread and a breast of fried chicken she had brought to him. Both were laid out on a linen napkin upon a little shelf projecting from the rock.

"Why do you say that, Mr. Jane?"

"Well," he said, pushing a pebble with the side of his boot. "Cowboyin' is 'bout all most o' us know, and there ain't none o' us gonna git rich off it."

"But you take pride in it," she said. It was not a question.

Clayt knew by her tone that he need not answer. Down below, he spotted Harry, scanning the horizon. Whit and Johnny were somewhere down there, too, and he had no doubt that each of them was just as vigilant. He was speaking for all of them, he knew. For Chalky and Nestor behind him. Even for Rascher.

The cigarette was only half burned, but he pinched the coal dead again and slipped it into his pocket. The mustangs were gone now, the only evidence of their passing a cloud of pink dust ascending against the distant gray of the Laramies.

"This must be what heaven is like," she said.

Clayt smiled at these words that fairly served as an anthem to his life. After a time he looked at her. The bruise below her eye was now an inverted rainbow of colors.

"Or . . . might be," he said quietly, "this is it, ma'am."

Her smile reduced the multicolored bruise under her eye to an insignificant blemish, and she carried that smile out to the plains in the direction the horses had run.

"Do you think you might call me 'Isabella'?"

Clayt pushed out his lower lip and nodded. "Yes, ma'am . . . I can do that."

Her smile tightened, and her eyes brightened as though she might laugh. "It would take the place of 'ma'am,' you know," she said.

When Clayt looked down at his boots, he felt her gaze hold on him. Staring at the lines he had drawn in the sand, he remembered the nights he and Grady Brooks had worked with pencil and paper to come up with the simple brand.

"And may I call you 'Clayton'?" she added.

When he looked up at her, he saw by the personable expression on her face that the question was an honest one. She took nothing for granted.

"Friends call me 'Clayt.' Maybe you could call me that."

"Thank you," she said and smiled as though she had been handed a gift.

Her words, he realized, were collecting inside him, amassing like the mystifying marks that tracked across the pages of a book. He knew that he would retrieve these words later, play them over again in his mind, and think more about their meanings.

"It's interesting," she said, "how small I feel standing up here before all this open space." She swept her hand toward the prairie. "Yet, up here, I feel that I count." She held her hair from her face and turned to him. "Do you know what I mean?"

Clayt looked at the gray haze clinging to

the Laramies, seeing it as a shield that protected him from his past. He knew exactly what she meant.

"Lot o' that irony out there, ain't it?" he said.

CHAPTER 21

"It's gittin' damned cold out there," Short-Stuff announced, backing into the bunkhouse. Cradling hen's eggs inside the sling on his arm, he closed the door with his backside and moved carefully to Swampy's sideboard. One by one he laid the eggs in a pan.

Shirtless in his trousers and socks, Clayt shaved before the mirror over the wash basin. As he scraped the blade down one cheek, he saw Short approach and stop behind him as if to check his progress with the razor.

"Mr. Aff's wantin' to see you, Clayt."

Clayt swirled the blade in the hot water, and the steel came out glistening and steaming, and he began another pass under his chin. "He at the house?"

"Dairy barn," Short said and leaned in to watch. Then he studied himself in the mirror as he fingered the gray scruff that covered the lower half of his face. "How the hell do you do that without cuttin' yourself? I'll draw blood ever' time."

Clayt stretched his chin forward and moved the blade along the contour of his jaw. He cleaned the blade in the water again and nodded toward the strop on the wall.

"Put time in on the leather first. Sharper the razor, less chance o' gittin' cut."

When Short frowned at this questionable logic, Clayt smiled at him in the mirror. "It's what you call 'irony,' " he explained.

Short stared at the razor and deepened his frown. "Ir'ny? I thought they was made o' steel."

Clayt turned and looked at Short's damp shoulders. "Is it rainin'?"

"Snowin . . . if you can call a wet slap in the face 'snow.' " Short frowned and shook his head. "It ain't gonna last long."

When Clayt turned back to the mirror, Short-Stuff huffed a laugh. "Last I shaved, looked like I'd stuck my face down a badger hole. Main reason I wear this pitiful thing." He ran his fingers through his disheveled beard.

As Clayt toweled off, Short-Stuff took the opportunity to study the scar that puckered the flesh below Clayt's left collarbone. "Got damn near the same wound, you and me."

When Clayt said nothing and put on his shirt, Short cleared his throat and lowered his voice. "Grady seen Mr. Aff's sister walkin' out past the chicken coop last night. Said he would'a gone on up to her and escorted her back to the house but said she was sick or somethin'. He couldn' tell if she was losin' her meal or cryin' or both. Reckon we oughta say somethin' to Mr. Aff? You know, 'bout bein' out by herself?"

Clayt stuffed the shirttails into his trousers and snapped his suspenders over his shoulders. "I'll see to it, Short," he said and sat on his bunk to pull on his boots.

Afton stood at the far stall of the dairy barn talking to Grady Brooks, both men dressed heavily against the frosty morning. When the Englishman saw Clayt, he held up a finger, quickly wound up his conversation, and walked half the length of the barn in his quick, purposeful stride. Stopping smartly, Afton slapped a pair of gloves across his palm.

"Well, you can always count on one of these wet miserable snows just when you think that spring has finally settled in."

Clayt shook his head. "Doubt it'll amount to much. Clouds are too strung out."

Afton looked out the front entrance as if — on the strength of Clayt's words — he

323

already expected to see a change in the weather. He slapped the gloves again smartly and reached into his coat.

"This is today's supply list. Send in two more of the men to Ivinson's. Make sure they know to sign." Clayt took the paper, and Afton twisted at the waist to check on their privacy. Grady was head down, occupied with shoveling manure in the far stall. When Afton turned back to Clayt, his eyes were all business. "Wallace Dunne wants to meet with you," he said quietly. The Englishman waited for some reaction, but Clayt's jade-green eyes showed nothing. Afton began slipping his fingers into a glove. "He'll be at the old windmill out at the Pender place an hour before dark."

Watching the snow fall wetly past the doorway, Clayt sucked in his cheeks and considered the request. "Why don't he just come out here and talk?"

"I want you to go out and see him, Clayton," Afton instructed. "I want to cooperate in this by every means possible."

"What about today . . . b'fore I do that, I mean?"

"My brother-in-law and I are going into town to meet with some merchants."

"And what about your sister? And the boy?"

"Thomas will be going with us." Afton sniffed and cleared his throat. "His father is grooming him for business," he said matter of factly, trying to lend reason to the idea.

Clayt nodded. "Reckon me and the boys in the bunkhouse will ride out to the south pastures. Spell some o' the crew ridin' herd out there."

"No," Afton replied quickly. "I want you here. My sister will be here. If Chatka gets it into his head that he will bring a fight to the ranch, I want you here to organize things. Keep whatever men you need. I'll want only a few as an escort into town."

Clayt looked down into the palm of his hand and narrowed his eyes. "You know that ain't likely 'bout Chatka. Ain't no half-starved Sioux gonna take a chance like that 'gainst a outfit our size."

Afton tamped his hands deeper into the gloves by scissoring each set of fingers and forking them together in smart little jabs. "Nevertheless, that's what I want," he said curtly. After hesitating a moment, he started out the main door of the barn, his stiff walk faring badly on the rutted yard.

"Mr. Afton," Clayt called to his back.

Afton stopped and turned. He clasped his hands behind his back and raised his chin in his false show of patience where patience was wearing thin. The big flakes of snow fell around him like patches of damp, gray cloth dropping from the sky. Clayt walked out to him, and they continued shoulder to shoulder toward the house.

"Anythin' I oughta know 'bout your sister's health?"

Afton stopped and turned, his face knotted with concern. "What do you mean?"

"I reckon it might have some bearin' on how far out we oughta be ridin'."

"Her health is fine," Afton insisted, his cheeks showing some color. He glared at the main house, turned up his coat collar, and brushed the snow from his sleeves.

"Somethin' ain't right, Mr. Aff," Clayt said. Afton's eyes flashed white as he looked away. Then he took a deep breath and closed his eyes. Clayt stepped closer to him and lowered his voice. "Her husband . . . he's beatin' on 'er, ain't he?"

Afton opened his eyes but would not look at Clayt. In profile his face was like a clenched fist. The wet flakes of snow clung to his hat and coat, and he stood like a man defeated by some unseen adversary.

"She has never said that!" he snapped, his tone anything but convincing.

Clayt stepped around in front of him to talk eye to eye. "We cain't be lettin' that happen, Mr. Aff."

Afton's color darkened, and his expression turned indignant. "These are adults, Clayton! Husband and wife! I can't presume to intercede in their affairs!"

"She's your sister, Mr. Aff. When a man treats a woman thataway, that man loses some o' that consideration you might ordinar'ly afford 'im."

Afton's breathing whistled quietly through his nose. He shook his head so smartly that water flung off the brim of his hat.

"Damn it, Clayton! I cannot bloody well reprimand the majority shareholder of New Surrey Downs."

Clayt shook his head. "Don' know nothin' 'bout shares, but she's your sister, sir."

"Damn it, man," Afton huffed in a whisper, "don't you think I —"

A sound at the front of the house turned Afton. Tom stood in his shirtsleeves on the porch, his dark hair laced in a net of snow and his cheeks blooming with red. Afton affected a laugh, but Tom's worried eyes darted from one man to the other.

"Thomas, my boy, you shouldn't be out here without a coat." Afton hurried up the steps and shunted his nephew toward the door. "What are you doing out in the cold?"

Tom resisted and stopped. "Uncle John,

do I have to go in a wagon today? Can't I ride Black Knight? I can ride her real fine . . . you can ask Clayt."

Afton straightened and lifted his arms from his sides only to let them fall back with a slap. "It's your father's wishes, Thomas. He's thinking about the way the two of you will conduct business back home." He reached past the boy and opened the door.

"But we're *not* at home." Tom looked to Clayt for support, but Afton ushered the boy to the door with a hand between his shoulder blades.

"Let's get you back where it's warm," Afton said.

As soon as they had gone inside, Henry Walsh filled the doorframe, where he eyed the day with disapproval. Without altering his expression, he glanced at Clayt, turned, and disappeared into the house, closing the door behind him.

Clayt walked into the bunkhouse, stepped to the center of the room, and propped his hands on his hips. All the boys were up now, getting dressed by the wood heater, a few waiting at the chow table in the vain hope that their presence would hurry Swampy.

"Whit, Harry, Stiles, Rascher," Clayt began, "you boys are goin' into Laramie with Mr. Aff and his brother-in-law and the boy. You'll be their protection, so take along the ammunition you might need. When you hit town, Stiles and Rascher, you're to git these supplies at Ivinson's." He dropped the list on the table. "Be sure and sign for it . . . both o' you." The men were quiet and still, each holding a perplexed expression on his face. "G.T. and Chalky will stay here with me an' Grady at the ranch. The rest o' you boys can ride on out to the south pastures," Clayt said. "Work out a rotation with Lou and Buck and the rest o' the crew."

Clayt waited long enough to see if anyone had something to say. When Swampy clacked down a platter of eggs on the table, all heads turned, but no one made a move toward the benches. When Clayt walked out the door and closed it, he still heard no rush to the table. Crossing to the barn, he hunted up a stiff brush and began grooming Skitter.

He was rasping his mare's back hoof when Nestor walked through the stalls toward the corral carrying his bedroll. Neither spoke as they went about their work, but there was an unnatural feeling to the silent duet — one gearing up for the range, the other settling in for a day at the ranch. When Nestor booted into his stirrup and perched on his horse, Clayt led his dapple-gray into the paddock and then led out the two Morgans to the wagon in the yard, where he hitched them to the traces.

Nestor broke the silence. "So what is it *you're* doin' today?"

Clayt threaded the cinches and tightened the hip straps. "Damned if I know."

While the others assigned to work in the south pasture saddled up and mounted, Clayt filled canteens for the party going into town. He stashed them in the boot of the wagon and looked at no one as he went about his work. The cowboys exchanged glances, pulled up their collars against the weather, and, following Nestor's lead, rode east out of the main gate and then turned south along the creek.

An hour later Clayt was forking hay from the loft when Afton, Walsh, and Tom boarded the wagon. Their entourage of four riders squared off around the wagon and waited as Afton held the reins with one hand and buttoned the collar of his coat with the other. Then together as a unit they started toward the main road, the wagon rattling and the horsemen holding back their mounts to match the plodding pull of the Morgans.

The snow had let up, but the gray day held to its chill. Clayt finished feeding the horses and carried a shovel to the garden, where he cut fresh walls into those sections of irrigation ditches where last winter's freezes had collapsed the channels. Behind him in the barren garden bed, Grady swung a pickax, preparing the soil for the spring planting.

When the ditches were repaired, Clayt checked the water troughs at the paddock, and, finding them sufficient, he stood by the gate for a time, watching the easy rhythm of the horses as they moved contentedly among themselves. Skitter approached, her head bobbing lazily, but her eyes fixed on him. She lifted her muzzle over the gate, and Clayt let her velvet nose nuzzle his face until a sound from the mill shed turned his head.

He walked to the door of the shed and stopped when he saw Isabella Walsh standing alone in the room, her back to him, her body as still as one of the mannequins in Ivinson's store window. She wore a blue shawl around her shoulders and a long sand-colored dress. He knew she was looking at the easel. It stood in the back of the room, its legs spread into a perfect tripod. She moved toward it at a halting pace and touched the stand along one of its wooden braces.

331

Clayt backed away, walked quietly into the barn, took up the spade shovel, and walked across the yard back to the garden. When he began loosening the soil at the far end of the bed, Grady watched him for a time but said nothing.

At the noon hour Clayt and Grady cleaned up at the bunkhouse and ate a meal of hot soup and warmed-over biscuits. When Swampy came back inside after taking the soup bone to the dog, he fixed worried eyes on Clayt and poked a thumb back at the door.

"That there sister o' Mr. Aff's . . . she's saddlin' up one o' the horses."

Clayt stared at Swampy for two heartbeats, set down his coffee cup without drinking, and pushed up from the table. Without veering toward the coat rack, he walked purposefully out the door and closed it behind him.

When he reached the barn he stopped in the doorway. She wore the same riding clothes she had worn yesterday. A heavy overcoat lay draped over a stall gate. She had tethered the chestnut mare to a post and thrown up both blanket and saddle. The mare stood for it as if readying for a day's work.

Isabella Walsh looped a stirrup over the

saddle horn, bent low to tighten the cinch, straightened, and let fall the stirrup. Reaching up she tested the fit of the saddle, one hand on the horn, the other on the cantle. It was plenty snug.

Bareheaded, Clayt stood quietly in his shirtsleeves, his skin prickling from the cold. "Ma'am, are we ridin' out some'res today?"

She did not turn at his voice but pushed her arms into the coat and untied the reins to part them around the mare's neck. Crossing them over the withers, she turned to look at him, her left hand covering the horn with the reins threaded through the fingers. The bruise above her cheekbone was like a purple shadow, so dark it made the white of her eye glow like a sickle moon.

"I thought we'd gotten past 'ma'am.' "

The stirrup hung more than halfway up her thigh, but she nimbly hiked her leg and hoisted herself into the bow of the saddle in a continuous gliding motion. She sat the horse with a visible sense of pride, as though her success with the tack surprised her. The horse threw its head down and snorted, jangling its bridle. When the chestnut shifted its weight, the woman played out the reins to let the animal act out its ritual of anticipation.

"Are you plannin' on ridin' out from the

ranch?" Clayt said.

She stared down at the reins in her hand. "I hadn't really made a plan."

He started to take hold of the cheek strap of the bridle but then thought better of it. "If you're headed out on the prairie, we might like to round up a few o' the —"

She kicked her heels into the horse's flanks, and it high-stepped smartly past Clayt out of the barn.

"Ma'am?" he called, following her on foot. "Isabella?"

When she prodded the mare into a canter, he watched helplessly as the horse gathered momentum and broke into an easy lope down the road toward the front gate. The passage of horse and rider was dreamlike, cutting against all logic.

"Damnit," he whispered, his voice thin and meaningless. He ran for the paddock. By the time he had saddled Skitter and mounted, Swampy had carried Clayt's coat and hat out into the yard. Clayt reined up to receive them, and the two men looked at one another, each mirroring the other's face of taut consternation.

"I got no idea," Clayt said to the unasked question. He took the coat, then the hat.

Swampy just shook his head and looked down the road where the woman was almost out of sight. When his eyes came back to Clayt, he handed up a sack.

"Here you go," he said. "Case you need somethin' to eat out there." Then, venturing a smile, he added, "Good luck."

Clayt caught up to her on the main road half a mile shy of Shin Bone Creek, where the land dipped low and was shaded by a colonnade of big cottonwoods. Not knowing what to say, he merely fell in beside her and let Skitter follow her equine instincts to match the other horse's gait. The riders remained silent. The awkwardness of the situation was somewhat balanced by their shared assessment of the terrain around them: Clayt searching for signs of unshod hooves, the woman, no doubt, exploring her surroundings for their inherent beauty and potential on canvas.

After fording the creek, they turned north to follow the path under the trees. With the leaves just budding, the cottonwoods still laid down a winter maze of crisscrossed shadows. The moving water provided a constant boil that filled the silence between them.

At the willow flats they watered their horses, and she gazed at the bluffs billowing up against the sky like gray clouds hardened to stone. "May we go there?" she said, pointing up toward the rim of the canyon.

After following her whim of an escape from the ranch, he thought it odd that she would ask. He watched her admire the cliffs and saw for the first time that the bruise on her face had ruptured and formed a scab across her cheekbone. A bright bead of blood clung to the scab like a tiny red rose emerging from a rock outcrop. When she caught him looking, her hand went unconsciously to the wound and the light touch made her wince.

"Are you aw-right?" Clayt asked. When she looked away, he snapped off the supple tip of a green willow branch and stripped it of its slender new leaves. "Chew on this and swallow the juice."

She frowned at the sprig but did as she was told, wrinkling her nose at the taste.

"Keep with it till it ain't bitter no more," he said. "Then spit it out. It takes a long while to kick in, but it'll help with the pain when it does." To afford her some privacy, he squinted up at the angle of the sun over the rim of the cliff.

When she leaned and spat out the dregs of the medicine, he pointed through the willow thicket to the mouth of the canyon. "There's somethin' I'd care to show you up there."

CHAPTER 22

He led the way past the seeps and veered toward the rock springs that marked the trail to Shannonhaus's southernmost line shack. Fresh tracks abounded in the sand, from both boot and hoof. Closer to the cliff, beneath an overhang, he found two cigarette butts.

"Is this part of John's land?" Isabella asked.

Clayt shook his head. "Don't b'long to nob'dy."

She gazed at pieces of charred wood half buried in the sand. "Was this a fire?"

He pointed to a shallow depression under the overhang. "Somebody slept here."

He started into the canyon, and she followed him through the breach in the rock, where the canyon mouth opened like a palatial hallway and then narrowed into a winding defile. The sound of their horses' hooves amplified off the walls and filled the air, as though they were moving past long shelves filled with grandfather clocks. They traveled without words up the natural stone steps, the horses moving in and out of the narrow ribbon of drainage that trickled through the center of the trail.

When they approached the entrance to the dark-ceiled room, Clayt dismounted and indicated that she do the same. He tied both sets of reins to a stick of sun-bleached wood and jammed the stick in a narrow crack between two boulders. Walking into the crepuscular light of the room, they quieted their steps so as not to intrude upon the stillness in the air. There was no water dripping today. The dark pool imbued the room with a sense of absolute serenity. Cool air rose off the glassy surface.

He pointed to the far side of the pool, to the stark, bright edges of stone that appeared rimed in incandescent gold. The contrast of these vivid lines to the dark of the room was like witnessing a resurrection of life.

They stood without speaking, she moving her head slowly to soak up every detail, and he trying to see it as she might. He imagined the fine stroke of a brush capturing this element of rock or that reflection of water . . . and the play of light that somehow emanated from the darkness like fine sparks coming to life in a pile of ash.

"Thought you might like this place," he whispered and pointed again. "The way that light burns along the edge of the rock." Though he had spoken as quietly as possible, his words returned as a whispery echo in the darkness.

"It's called 'chiaroscuro,' " she said and moved her finger through the air as if tracing the outline of the boulder. The rock's blackened form was etched along one side with a thread of light that resembled a heated wire.

Chiaroscuro.

He tried whispering the word so as to remember it, but it did not fare well on his tongue. With the room settled into its natural quiet, he ventured the question he had not been able to muster in the light.

"How is it you don't paint no more?"

She did not speak for so long that he feared he had overstepped some proprietary boundary. But in the cavern's dead calm, her answer did come, clear and resigned.

"My husband," she said. "He forbids it."

Clayt shallowed his breathing to hear anything else she might offer on the subject, but for a full minute she simply gazed across the water.

"How's that work 'xactly? One person sayin' another'n cain't paint?"

She smiled and bowed her head. "Oh, scandal will do." A dry, airy laugh brought up her head. "I have become the tasty morsel of gossip in Surrey." She turned to face him. "Don't you want to know?"

Clayt shrugged. "I reckon some people always gotta be talkin' 'bout somethin'."

Isabella sat on the nearest boulder, took in a deep breath, and expelled it. "A painter paints," she said, her voice taking on an edifying tone. "It doesn't matter what she paints. Inspiration can be buried in the simplest of things. Every form contains its own beauty, and perhaps there is nothing so beautiful as the human body."

Quietly, Clayt lowered himself onto the rock. Sitting side by side they waited for the silence of the room to gather around them again.

"I brought models into the house," she continued. "Into my studio. I paid them, just like the best schools in Europe pay their models. Men and women alike. The real people who work as seamstresses, or sail-makers. The farmers and stone masons. You can probably guess the rest of the story."

"That when he started in on hittin' you?"

Now it seemed the whole of the cavernous room was holding its breath. She did not flinch or pretend any denials. The quiet of the room was answer enough, and both knew that the nature of their relationship had changed. Now they were confidants.

"Why does he keep on doin' it?"

"Because I will not break," she said, her voice harder now.

"But if you ain't paintin' no more . . ."

She lowered her head again. "A woman has her own ways to deny a man what he wants," she said plainly. "I'm not just talking about the private life of a man and woman in their bedroom. In upper-class England, a wife's purpose is to define her husband in those terms by which he wants to be defined. That, of course, being part of the rules as defined by the men." She shook her head. "I won't play by those rules. He can take away my paints and brushes . . . but not my soul."

"He can take your life. It's on account o' that I'm bound to help you."

She turned quickly, and he could see fear in her eyes. "No, you mustn't. It's not done that way."

"I ain't carin' too much 'bout how it gits done. Just that it gits done."

She was shaking her head even as he spoke. "I don't wish to talk about this anymore. I know you mean well. And I thank you for your concern but —"

"I knew a man kilt his wife back in Tennessee. Made 'im 'bout half crazy. Said he didn' intend on the killin', but she was still dead, intended or not."

"It won't come to that," she said. "You must promise me you won't interfere."

Clayt said nothing. Leaning, he picked up a stone and tossed it into the water. The sound of the pool swallowing it was like a quick musical note from a bird on the wing.

"You give any thought to what this might mean to your boy?"

Her eyes pinched in surprise. "He knows nothing about this."

"Maybe. He will though, if he ain't already figured it out. There's only so many times you can trip over a chair."

Her expression turned pleading. "You mustn't talk to anyone about this. Please."

"I aw-ready talked to your brother, but he won't admit to it happ'nin'. Says it ain't his place to butt in."

"You talked to John?"

Back in the open canyon the horses nickered, and their hooves clattered on the rocks. By the nervous tension in Skitter's throat, Clayt knew she would be backing against her tether, trying to pull herself free.

He quieted Isabella with an open hand raised between them, and they sat unmoving, listening. When Clayt pushed away from the rock and started back the way they had come, she followed.

Two men rode up the canyon, their legs stiff as they stood in their stirrups, their eyes fixed on the horses up ahead. From the dark of the cavern Clayt watched them long enough to recognize Leland Shannonhaus on his buckskin mare. The other man was half a head taller and dressed in a gray duster open at the front.

The tall man rode a big blaze roan, its forehead glowing white as a banker's shirt. The rider twisted at the waist and pulled a blue blanket from behind his saddle. One-handedly he unfurled it and laid it across the horse's rump behind the cantle.

"Stay in here," Clayt whispered to Isabella and walked out into the light.

When the two horsemen reached the tier where Skitter and the chestnut were tied, the man in the duster pulled up short, letting Shannonhaus approach alone. The stranger's saddle blanket showed the same color as the blanket draped over the horse's haunches. Clayt nodded but got nothing from either man.

"Something you need?" Leland said.

Clayt said nothing, just shook his head. Leland squinted at the opening of the arched room. The other man coaxed his horse to one side for an unobstructed view of Clayt without Leland in the way. The high, curved cantle of his saddle reached to the man's lower back. Contrasting against the drab color of his coat, the blanket of blue showed a thin, red border around its perimeter. A long rifle scabbard angled across the roan's ribs, its open end covered by the blanket.

"This canyon don't go nowhere but to our place," Leland said, still waiting for an explanation. When Clayt only nodded, Leland shifted in his saddle. "I don't see that you got any business bein' here."

Making no response, Clayt held his gaze on Leland but kept a peripheral view of the second man. When Leland dismounted Clayt unbuttoned the front of his coat, feeling the muscles of his shoulders start to gather.

"Half the Laramie Plain ain't enough for Afton?" Leland checked the ground for tracks, but the canyon floor was solid rock here. "You working cattle through here?"

Clayt kept his voice even. "That'd be a poor choice." He leveled his thumb back toward the dark cavern. "Water's tainted.

344

Beyond that, the terrain ain't good for livestock up this way." The implied insult might have been lost on Leland. Clayt couldn't tell.

Leland spat off to one side. "Then what're you doing in a place that leads to Shannon-haus land?"

Clayt managed a smile. " 'Leadin' to' and 'bein' part of' ain't the same thing."

Leland glared, but his hostility did not fare well against Clayt's easy manner. "Who's that belong to?" Leland barked, turning his wrath on the chestnut mare.

"One o' ours," Clayt replied. "Brand's clear enough."

As Leland studied the horse, Clayt took the moment to examine the other man. In his long duster, the tall man sat his roan as still as a statue. His face was scarred with tiny craters along the sunken hollows of his cheeks — like a tin plate that someone had banged with a small hammer. His eyes seldom blinked and never strayed from Clayt.

"Git your man out o' there and ride out," Leland said. "We don't like trespassers."

Without seeming to make a deliberate move, Clayt arranged the drape of his coat so that the butt of his gun touched the inside of his forearm. The stranger's hand flattened on his thigh.

"I'll leave when it suits me," Clayt said pleasantly. "It don't suit me yet."

Leland glared at the extra horse. It was clear that he didn't know what to say next. He looked back at the tall man, whose pocked face remained as aloof as a distant moon on a cold night. Flustered, Leland turned back to Clayt and bared his teeth.

"Maybe you an' Afton think you got some say-so up in these parts," Leland said. Abruptly, he mounted his horse. "But what you think don't mean shit up here, and it *suits me* that you stay away from Shannonhaus land." Leland jabbed his heels into the buckskin's flanks, coaxing his horse toward the dapple-gray and the chestnut. When he pushed his way between the animals and the boulder where they were tethered, the animals backed away, snapping the picket stick wedged in the crack. When the chestnut turned to run, Skitter held her ground and snorted, and the chestnut hesitated.

Leland reined around his buckskin and snorted a laugh. "You ought to tie up your animals better," Leland advised with another white flash of his teeth.

Clayt remained standing exactly as he had been. "Appears I should," he said, "long as

346

people in these parts are as careless as they are."

The tall man's steady gaze broke now, his eyes angling past Clayt toward the sound of light footsteps echoing from the cavern. Isabella walked from the shadowed room into the open light of the canyon. Leland wheeled his horse around at the unexpected appearance of a woman. The tall man's focus had already returned to Clayt.

"Do you own this canyon, sir?" she demanded, raising her chin at Leland. She kept moving toward him, glaring, not even looking down to find her footing.

Leland sniffed and tilted his head up the canyon. "I own up on the high ground."

Isabella stopped inches from his stirrup and thrust out her hand, fingers stiff as the tines of a pitchfork, her thumb pointing at the sky. "I am Isabella Walsh. And you are?"

Reluctantly, Leland took her hand. "Shannonhaus," he mumbled.

The line of Isabella's jaw cut a hard angle against the smooth texture of her flushed neck. "But you don't own this land we are standing on . . . is that correct?"

Leland looked uncertainly toward the canyon room and opened his mouth, but she did not give him time to answer.

"Then I suggest you two gentlemen ride

on." She spun to Clayt. "I think we had better gather our horses and keep them close at hand," she said and turned back to Leland, ". . . as long as there are careless riders about."

She marched in a determined line toward the chestnut, but the frightened animal backed away, its hooves clacking on the shelf of stone. She stopped, flustered, put her hands on her hips, and looked back at Clayt, her face darkening with enough color to hide the bruise below her eye.

"Are you coming?" she said.

"D'rectly," Clayt said, still facing the two men on horseback.

The tall man reined his horse around at a slow walk and herded the chestnut back toward the dapple-gray. He waited as the woman stepped forward more carefully and grabbed the reins of her horse. The rider tipped his hat as he passed the woman, and then he let his horse pick its steps up the canyon toward the Shannonhaus spread, the blue blanket over his saddlebags swinging with the horse's gait.

Leland Shannonhaus jerked his horse's head smartly so that the animal bared its teeth on the bit and tossed its head high, the mane whipping over its neck. He kicked the horse into submission with his boot heels and followed the other man up the canyon.

Clayt walked to Skitter and led the dapple-gray down the first few ledges on foot. When he stopped to toe into the stirrup, Isabella — now mounted — kicked her horse into a smart walk past him and clattered down the trail alone. He mounted and caught up with her where the canyon widened a hundred yards shy of the mouth, but they did not speak all the way back to the willows.

On the flats beside Shin Bone Creek she started for the gap in the low hills whence they had come. Clayt advanced beside her and forced her horse to veer.

"We need to follow the creek down to the main road," he said. "There's some business I need to tend to."

She made no response, but neither did she resist. With Clayt in the lead they forded the creek and traced the route the cattle had taken to the south pastures. The sky had cleared. The sun was making its way toward the crest of the Snowy Range. The slanted rays touched the whole of the prairie, bringing out the silver sheen of the grass as it rippled in long, flanking waves in the wake of the wind.

They rode for miles in silence to a boulder field burned to amber by the angle of the light. There the ground itself appeared to glow as though the baking of the prairie sun had endowed the earth with this hour of ambient return.

Topping a low hill they stopped. From there they saw the main road spool away like a wobbling ribbon for a half mile to the east. To the west a stand of cottonwoods marked the arc of the creek that bowed toward them. Somewhere to the south a coyote yelped and yammered, rendering a mournful ululation. Isabella stilled at the sound and looked off in the direction from which it came.

"Ki-yote," Clayt explained. "It's the end o' their matin' season. That'n's havin' a hard time lettin' it go." He pointed toward the road. "I need to check for tracks." When she said nothing, he urged his horse forward, and again she followed. Bottoming out on the road, Clayt dismounted and walked east a few paces. He stood for a time, examining the road, and then he knelt to touch the dust that had accumulated in a wheel rut.

"I'm s'posed to meet a man here," Clayt said. "We can wait down by the creek an' let the horses drink."

She dismounted and surprised him by handing him her reins and walking back toward the knoll where they had first spotted the road. He led the horses to water to take their fill, and as they did he looked over their backs at the woman seated on the rise fifty yards away. Her head was turned to one side as though she were using the last rays of sun to warm her neck and cheek. He tied off the horses and started a slow walk toward her.

As he approached she held her head at an angle that seemed at once both defiant and thoughtful. He turned his head to see what she might be looking at, and there in the wind-pruned scrub hovered the haze of blue that the twilight delivered to the prairie.

He stopped a few yards from her and checked the road to the east. Then he studied the sky. There would be enough light from the first quarter moon to illuminate the trail after sunset. He looked down the road again, hoping to see Afton's wagon returning from town. Afton would be angry about his sister being so far from the ranch this late, but there was nothing else for it.

"Were you so ready to risk your life for something so silly as a line on a map?" she asked. The fraction of her face that he could see glowed with heat. "Did you think at all about my presence there?" She glanced at him with hurt eyes and then laid her brow upon her forearms propped across her knees.

"It's boundaries that stake out who and what you are out here," Clayt explained in a voice instructive but gentle. "Those lines are important. And more important is what you let another man know 'bout what he can and cain't do to you."

She looked up at him sharply. "That man, Leland . . . he was ready to fight, wasn't he?"

Clayt pushed up the brim of his hat to let her see the earnestness in his eyes. "He's mostly a lotta talk. I would'n'a let nothin' happen to you."

Tears welled in her eyes and spilled down her cheeks. She swiped her palms roughly across her face and looked out at the evanescent blue color of the plain.

"Nothing happened because I defused the situation. I suppose you men would have seen it through until one or two of you were dead." She turned with an accusatory glare. "Just like those books that Thomas devours," she said. "My God, it's all so puerile."

Clayt didn't know the word, but he understood her meaning. He sat down next to her, laid his hat between them, and gazed out at the blue tint of the world.

"Leland's got a hot head and a quick mouth, but he don't never back it up."

"And the other man? Did you know him? He was — I don't know — disturbing."

Clayt nodded to her judgment. She had known which man had posed the danger.

"You and me," Clayt said, "we just saw different as to how it oughta go."

She glanced at him only long enough to show her disappointment.

"I reckon you're right to be angry at the way men make the rules. What you gotta understand is that I gotta live with 'em, too. I weren't just throwin' out words back there. I was speakin' as much for your brother as I was for myself. Long as we ain't crossed their line, we cain't be lettin' Shannonhaus tell us where we can and cain't go."

"Of course not!" she quipped. "Men must never give in."

Clayt picked up his hat and turned it in his hands. "I reckon it's hard to understand," he said quietly. "Maybe things are different out here compared to where you come from." He stilled the hat and stared out at the land. "The reason Leland ain't gonna start real trouble . . . is 'cause he knows I won't back down from it."

She buried her face in her hands and

pressed the heel of each thumb into her eyes. When she looked up at him, her eyes were raw and filled with bewilderment.

"Listen to yourself. You're like children in a schoolyard."

Clayt had never been in a school, so he had nothing to say about that. He looked down the road — hoping to see the wagon . . . and hoping not to.

"I reckon there's things a woman like you cain't know 'bout."

"Really," she replied and made a tight smile. "And *what* can't *I* understand?"

Clayt felt the answer rise in his throat like a defiled sacrament intruding on the soft blue halo of the evening. He had to look away from her to say it.

"There's men who will kill 'cause they ain't never known how to put any value on a life. Not even their own."

"And so you play by their rules," she said. "Doesn't that make you like them?"

Clayt pursed his lips. "A man don't always have a choice, you know."

She canted her head in a pleading pose. "You always have a choice, Clayt."

"No, ma'am. Not in a war."

"A war?" Her forehead creased with three clean lines, but as she stared at him her face gradually smoothed out. "You were in the war?"

He nodded.

"How old were you?" she asked, her voice a whisper.

He shrugged and watched the last of the blue tinted air hover over the prairie. She leaned forward to better see his face.

"Then why test a man like Shannonhaus?" she asked without anger.

"It weren't me doin' the testin'. Standin' up for yourself is part o' stayin' alive out here." He turned to face her, trying not to show the misery he carried from the war. "I know the bad a man can do 'cause I know the same thing's inside o' me. I prob'ly ain't the person people think I am. I reckon you need to know that." He looked back at the blue sanctuary of the prairie. As it always did, the color began to evaporate, to yield to the inevitable night. He turned to her again. "I done more'n my share o' killin' in the war."

That he had confessed this to her seemed beyond comprehension. Yet at the same time it had seemed necessary. A stillness crept over them, and for a long time they sat without the intrusion of words. When the coyote yowled again, it gave them a common point on which to fix their bearings.

She put her hand on his arm, and for him it was like a final rope lowered to him in the pit he had fallen into more than a decade ago.

Before she could speak, Clayt heard the wagon. He stood and put on his hat.

"That'll be Mr. Afton."

She rose and brushed at her trousers. Clayt walked to the road and raised his arm to the approaching party. Whit was out front, slowing, sliding his carbine from its scabbard. When Clayt cupped one hand to his mouth and called out from the semi-dark, Whit relaxed, lowered the weapon across the bow of his saddle, and came on at a trot.

"Hey, you Sorry-Damn cowboy. What the hell're you doin' out here on foot?"

When Clayt made no reply, Whit turned his horse, and together they waited for the wagon. The two-horse team came on at a fast clip, its wheels jarring on the rocks and ruts in the road. When it stopped, Afton, Walsh, and Tom stared expectantly at Clayt. Their white shirts seemed impossibly bright in the dying light. Then their heads turned as one toward the movement on the hill, where Isabella picked her way through the scrub brush and stepped onto the road.

"What the bloody blazes?!" Afton demanded.

"We been waitin' on you," Clayt said.

Harry, who had been riding behind, joined the parley and sat his horse. He saw the high color in Afton's face and then studied the reins in his hand.

"Surely you're not out here alone!" Afton exclaimed. "My God, Clayton! What were you thinking? There's talk in town about Indian attacks escalating."

Clayt weathered the rebuke without excuse. "I figured you could escort your sister back to the ranch."

Henry Walsh glowered at Isabella. "Get in this wagon right now!" Walsh ordered. Tom climbed over the seat into the bed, but Isabella remained standing in the road, her arms folded, her hands clasping her upper arms. "Isabella!" Walsh barked.

When she turned and walked down the road toward the creek, Walsh cursed under his breath and heaved himself out of the wagon. Clayt sidestepped into the man's path.

"Clayton!" Afton gasped, his voice full of reprimand.

Clayt ignored Afton and looked directly into Henry Walsh's incensed face. "Her horse is over there in the trees. Maybe you oughta just let 'er git it."

357

Shocked, Walsh looked back at Afton, who was tying the leads to the brake handle. Walsh snapped his coat taut by the lapels and gave Clayt a loathsome sneer.

"If you hope to work for me, you will remind yourself of your station."

Clayt kept his voice flat and expressionless. "I work for Mr. Afton."

Walsh's smile widened, and his eyes narrowed, as though there was not room enough on his face for such pleasure. "And Afton works for me," he said. He made a backhanded wave of his fingers, indicating that Clayt was to step aside. Clayt stood firm.

Afton climbed down and hurried around the team. "This will not do, Clayton!" He took his foreman's arm, and Clayt allowed himself to be turned.

"What's he mean by that?" Clayt said. "You . . . workin' for him?"

When Walsh tried to walk around the two men, Clayt sidestepped, blocking him again. Afton tightened his hold on Clayt and tugged, but the foreman did not budge.

"Get a grip on yourself, Clayton!" Afton implored.

Again, Walsh veered around them, but Clayt broke free, caught Henry Walsh by his elbow, and turned him. "You ain't gonna

358

hit her no more," Clayt said quietly.

Afton gripped a handful of Clayt's coat. "Clayton! This is not your business!"

Walsh took the opportunity to jerk his arm free. Brushing the fabric of his sleeve with his hand, he continued toward his wife.

"This ain't got nothin' to do with bus'ness," Clayt said to Afton. He started to follow Walsh, but this time Afton maneuvered in front of him.

"You *do* work for Henry, Clayton. He is the one we all answer to. Please!"

The skin around Clayt's eyes pinched. "I work for you, Mr. Afton. Goin' on eleven years now. And you know why I stuck by you? You been a fair man. Someone a feller could depend on to see things git done the right way." Clayt nodded toward the creek. "But you ain't wantin' to see what's happ'nin' right here."

"It is not your affair!" Afton intoned in his most commanding voice.

Clayt winced. "For God's sake, Mr. Aff! She's your sister!" He looked down at Afton's grip and then jerked his coat free. "If you wanna grab somethin', grab him." He nodded in the direction Walsh had gone. The Englishman stood transfixed, like a man watching his house burn to the ground.

The nervous nickering and the shuffle of

hooves on the track ahead pulled everyone's attention. "Let go of me!" Isabella demanded. Mounted on her horse she floated toward the wagon — her dark silhouette etched out from the faint glow of the road. Walsh followed in an angry stride. Marching past his wife he climbed into the wagon, sat with a grunt, and looked straight ahead. Tom knelt quietly in back, watching his mother.

"Get in the carriage, Isabella," Walsh ordered. "We're leaving."

"When I go . . . and how I go," she said, "it will be of my own volition." She turned coolly to her brother. "John, I'm riding back alongside you. Are you ready?"

"Well, yes, we need to get going," Afton said, trying to muster some authority. "Get your horse, Clayton. We're late as it is." Afton climbed back into the driver's seat.

Clayt stepped beside him. "I got a appointment at a windmill, remember?"

CHAPTER 23

The wind picked up, and a gauze of clouds unrolled across the sky, dulling the moon. The stars broke through only in sparse patches. Clayt made a circle around the windmill and then spiraled outward two more turns to check the ground. There were no tracks. He stared off at the race of clouds that dappled the prairie with running moon shadow. All the land seemed in motion.

He braced the crown of his hat as a sudden gust whipped his coat around him and rattled the broken blades in the windmill. He thought about the other windmill that stood down by the Chimney Rock fork and wondered if Dunne might have confused the two.

After sliding his Henry rifle from its scabbard, he levered a cartridge into the chamber. One handedly he fired off a round into the sky, and right away the wind wrapped around the sound and whisked it away.

"Mr. Jane!" Dunne called, his voice barely cutting through the rush of the wind. He appeared bleary eyed, on foot, walking from a cluster of boulders north of the road as he dusted off one side of his body with quick swipes of his hand. The Scotsman looked small and helpless out here in the prairie, picking his way carefully through the brush in his brown-checkered suit and city shoes. "Come back behind these rocks," Dunne called out and pointed. "Let's get oot of this blasted wind."

The rocks made a three-sided room that cut out the blow of dust and sand and much of the sound of the wind. Just beyond the boulders in a gully, a black gelding stood tethered to a shrub of sage. Against the back wall, sticks of squaw wood were stacked a foot high. Dunne squatted by a bed of coals and spread his palms.

"Fire's about dead," he said, shrugging an apology.

Clayt studied the unburned sticks ringed around a few struggling embers. "How long you been waitin' out here?"

The detective removed his odd little hat and leaned to blow on the coals. "A few hours. I didn't want to be seen from the road, so I nestled in here and must have fallen asleep." He looked up at Clayt. "I have even moore reason nae to be seen with you now."

Clayt forced patience into his voice. "That right?"

Smoke began to swirl inside the little rock room until it found a way to race off into the wind. When a flame appeared, Dunne sat up and opened his hands to the meager source of heat.

"I understand you have a man woorking for you by the name of John Waites."

Clayt sat and crossed his legs. "What 'bout 'im?"

"I need you to verify something for me," Dunne said. He brushed off his hands and reached into his coat pocket. "I'm going to read a phrase to you. I'd like you to tell me if that phrase makes you think of anyone in particular." He unfolded a small, yellow piece of paper and held it at an angle to the meager flame. Clayt could see it was a telegram. Folding the paper back up, Dunne focused intently on Clayt's face. " 'If you follow my way of saying it.' " Dunne paused and dipped his head with his question. "That's the phrase. Do you know anyone who uses it?"

"I've heard it. It's common enough."

"Does Waites use it?"

Clayt turned to the cloud-shadow skating

across the moonlit prairie. "I reckon he does. But like I said. It's a common sayin'. Lotta men use it."

Dunne poked at the fire with a slender stick. "Can you name another who does?" He watched Clayt's face carefully, as the flames grew to throw flickering light upon each man. "So," Dunne said, smiling, "you're nae going to lie to me . . . but you're nae going to make it easy, are you?" He tossed the stick into the flame. "Afton wants you to cooperate with me in every way, Mr. Jane."

Clayt took a cigarette stub from his pocket. "What've you got ag'in Waites?"

Dunne shook his head. "It would serve nae purpose to divulge that. I want you to send Waites into Ivinson's tomorrow. Have him sign for supplies."

Clayt leaned and picked up a burning stick to light the cigarette. "I'd need a reason for that. Johnny and me go back a few years."

"What does it matter, man? You're going to send in *everyone* before it's over."

Clayt drew on the smoke, exhaled, and studied the side of his cigarette. Shaking his head, he laughed quietly to himself.

"Seems like I light up one o' these ever' time I ain't too sure what I'm 'bout to do."

He tossed the cigarette on the coals. "Never did much like the taste."

Dunne made a wry smile. "What are you unsure about, Mr. Jane?"

"Like I said, Johnny Waites is a friend o' mine."

Dunne's face hardened. "He might be the friend who is plotting to murder the president of the United States."

Clayt pursed his lips and shook his head. "Nope . . . not Johnny."

Dunne laughed a single quiet hiss through his teeth. "Your word on that won't help me much if Waites kills the president, now will it? Besides, if you're so certain, what is the harm in sending him into town tomorrow? It could prove me wrong."

The wind made a whipping sound out in the darkness, curling upon itself like a flag snapping taut on its pole. Dunne laid more wood on the fire and waited.

"Mr. Afton says I'm to cooperate with you," Clayt said, "but I ain't feelin' too good 'bout offerin' up a friend o' mine for inspection 'less you got good reason." He nodded toward the telegram in Dunne's hand. "I'll be needin' to know what's in that."

Dunne pocketed the paper. "I'm not here to make deals with you."

Clayt rubbed the back of his neck, nodded, and stood. "Reckon I'll be headin' back to the Rollin' F then." He stepped out into the wind and took up the reins hanging from Skitter's bridle.

"Damnit, man," Dunne yelled over the wind. "If you don't send in Waites, I'll just have to come out to the ranch. I could get a warrant and arrest him."

Clayt mounted. "Then do it, Mr. Dunne. It's a better way to come at a man . . . through the front door . . . 'stead o' me sneakin' you in through the back."

Dunne took in a deep breath, purged it, and slipped the folded telegram from his pocket. With the back of his free hand he slapped the paper and then held it up between them. "What good is it to shoo this to you? You can't read the first wee bit of this telegram. If I were to read it to you, how would you knoo I'm reading it truthfully?"

Clayt looked the man squarely in the eye. "Read it to me backwards. It's been my experience that a man can't think fast enough to do that and lie at the same time."

Dunne's face soured as he unfolded the telegram. "All right. Come back to the fire where I've got light."

They settled again by the small flame, and Dunne read the words from bottom to top in a halting cadence. Then he looked up expectantly.

"Now forward," Clayt said. "Don't stumble. Just read it quick."

Dunne breathed in deeply and then spewed out a whisper of air. " 'New threat by mail. Following phrase used four times: If you follow my way of saying it.' " Dunne looked up from the paper. "Satisfied?"

Clayt nodded. "Now read it slower."

Dunne repeated the message, spacing the words as though dictating to a child. When he finished he opened his hands, palms up, and waited for Clayt's appraisal.

"Well?" Dunne chirped. "I've been told Waites uses that phrase on a regular basis. Is that right?"

Clayt stared at the fire and frowned. "I ain't never read or wrote a lick, but somethin' 'bout this don't seem right. Those are words you'd say without much thought to it, but it don't seem to make much sense to bother writin' it out in a letter."

"Nevertheless," Dunne said, "it was part of a threat. I talked to the bartender at Sorohan's. He was the one who told me that Waites uses the phrase."

Clayt pursed his lips. "Ain't much to go on. One man can use another'n's words."

Dunne stuffed the telegram into his

367

pocket. "Look, man, I've been fa'r and squar' with you. Now, it's your turn. I want Waites in town tomorrow to sign for goods." He pointed a stiff finger at Clayt. "Your Mr. Afton agreed to help me in every way."

Clayt stared out at the wind-torn night. Now there was not a star to be seen.

"I'll send Johnny in tomorr'," Clayt said, letting conviction show on his face. "But I'll take an oath that Johnny Waites ain't the man you're lookin' for."

Dunne leaned forward. "And you woon't say anything to Waites about this?"

"I'm puttin' myself in your shoes, Mr. Dunne. This little trick at Ivinson's . . . it's 'bout all you got, I reckon. And you ain't got much time to figure it out."

"Eight days, to be exact," Dunne reminded.

Clayt nodded. "I wish you'd take me at my word 'bout Johnny. He's a waste o' your time."

Dunne shrugged. "I have to check out every lead, doon't you see? But I *will* take your woord," he said, offering his hand over the fire, "that you woon't talk to Waites about this."

Clayt eyed the Scotsman over the fire. Dunne was a picture of sincerity.

"You got my word," Clayt said and shook

368

the man's sinewy hand.

Leaving Dunne to the shelter of the rocks, Clayt stepped out into the night and mounted his horse.

"You be careful now, lad," Dunne called out. "There was talk in Sorohan's today about Indians stirring up trouble down on the river below town."

Clayt paused and frowned at the Scotsman. "What kind o' trouble?"

Dunne stood and approached from the rocks. "There was a skirmish with a timber crew. Twoo of the red devils were cut down, and the rest took off into the hills. They're saying it was that one called 'Chatka.' The crew foreman organized a ragtag troop, and they went oot in pursuit, but the savages were waiting for them along the road." Dunne shrugged. "That's all I know about it."

Clayt eased Skitter closer to the detective and reined up. "I reckon you got no cause to believe me, Mr. Dunne. But I don't wanna see the pres'dent kilt neither."

Dunne showed no reaction. "You truly hold no grudge from the war?"

Clayt leaned forward on his pommel. "Me an' Grant been through the same war. I reckon we both got a lot o' blood needs washin' off o' our hands." He stared at

Dunne for a time, and then he straightened. "I cain't wish an early grave for nobody that fought in that war. We all spent enough time in hell already."

A mile shy of the ranch, John Afton pulled up on the ribbons and brought the team to a stop. The cessation of motion woke Tom and brought Henry Walsh out of his disengaged sulk. Isabella reined up on the chestnut and waited. Ahead of them two riders approached at a gallop. Harry saw them and caught up to the wagon from the rear.

Nestor reined up, his big roan sliding to a stop. Then Whit arrived, his horse in a frenzy. The equine energy was like contagion passing through the other animals. The two draft horses snorted and balked at standing still, and Isabella's chestnut sidestepped off the road before she regained control.

"Mr. Afton," Nestor said excitedly, "Chalky's got himself shot right through. Took a arrow right here." He tapped a finger to his ribs. "Comin' back from the south pastures." Nestor shook his head and looked away. "Ain't never seen so much blood."

"How bad is it?" Afton asked.

"They're sayin it's his *lung*." Nestor winced at the word. "He rode out to scout and come back with that arrow in him. You could see both ends stickin' out." Nestor waited for Afton to say something, but the Englishman stared off into the night and pushed his lips out and in. "Chalk said he just rode right up on 'im. Said they must'a surprised each other." The young cowhand's face compressed with misery. "Sir, there ain't no way he can make it with a hole in his lung, is there?" Nestor's voice was beseeching, prayerful. "He's coughin' up blood somethin' terr'ble. He's askin' for Clayt." Nestor looked around at the startled faces. "Where *is* Clayt?"

The horses shifted restlessly and nickered, forcing Afton to put tension on the reins. He looked off toward the ranch and hissed air through his teeth.

"Where *is* he?" Nestor demanded, looking from face to face.

"Bloody hell," Afton grumbled and tied the reins to the brake handle. He stepped down from the wagon and walked to Isabella. "I need this horse. I need you to get into the wagon." She was already dismounting when Afton turned to Whit. "Tie your horse to the wagon and drive these people to the ranch." He began letting out the stirrups.

"Shouldn' somebody oughta git the doctor?" Nestor said.

"I'll do that after I find Clayton," Afton snapped.

Harry reined his horse next to Afton. "You don't want me goin' with you, sir?"

"No, damn it, I want all of you back at the ranch." He mounted, and the chestnut slewed a circle in the road before Afton got the horse under control. "Mr. Purdabaugh, take the lead. And keep your eyes sharp. Let's have no more surprises."

Harry walked his horse closer. "You don't wanna be out there alone, Mr. Afton."

"Do as I tell you!" Afton ordered.

Isabella climbed into the back of the wagon with Tom. Whit tethered his mount to the tailgate and took his place at the reins. He turned to check on his passengers.

"Go!" Afton commanded.

When Whit snapped the reins, the wagon lurched forward. Afton kicked his heels into his mount's ribs and started at a gallop in the opposite direction.

"Be careful, John," Isabella called over the clatter of the wheels.

CHAPTER 24

After a circuitous route that took him by the old buffalo wallow, Clayt rode into the ranch from the northeast. He had taken his time, stopping often to listen, traveling much the way he had as an outrider for Forrest in the war. Coming out of the trees at the creek he was surprised to see so many lamps burning in the windows of the buildings.

Of the hands clustered at the front steps of the main house, it was Nestor who spotted Clayt. The boy started running but stopped halfway across the yard. With fearful eyes he waited until Clayt was close enough to hear him whisper.

"He's been askin' for you, Clayt."

Clayt reined up and checked the somber faces on the porch. "Who has?"

Nestor's pained face collapsed into a deeper dread. "Mr. Aff didn' find you?"

The men on the porch stood quietly, yet a

373

restless tension ran through them. Clayt set his jaw for bad news. He used his foreman's voice to calm the boy.

"What's happened, Nestor?"

Nestor jammed his hands into his back pockets, looked down at his boots, and came up shaking his head. "It's Chalky, Clayt. Took a arrow through his lung." His face tightened like a twisted rag. "They're sayin' he ain't gonna make it, Clayt."

"Where is he?" Clayt said.

When Nestor pointed to the house, Clayt dismounted and handed his reins to the boy. "Would you see to my horse for me?" He climbed the steps, and the men parted for him in a slow shuffle, their heads lowered so that their hat brims covered their faces. Without knocking he opened the door and went inside.

Lou was in the hallway buttoning his coat, his face set hard, his eyes fixed on the wall. His hands stopped at the top button when he saw Clayt. Then he opened his mouth to speak, but he couldn't find the words. He just shook his head.

Clayt moved past him toward the low murmur of voices in the study and found Mrs. Afton, Cora, and Isabella huddled on the floor by the hearth. Chalky was stretched out on a pallet of blankets, a white bed sheet covering the lower half of his body. The firelight reflected off his dark face and shoulders in soft flashes. His eyes were closed, his face as peaceful as when he napped after a noon meal. Isabella rose up before Clayt.

"We've just lost him," she whispered.

The misery in the room funneled into Clayt like a wind out of the north. His legs moved forward of their own accord. The bandaging wrapped around Chalky's chest glistened wetly and seemed so alive with tiny arcs of reflected light that he thought these people somehow terribly mistaken. Cora dipped her hands into a porcelain basin and washed herself as she sobbed.

Leaning over the body, Mrs. Afton held her head at an angle so as to align her face with Chalky's. Her head shook in palsied increments of denial. Her eyes roved nervously across the room as though she needed to explain the sanguinary state of her study. When she saw Clayt, her face took on a bewildered expression.

"He wanted very much to see you," Isabella whispered and touched Clayt's arm.

Henry Walsh entered the room wearing a fresh white shirt. A lighted pipe was clamped in his teeth. When he caught sight of Clayt, he stopped, jutted his chin forward, and removed the pipe from his mouth.

"Where's John?" Walsh said. But Clayt did not answer.

Moving through a tunnel of silence, Clayt reached Chalky and knelt to the pinewood floor. He touched his fingertips to the strong, char-colored hand that had guided tools and horses so effortlessly. Chalky's flesh was still warm.

Walsh cleared his throat. "Isabella, where is your brother?"

Isabella sat down in Afton's chair, settling her head back on the cushion and closing her eyes. "Mr. Sullens has died, Henry," she said quietly. "I don't know where John is."

Walsh stood awkwardly for a moment and then moved to the front window, where he parted the drapes and took long draws from the pipe. Clayt looked at Mrs. Afton and waited for her to meet his eyes.

"I'll git some o' the boys, and we'll take care o' the body. I'll make a box for 'im. We can do the buryin' come tomorr'."

Only Cora seemed to hear Clayt. She helped Mrs. Afton up from the floor to sit on the hearth, where the dazed woman began rocking front to back.

"He's going to stay right here tonight," Cora announced through her tears.

"You got enough to clean up here as it

is," Clayt said. "I can tote 'im to the barn."

Cora swiped at her wet cheeks with the backs of her plump wrists. "You'll do nothing of the kind." When she began to sob, Clayt stood and stared down at Chalky.

"I want to know where John is," Walsh said from close behind Clayt.

Clayt turned and stared at the man's insistent eyes. "I ain't seen him since crossing paths with the wagon."

Walsh frowned. "He left us to find you and summon a doctor."

Clayt kept his voice flat. "He didn' find me. Must'a gone for the doc."

Walsh's eyebrows lowered. "Well, send someone out to find him." He pointed with the pipe at Chalky. "Now that the Negro is dead, we won't need a doctor."

Clayt's face was wooden. "Chalky," he said in a quiet, even voice.

"I beg your pardon?" Walsh said, frowning.

"Chalky Sullens," Clayt informed him. " 'The Negro.' "

Walsh's frown deepened, and his eyes glanced toward the corpse and back. "Yes, well —" He waved the pipe in the air. "Someone needs to find John."

Clayt walked past Walsh into the hallway, but before he had opened the door he heard

Walsh issue a harsh command in the study. Clayt hesitated, his hand on the knob.

"Take your hand off me, Henry!" Isabella said sharply. There was a swish of fabric that delivered her into the hallway. Then she was standing so close that Clayt could see the pulse in her neck.

"Isabella!" Walsh called from the study. "Come here!"

She put her hand on Clayt's and turned the knob. Keeping a grip on his hand she pulled him out behind her into the dark. The yard was vacant now. Clayt knew that Lou would have told the boys to get some sleep. That there was nothing to be done for Chalky. When Clayt left the door ajar, Isabella reached past him and closed it.

She cradled his hand in both of hers and looked down at it as if it were a wounded bird she had picked up from the grass. Clayt let his hand lie there, lifeless and needing. Her fingers ran across the tendons that ran to his knuckles, and he looked down at the caress. He had never felt such a perfect touch in all his life.

"Mr. Sullens wanted so badly to talk to you," she said. Seemingly composed, she lifted her chin, but then her hands flew to her face as she began to cry. Clayt's hand hovered between them as though she were still supporting it. Slowly, he lowered his arm to his side and simply stared down at the top of her head as she wept.

"He would'a wanted you to call 'im 'Chalky,' " Clayt said.

When her hands came away from her face, she tried to smile through her tears.

"Me and Chalk . . . we were . . ." Clayt looked toward the bunkhouse and shook his head. "I started to say like a father and his son. Only Chalk let it go past that to two men on equal footin'."

Clayt thought of a night almost a decade ago, when just the two of them sat by the wood heater while the other hands gathered at the main house and worked on a peach pie that Mrs. Aff had volunteered. He remembered Chalky's kind face, neither judging nor absolving but attentive as Clayt disclosed his part in the war. Chalky had listened to it all, never showing his repulsion, just allowing the past to be what it was.

"When I first come out here," he continued, "your brother's the one threw me a rope to pull me outta the hole I'd dug for myself . . . but it was Chalk who pulled me up. He dragged me outta a dark place." Clayt looked back toward the house. "One man never owed another so much as I owe him."

Isabella placed her hand on Clayt's coat and pressed firmly over his heart. "He loved you very much," she whispered. "He knew you loved him."

He watched his hand rise and go to her face to wipe the wetness from her cheek. She raised her face to his and spoke in a voice so quiet they might have been standing in the cavern again, listening to their words travel across the smooth surface of the blue-green pool of still water.

"When it looked as though you would not make it here in time to see him, Chalky looked at me and smiled and spoke your name. I don't know how he could do that . . . smile *or* talk. He was having such a difficult time breathing. Whenever he tried to talk, blood came up from his mouth, and he coughed terribly." A sad smile softened her face. "He wanted so badly to see you."

Clayt nodded and then looked off toward the paddock. "We had this agreement, him and me. Whoever went first — if the other'n could be around to hear it — we were to say what there was to see about leavin' this life and headin' into another'n." Clayt's head tilted back, and he studied the night sky. "When we was out under the stars on a night shift with the cattle — just him and me — we used to talk 'bout that . . . wonderin' where we might be bound after this life. Didn' neither of us know much 'bout a heaven or some such place, but still I reckon we held out some hope for it. We figured a man couldn' really be 'xpected to know 'bout such things, but if we could catch sight o' somethin' there at that last hold we had on this life, we promised to let the other'n know."

He cradled her face in both his hands — a movement as natural as blowing warmth into his fists on a cold morning. She reached up and took his hands in hers, her fingertips digging into his palms. Pulling his hands down she nestled the knot of their collective grip beneath her ribcage.

"He kept saying 'this is it . . . right here . . . this is it'," she whispered. "And 'chursh it.' I think he was trying to say 'church.' " Her eyes were sharply focused as she brought up the memory.

" 'Cherish,' " Clayt said. "He was sayin' 'cherish.' " Clayt began nodding. "He was tellin' you what he couldn't say to me." He looked at the connection of their hands and nodded. "He would know to say it to you instead. Chalk could always see right into me."

Across the yard the nearest bunkhouse door opened, and a dim rectangle of light bled out onto the rutted ground. Someone stepped out under the awning and stood head down as he checked his pockets. A lucifer flared illuminating Lou Breakenridge's face. Clayt slid his hands free and waited as Lou crossed the yard toward the house. When Lou saw them on the porch he stutter-stepped and took off his hat.

"Oh, hey," Lou said, smiling his apology. He looked at his hat in his hands. "Me and the boys was wond'rin' if there was anythin' needed doin'. Maybe help Miss Cora clean up?"

"We'll take care of that, Mr. Breakenridge," Isabella said. "Thank you."

Lou nodded, checked Clayt's face, nodded again, and then studied the front of the house as if it were his first time seeing it. "Chalk made that door, didn' he?"

"Ever'thin' *but* the door," Clayt said. "Mr. Aff shipped that in from England."

Lou took in the whole of the front of the house, drew on his cigarette, and flicked the ashes downwind. "The boys are wantin' to start out in the mornin' and track down Chatka," Lou said and lifted one eyebrow. "Gonna be hard sayin 'no' to that."

"That's the army's job," Clayt said.

Lou gave him a look. "Them shirkers cain't hardly find their way outta Sorahan's saloon after a night o' drinkin'."

"There'll be regular shifts tomorrow like always," Clayt said. "Ain't nobody runnin' off half-cocked up into the mountains to git shot up by Chatka or anybody else."

Lou sucked on the half-smoked cigarette, threw it into the yard, and nodded.

"You wanna ride out with me to find Mr. Aff?" Clayt said.

"Rascher rode out coupla hours ago. His idea . . . if you can believe that."

Clayt frowned. "Alone?"

Lou shrugged. "Yeah, he just lit out soon's the wagon come in without Mr. Aff. Whit said you were meetin' somebody at a windmill so we figured it had to be either Pender's or the one down at the Chimney Rock fork. Rascher rode to Pender's, so I sent Buck, Harry, and Whit down to the other'n."

Clayt nodded. "Who's with the herd?"

"Most o' Buck's crew. I sent out Waites, Stiles, and the Texan, Bud, to join 'em. I put Waites in charge o' that." Lou raked his upper teeth over his lower lip. "You reckon Chatka will make a run at the cattle?"

"Cain't never know that for sure. They'll more'n likely hole up for a while."

Lou nodded and continued to study the

front of Afton's house. "Least they could'a done was choose a white man to shoot. I never know'd Chalk to hurt a soul." When Clayt made no reply, Lou fitted his hat to his head. "Well," he said and made a move as though to leave.

"When will Waites come back in?" Clayt asked.

Breakenridge shrugged with a question on his face. "We'll go out and relieve 'em in the mornin'. He should be back at the bunkhouse b'fore the noon meal."

"I want you to send Johnny Waites into Ivinson's when he comes in. I need to make a box for Chalk."

Frowning, Lou propped his hands on his hips. "We got lumber in the loft."

"I need some six-penny nails. Better send his two friends 'long, too."

Lou's eyes narrowed. "Oughta be some nails in the mill shed."

Clayt let Lou see the authority in his face. "Send 'em in, Lou."

Lou looked down at the ground, his tongue running across the front of his teeth. "Three men," he said flatly and looked up at Clayt. "For nails."

"Six-penny," Clayt reminded. "Make sure they sign for 'em."

Lou carried his flat expression back to the

house, exhaled a long sigh, and nodded again. "Sure you don't need no help inside?"

"Cora says they'll keep Chalk inside the house tonight. We'll figure on buryin' 'im tomorr' late afternoon when the boys in our bunkhouse are in. I'll put Buck's crew on the cattle then. They didn' know Chalk as well as we did."

"You want some help with that box?"

Clayt turned and gazed at the woodwork on the front of the house — the doorjamb, the windows, the fine trim over the porch. All of it done by the hands that had taught Clayt everything he knew about a carpenter's tools.

"No, I'll take care o' it."

"Well," Lou said and adjusted his hat as though he were expecting a gust of wind. "Me and G.T. and Nestor'll be startin' the corral for the mustangs in the morning. We'll come in with the others for the buryin'." He pulled down on the brim of his hat and nodded to Isabella. "G'night, ma'am." Then he offered his hand to Clayt. They gripped with a strength that each knew reflected their common bond with Chalky. Then Lou crossed the yard and went into the bunkhouse. Now the yard seemed quiet without him.

"Life goes on, doesn't it?" Isabella said.

Clayt touched the smooth finish of the handrail at the steps. "Reckon it's got to."

She stepped beside him, and together they faced the yard. "You'll miss him," she whispered.

They listened to the quiet of the night. The wind had died, and there was not a sound of man or beast from any quarter of the compound or the grasslands beyond.

"When a man dies," Clayt said, "if there ain't nobody who really knew him, ever'thin' just keeps on like it is. 'Nother day comes along. 'Nother year." He paused, inhaled deeply, and let the air ease from his chest. "But if he leaves somebody behind . . . there's just this big hole in the world. Don't nothin' fill it. Maybe time blurs the edges . . . but don't nothin fill it."

She looked north up the valley, though there was nothing to see but darkness. "Maybe there is a place where we all meet again," she said.

Clayt turned to her. " 'Member that purple-blue color we saw? Just before dark? How it seemed to rise up right out o' the prairie?"

"Yes," she whispered. "I do."

"Chalky used to say that was the proof . . . that color . . . that we might already be in heaven here in this valley. He said weren't no reason for God to make that color rise up like that lest it was for a good reason. That color singles out this land. Chalk said it was why he knew to live out each day with nothin' but gratitude just for bein' here."

A silhouette passed behind the window curtain, and they could hear Cora putting away bottles into the medicine closet. When her footsteps faded to the back of the house, Isabella lifted her hand and rested it on Clayt's arm.

When her hand slid away from his sleeve, she wrapped her arms around her midsection. Still she remained standing so close he could feel her breath on his shoulder.

"I wasn't angry with you today. I'm sorry for riding off the way I did."

He shook his head. "You got as much right to ride out as anybody else. It's just that I got the job o' goin' with you."

She laughed quietly. "A thankless job. Now I've made trouble for you with John."

Clayt squared himself to her face to face. "You don't make trouble for me." The simple statement seemed to hang in the night air like the last note of a church bell.

"You stole my partin' line today, you know," he said holding a poker face. "If you're gonna use it, you gotta do better at gittin' it right."

"Your 'parting line'?"

He lifted his face to the sky. "I believe it went somethin' like . . . 'when I go, it will be of my own volition.' " He shook his head. "S'posed to be . . . 'I'll leave when it suits me . . . and it don't suit me yet.' "

She laughed outright. "We English have our rules, you know. Make everything sound more important than it is."

Afton's door opened, and the light from the hall lamp silhouetted Henry Walsh. He stood for a moment, unmoving. Then he took a heavy step onto the porch.

"Come inside, Isabella. You have no wrap." His voice was stern but sterner still when he addressed Clayt. "Have you sent someone after John?"

"It's took care of," Clayt replied.

Walsh cleared his throat. "Isabella, would you come inside? Please!"

She tightened her arms beneath her breasts and turned to face him. "Henry, a good man has died tonight. There are words that need to be spoken. Go sit with your son and help him to understand what has happened."

The quiet of the night seemed to gather on the porch as these three formed an uneasy triangle. After sniffing sharply through his nose, Walsh turned, went inside, and closed the door. They heard his heavy gait make the floorboards groan as he marched deeper into the house.

"I better git some sleep," Clayt said backing away.

"Clayton?" she said. "Was it you who made the easel?"

He looked down at the ground for a moment before answering. "Is it aw-right?"

She took a step toward him. "The place you bury Chalky. I would like to paint it."

"Chalk would like that." He tipped his hat and turned for the bunkhouse. He had covered half the distance and still had not heard her close the front door.

"It was indigo," she called to his back.

Clayt stopped and faced her again. "Pardon?"

"The color on the prairie this evening," she explained. "It was indigo. I thought you might like to know."

CHAPTER 25

Clayt lay on top of the old orange blanket, his legs crossed at the ankles and his hands clasped behind his head. Staring up at the darkness around the rafters of the bunk-house, he watched the faint light flicker from the woodstove, making the underside of the roof flash with soft shudders of yellow. Though worried, he would give the boys an hour or two to bring in Afton. Failing that, he would ride out again. But for now he pushed Afton and the Walshes from his mind. For now, he wanted to think only of Chalky.

When he heard horses, he lay very still and took the measure of the animal strides, painting their picture in his mind. In the image he saw three horses — ridden hard and winded — breaking from a gallop to a nervous walk out in the yard. When the horses moved past the bunkhouse toward the main house, Clayt rose up on one elbow.

Soon he heard someone banging on Afton's door. Clayt pulled on his trousers and slithered into his blouse. In seconds the sound of hooves came right up to the bunkhouse and stopped.

"You reckon that's Rascher and Mr. Aff?" Lou said from his bunk.

The door opened and Buck's gritty voice filled the room. "Clayt!"

When Lou lit a lamp on the long table, Clayt was standing in the center of the room in his stockinged feet, his Colt's pistol in his hand. "What's the matter?" Clayt said.

"Mr. Aff ain't come back, and he ain't in town. Where was it he was to find you?"

Clayt walked past Buck and looked out into the yard. A single light burned in a window of the house. Rascher sat his sweat-soaked horse, but Whit dismounted and strode toward the bunkhouse.

"Who'd you talk to at the house, Buck?"

"Cora," Buck said. "He ain't there, and his horse ain't back. Where was he goin'?"

Clayt nodded northeast. "That broke-down windmill out by the old Pender place."

"Hell, we rode by that goin' out and comin' back in. Didn' see nobody."

Clayt frowned. "Did you check those big rocks north o' the road?"

Whit stood in the doorway now. "That's

391

where I thought I smelt some smoke."

Buck spun and glared at him. "Well, why'n hell didn' you say somethin'?"

Whit scowled. "Hell, I ain't never know'd Mr. Aff to make a fire on his own."

Buck presented his "can-you-beat-that" look to Clayt and breathed through his nose like a bellows. Clayt gestured toward the main house.

"Buck, go back and tell Cora not to bother Mrs. Aff with this. Me and Nestor and Short'll go out and find 'im. Did you talk to the sheriff when you were in town?"

"Didn' figure we oughta. Didn' think Mr. Aff would'a wanted us to. Besides, we thought we might still run into him on the trip back."

Clayt nodded and checked the sky. "Git some sleep. Lou can go out with your crew at daybreak. You take the night shift again. We'll square up on that later."

"It's a damn circus out here," Short snorted, pointing at the tracks around the windmill. "They're blowed over with the wind some, but they're fresh." He extended his finger at another set of tracks. "That'n there's a little older. Same horse goin' 'round and 'round."

"Those're mine," Clayt said, dismounting. He knelt by the tracks that had cut across his own, the low rays of the morning sun marking them clearly with shadow. This horse had stood for a time by the windmill before moving off toward the boulders.

"This'n looks like Mr. Aff's horse," Clayt said. He picked up a small clod of dirt and shook it inside his loose fist. Tossing it aside, he stood. Leading Skitter, he walked to the boulders where he and Dunne had parleyed. When he did not reappear after a minute, Nestor and Short-Stuff followed.

They found Clayt standing in the grass, his back to them, one arm outstretched to connect to a boulder, his other hand holding his hat by his knee. He was facing east, but there was nothing to see out in the morning haze. Nestor reined up and started to speak, but something in the stillness of Clayt's body made him dismount. As soon as he walked around the corner of the boulder he saw the bodies.

"Oh, Sweet Lord in heaven," Nestor whispered.

John Afton's body slumped against the far wall, his chin pushed deep into his ascot, a dark stain of blood crusted into his blouse. Dunne lay sprawled across the cold ashes of his fire. His brown suit was singed black along one side.

Nestor started toward the bodies but

stopped when a buzzing cloud of flies lifted from Afton's lap, where blood had pooled. Nestor's hand slapped to his mouth.

"God A'mighty, Clayt?" he said through his fingers. When Clayt did not turn, Nestor looked back at Short, who still sat his horse and stared tight lipped into the cavity.

"God damnit to hell," Short-Stuff growled and dismounted. He stood before the garish sight and gritted his teeth. "God damnit to hell!" he said again.

With his head down, Clayt walked out into the prairie, covering the ground in ever-widening semicircles. He moved methodically until his sweep followed an arc a full forty yards from the boulders. There he stopped and looked a hundred yards off into the distance where another cluster of boulders sat isolated in the grass and scrub.

He gazed up into the sky. Three vultures glided high against the clouds in the north, their desultory drift seeming to coalesce into a purposeful pattern until they circled overhead like a lazy wheel turning on a well-greased axle. Clayt looked again at the distant boulders and turned toward Short and Nestor to appraise the line of sight connecting the two rock clusters. When he walked back to the bodies, his eyes were sharp and focused.

"Short, go back to the ranch and bring back the wagon. Send someb'dy out to the south pasture to let Lou know. He'll need to come in and see to things at the ranch. Let him be the one to tell Cora. I reckon it'll go better if Cora and Mrs. Walsh break it to Mrs. Afton. Nestor, you ride into town and tell the sheriff. He needs to see this hisself."

Making no move to leave, the two cowhands stared at Clayt. He was looking into the shelter of stone, nodding as though the scene before him was something he had expected all his life.

"What're *you* gonna do?" Nestor said, whispering as if he might awaken the dead.

Clayt fixed his gaze on a swale of dark grass to the north, where Afton's and Dunne's horses had wandered into view. They grazed in typical fashion, as though nothing unusual had happened, their saddles perched meaninglessly on their backs.

"I'll stay here and keep the buzzards and ki-yotes off 'em." He pointed north. "And I wanna walk out to those boulders and look 'round some."

By late afternoon they were gathered in Sheriff Abel Teague's office, spread out in a somber half circle before his desk. Henry

Walsh and Doc Buell claimed the only chairs. Short-Stuff, Nestor, Whit, and Clayt stood flanking them. Behind them all, Frank Maschinot, Teague's deputy, leaned against the wall with his arms folded.

Standing, the sheriff leaned over his desk, head down, his palms flat on either side of the coroner's report. He began shaking his head slowly. The wet strands of iron-gray hair covering his bald spot fell away one by one until the crown of his pale head shone like a featureless face caught in blank surprise.

"This is a helluva thing," he mumbled, "a helluva thing." His voice was thick, his demeanor tired and beaten, the way a man ought to sound after a day of hard physical labor. "And just a damn week before the pres'dent is due to come into town."

Teague heaved himself upright. The veins in his flaccid jowls made a tangle of blue and red threads, and the lower lids of his eyes sagged like a loose-skinned hound's. The imposing frame of his body still radiated strength, but the great cannonball swell of his stomach gave him a look of sedentary ballast and limited mobility. He raked his hand over his scalp and patted the streaks of hair. Then his eyes fixed on Clayt.

"So . . . Mr. Afton told you to meet with

this Wallace Dunne out there by the windmill. Well, what in hell was that about . . . meetin' like that after dark out there?"

Clayt had been thinking about this moment all morning. He would need to tell the sheriff everything about Dunne, but, now, with every eye in the room turned on him, he felt the need to preserve Dunne's secrets until he could talk to the sheriff alone.

"Reckon I'll need to talk to you in private 'bout that, Abel."

Walsh strained to turn in his chair to let Clayt see the glower on his face. "We're here to find out what everyone knows, Mr. Jane. As the owner of New Surrey Downs, I have a right to know everything. And, of course, so does the sheriff."

"He's right, Clayt," Abel Teague said. "Let's just get it all out on the table."

Clayt looked around the room at the curiosity pasted on each face. John Afton's death, it seemed to him, did not alter the loyalty Clayt had afforded the man.

"Dunne came to Mr. Afton 'bout some mineral rights. He talked 'bout locatin' coal on the Rollin' F. A meetin' was set up, but Mr. Afton couldn't go on account of his guests. So I went for him . . . representin' the Rollin' F."

Teague pursed his lips until his nose nestled into his thick moustache. He cocked his head and made a pained expression.

"So you went out alone. Well, why the hell did Afton go out there alone later? Why didn't he send someone else? Or take somebody with him?"

Clayt pretended to think about it. "Don' know."

Teague shook his head and frowned down at the report, but his eyes did not move across the page. His breathing made small whistling sounds in his nose.

"How long were you out there with Dunne?" the sheriff asked.

"Couldn'a been much more'n a quarter hour," Clayt said.

"Why the fire then?" Teague grilled.

Clayt shrugged. "Dunne had the fire goin' when I got there."

Henry Walsh slapped his hands to the knees of his dark trousers and sat forward. "Sheriff," he said formally, "it would seem to me that establishing a search of the countryside would serve much better than holding interviews inside an office."

Abel Teague nodded deeply, as though he had heard good advice. He walked around the desk and sat on its front edge.

"Mr. Walsh, the first thing is always to get

as much information as you can. That way you can maybe eliminate some possibilities. Then we don't waste time flyin' off half-cocked in the wrong direction." He gave Walsh a generous smile. "Now I understand how you could be anxious in all this. It's a helluva thing. Worse when it's kin. Your brother-in-law was a very important man here. We're gonna go about this the right way."

Walsh sat back, only marginally appeased. Every other man appeared mystified at such a speech coming from Sheriff Teague.

"Well," Walsh said, "shouldn't you be out there looking for some evidence?"

Abel Teague managed a diplomatic nod. "Mr. Walsh, you're a businessman. You know more about whatever it is you do than I ever will. I'm an officer of the law. I been doin' this a long time. Guess I'll keep on with it as long as the people vote me in." He lifted an arm and pointed west. "My man Mooney is out there right now at Pender's windmill. Mooney's my tracker, half-Shoshone and good at what he does. Could prob'ly track a fish through water. If there's something to be found, Mooney'll find it."

Throughout the lecture, Walsh had been stiff lipped. Now insult washed over him.

"You've got an Indian out there? Good

Lord, man, how do we know it was not a bloody Indian who killed John . . . the same one who killed the Negro."

"The horses were shod," Clayt explained. "And there weren't no pattern to it that would fit a Ind'an's ways. Whoever done it just sat out there and squeezed off shots. Nothin' got stole. And weren't no honor to it."

Walsh spewed air through his lips. "Are you trying to tell me that these Indians could not have been on horses with metal shoes? They are known to steal horses all the time, are they not?" The Englishman sat back heavily. "I don't understand you people." He swept his arm toward the window. "You have soldiers right here. A fort, for God's sake, just outside of town. And yet you allow these savages to run rampant all over the countryside. Killing people. Stealing cattle."

"It's a big country, Mr. Walsh," Teague said. "One o' the reasons we like it. It ain't crowded here. Not many outsiders comin' in."

The insult was not lost on Walsh. He forced a smile but kept his eyes hard.

"Yes, John liked it, too. And, outsider or not, look where it got him." Walsh's face flushed with a private realization, and he eyed the others in the room. "Is that it? That John was an Englishman, and this doesn't warrant an intensive investigation?"

"Now wait a damn minute," Teague growled and stabbed a finger in the air at Walsh. "John Afton was well respected, and we're gonna see to it that whoever murdered him and this Dunne fellow are gonna be accountable to the law." With all diplomacy abandoned, the sheriff straightened and tugged up on the waistband of his trousers. Glancing at Clayt, he made a show of composing himself. "Look here, Mr. Walsh," he said, his voice under control now, "Mr. Afton was as much Wyoming as any man here."

Teague reached to the desktop behind him, produced a mangled knot of metal no larger than the butt of a cigarette, and held it up between thumb and forefinger. "The doc took this outta Dunne's back. Looks like a piece of a rifle slug. It entered through the chest and lodged just under his skin in his back. That about right, Doc?"

Doc Buell donned spectacles and tilted back his head. "Yes, it shattered the spine and in the process broke into fragments. This piece is too misshapen to identify."

"What 'bout Mr. Afton?" Clayt said.

"Again, just one bullet," Buell reported.

"It passed through his heart and exited the body. The bullet has not been found."

The sheriff set the fragment aside and began shuffling through papers. "I got a few things need clearin' up," he said and studied a paper for several seconds before looking up at Whit. "What time did Afton leave the wagon party to look for Clayt?"

"Right at dark," Whit recalled. "Sun was almost an hour below the Medicine Bows."

The sheriff nodded. "All right, so Afton started off by himself for the old Pender place . . . say somewhere 'round eight o'clock." Teague looked from one cowboy to the other. "What time did you boys start a search for *him*?"

Whit spoke up again. "Me, Harry, and Buck went out. And Rascher. This would'a been a coupla hours after Mr. Aff rode off. We didn' find nothin'. Weren't all that sure 'bout which windmill to ride out to."

When the sheriff looked at Nestor, the boy widened his eyes and cleared his throat. "Then me and Clayt and Short rode out," Nestor added. "That would'a been a coupla hours b'fore daylight. We found 'em just after first light."

The sheriff twisted around to write on the paper, and then he turned to Clayt. "What time did you leave Dunne at the Pender windmill?"

Clayt brought up the memory of the night sky and the few stars he could see. "Say nine or ten o'clock . . . or thereabouts."

Teague's grizzly eyebrows rose to an inverted V. "Well, how is it the two o' you didn't meet up on the road . . . you and Mr. Afton?"

"I didn' take the road," Clayt said. "Dunne told me 'bout the Ind'an skirmish so I rode off in the brush and made a swing out to the north. Up by the old buffler waller."

"What I find odd," Henry Walsh said to no one in particular, "is all this secrecy. Why a clandestine meeting out by a windmill in the dark of night."

The room went quiet, the silence broken only by the sounds of boots on the boardwalk outside. Clayt kept his attention on his hat in his hands, but he knew the Englishman was studying him. In this awkward stall in the proceedings, the sheriff dropped the papers on his desk, walked back to his chair, and sat. A new silence filled the room as all eyes settled on Clayt.

"What about that, Clayt?" Teague said.

Clayt looked up. "I was followin' Mr. Aff's orders."

Teague looked from Whit to Nestor. "And

none of you ever heard any gunshots? Or saw anybody out on the road?"

"No," Clayt said. Nestor, Whit, and Short shook their heads in agreement.

Teague sighed. "Well . . . that should do it for now. When I get more information from my tracker, I might be asking you boys to help with a posse. Can you stay in town?"

"Abel?" Clayt began and took a step toward the desk. "If you and I —"

"Yes," Walsh interrupted, "they can stay in town. I'd like to have a private word with you, Sheriff." Before Teague could respond, Walsh stood and faced the Rolling F men, his eyes intent on the black leather gloves that he pulled on. "You men wait for me outside." Without waiting for a response he turned his back on them and strolled to the map of the county that was tacked to the wall.

The ranch hands followed Doc Buell out the door. On the street they loitered by the wagon and watched the town go about its business. Some passers-by nodded their condolences, but no one stopped to question them. Every Sorry-Damn cowboy wore a hangdog expression, as though each had privately endured a personal insult.

"I ain't so sure I wanna work for that stiff-necked, jack-leg nobility," Whit said.

Short-Stuff grunted. "Amen to that!"

Nestor leaned on the wagon and slapped his hat against his leg. "What'd he mean 'bout a secret meetin', Clayt?"

Clayt propped one boot on the rear wheel hub and rested an arm on the side wall of the wagon bed. He could feel every one of the Rolling F crew waiting for his answer.

"Mr. Aff held lotta meetin's. This is just one he asked me to handle. Look, we need to be thinkin' 'bout Mrs. Aff. She'll be needin' to depend on us just like Mr. Aff did. This ain't no time to draw your pay and cut out."

"Might *be* 'cut out,' like it or not," Whit said and gestured toward the sheriff's office. "Mr. High-Britches in there might show us the back gate o' the Rollin' F."

Down the sidewalk in front of Sorohan's, Tessa raised her hand and waved. Clayt could see she had been waiting for him to look her way. When he only nodded, she began walking toward him in slow, measured steps, her head down as though working out a problem, her arms wrapped around a ledger book pressed against her stomach. The boys straightened and watched her approach.

"I'm so sorry about Mr. Afton," she said quietly to the group. Singling out Clayt, she

405

lowered her voice to a whisper. "And your friend, the Negro."

"Chalky," Clayt said.

"Yes." The tenor of her voice on the sidewalk was no different from her whispers in the darkness of her bedroom. "Are you staying in town tonight?" she said looking at all of them, but each man knew the question was meant for Clayt.

"Looks like it," Clayt said.

"Come by for a drink," Tessa said and smiled. "On the house." And this time they knew she was speaking to all of them.

The door to the sheriff's office opened, and Henry Walsh emerged onto the boardwalk. Stopping at the edge of the planks, he looked both ways on the main street and checked his pocket watch as though he might be late for an appointment.

"I want you men back at the ranch as soon as the sheriff is through with you." Showing each man his face of authority, he ignored Tessa. "The men watching the herd will need relief."

The sheriff appeared in the doorway and pointed a finger at Nestor and then Whit. "Lemme see you two boys inside," he said in his no-nonsense voice.

The two cowboys pushed away from the wagon, and followed the sheriff into his office. The door closed softly and clicked shut.

"I'll be back in ten minutes," Henry Walsh announced to no one in particular and walked toward Ivinson's.

"Is that the brother-in-law?" Tessa asked, watching the Englishman's back.

"And our new boss, looks like," Short-Stuff volunteered.

The glass in the sheriff's door rattled again, and Frank Maschinot strode out of the office, closed the door, and leaned against the awning post. "Tessa," he said tipping his hat. Clamping an unlighted cigar in his teeth, the deputy idly gazed down the street.

Tessa touched Clayt with the edge of her book. "Don't forget that drink."

When she had walked from earshot, Maschinot stepped down heavily to the street to stand in front of Clayt. "What the hell's goin' on with you and this English feller?" When Clayt did not answer, Maschinot removed the cigar and looked at it as though its taste had gone bitter. He spat dryly into the street and quietly laughed to himself. "Well, I'm s'posed to come out here and keep a watch on you, if you can believe that."

"Me," Clayt said flatly, as if the word needed clarification.

"Sher'ff says I'm to stick with you like a tick on a dog's ear." He stuffed the cigar back into his pocket and scowled at the world. "You ask me, it's a damn bad business all 'round." Turning to face Clayt, his eyes lost all their skepticism. "Want you to know, Clayt, I'm right sorry 'bout Chalky. I know you two been partnered up a lotta years. Hate to lose a good man like that. Afton, too."

Clayt stared at the deputy. "What'd Walsh and the sheriff talk 'bout, Frank?"

Maschinot made a pained expression as he rubbed his hand across the rough whiskers on his face. "I ain't s'posed to pass on that kind o' information, Clayt. You know how it goes." He leaned in closer. "What happened with you and Afton? The two o' you lock horns on somethin'?"

Clayt kept his voice flat. "Is Abel thinkin' I'm libel to run off?"

Maschinot turned his worried look away, craning his neck as though searching for someone down the street. "Aw, you know Abel." Facing Clayt he tried for a smile. "I ain't never sure what he's thinkin'. Last coupla weeks he's been like somebody's old maid aunt . . . frettin' over all this hoo-haw 'bout the pres'dent." When Clayt started down the street, Frank's wan smile broke into blank surprise. "Hey, where're you goin'?"

Clayt angled across the thoroughfare toward Ivinson's, stepped up on the boardwalk, and passed through Ivinson's door in three strides. Stopping just inside he let his eyes adjust to the room. Sunlight speared diagonally from the high window above the rows of storage shelves. Dust motes drifted slowly through the beam like sand suspended in a pale-yellow stream. The smell of denim and canvas and tool oil mixed in the air, giving Clayt the pent up sensation that usually drove him back out to the street. Behind him, Maschinot was so close that Clayt could feel his labored breathing on his neck.

"Clayt?" the deputy said, trying to contain his problem inside a whisper.

Walsh was in the back of the room waiting for Ezra — the young black boy who worked for Ivinson — to climb up a ladder propped against the shelf with the hatboxes. Two of Tessa's girls chirped like songbirds as they fussed over bolts of cloth displayed on the wall to the right. And Tessa was there, reading the labels of medicinals. Ivinson was seated behind his counter, tightening the screw on a pair of scissors.

When he felt the crackling energy in his

chest coalesce into something purring and manageable, Clayt walked the length of the store, stopping an arm's length from Walsh. The Englishman pushed a wide-brimmed hat onto his head and leaned toward the wall mirror to inspect himself.

"You have somethin' to say 'bout me to the sher'ff?" Clayt challenged.

Walsh removed the hat and stood upright but kept his back to the foreman. His eyes met Clayt's in the mirror.

"I simply told the sheriff what I saw. I'm ruling out nothing in this investigation."

"Meanin'?"

Walsh raised his chin and sniffed. "It means a man who argues so vehemently with his employer ought to be given a close look in the event of that employer's death."

Frank Maschinot eased beside Clayt and looked from one man to another. "Now, gentlemen, let's don't have no trouble here."

Bolstered by the deputy's presence, Walsh turned and screwed up his face with disdain. "Furthermore, in my book, a man ingratiating himself to another man's wife is not to be trusted . . . by anyone." Walsh tapped his index finger to the front of Clayt's jacket. "You will stay away from her . . . and my boy, too . . . do you understand?"

The man's touch on Clayt's chest might

as well have been a rail spike driven into his breastbone. The skin on Clayt's back prickled as though a nest of spiders had spilled down his shirt collar. Maschinot raised his palms in a placating gesture.

"Clayt," the deputy suggested in a hoarse whisper, "why don' you an' me head back down to your wagon."

Clayt took a half step forward, his face now only inches from Walsh's. "How 'bout a man that beats his wife? Where does *he* fall in your book?"

Walsh's mouth twitched, and he flattened his hand against Clayt's chest. "You are forbidden to be with her. Do you understand that? And I will no longer need you as an employee. You can pick up your things at the ranch and vacate by the end of the day."

Clayt's face appeared carved out of oak. "You'll wanna take your hand off me."

Walsh's hand backed away as if he had touched a hot stove. Embarrassed, he stiffened his back.

"As I said, Mr. Jane," Walsh snapped. "Your services will no longer be needed."

"I reckon *Mrs.* Afton'll have somethin' to say 'bout that."

Walsh's face filled with vindication. "She'll have *nothing* to say about it. The business is in my hands." His chest expanded. "I am now the sole owner of New Surrey Downs, and you —" His arm came up again, the index finger extended toward Clayt's chest, but this time Clayt's left hand shot up and clamped on the man's wrist so quickly that the hat Walsh held in his other hand dropped to the floor. Walsh's eyes and teeth flashed white as he grimaced.

"Leave off, Clayt!" Maschinot yelled, his voice cracking as he tried to pry the two apart. "Do you hear me? Leave off!"

Walsh dipped one shoulder toward the floor, trying desperately to relieve the angle of discomfort, but Clayt held fast until Walsh sank to one knee. The Englishman's panicked eyes turned to the deputy.

"For God's sake, do something! Arrest him!"

Maschinot widened his stance and applied his weight, but Clayt's arm was stiff as angle iron. The deputy's boot slipped on the glossy floor, and he backed away taking a grip on his pistol.

"Goddamnit, Clayt! Leave off!"

The fear on Walsh's face rose up like a stench that fueled Clayt's anger. He squeezed tighter, wishing he could show this pleading face to Isabella to reveal the coward who lived at the core of a cruel man.

"Clayt!" Maschinot yelled and, getting no response, swung his pistol.

The need for violence had begun to roar in Clayt's ears like a locomotive, but now the sound coalesced into the ringing of a great bell, a single heavy note that trailed off into blackness. Into this dark, Clayt fell.

CHAPTER 26

"You still with us, son?"

Clayt stirred and strained to raise his head from a musty blanket rolled under his neck. The pain in his head sharpened, and he lowered himself by reflex. He lay on a cot hard up against a plank wall of rough-sawn pine. The pallet was tobacco-stained and reeking of bile and urine. Across the small room light filtered from a barred window and spoked shadows across the dirty floor.

"Didn' leave me much of a choice, Clayt. You're too damn strong for me, son." Frank Maschinot stood outside the cell door, grasping two bars in his fleshy fists. When Clayt was able to sit up, he propped his elbows on his knees and lowered his head into the cradle of his hands.

"Wasn't nothin' to do but crack that hard head of your'n." Frank was shaking his head, the loose skin on his jowly face swaying with the movement. So contrite was he that his voice took on a whining sound. He folded a soot-stained bandana, lifted a black kettle from the floor by its wire bail, and nodded toward the window. "Bring me that cup yonder, and lemme pour you some coffee."

Clayt stood slowly and gripped the bars of the door. "We're buryin' Chalk today, Frank. I need to head back to the ranch."

Embarrassed, Maschinot pushed his mouth to one side and gestured to the cup again. "Go on now and git the cup." He raised the kettle. "I brewed this up last night."

Clayt stared at the deputy for three heartbeats. Steady on his legs, he crossed the cell and retrieved the cup. When he held it through the bars, Frank filled it.

"Son, you might as well git straight on this right now," Frank said, his head weaving with apology. "You ain't goin' anywhere. Sher'ff's keepin' you here a while."

Clayt sat down, balancing the cup before him. The coffee was the color of scorched wood. A wisp of steam rose to his face, and the scent was a violation to his nostrils. He set the cup on the floor.

"How long?"

Maschinot shook his head and set the pot on the corridor table next to a lantern.

"Don't rightly know." He folded and un-folded the bandana twice before stuffing it into his back pocket. "Tessa's been down here to see you. I reckon 'bout three times."

With the window so high, all Clayt could see outside was the blue of the sky. Down the alley he heard the trundle of a wagon and the rattle of its traces.

"What time is it, Frank?"

"You been in here 'bout two hours. I was thinkin' I might have to pour some cold water on you, son." Maschinot checked his pocketwatch. "Why don't you just take 'er easy a few hours till the sher'ff comes in to talk to you."

Clayt looked around the cell. A dented chamber pot squatted in the shadow of the back corner. Prisoners from the past had scratched letters into the wall below the window, but they held no meaning for him. Leaning forward he spotted his hat under the cot. Someone had groomed the center crease, but he could see the mark near the top of the crown where the gun had crashed down on his head. The cellblock was as still as an empty church. He could only see the vacant cell directly across from him, but by the dead quiet around him he guessed the others to be empty.

"I need to git out o' here, Frank. Let me

talk to Abel."

Maschinot breathed in airily through his teeth, as though he had taken in a mouthful of sizzling meat just off the flame. Pushing a rolled blanket through the bars, he waited for Clayt to take it.

"You know the sher'ff 'bout as well as I do, son. He'll see you when he's ready." Maschinot shrugged. "Looked to me like he ain't gonna be ready for a while."

"Is Walsh pressin' charges?"

"Ain't 'bout Walsh. Abel's holdin' you for questionin' . . . 'bout Mr. Afton." Frank looked quickly at Clayt, watching for a reaction. When he saw none, the deputy wrinkled his brow. "I never know'd the two o' you to cross words b'fore." Frank shrugged. " 'Course I never figured on crackin' your skull with my shooter neither." He hung his head and shook it from side to side. "Hope you don' hold it ag'in me." He turned to leave. "You take 'er easy, son. Like ever'thin' does, this'll pass."

"Frank?"

"Yeah," the deputy said, stopping at the door.

"Do me a favor?"

"If I can."

Clayt looked at him through the bars. "Can you quit callin' me 'son'?"

417

■ ■ ■ ■

Clayt was lying on the cot in the dusky cell when Abel Teague made his entrance into the corridor of the cellblock. He took his time walking down the hall, his chin resting on his chest, causing the flesh of his neck to billow. A toothpick angled from his clamped mouth upward through his moustache. Digging into his vest pocket, he produced a lucifer, struck it on the lock housing, and carried the flame to the lantern on the table outside the bars.

"Gits kind o' cold back here at night," he said. "You need another blanket?"

Clayt sat up on the cot and shook his head. A plate of food sat untouched on the floor. Nudging the meal aside with his boot, he watched Teague pull a chair in front of the cell and straddle it backwards with his arms crossed over the backrest. The sheriff's stomach swelled out and tested the slats of the chair.

"Tell you what we got here," the sheriff began, as though he were addressing the city fathers at a council meeting. "We got a foreman that's worked for a man more'n ten years, and all of a sudden he's done blowed up with his boss twice inside the

418

same day."

Clayt started to speak but Teague raised a cautionary finger. "Seems this foreman rode out alone at night for some kind of secret meetin' with a feller from back East . . . feller lookin' to mine for coal on the boss's land. So the boss rides off to this meetin', more or less unannounced, and along with the mining man gits hisself shot dead. Foreman shows up back at the ranch and don't appear to know nothin' 'bout it."

The sheriff removed his toothpick and studied it. "So this foreman goes back out to the scene with two o' his crew. They find the bodies of these two men, and the foreman sends these boys off on errands while he hangs around the murder scene."

Teague had been talking with his head cocked to one side. He paused and rolled his head to the other shoulder.

"That might give him a chance to look around in the daylight for anything he might not want found, now wouldn' it?" Teague stared at his prisoner with a curt smile. He flicked the toothpick to the floor. "Your Henry rifle's been fired recent."

"Weren't my Henry that kilt Mr. Afton," Clayt said. "Did your man check for sign out amongst those boulders to the north? 'Bout a hun'ert'n forty yards out?"

Teague frowned at the distance. "Mooney didn' find no other tracks at that meetin' spot but your'n." The sheriff nodded toward Clayt's boots. "Your left heel has got a little notch tore out one side." Teague's eyebrows floated up with this news. "Mooney come in an' checked your boots while you was sleepin' off your headache."

Clayt gave him a hard look. "Somebody could'a laid up in them rocks and then left the place lookin' natural."

Teague let his eyes relax with blatant skepticism. "Well, who the hell else knew 'bout this meetin' so they'd know to wait out there? And who the hell's gonna be shootin' from that far out? In the dark? With considerable wind? Who would do that?"

Clayt stood and leaned into the bars. "It takes a different kind o' bullet to travel that kind o' distance. I walked out there to them far boulders. Didn' find no ejected shells or nothin' like that . . . but didn' 'xpect to neither. I could see where a man might'a set up lyin' on his belly. But grass won't hold a track for long. 'Specially with all that wind."

Teague made a show of patience by smiling and lowering his eyes to the floor. "Well," he hummed. Then he looked squarely into Clayt's eyes and all amenities

420

were cast away. "I don't reckon a track like that's gonna be much help to us then, is it?"

They kept their eyes locked on one another, neither man blinking. "It might go better on you," the sheriff said, "if you'd just tell me the whole thing. 'Bout Mrs. Walsh."

Clayt's eyes turned cold as glass. "She ain't got nothin' to do with this."

Teague widened his smile. "Then what was it to do with, if it weren't her?"

"You've knowed me all this time, Abel, and you're willin' to listen to Walsh like his word is gospel."

"He's your employer, ain't he?"

"That don't make him anythin' more'n a man," Clayt replied. "Maybe you oughta know a little more 'bout *him* and how he treats his wife."

Teague sighed, braced himself on the backrest of the chair, and heaved himself up. "Maybe I know better'n to pry into a man's private life with his wife." He lifted the chair and swung it back to the wall. He gestured with a hand toward the corridor door. "Lou Breakenridge is out there. He's been waitin' to talk to you. I'm gonna let 'im in now, but Frank's comin' in, too. I'm gonna give you five minutes." Teague tugged

421

his trousers higher on the bulge of his stomach and tucked in his shirt. "You decide you wanna talk some more, I'll be back here in a coupla hours."

When Lou came through the door, he walked quietly over the rough plank boards, his hat pressed to his stomach. He peered first into the dark cell on his right before seeing Clayt on his left. He stopped at the cell door and looked around at Clayt's living quarters.

"You aw-right, pard?"

Clayt nodded. Maschinot shuffled in behind Lou and moved down the hall to the lantern. He bent low to adjust the wick, his movements awkward and directionless.

"What 'bout your head? You hurt bad?"

When Clayt said nothing, Lou carried a frown to Maschinot. The deputy lowered his eyes and studied his boots.

"Did you boys bury Chalk today?" Clayt asked quietly.

Lou nodded. "Figured we should go ahead with it." He looked around the dirty cell again, at the slop bucket. "I took care o' Skitter. She's down at the West End Livery. Nestor brushed 'er down and fed and watered 'er."

Clayt nodded. " 'Preciate that." He leaned on the bars. "Tell me 'bout the burial."

Breakenridge stared down at the floor, his face sober with the recollection. "It was 'bout what Chalk would'a wanted, I reckon. Grady spoke over the grave. Seemed like the right words to me."

"Mrs. Aff git out to it?"

Lou winced and hitched his head. "She ain't farin' too good. We ain't seen her since . . . well, since b'fore things went to hell." Lou looked away and swallowed. When he turned back to Clayt, his face compressed with a pained expression. "Clayt, what the hell's goin on . . . you bein' in jail and all?"

"It's Walsh. He's got the sher'ff's ear. Maybe even bought it. He's talkin' 'bout me an' Mr. Aff buttin' heads and tryin' to tie that in with the shootin's."

Lou's face filled with wrinkles. "They're thinkin' you done the shootin'?"

"Ain't nobody said it that straight, but I figure that's the way people could see it."

Lou's lips pulled back, baring his teeth. "That don't make no sense a'tall."

"Lou, where'd Buck hook up with Rascher that night?"

Lou frowned and chewed on the inside of his cheek for the time it took him to remember. "Buck said Rascher caught up to *him*. Said Rascher'd followed some tracks headin'

423

north thinkin' it was Mr. Aff. Rascher rode all the way up to the Shin Bone. He caught up with Buck, Whit, and Harry where the creek crosses the road."

"There ain't no windmill up around the flats," Clayt said. "Didn' Rascher know to go lookin' 'round one o' the windmills?"

"That's all anybody *did* know," Lou said. "Just didn' know which windmill."

Clayt gripped the bars. "I need you to do me a favor, Lou."

When Lou sidled closer, Frank Maschinot circled around until he could see the faces of both men.

"Tomorr', when you got some good light, go out to where Mr. Aff was found and see can you find a spent bullet . . . or a piece o' one."

"I'll ride out at first light," Lou said, eagerly grabbing at a tangible thing to do. He waited for more instructions, but Maschinot cleared his throat and checked his watch, a signal that visiting time was over. "Well," Lou said, "ain't there anything else I can do?"

"How is Isabella handling what's happened . . . 'bout her brother, I mean?"

"She's stayin' close to Mrs. Aff. Her and Cora. She come out to the burial — her and the boy — but I didn' really talk to her."

Lou shifted his weight and turned his hat in his hand. "They'll be buryin' Mr. Aff to-morr', late afternoon in the town cemetery." Lou's words — quiet as they were — hung heavily in the stillness of the cellblock. Beyond the window, the sounds from town drifted to them hollow and meaningless.

"Frank," Clayt said turning to the deputy, "I 'xpect to go to that funeral."

Maschinot slid his hands into his pockets and frowned. "I reckon you do, Clayt. But you gotta talk to the sher'ff 'bout that. You know I ain't got no say in it."

"Lou, you better bring me a clean shirt. I'll see can Frank git me a razor."

"Hell, yeah," Frank said, his face serious now. "I'll bring you my own damn razor to use." He nodded toward the front office. "I can heat you some water, and we got a mirror we can hang on your wall." Frank cleared his throat. "I reckon it's 'bout time we end this confab. What you say, Lou? I was off duty half a hour ago."

Lou gave Clayt a wan smile, raised his hat to his waist and fanned the air. "Aw-right, pard. You take 'er easy now."

"Lou," Clayt said, stopping both men. "Tell Mrs. Aff I'm sorry 'bout Mr. Aff. Tell her I'll see her tomorr'." Clayt moved along the bars, and Breakenridge waited because he could see there was more that Clayt wanted to say. "Can you tell Isabella, too? Tell her —" Clayt frowned, not sure how to go on.

Lou fitted his hat to his head. "I'll tell 'em both."

When the door closed shut, Clayt walked back to the high window, stood on the rusted chamber pot, and gripped the bars. Pulling up to the cool fresh air, he inhaled deeply. He could not see beyond the backs of the buildings that lined the alley, but by the light from the sky he knew that the prairie would be burning with color now.

Indigo.

He liked the word. Liked the way it fell off his tongue. Liked it that the word was connected to Isabella. That soft bluish flame seemed as transitory and unpredictable as the fragile terms of life itself. He lowered himself to the bucket and listened as the evening sounds of saloons took their claim on the night. He was still perched there when the door scraped open and the night-duty jailor came in unrolling Clayt's old orange blanket, examining it. With the wool unfurled, he crossed his arms to inspect both sides and then folded it into a smaller square.

"You ain't thinkin' on squeezin' outta

there, are you, Clayt?"

Clayt stepped down from the bucket. "Thinkin on it and doin' it ain't the same."

The deputy pushed the blanket through the bars and dropped it on the cot. "Took it off your rig at the stable. Figured you wouldn' care. Sher'ff said you might need it."

" 'Preciate it," Clayt said.

The jailor nodded toward the plate of cold food on the floor. "You'll have to miss more meals than that'n before you can fit between them bars. You want me to take that away or do you figure on eatin' somethin'?"

Clayt picked up the untouched meal and slid the plate through the gap at the bottom of the door. "Tell Abel, when he gits in I need to talk with him."

At midmorning, carrying a cup in one hand and the black coffee pot in the other, Sheriff Abel Teague kicked the door shut behind him as he entered the cellblock. In his white shirt and red ascot folded into a lopsided triangle, he looked more like a banker than a lawman. His hair was slicked down as if it had been painted on his scalp.

"How 'bout some fresh coffee?" He set his cup on the table. "Pass me your cup."

Clayt extended his cup through the bars

and waited as the sheriff poured for him. Taking it in both hands, Clayt sat on the bunk.

"I hear you wanna have a little talk," Teague said, his voice light, friendly.

Clayt sipped off the top of the cup, and the warmth spread through him in a welcome wave. "I'll be wantin' to go to the burial today, Abel."

Teague cocked his head with a gambler's smile. "We can talk about that." He leveled his eyes on Clayt. "We got anything else to talk about first?"

Clayt cradled his fingers around the smooth curves of the cup and watched the steam rise from his coffee. "You made any contact with Dunne's people back East?"

Teague sipped coffee and watched his prisoner over his cup. "I did."

Clayt looked up. "And?"

Teague raised his eyebrows. "Body will be on the noon train headed to Illinois."

"Who was it you sent off the telegram to?"

"U.S. marshal in Chicago. Just got the reply this morning."

"Chicago ain't in Pennsylvania," Clayt said.

Teague sat back in his chair and cocked his head to one side. "Meanin'?"

"Dunne weren't no Pennsylvania minin'

man, Abel," Clayt said in a low tone. "He was a Pinkerton detective."

Clayt waited for a reaction, but the sheriff's expression did not change.

Teague finally grinned. "And how'd you come by that piece o' information?"

"Dunne told me and Mr. Afton. It's why I ain't been free to talk. He was here lookin' for a man who's gonna try an' assass'nate the pres'dent."

Teague looked down into his coffee. "So, this Pinkerton man, as you say, comes into Laramie, skips right over the county sheriff, and opens up his plans to a rancher and his foreman. That about it?" Teague looked up with a specious smile.

"Dunne didn't know who to trust, Abel, except Mr. Aff, on account of the people in Washington that know 'im. There's been some letters sent . . . threats. Somebody aims to kill Gen'r'l Grant when he comes into Alb'ny County."

Teague pretended a look of concern, but the light in his eyes fairly danced with amusement. "Let's see if I got all this. Somebody writes a letter sayin' he's gonna assassinate the president, so they send *one* man out here. And rather than hook up with the law, he runs out to Afton's and spills his guts." The sheriff huffed a laugh. "Way I hear it, you and this Dunne feller been struttin' 'round each other with your feathers up ever since he come into town. Now he's lyin' in a box on the loadin' dock at the depot."

"Who's payin' for the train ticket, Abel? Are Pinkertons footin' the bill?"

Teague sipped coffee again, taking his time. "Dunne paid up at the hotel two weeks in advance. I used that and purchased the ticket myself."

"Will you at least wire the Pinkertons? An' ask 'em 'bout Dunne?"

Teague shook his head. "Even if *you* believe ever'thing you told me was true, you ever think maybe you got slickered by this Dunne? A man lookin' to dig for ore on another man's property can come up with a heap o' reasons why it oughta git done."

"He weren't here for minin', Abel. He didn' care nothin' 'bout that."

"Then why the hell didn' he come to me?" whined the sheriff, his jowly jaw trying to knot. "I'm the law here, ain't I?"

"I cain't say why, Abel. I reckon he had to be careful."

The sheriff sucked on a tooth and let his skepticism show. "So he chooses you and Afton over the law. That about it?" He threw back the rest of his coffee and rose to leave.

430

"What 'bout the burial, Abel? I need to be there."

Teague tilted his head to one side and squinted as though he had heard unexpected news. "You're in jail, son. For murder. You better git that into your head."

"Mr. Afton was like a father to me. There ain't nothin' I wouldn'a done for 'im."

The sheriff had started to leave, but now he stopped and leaned one arm against the wall. "Wonder what Afton thought about you and his sister, Clayt?"

When Clayt offered no reply, the sheriff backed away and closed the door.

CHAPTER 27

A church bell tolled from the east side of town and rolled across Laramie like a soulful prayer. Clayt walked to the window and looked up into a clear azure sky. He could imagine Elizabeth Afton's face, hidden inside folds of dark lace, carrying a misery whose far-reaching implications she was not equipped to handle. Cora would be with her, a strong grip under her arm. And Isabella.

He could picture the boys in their attempts to dress proper, and he imagined their discomfiture inside the hushed maw of the church . . . and, at the same time, their absolute need to be there. Clayt figured most of the town would attend the service.

He had seen no one since his talk with the sheriff, except for Frank Maschinot, when the deputy had escorted him to the outhouse for the morning ritual of emptying the chamber pot. Twice Clayt had heard

Tessa's voice through the closed door to the office, but they had not let her in. Another time he thought he recognized Lou's quiet drawl. When Clayt asked about visitors, Maschinot shrugged and would not meet Clayt's eyes.

The day dragged on. He lost track of time. In the late afternoon a light clink of metal rang out at the window, and several small stones showered down on the plank floor. Clayt stood on the bucket and pulled himself high enough to see Lou squinting up at him from the alley. He wore clean trousers, a dark coat that he rarely brought out, and a white shirt buttoned up to the lump in his throat. His boots were polished to a high sheen. His hat was the only thing that looked normal.

"Clayt!" Lou called up in a raspy whisper. "I didn' find anythin' at the windmill! I looked ever'where!"

Clayt exhaled the breath he had been holding. "They 'bout got me nailed up in a box for this, Lou. I need to find one o' them bullets. I'm satisfied somebody shot Mr. Aff from them boulders standin' 'bout a hun'ert'n forty yards north up the valley."

Breakenridge stared up into the window, his teeth pulling at his lower lip. "That's a damn long way for a shot on a windy night,

433

ain't it?"

Clayt pulled his face closer to the bars. "Listen to me! Dunne weren't what he said he was. He was a Pinkerton."

Lou frowned. "He weren't a minin' man?" He turned his bewildered expression down the alleyway and then looked back at Clayt. "You tell that to the sheriff?"

"Abel don' wanna hear it."

"How the hell'd *you* find out?"

"Dunne told me an' Mr. Aff. We were helpin' 'im. It's 'bout the pres'dent."

Lou thought about that for a time. "Hey!" he said, looking up. "So maybe this is 'bout *him* . . . Dunne, I mean. Might be Mr. Aff was just with the wrong company." Lou took off his hat and swatted it against his leg. "Well, hell, that ain't gonna look any too damn good for you. Ever'body thinks you and Dunne was like flint and steel." He took a step closer, his face set hard with purpose. "Just tell me what you want me to do."

"All I know to do is go back out there and find a piece o' that lead. Least it might prove it didn' come out o' my Henry."

Breakenridge shook his head. "Hell, Clayt. There's a damn poor chance of finding somethin' like that." He pulled his hat down on his head. "But I'll go out and look

434

again." Lou held up an index finger as he backed away. "Wait a minute. Don't go no-where."

"Wasn't plannin' on it," Clayt muttered to himself.

In a few seconds Isabella came hurrying up the alley, holding the front of her dress out of the dirt. Her dark-blue outfit was complicated and stiff and rustled like paper. Her hat was made of the same blue mate-rial. Her hair was done up the way he had first seen her at the train depot. She stopped below his window, her eyes full of regret.

Holding himself up by the window bars, he tried to smile. "Mrs. Aff doin' okay?"

She shook her head as if a bee were wor-rying her. "She doesn't know what to do. Neither do I."

"She knows I didn' do what they're sayin', don't she?"

Isabella nodded. "Cora and I won't let her think that way." She stepped closer. "Clayt? What is going to happen?"

He wanted to show her more hope than he felt, but he couldn't see the sense in ly-ing to her. "They're trying to put my name on this. Might do it, too, 'less I can come up with a reason they cain't."

When tears formed in her eyes, she low-ered her head until her chin dug into the ruffles of her dress. "We should never have come here," she whispered.

"Well, that ain't right," he said, giving the words what lightness he could muster. "Weren't much chance o' me comin' over to England."

When she smiled, it was like a gift delivered to his door. He couldn't have wished for a better boost to his morale. Then as quickly as it had come, the gift was gone.

"This never would have happened if I had not ridden out from the ranch."

"It ain't no good to waller in it, Isabella. We got to think straight." He strained to see her face. "Is he hittin' you? 'Cause if he is, you tell Cora to let G.T. know 'bout it. The boys won't stand for it."

"He's thinking of staying on. To run the ranch, he says. But he only wants to give things the appearance of running well. Then he'll sell New Surrey Downs. I know him."

"Sell it?" Clayt said, his voice rising above a whisper. "What 'bout Mrs. Aff?"

"Elizabeth is talking about returning to Surrey." Isabella rubbed at the tears streaking down her face. "What's going to happen, Clayt? The sheriff is telling people that you'll stand trial for the murders."

"I reckon that's on account o' the pres'dent. Ain't gonna look good to have him comin' into town with a killer out loose in the territory."

"It's not right," she said. "Henry could convince the sheriff you didn't do this. I'll have a talk with him tonight."

"No! Ain't nothin' good will come o' that. That'd just make me worry 'bout you."

Tears ran freely down her face now, and she swiped roughly at her cheeks. "All of this because of something he imagines. He doesn't know anything about us. We haven't done anything to be ashamed of."

"You ain't. But I cain't argue what he's thinkin' 'bout me."

The startled look on her face gave way to an earnest plea that was close to anger. "Clayt, that's nonsense. You are more a gentleman than any of that class of pompous Englishmen who claim the title for themselves."

"Isabella, he's a fool to hit you like he does, but I cain't fault him for what he's feelin'. No man likes bein' on the losin' end o' things."

"Oh, Clayt," she whispered, "he had already lost me back in Surrey." When he made no reply, her eyes took on a pleading look. "Clayt, we've done nothing wrong."

"It don't matter what we done or ain't done," he interrupted. "It's what we know."

Her tears flowed freely again. "I'm so sorry for all of this, Clayt."

"Not all of it, I hope," he said, and, for the second time since arriving at his window, she smiled.

Lou appeared from the mouth of the alley and signaled to her. Isabella took a step closer to the building and stared up at Clayt through her tears. Her smile relaxed, giving her face that same earnest expression she had worn on the bluff when overlooking the Laramie Plain.

"Not all of it," she said.

CHAPTER 28

Two days went by, and he saw no one but the two deputies on their respective shifts. Clayt got out into the fresh air only for the morning walk to the privy. Each time, he emptied the chamber pot and flushed it with a bucket of water. Then he washed his face and hands at an outdoor basin and returned to his cell, the stench waiting for him there hardly better than the fumes of the outhouse.

Whenever Clayt asked about a lawyer, Frank Maschinot promised to take it up with the sheriff, but when Teague at last visited the cellblock he asked only one question: "You ready to tell me about it?"

Clayt ignored the question and issued his demands for counsel. Teague simply turned on his heel and left, shutting the door quietly behind him.

On the next morning when the corridor door opened, Maschinot carried in a tray of food and a slatted chair. He set down the meal before the door and slid it into the cell with the toe of his boot. Then he positioned the chair to face Clayt's cell and swung the other chair from the table next to it.

"You need to eat somethin', Clayt. That there is some good stew. I had some myself. That Chinaman's wife over by the depot made it."

Clayt watched Frank arrange the chairs just so. "What's goin' on, Frank?"

Frank would not look at him. "Sher'ff's comin' to talk. Got a feller with 'im."

As soon as Frank had walked out, Sheriff Teague came into the hall with a wiry man dressed in a tweed businessman's suit. "This here is Mr. Hester, a business partner to Mr. Dunne," Abel announced. "He's got some questions, and I want you to cooperate."

The man named Hester lowered himself into a chair and smiled, but there was loathing in his eyes. "Mr. Jane," he began, putting some punch into it as though he were calling off a name from a roster. "I'm with Pennsylvania Consolidated. I understand you and Wallace Dunne did not see eye to eye on some matters."

The sheriff sat and stroked the strands of hair on his balding head. Clayt looked from

440

one man to the other and settled his gaze on the new visitor.

"You tell 'im who you really are, Mr. Hester?"

Hester sat unperturbed, as though prepared for anything Clayt might throw at him. "Just as I'll tell you," he said formally. "Payton Hester with Pennsylvania Consolidated."

"No," Clayt said. "If you're with Wallace Dunne, I reckon you're a Pinkerton."

Hester was a rock. In the silence, the sheriff's mouth puckered to an amused grin.

"What'd I tell you?" Teague said in a tired voice.

Hester kept his eyes on Clayt. "You're here for killing an associate of mine."

Clayt held the man's stare and shook his head. "I was helpin' 'im."

Hester lifted his chin. "Your employer . . . Mr. Afton . . . I know he was contacted by Mr. Dunne." He tilted his head like a man sighting down a rifle barrel. "There was no mention of you."

"Mr. Hester," Clayt pressed, "you need to tell the sheriff what this is all about. Your friend Dunne came to trust me. So just tell the sheriff who you are."

Teague leveled a finger at Clayt. "We'll tell you who needs to say what to who, Mr.

441

Rebel Spy. I know all about you ridin' with Nathan Bedford Forrest in the war."

Clayt gripped the bars. "I know why you're here, Mr. Hester. It's 'bout the pres'dent. Dunne told 'bout the letters. He was tryin to match handwritin' and habits o' speech to find his man. Mr. Afton and I was helpin' him. An' Ivinson had to be in on it."

Hester allowed a minimal smile. "Mr. Dunne told *you* all this?" His eyes were sharp and mocking. "May I conclude from your accent that you are from the South?"

"Georgia," Clayt said. "And, yes, I fought under Forrest. Spied for 'im, too. Dunne knew all this 'bout me and still knew to trust me."

"Indeed," Hester purred. "And look where that trust got him."

Sheriff Teague shifted his weight in his chair and frowned. "I checked with Ivinson. Says he knows nothin' 'bout all this, 'xcept Dunne warned 'im to start requiring signatures for purchases on credit. Said a merchant back East lost a bundle o' money when a customer refused to pay for charges that bore no signature by his employees."

When Clayt made no response, Teague leaned to one side and dug into the side pocket of his coat. When he brought out his

442

closed fist the black beads of his eyes fixed on Clayt with the sly vindication of a prosecutor.

"My deputy, Mooney, went back out there to look around at the Pender place . . . case there was somethin' to that cockeyed story of yours. While he was up there in them far off boulders, who come 'long but Lou Breakenridge. He saw Lou pick this up."

Teague opened his hand and revealed a spent cartridge casing. The yellow metal gleamed like it had just come out of the box.

"Forty-four caliber," the sheriff said, feigning surprise. "Looks like it'd slip right into that Henry of your'n, don't it?"

Clayt stared at the hollow casing. "I awready searched that place. Someb'dy went back out there and dropped that." He turned back to Hester. "You're dead wrong to think the president's safe on account o' me bein' in here."

Hester sat forward and allowed the composure of his face to be replaced by disgust. "*If* that were my job, Mr. Jane." He made a tight smile. "I'm a mining man," he said and started to rise.

"I can prove what I'm sayin'," Clayt said and waited for Hester to settle back into his chair. "Dunne told me what he was lookin' for." Clayt prayed a silent apology to Johnny

443

Waites and spaced his words carefully. "If you follow my way o' sayin' it."

Hester's brow lowered over his eyes as the recognition of the phrase sank in. "You just hanged yourself, Mr. Jane." He stood and stared at the prisoner through the bars. Turning to Teague he threw out a sharp order. "I want you to remember the words he just used, Sheriff. Memorize them!"

Clayt frowned as he realized what had happened. "Now, wait a minute, that —"

"Shut up!" Hester shrieked. "I don't need to hear another word from you!"

Clayt turned to Teague. "Abel, I'm only tellin' you what Dunne —"

"The man said to shut up!" Teague shouted. "For once do as you're damned told."

Clayt didn't sleep. The music from the saloons tinkled in the distance, and the clop of horses' hooves passed infrequently past the mouth of the alley. The cool of the night brought some relief from the stench of the cell but forced Clayt to wrap up in the old woolen blanket. Staring up at the dark ceiling, he was resigned to wait out the night.

Something tapped sharply on the floor, bounced toward the barred door, and rolled to a halt. Sitting up, he listened until

444

someone hissed his name outside the window. He crossed the floor in his stockinged feet and hoisted himself up to the sill.

"Clayt! It's Nestor!"

It was so dark in the alley that Clayt could barely make out the boy's silhouette.

"Things ain't right at the ranch," Nestor reported. "I ain't sure what to do." He wiped his mouth with the back of his hand. "Are you aw-right, Clayt?"

"Tell me 'bout the Rollin' F."

Nestor glanced toward the street and quietly cleared his throat. "Mrs. Walsh . . . she rode off the other day . . . by herself. Didn' none o' us know till it was too late. A few of us rode out, but it took us half the day. Hell, cain't none o' us track like you and Chalk. She was ridin' back and met us after dark out on the trail out to Chalky's grave."

"She aw-right?"

"She was then. Once we got her back, ain't none of us seen her again. The boy neither. Grady says he can hear her cryin' from the house sometimes." Nestor waited for Clayt to say something, but then he himself broke the silence. "Walsh's got me and Lou down in the south pastures. Mrs. Aff is stayin' here in town in the hotel." He paused again. "Whatta you want me to do, Clayt?"

Clayt could not think straight. Holding himself to the barred window his muscles were burning. Someone yelled from the street, and Nestor started backing away.

"Clayt?" Nestor added, "Tessa said to tell you she's wired a lawyer in Cheyenne. I got to go."

Clayt pulled his face to the window bars. "Nestor!" he called in a whisper, but the boy had broken into a run toward the back of the boot shop. Within seconds Frank Maschinot appeared in the alley, and Clayt lowered himself back into the dark of the room.

Working quickly he whipped the dirty mattress off the bunk, tore the ticking, and grabbed a handful of cotton stuffing. This he crammed into the chamber pot. Kneeling to the untouched tray of food, he spooned the stew into the bucket, filling it to the brim.

Just as he threw the mattress back on the bunk and lay down, the cellblock door opened. Holding a lighted lantern, Frank Maschinot looked through the bars at Clayt stretched out under his orange blanket.

"You awake?" the deputy said. "Who was that outside your window just now?"

"I'm sick," Clayt rasped. "Need to git to the outhouse."

"Cain't do it, Clayt. I'm just now comin' on duty, and there's half a dozen things I gotta do first. You got to use the slop bucket back there in the corner."

"It's full," Clayt said. "I been sick for hours."

Frank lifted the lantern high and rose up on his toes to inspect the pot. With a groan, Clayt sat up and began pulling on a boot.

"I gotta git out there, Frank, or I'm gonna empty my gut all over this cell. Open up, will you?" He slipped into the other boot and lowered his face into his hands.

"I ain't s'posed to do that, Clayt."

Clayt looked up quickly and saw that his jailor wore no gun. "You want me to soil the floor, Frank? I reckon you'll be the one havin' to clean it up."

The deputy winced. "Damn it to hell, Clayt. I gotta have someb'dy else here to —"

Clayt clutched his hand to his stomach. "It's comin' on again, Frank!"

Maschinot set the lantern on the table, dug the key from his pocket, but hesitated at the door. "Hell, let me just bring you another pot," he said and closed his fist around the key.

447

Clayt leaned against the bars. "Frank, that ain't even the right key you got there."

Frank frowned, opened his hand, and stared down at the key. It lay on the flat of his palm, its small loop of brown cord tangled beneath it. Clayt's right hand shot down from the bar, his fingertips punching into the deputy's palm, surrounding the key like a cage. Grabbing the key, he used his other hand to snatch a handful of the deputy's shirtfront and jerk him into the door. Frank's head rang on the bars.

"Goddamnit, Clayt! What the hell're you doin'?"

Clayt worked the key blindly and pushed the door open. When he pulled the deputy into the cell, Frank hit the wall and raised his hands defensively before his face.

"I don't mean to hurt you none, Frank, but I cain't stay in here no more." He frowned into the deputy's cringing face. "What the hell am I gonna do with you?"

"Well, damnit, you ain't gotta kill me, do you?"

Clayt took him by the upper arm and led him to the cot, where the deputy sat heavily. "I ain't kilt nobody, Frank. Not since the war."

Like a child fearful of his punishment, Frank looked up at him with pleading eyes.

"Well, I'd like to think you ain't gonna start now."

"I'm gonna need this," Clayt said and took his orange blanket. Rolling it under an arm, he gave Maschinot a nod. "Can you give me your word you won't yell out, Frank?"

Maschinot took on a pained expression. "Hell, you know I cain't promise that. I reckon you better give me a rap on the head. I cain't be losin' my damn job."

"You can tell Abel that I had a gun . . . that you didn' have no choice."

Frank nodded, but he didn't look happy about it. "I reckon you better hit me."

Clayt lifted Frank's chin with his fingertips and considered the scrape on his forehead and cheek where he'd hit the bars. The skin was torn above his eye and blood had beaded in the thicket of his eyebrow. The flesh around his eye had started to swell.

"I reckon that'll pass for a knockout blow. Cain't you be quiet for me a coupla hours? It's early yet. Maybe you could get some sleep."

"Damn it all," Frank hissed and shook his head. He leaned his forearms on his knees and let his head sag from the shoulders. "Yeah, I reckon I can be quiet." He looked around. "I don't know as I can sleep though. This cell is rank, ain't it?"

449

Clayt emptied his shirt pocket of tobacco and rolling paper and dropped them on the bed. "There you go. That might help some. You got lucifers?"

Maschinot waved at the air with his hand. "Yeah, I got some." He probed his forehead with his hand and checked his fingertips for blood. "I reckon I can give you a hour before I start to yellin'." His face filled with regret. "Me an' Abel an' Mooney . . . we'll prob'ly be comin' at you with a posse, Clayt. I'd hate to see it come to that."

Clayt nodded once. "We all gotta do what we gotta do, Frank."

Maschinot took in a deep breath and expelled it. "I reckon we do."

"Where're my guns?"

Maschinot looked toward the office. "In there . . . in the case. It's unlocked."

Clayt stepped out of the cell and closed the door. "I'll need to lock you in, Frank."

Maschinot lay back on the bunk and sighed. "Hell, I know it."

By the light of the lantern he found his Colt's and Henry rifle in the front room. After wrapping both weapons in the blanket, he snuffed out the lantern, walked back into the cellblock, and leaned in to check on Frank Maschinot. The deputy was stretched out on the cot, snoring.

Clayt slipped out the front door to find the street empty. Still, he sidled along the boardwalk and dodged into the dark alleyway to make his way to the West End Stables.

CHAPTER 29

He rode hard, relishing the taste of the cool night air and the clean smells of the prairie. Skitter was spirited and frisky, snorting with throws of her head as though she had been craving such a run. They traveled as they always had, joined as a single mind, deciding together when to slow and when to settle into the rhythm of a lope or an easy gallop.

When he reached the ranch, there was not a light to be seen in any building. He went straight to the barn, rubbed Skitter down in a stall, and threw a scoop of sweet grain into the feed trough. In the paddock he slipped a hackamore over the surefooted skewbald and led it to an adjacent stall.

"You two girls are gonna be seein' a lot o' each other from now on," he said and doled out more grain for the sure-footed mare he had chosen as his packhorse. He half-filled a burlap sack with more grain and stacked it next to his saddle, rifle, and bedroll. Then he carried another sack, his canteen, and saddlebags to the bunkhouse.

By the faint orange glow escaping from the door of the wood heater, he saw that every bed in the main room was empty. Stopping to listen, he heard Swampy snoring in the back. Clayt collected a few personal belongings, boxes of ammunition, and the winter coat with sheepskin lining that Afton had given him when he had made foreman.

A Dutch oven sat atop the cook stove — its contents keeping warm for the night crew when they came in. Standing by the stove, Clayt ate his fill in the dark, dipping the ladle and eating from it like a beggar stealing his last supper. At the larder he packed coffee, sugar, flour, salt, cornmeal, a jar of rendered fat, a bottle of syrup, a slab of salt pork, five cans of beans, and two of peaches. He filled his canteen from the pitcher pump and carved a section of lye soap, which he wrapped in paper. Swampy continued to snore.

When both horses were outfitted, he walked to the back of the main house and listened. Above him the stars dusted the great arch of the sky. There was not yet even a blush of light in the east. The tranquility of the night surrounded him, as he felt every familiar habit of ranch life leaving him, like pieces of the spirit prematurely rising from a dying body. After trying the locked door, he stepped back and kicked it in, splintering the jamb and cracking two panes of glass. He walked through the kitchen and down the dark hallway like a man pacing off a measured distance across open land. Turning at the newel post, he climbed the stairs and stood looking at four closed doors.

"Walsh!" he called out, loud enough to be heard in any of the rooms.

The first door to his left *clicked,* and Tom's silhouette showed in the crack. The door opened wider, and Isabella appeared behind the boy, a lighted candle flickering in the room behind them. Her questioning eyes darted to the door across the hall.

Clayt's eyes never left her face. He stepped toward her and turned her cheek with his fingertips. Even in the dim light, he could make out the marks on her face. The door across the hall opened, and Walsh's voice came tentatively from the dark.

"Isabella? What is it?"

Walsh wore a shiny robe that threw off tiny sparks of light from the lamp he held. When he saw Clayt, his face froze in shock. Setting the lamp on a small table, he moved

into the hall bringing up one of Afton's
fowling pieces — a double-barrel sixteen-
gauge with fancy scrollwork carved into the
stocks.

"What are you doing here!" Walsh demanded. "How did you get out of jail?"

Clayt spoke to Isabella. "Take Tom inside
and close your door."

She pulled Tom to her but remained
standing. "Clayt, what are you going to do?"

Clayt took the knob, nodding to her as he
closed the door on mother and son.

"You don't work here now," barked Walsh.
"You should not be in this house."

"Prob'ly b'long in it more'n you," Clayt
said and held up his hand to quiet the man.
"I don' care to hear what your pieces o'
paper say. I'm here to tell you somethin'."

Walsh gripped the shotgun with both
hands, his fingers opening and closing on
the weapon. "Say it and get out!" Walsh
yelled. "Don't think I won't shoot you."

"I don't rule out nothin' with you. A
coward's likely to do anythin'."

Walsh's nostrils flared. "I have the right to
protect my —"

Clayt held up his hand again. "I'll be the
one talkin' this time . . . and you'll be the
one listenin'." Clayt jerked his head toward
the bedroom behind him. "You won't be

hittin' her no more. Ever. This is the last warnin' I'm givin'. Lay your hand to her just one more time, and I'll come back here, and I will kill you." Clayt's voice was ice.

Walsh snorted. "Is this your solution to everything? Just killing everyone?"

"This ain't up for negotiation," Clayt explained. "I ain't gonna deal with you like you was a reasonable man. You ain't earned that."

"Who the bloody hell do you think you are!" He waved the shotgun barrel in an arc through the air. "All this is mine. And I *have* earned it. You don't know the first thing about building an empire with investments and —"

"That ain't what we're talkin' 'bout here," Clayt interrupted. "I'm talkin' 'bout the proper respect to a woman. Before I leave here, I'm gonna hear you make an oath. You're gonna swear not to lay a hand to her. You're gonna swear it to God Hisself."

"You can't lecture me about things where you have no business! I won't stand for it!" Walsh lifted his thumb and crooked it over the spur of one of the shotgun's hammers.

Clayt's hand dropped to the butt of his Colt's. "Try an' cock that hammer, and I'll make good on that promise right now. I don't care how fast you think you can pull off a round with that birdshot. You're gonna die right here."

Walsh pointed the barrel of the gun at Clayt's chest, lowered his brow over his panicked eyes, and screamed, "Get out of my house!"

"When I'm ready," Clayt said. He reached up slowly, wrapped his fingers around the barrels of the shotgun, and took it from Walsh as easily as sliding it out of a loose scabbard. Walsh straightened and glowered, standing impotently now in his shining robe. "Make your oath," Clayt hissed. "I'm waitin'."

"Go to bloody hell!" Walsh shrieked, flecks of saliva popping from his mouth like fat from a hot skillet.

Clayt propped the shotgun next to the table and lamp, turned, and quick as the snap of a whip drove his fist into the man's eye. Walsh's head jerked back, and his arms flailed for some imagined support behind him. He fell back into his room and crashed heavily to the floor. Clayt followed into the room, bent forward, and pulled the man up by the lapels of his robe.

"I'm waitin," Clayt said into Walsh's face.

Walsh made a two-rail fence of his forearms in front of his face. When he saw that Clayt was not winding back for another blow, he gingerly touched his trembling eye.

"What if a man was trying to steal *your* wife?" Walsh whined.

Clayt allowed the thinnest of smiles. "Reckon I'd try an' love 'er more," he said. Then he replaced the smile with a hard glare. "Now say it!"

Clayt watched a vein in the Englishman's throat pulse six times. Then he hit the man again. Walsh crumpled to the floor and moaned, both hands cupped around his nose.

When Clayt reached for Walsh again, the Englishman broke. "I won't hit her," he croaked, covering his face. "Before God, I swear it."

Clayt turned to the shuffle of feet behind him. Tom stood in the doorway, his face pale as a bedsheet, his eyes reflecting the lamplight like bright coins.

"What are you doing to Father?" he cried.

Behind the boy, Isabella's battered face winced. "Oh . . . Clayt . . . no."

Clayt spoke to both of them but kept his eyes on Isabella. "This here's the best I can do. I cain't be here to watch out for the two o' you. I'm gonna be livin' outta my saddlebags for a while . . . up in the mountains." He turned his head to include Walsh, who had pushed himself up to sit cross-legged on the floor. "I'll be in touch with the boys here," Clayt explained. "If I find out he's broke his word —" Clayt completed the ultimatum with the hardness of his eyes.

Clayt knelt to the boy. Tom's mouth quivered, and his eyes shone wetly.

"Maybe one day you can understand this, Tom, what I done here tonight. It was for you as much as for your mother. You'll be a man soon enough and take care o' things on your own. Right now, you need a lil' help, an' I'm the one bound to provide it."

He pivoted back to Walsh, who raised his arms again like a shield. "Say it again, Walsh. I want them to hear it."

Walsh could only afford his family an oblique glance. Lowering his bleeding nose into his hands again, he spoke with a hollow sound.

"I won't strike you again! I swear it before God!" He let his head sag lower until his hands covered his face. "I'm sorry," he said, and his shoulders began to shake.

Tears poured from Isabella's eyes as she hugged the boy to her.

Clayt stood and softened his voice. "I know this ain't your way, beating words from a man. But, bein' on the run like I am, it's the only way I know how to handle this."

Though he knew he had disappointed her, Clayt felt a weight lifted off his shoulders. In this moment he knew she could see all that he was. Nothing was hidden. Every dark fold of his fabric had been stretched flat and laid bare to the light.

"I know who you are, Clayton Jane," she whispered. "I do."

"I won't be seein' you two for a while," Clayt said. He laid his hand on Tom's head, and the boy tensed and pressed harder against his mother. Clayt knelt and gently squeezed both of Tom's shoulders. "You take good care of your mother, Tom."

With his face pushed into his mother's robe, the boy nodded. When Clayt stood, the boy swung around and heaved himself forward, wrapping his arms around Clayt's hips, pressing a cheek hard into his coat and sobbing in spasms that telegraphed through Clayt like a tender memory lost from his past.

"Thank you," Clayt said quietly to Isabella, "for ever'thin' you taught me."

When her eyes tightened with a question, he disengaged himself from the boy, turned, and walked down the stairs and out of the house.

As he crossed the yard for the barn, he forced his mind to inventory the practical items he would need in the mountains. The axe in the mill shed would serve him well for firewood and for building a shelter. And rope. Lots of it for lashing together the roof poles. And a fry pan for rabbits and grouse, and such.

Inside the mill shed he struck a lucifer and touched it to the wick of the oil lamp. When the flame settled, a confined square of subtle colors at the center of the room surprised him. Propped on the easel was a piece of canvas stretched over a crude frame and nailed in place. There were bone-yellows and olive greens and smoky grays, nothing too bright. Every part of the composition was muted and bound to the whole of the painting by a lack of any brilliant hue. But weaving through it all was that lambent blue-violet of the prairie. The tinted air that lifted off the land at twilight. In the painting the indigo stratum infused the grasses like a mist hovering over the earth. He stepped closer and made out landmarks familiar to his eye. A lone oak bent like a thick elbow. A massive rock face shaped like the crown of a hat, all of it bathed in the shadow of mountains. Jutting from a patch of bare earth was an upright stone etched with carved markings.

Clayt touched the wrinkled apron of the

canvas and recognized it as a piece of old tarpaulin they had used to cover a supply wagon. On the workbench to his right was a motley array of jars, their contents ranging from pale yellow to ocher and jade. On the cold wood heater sat a dented pot, its interior residue cracked like a dried-up mud hole.

Looking back at the painting again, he shook his head in awe of the artist's talent. He did not understand how such a picture could be created from nothing at all on a dirty piece of canvas. How could she capture that elusive twilight by using a brush and paint?

"Indigo," he said, wanting to hear the sound of the word.

Hearing horses near the gate, he blew out the lamp, picked up the axe and three coils of rope, and walked to the barn. There he led the skewbald into the yard and tethered her to the corral fence. Nestor and Johnny Waites materialized out of the dark, holding their horses to a walk as they approached. Neither man spoke. When they reined up at the barn, Clayt acknowledged both men with a single nod, lashed the axe and rope to the packhorse, and then walked inside to the stalls.

Nestor turned a puzzled face to Johnny,

but Waites only studied the packhorse loaded for travel. Nestor dismounted and followed Clayt into the barn.

"So you're out o' jail?" he asked.

Clayt tightened the cinch on Skitter and checked the lashings on his bedroll. "Out o' jail but not out o' trouble. The sheriff will be lookin' for me." He led his horse outside.

"Ever'thing aw-right, amigo?" Waites said, still sitting his horse.

"Seems like there ain't nothin' right at the moment," Clayt said. "I got to disappear up in the mountains for a while." Clayt mounted Skitter and took up the lead rope of the packhorse. "I won't be seein' you boys for a while."

Johnny squinted an eye and grinned. " 'Less you think you'll need some help."

A light showed in the front window of the Afton house. The front door opened, and Henry Walsh came marching down the steps in trousers pulled up under a billowing sleeping gown. His bare feet were pale as snow. His awkward gait would have been comical were it not for the shotgun braced against his shoulder.

He was a garish sight with blood smeared across his cheeks and one eye swollen shut. Stopping ten yards away, he bared his teeth and breathed hoarsely, his gun fixed on

Clayt. He cocked both hammers of the gun, the sound sharp and ominous in the yard.

"Mr. Walsh!" Nestor said and took a tentative step toward the man. "What're you doin?" Johnny Waites coaxed his horse away from the line of fire.

"Move aside!" Walsh shrieked. "That man is a fugitive. He tried to kill me."

The horses shied at the high-pitched grate of his voice. Skitter stamped a hoof at the ground and stiffened her ears.

"Take out your weapons and help me hold him here!" Walsh commanded.

Nestor's hand moved reflexively to his pistol butt, but he did not grip it. Johnny Waites pushed his hat back on his head.

"Mr. Walsh," Waites said, "we cain't be pullin' no gun on Clayt."

"You work for me!" Walsh shouted.

Johnny shook his head. "No, sir, I don't. Not if it means throwin' down on Clayt."

Clayt laid over the reins, but Skitter balked, pawed the earth with a front hoof, and snorted. Walsh craned his head toward Nestor.

"Pull your gun, boy! That's an order!"

Nestor raised empty hands and shook his head. "Cain't, Mr. Walsh." Nestor turned to Clayt as if Walsh were not there. "That cartridge Lou found . . . he says it weren't there that first time he looked. He's sure o' that."

"Henry!" a high-pitched female voice yelled from the front porch. Every man turned to see Isabella Walsh running across the yard in her bare feet and nightgown.

Her appearance seemed to throw Mr. Walsh into a panic. "Damn you!" he spat at Clayt and stepped forward. "You are a nobody, a common laborer!" Stumbling on a wheel rut, he had almost recovered his balance when Isabella grabbed his arm. In pulling away from her, he reeled, and the shotgun muzzle stabbed into the ground and discharged, throwing up a shower of dirt that rattled a sandy report against the dry boards of the barn. The horses swirled into motion, Skitter rearing and flailing her front hooves at the air.

A second shotgun blast illuminated the dapple-gray's chest, and Walsh stood splay-legged blinking over the barrels, fear and surprise widening his one good eye. Isabella stared at Clayt, her hands pressed over her mouth. Clayt, still holding the lead rope for the packhorse, swayed in the saddle, almost falling. Skitter made a high, wrenching sound and wheeled on her rear legs. When she bolted for the gate, Clayt hunched low over the horse's withers and held tightly to the packhorse rope.

"Goddamn," Johnny breathed, "you done shot Clayt!"

Isabella ran down the road after Clayt. Halfway to the gate she stopped to listen, her arms hovering out from her sides like broken wings. There was just enough light to see the shape of horses and rider meld with the dark scrim of trees by the creek.

"Clayt!" she yelled. But her voice was like the cry of a tiny bird lost in the vastness of the prairie. The rhythm of the two horses' hooves clattered from far down the road, and then the sound faded into a vague and distant pulse, more felt than heard.

Johnny spun his big blue roan around and held it in check, stutter-stepping before Walsh. "I'm goin' after him. Goddamn you, I think you hit his horse, too."

Walsh thrust out his chin and, one-handedly, began tucking his nightgown into the waistband of his finely tailored pants. "No. Your job is here. To protect us. He is a fugitive." He pointed toward the creek. "That man burst into our house and attacked me."

Johnny winced as though he had met with a foul odor. "It ain't up for argument," he said plain enough. "I'm goin'."

Walsh stepped forward, his back as stiff as

a fence post. "No!"

Johnny spat off to one side and glared at Walsh. "You gonna shoot me, too?" He dug his spurs into the roan's flanks, and the horse plunged into a quick start, fairly leaping into a gallop from a standstill.

CHAPTER 30

Beyond the creek, Clayt turned north, away
from the pink nimbus of light rising behind
the Laramies. He followed the trail toward
Looking Glass, as Skitter huffed plumes of
steam and thrust her head with each stretch
of her stride. The skewbald followed behind,
obedient to Clayt's tug on the lead rope.
Together they ran, and to Clayt it seemed
that all his future was now behind him.

A mile north of the ranch, when the first
rays of sun streamed through the valley and
touched his shoulder, Clayt reined up and
examined the welts burning on his left leg.
The trouser leg was dark with blood and
pasted wetly to his skin. Seven holes were
torn into the material, making an arc along
the thigh up to his hip. Gritting his teeth,
he dismounted from the right side and
limped to a tangle of brush. There he tossed
the lead rope of the packhorse into the
branches and turned back to Skitter. Her

neck, chest, and legs glistened with red, as though she had been slathered with fresh paint.

"Damn, girl," he breathed, watching her life blood seep from the small holes scattered across her. He pulled off his bandana, wadded it into a compress, and pressed hard against the wettest wound. Skitter's head hooked over Clayt's shoulder, and she blew out a long breath.

"It's aw-right, now," he said, stroking her cheek. "I'll take care o' you, girl."

When Johnny crested the rise, Clayt was sitting in the road, lashing a strip of orange blanket to his leg. Around the dapple-gray's neck was a similar bandage tied into a thick knot before the pommel.

"You hit bad?" Johnny said, dismounting.

"I think my horse took the worst of it."

Johnny whistled a sliding note when he saw the blood soaking through the bandage on Clayt's leg. "You need to git that lead dug out before it can fester."

Clayt shook his head. "I cain't be goin' into town," he replied. "Help me up on my horse, would you?"

Johnny turned, squinting at the rise and fall of the land around them. "Where's your packhorse?"

When Clayt struggled to stand, Johnny

gripped him under the arm and got him to his feet. "I reckon she's run off," Clayt said.

"Damn, Clayt, you cain't just ride out o' here carryin' lead in your leg."

"I reckon I can," he said and stood on his own.

"Well, hell," Johnny protested, "your horse is shot up. You want mine?"

Clayt shook his head. "Just gimme a hand up."

When Johnny boosted him up, Clayt set his face hard against the pain.

"I'll bring Doc Buell out here," Johnny said. "You tell us where to meet you."

Clayt frowned and shook his head. "He won't come."

"He'll come. I ain't gonna ask 'im. Just bring 'im." Johnny waved at a fly that was worrying Clayt's thigh. "Listen, Clayt, you gotta take this serious. If you don't git that scattershot cut out o' you, it ain't gone matter 'bout your packhorse runnin' off with your supplies, if you follow my way o' sayin it."

Clayt looked west toward the Snowy Range. "I'll find the packhorse. I'm gonna try and git myself up to the salt lick. If you can git the doc, bring 'im there."

Johnny let go the bridle and stepped back. "I'll git 'im."

470

Clayt leaned forward and pressed his hand to the bandage on his leg. The sting of the pellets spread into a deep inclusive pain of inflamed tissue and bruised muscle. Maybe bone, too. The swelling tightened the area, making it feel as though an iron bar had been hammered into his upper leg, wedged alongside the bone.

After tracking a half mile he found the packhorse and began the trek to the mountains at a walk, keeping his weight off the left stirrup. When they reached the lake, he was slumped forward in the saddle, his hat brim brushing Skitter's mane, only his grip on the pommel keeping him up. He wondered how much blood a man could lose and still be alive. His left foot was sodden with blood inside the boot.

When he reached the spring at the sycamore, he let the horses drink as he kept an eye on the trail behind him. He did not dismount for fear he could not regain the saddle. His thoughts veered off on strange tangents. Looking at the sun, he tried to remember if it was rising or sinking and knew then — without any true sense of loss — that he had surrendered his grasp on time and direction.

The day was warming, but his teeth clicked together as a shiver rippled up his spine. His lungs fought against the illogical cold, his breathing coming in broken surges between spasms in his chest. He buttoned his coat up to his chin and looked up at the cliff. As he angled his head back, a curtain of black ink spilled behind his eyes. His body went light, and the strength in his arms slipped away. His falling from the saddle seemed so slow that at first he believed himself somehow suspended above the earth. Like a hawk facing into the wind, hovering, stopping the world.

The dream teased him, drifting in and out of his mind in broken parcels. There seemed no end to it, a chain of scenes eddying through his head in cycles. Horses. A herd of them. Horses of every color running wild over open grassland. Throughout this flicker of images, the earth released its indigo blue, purling around the animals' hooves like dust kicked up from a painted land. The air was cold and penetrating.

He was on foot amongst these horses, keeping up, catching glimpses of the dapple-gray that led the herd. His leg burned with each stride, a heat stolen from every other part of his body, leaving ice at the core of him. Even as he trembled, sweat beaded on his brow. He could smell his own heat swirling around him like smoke.

Convulsing in a violent shiver, he heard himself cry out, but his voice was lost in the boundless arch of the sky. The sound of the hooves was all wrong, but he did not question it. It seemed more a language, relaxed and wholly unbefitting the thunderous race across the prairie. As many different voices as there were horses. One voice spoke so close to his ear that it startled him, and he tried lifting his heavy eyelids.

The dream disassembled, and above him the blur of light went dark as someone leaned over him and pressed a cool hand to his brow. The touch quenched something in him, like branch water to a parched throat, and yet he was still burning.

His eyes could not focus more than to see a woman, the skin on her hollow-cheeked face deeply lined — skin the color of smoke-cured leather. Her hair made him think of spider webs. She spoke in such an offhand way that he looked to see what other person might be there. Her voice crackled like boot soles walking across broken glass.

Hands slipped behind the curve of his skull and raised his head until his lips found a wooden bowl. A warm, meaty aroma steamed up into his face, and he felt his mouth moisten to the salt scent of it. He tried to drink greedily, but she allowed him only sips. When the bowl was empty, she pulled a blanket to his chin.

"Where am I?" he said, surprised at the hoarseness in his voice.

She remained there, hovering over him on her knees, humming softly. She touched his neck and cheeks with the backs of her fingers. Her hand felt like the dry talons of a bird. Cold, scaly, and withered.

"Eesh-tee-mah," he heard her say, her voice a nurturing whisper. She repeated the phrase and gently swept her hand downward across his eyes, keeping the hand in place to let him know to sleep . . . or, perhaps, die. With the warm broth settling in his stomach, he dropped again beneath that swirling surface of consciousness and began to scour the broad horizons of his dream for that herd. He wanted to see again the dapple-gray out front who ran like the wind.

He awoke in dim light. Whether dawn or dusk, he did not know. Rising up on an elbow, he lifted away the orange blanket and inspected his leg. The throbbing limb appeared to be less a leg than something borrowed from a tree. The trouser material was cut away and the thigh sheathed in leaves that molded to the curve of his leg, all of it held in place by the loose twining of braided rootlets — spruce by the smell of them. Beneath him was a cushion of pelts. His inverted boots were propped up on two stakes driven into the earth next to a small fire. Suspended by a crude tripod set up near the fire was what looked like the dried stomach of an animal, tied off at the bottom and open at the top. Hanging next to it was a bright tin can — about the right size for peaches. The can had been helved by a carved stick to form a crude ladle.

Above the fire a shelf of rock extended like an eave. There the smoke billowed momentarily before streaming away into the trees. Inside the large cavity of the rock he saw his saddle, his hat hooked on the pommel. Missing were his Henry rifle and scabbard and his cartridge belt with the Colt's.

The sun was low in the spruces, and he knew it to be the waning light of day's end, which put him on the west face of this mountain. Beneath the sloped branches were shaded patches of snow pooled around the tree trunks. Looking down the side of the mountain he recognized nothing in the landscape, but through the evergreens he saw movement. Someone approached.

The white-haired woman climbed the hill toward him, and now he could see the habiliments of her culture. Her shapeless dress was yellow-brown and supple with the soft nap of kneaded deerskin. It fitted her emaciated body like a blanket thrown over a coatrack. Her moccasins flashed brightly with colorful patterns stitched into the leather — porcupine quills dyed white, red, and black. Behind her walked a lean man with graying black hair that draped over each shoulder. He climbed the trail like a cat, his legs cushioning each step with such poise that his body appeared to float up the hill.

The woman peered down at Clayt as she circled him, her inspection empirical and appraising, the way a rancher might assess livestock at an auction. She dipped the can into the cooking bladder and poured the contents into the wooden bowl.

The man stood at Clayt's feet and said nothing. He was older than the outline of his body had suggested, his face as seamed and weathered as cracked rawhide. Tendons stretched beneath the skin on his chest and arms like taut fence wire. A shy grin pulled his lips back to reveal three crooked teeth. His eyes were dark and intelligent, ageless and alert, missing nothing.

"Sheeh-nah-zhee-shah," the man said softly.

Clayt looked into his dark eyes. The Indian stepped closer and squatted. His face radiated quiet confidence, and the stillness in his pose showed that he was comfortable in such close proximity to a white man.

"Sheeh-nah-zhee-shah," he said again. His hand went to Clayt's blanket and gathered a pinch of the orange wool between thumb and finger. He raised the material and rubbed slowly, as though demonstrating the suppleness of the wool.

He stood and spoke to the woman in choppy phrases. There were nasal sounds and clickings from his throat interspersed throughout the words. She replied in kind, and the man turned back to Clayt. Whatever he said then, the message was clearly not hostile. It was, in fact, personable. He turned to walk back down the trail.

"Why're you helpin' me?" Clayt said to his back.

The lean man turned, his eyes narrowing as though he might divine the meaning of Clayt's words merely through his stillness. He raised his chin, and, with a minimal gesture, he touched his thumb to his breastbone.

"Chah-tkah Wash-tay," he said. Though delivered in a hushed voice, the words — spoken so deliberately, so boldly — might have served a wolf standing over its prey.

Clayt stared hard into the black eyes that now smiled at him. "You're Chatka?"

The warrior nodded, and his hand rose again to point at Clayt. "Sheeh-nah-zhee-shah." Now a smile spread across his face. Chatka nodded as though a necessary transaction had been tendered. Then the man turned and descended the slope.

Through the trees Clayt saw four, five, six braves. And a reedy woman nurturing a baby at her breast. He could see no shelters down below and assumed that these people were making use of the overhangs and crevices in the rocks.

Chalky had told him about the rough country on the west side of the Snowys. No white man entered it alone, for few solo travelers had returned from it.

The old woman fed him broth, refilled the bowl, and fed him again. Before he finished it, she allowed him a bite of ashcake that he could have sworn had the texture and taste of corn. The warm food settled him.

Kneeling by his side, she lifted the blanket from his wounds and folded it over his good leg. Taking care to regulate the flow, she began dripping water from a rawhide pouch onto the leaf-encased leg. As the poultice material grew more pliant, she began the tedious process of peeling it away, leaf by leaf, never once pulling the skin. With the wounds exposed, she began swabbing the leg with a yellow-green liquid squeezed from a handful of herbs.

Clayt raised his head and for the first time saw the stitchwork on his thigh. Each wound that had marked the entrance of a shotgun pellet was now a closed gash, knotted together by thin, pale-yellow cordage that puckered the skin around it. It gave his leg the appearance of insects clinging tightly to the skin. The old woman probed the flesh and nodded, apparently pleased. Unfolding a swatch of leather she showed him a collection of shiny metal beads — seven of them. Recognizing the birdshot, he looked quickly at the woman.

"You dug them outta me? And my horse, too?"

From another pouch she sprinkled a pinkish powder onto the wounds, and, as she did, she spoke to him, bouncing her hands in the air above the wound like a piano player. When he tried to cover himself with the blanket, she took it from his hands and folded it back over the other leg again. Repeating the words, she fanned the air with a hawk wing, and he could feel a cool sensation on the damaged skin. He lay back, exhausted from the simple task of trying to communicate.

That night, a child — a girl no older than Tom — built up the fire, and the alcove of stone came alive, trembling with visual stories rendered in light and shadow. The girl's curious eyes covertly angled to Clayt but looked away each time he spoke to her. The old woman touched his ribs with her moccasin. She pointed up to the starless sky and uttered more of her chopped-up words. When she reached down to lift him to his feet, he helped as best he could; but in the end she carried his full weight, and the girl dragged his bedding under the rock.

Having his hip and leg support him was excruciating. After he lay down, it took a long time for the hammering pulse of pain to abate. The woman and the girl showed no reaction to his involuntary gasps. It was as if they knew that — no matter how his story played out — he would be whole again or he would die, and any fleeting discomfort he experienced on the way to a resolution would count as nothing in the end.

With three men behind him, Chatka led the way up to Clayt's den. All were Indian, but the two who flanked the center man clasped his upper arms tightly and ushered him roughly forward. When they stood before the fire, Clayt saw that this man's hands were bound behind him, and his attire was that of a white man. Boots, trousers, shirt, and coat. In the flickering light his gold-bronze face became familiar.

"Mooney," Clayt said. "You're Teague's tracker. I reckon you're after me."

The half-breed deputy raised his chin. "Was," he said. "Now I just try and save my own skin."

Clayt frowned. "I hear you got Shoshone blood in you. That a problem here?"

Mooney's stoic face broke for an instant as he smiled. "Shouldn'a been."

Chatka broke in with a sharp commanding voice, and Mooney turned his head to the leader. When the deputy offered a few halting syllables in Indian, Chatka nodded.

"You speak their language?" Clayt said.

Mooney shrugged. "Some. He want to know what we say."

"What's he know 'bout me?" Clayt asked.

"He knows I come after you for breaking jail. And for the murders."

"I didn' kill nobody."

Mooney shrugged. "He don't care what you done. He know you somehow."

"What's that mean?"

"He say you give his people meat when they starve."

481

Mooney turned to Chatka, and Clayt watched as the deputy translated their conversation. He could see the intelligence in the old warrior's eyes, absorbing every detail and storing it away.

"What's he aimin' on doin' with us?" Clayt asked.

Mooney smiled again. "Don' know. But maybe you better off than me."

The first drops of rain began to tap on the rock face outside. Thunder rumbled in the west, the distant sound making the overhang shelter feel warm and welcoming. Chatka spoke to Mooney with his words deliberately spaced for the deputy to understand.

"He say, you stay off that leg for a week before go home."

Clayt looked at Chatka. "Tell 'im I ain't got a home no more."

When he received Mooney's translation, Chatka looked at the fire. His mouth tightened, and a crease cut into the chief's cheek. If it was a smile, there was no humor in it. His reply was melancholy and brief. Mooney looked down at his boots.

"What'd he say?" Clayt said.

Mooney softened his voice. "He say 'like Lakota and Cheyenne . . . no home.' "

The rain came harder now and water danced off the rock like fat popping in a fry pan. The smell of wet stone mixed with the resinous fragrance of the spruces and the acrid woodsmoke. Chatka spoke to the woman, and, answering in a tone of deference, she turned back the blanket from Clayt's wound. Clayt looked to Mooney for an explanation.

"She cut out all buckshot. You have fever three days, but fever break."

Clayt and Chatka locked eyes on one another. "What's them words he keeps usin' when he points at me? 'Sheena zeesha?'" At Clayt's attempt to pronounce the words, Chatka raised his eyebrows.

"That is what they call you," Mooney said and pointed. "They know you by that blanket."

Chatka addressed the men holding Mooney, and the deputy's arms stiffened against their tighter grip. They started to drag him away.

"Hold on," Clayt said and propped himself on an elbow. He kept his eyes on Chatka as he spoke to Mooney. "Ask 'im how come his people was to kill Chalky."

"Who?" Mooney said.

"The colored man got killed on Rollin' F land."

After Mooney asked the question, Chatka searched Clayt's eyes, as though preempting the question with his own. After a time, he spoke in a low growling tone, his face showing nothing. Then he looked to Mooney to translate.

"He say, whites and Lakota always kill each other. That what they do." Mooney listened as Chatka spoke again, many phrases chained together into a quiet narrative. "He say Lakota check fish traps at river. White men open up with rifles on them. Of the Lakota who were kilt, one was an old man named Wooden Dog. Later, his son return home and run up on black white man, so he kilt the black white man."

Clayt locked eyes with Chatka. "That man was my oldest friend."

It was Chatka's turn to give Mooney a questioning glance. The deputy spoke in his halting Sioux tongue again. Chatka looked at Clayt and spoke in a whisper.

Mooney translated. "The old man who got kilt — Wooden Dog — he the father of Chatka's dead wife."

Chatka held Clayt's gaze for a time, and then abruptly he spoke to the two guards, and they jostled Mooney, pushing him out into the rain.

"Tell 'im I need you to git back safe," Clayt called out.

Everyone stopped. When Chatka heard

the translation he frowned at Clayt.

"Tell 'im," Clayt continued, "if somethin' happens to you, it'll go bad for me."

Mooney almost laughed. "He not believe that."

"Tell 'im!" Clayt ordered.

When Mooney translated, Chatka spat words more quickly than before, and the deputy's face went sullen.

"Says he has no use for Indian who works for the white man. Says nobody will trouble you when my body is found with my head lopped off next to my entrails."

Clayt pointed a finger at the deputy. "I need you to go back and study on them rocks set out north from where Mr. Afton got kilt. If you're any good at what you do, you'll see somebody laid up there and done that killin'. Then later, somebody dropped a shell casing out there that matched my Henry rifle."

Mooney's eyes angled away, as though he did not want to hear these things. Then his face took on the curious grin of a man holding back the last part of a joke.

"I already go back out there. Found tracks where a horse had been tied up in a gully near those rocks. Tracks come in and go out same way. I follow. Lead back toward Shannonhaus land. When I make Bear Springs, I hear rifle shots from west. Shots come at one-minute intervals, slow but steady. I go and look."

Mooney checked Chatka's face before continuing. "I find man lying down in shade of big juniper. He shoot at something maybe half mile away. His gun have tube mounted on top. His target is plank of wood set upright in ground. I know this only because I ride down to inspect it later." Mooney shook his head in wonder. "This gun, it shoot today and kill tomorrow. Man splinter that plank into kindling."

"Well, who was he?" Clayt asked.

The deputy shrugged. "Tall man in long coat. Ride back to Shannonhaus ranch."

"You see his horse?"

Mooney nodded. "Big roan. White blaze on face."

"And a blue bedroll behind the saddle," Clayt added.

Mooney's eyes narrowed. "Same blue on saddle blanket."

"Well, did you tell the sheriff about this?"

Mooney looked around at his captors. "I not only one drawn to them shots. After man with medicine gun leave, Chatka's men take me."

Clayt struggled to sit, his eyes fierce with the need to be understood. Staring at

Chatka he pointed at Mooney and spoke with an urgency that drew everyone's attention.

"You need to let 'im go!" Clayt implored, using his hands to render his meaning.

Chatka regarded Clayt's heated face, and then he considered the half-breed. He turned to face out into the rain for a time. All the while, Mooney was soaking to the skin and awaiting his verdict. Without looking at his prisoner or the guards and without a trace of passion, Chatka spoke. When he finished, the guards stepped away from Mooney. The deputy looked around as though expecting a trick. One of the guards pushed him farther out into the rain, and Mooney stood there staring at his captors, his hair molded to his skull. He half turned and offered his tied wrists to them, and Chatka stepped into the rain drawing a butcher knife from a sheath. He purred softly, communicating some last decree as he held the knife to Mooney's throat. When Chatka lowered the knife, Mooney backed away and began walking down the trail, his back and shoulders erect, his wrists still lashed at the small of his back.

A man led a horse up the incline, the horse walking blind with a cloth tied over its eyes. When the horse nickered, Clayt knew it to be Skitter. She was led underneath the rock where the firelight illuminated patches of gray poultice pasted to her neck and chest. She extended her muzzle toward him, blew, and bobbed her head.

"You're lookin' a sight better'n me, girl," Clayt said and stretched his hand to her. She brushed his fingers with the velvety skin below her nostrils and blew warmth over his hand. He lay back and closed his eyes, grateful for her and for the warmth of the fire.

CHAPTER 31

Morning broke. The rain had stopped. The tribe of rock dwellers broke camp under a clear sky. By the ease of their transition, Clayt assumed that relocating was their common practice, and he suspected this move had something to do with Mooney's release.

When all was ready for the journey, they came for him. Two dark-bronze men with wiry arms and washboard ribs transferred him to a stretcher of red osier wands lashed to a pair of shaved spruce poles. Wordlessly they hauled him to the shelf below and joined the rear of the procession.

After dropping into a dark valley, they followed a foaming creek until it joined a broader stream, which they forded and left behind to climb to a gap that delivered them to a valley farther west. In the saddle of the gap a new team of carriers replaced Clayt's escorts, who wandered off as quietly as they had traversed this rough terrain. Jarring as it was, Clayt slept through most of the journey.

When he awoke, the sun was several hours above the mountains to the west. On a dark floodplain thickly covered with evergreens they made camp, settling into the landscape as naturally as a flock of birds disappearing into the foliage of a tree. Wickiups sprang up on the valley floor — a smaller version of the tipis he had seen set up outside Fort Sanders. The old woman and the girl who had tended to Clayt erected their own frame and covered it with a tarp of sewn buffalo skins. His new home complete, these women built a fire and began preparations for a meal.

They remained in this valley for three days, then moved again, this time heading south and east to a glade that pushed back aspens to either side and opened to the great expanse of the plains. Clayt estimated that the south pastures of the Rolling F were less than three miles distant. He wondered how many times, over all these years, he had been observed by watchful eyes as he circumnavigated the herd, thinking he had been alone in his sector of the pasture, humming a melody intended for the ears of the cattle only.

Each day of his captivity, as twilight began to usher in the sounds of night, Chatka had come to sit with him. They did not attempt to breach the barrier of languages that lay between them, but Chatka used his hands fluidly to make his thoughts known. Much of it was lost on Clayt, but some of it he grasped, enough to know that the Sioux chief was a cautious and dedicated leader. Each late afternoon Clayt found himself anticipating the visit from the old man the same way he had treasured time with Chalky when Clayt had first arrived at New Surrey Downs.

In the graying hour of the next night in the glade, Clayt was limping back from the spring, where he had walked less for a drink than for testing his leg. Chatka waited for him at the shelter, feeding sticks into a small fire. Skitter and the packhorse stood behind him tethered to the shaggy juniper that shaded his living space.

Clayt walked to Skitter and stood before her, pressing his hands to her flat jaws, smelling her. The saddle and Henry rifle had been competently mounted on the animal. Looped around the pommel was his cartridge belt and holster — the Colt's looking as natural as if Clayt himself had hooked it there. The packhorse was bare.

Chatka pointed to Clayt's leg, exposed by the cut-away pant leg. Clayt bent both legs carefully. His scabbed leg and pale bare feet appeared to him as parts of someone else's sickly body. The leg was weak and painful, but he could feel the concinnity of muscle and bone functioning as it once had. He gave Chatka an assuring nod.

The old warrior spoke to the woman and left, leaving Clayt to stare questioningly at the two horses. The woman stepped before him, loosened the top button on his trousers, and spoke to him in her perfunctory way. After many hand gestures she persuaded him to remove what was left of his trousers. He wrapped inside his blanket, sat down, and watched the woman sew a buckskin legging to the trouser leg that had been cut away.

When she had finished the repair, it was dark. The stars crowded in thick clusters above the land. He dressed, rolled the orange blanket, and tied it behind the cantle of his saddle. By the time he had mounted, the woman had packed food for him in one of the burlap bags he had originally strapped to the packhorse. She presented it along with his canteen, which the girl had filled at the spring. When he looked through the bag, he selected a few strips of dried meat and handed the bag back to the woman.

"You people are gonna need this more'n me."

She took it without comment. He offered his hand, but the woman looked away and spoke in a droning chain of unintelligible syllables. Clayt put his hand on the new legging and stroked the supple deerskin that now covered his wounds.

"Thank you," he offered. "For my horse, too." He smiled at the girl. "And I thank you." The girl shrank in upon herself and looked back at him like a creature of the forest, both fearful and curious, staring from a distance.

He led the horses across the glade to the place where Chatka resided. There were two campfires burning there, and men, women, and children stopped their work to watch him. Silhouetted against the cast of the fire glow, Chatka stepped to the edge of the trees with three other men, each of them thin from malnutrition but straight with dignity. Clayt limped close to the leader and handed him the reins of the packhorse. Chatka nodded, and then his face grew stern as he stared into Clayt's eyes.

"Reckon I owe you a lot more," Clayt said quietly, "but this horse'll have to do."

He mounted Skitter and took her at a walk

down the length of the glade, all the while thinking about what future lay ahead for this band of renegades. How long could they keep picking up and moving on to remain invisible in this country? It was a hard life made harder still by his contact with them.

That was when the sedentary peace of the village struck him as an oddity. They were not preparing another migration. They were trusting him. He thought about that as he moved into the broad sweep of the prairie; and he wondered could he have been so trusting toward another man — especially a stranger . . . be he white, black, or Indian?

He skirted the south pastures and rode north to the Shin Bone flats, where he crossed the creek and stopped at the campsite by the rock spring. It was vacated. A cold ring of charred stones remained where a fire had been. Staying off the trail, he pushed on toward Shannonhaus's land on a route that would take him south of the line shack toward the main ranch house, careful to keep his silhouette beneath the backdrop of sky. Before topping the final ridge he dismounted and walked Skitter into a grove of chokecherries, where he tethered her in good grass.

Carrying his blanket and rifle into the

timber just below the ridge, he nestled in, prone between two logs in a stand of limber pines. From there he could see the main yard of Shannonhaus's ranch two hundred yards away. The house faced south, and four outbuildings comprised the rest of the compound. Only the bunkhouse showed a light in a window. In the paddock he could make out the individual shapes of the horses as they matched the stillness of the night around them.

Turning onto his back, he laid down the Henry rifle, spread the blanket over him, and let his head come to rest on a cushion of fallen needles. The musty scent of earth and the fragrance of the needles lifted him as if on an altar, clean and aromatic, connecting him to the freedom of the nomadic stars. Remembering the filth and stench of the jail cell, he drifted off into the kind of sleep that can only be had in open country.

When the sun broke over the Laramies, Clayt was fully awake, belly down, lying atop his blanket at the edge of the pines. He watched men straggle out of the bunkhouse one by one and make their way to the barn. One threw out hay for the horses, while others hauled buckets of water from the storage tank to the troughs. Though a steady breeze blew in from the northeast, the windmill next to the paddock stood dormant. On the few occasions Clayt had ridden up to the house, he had never seen the vanes turn, and he guessed that the well had long ago run dry, leaving the working parts of the structure unattended to rust and jam with sand. Above him on the ridge, gusts of wind whipped the pine boughs so that they swayed and brushed together with the sounds of a shallow river shoal.

A party of five men rode out to the north, and Clayt guessed them to be the day crew heading out to relieve men at the main herd. A bowlegged man with a rocking gait hitched up a team of gray Percherons to a wagon partially filled with wooden crates. Making three more trips to the barn by foot, he loaded more boxes into the bed. Each time he swung one in, it bounced lightly, the brittle sound reaching Clayt's ears seconds later. When he had finished, he mounted a bay and rode north like the others.

Old Man Shannonhaus and Leland emerged from the main house and talked in the yard. When the father and son boarded the wagon, a third man — tall and lank in a gray duster — walked from the barn in long, unhurried strides. He inspected the cargo

496

and rearranged the crates into some kind of order, and then he faced the pair in the wagon.

As Shannonhaus talked, the tall man produced a cigarette and lighted it. If he shared in the talk that followed, Clayt could not discern it. So indifferent were his movements that the men in the wagon might have been strangers to be tolerated.

Another man led a big paint from the barn. Even without the horse Clayt would have recognized Rascher by the rolling of his shoulders as he walked. Rascher parleyed briefly, mounted, and rode out under the wide, wooden sign that spanned the front gate.

Clayt wondered if Henry Walsh had fired Rascher. Or perhaps the cowboy had quit the Rolling F and its new owner. But another possibility presented itself when Rascher struck a course southwest, straight for Rolling F land: Maybe Rascher worked for both ranches.

The wagon rattled off toward the main road, and the tall man stood for a time pulling on his cigarette. His head pivoted in sharp increments, like a hawk perched high in a tree as it surveys a field. After tossing the cigarette into the hardpan of the yard, he disappeared into the barn.

Beneath the current of the wind in the pines, Clayt heard — or felt — a movement behind him. He turned so quickly that a searing pain shot up his leg and hip. His hand had gripped the shank of the rifle stock, but he froze with the barrel still resting on the ground. Deputy Mooney crawled up beside him and lowered his chest to the earth, his gaze fixed on the house below, a small field glass in one hand.

"Tall man who shoot the board from half a mile . . . he down there."

Clayt eased back onto his belly and kept watch on the barn. "I seen 'im." He turned his head to Mooney. "How long've you been out here?"

"Two days." Mooney nodded toward the ranch. "Tall man is only one who does not work cattle." He pointed to the barn where the blaze roan stood at the entrance, its hindquarters in the light, its forequarters in shadow. "You look," he said, offering the long-distance glass. "Gun that shoots today and kills tomorrow."

Clayt propped his elbows on the ground and peered through the lens. The rifle scabbard that he had seen partially hidden by the blue blanket now hung in full view from the tall man's saddle. The canvas sheath was long and roomy. A rag was stuffed into its unusually wide mouth.

"I saw a rig like that in the war," Clayt said. "Allows for a Whitworth rifle and scope. That cloth is to keep out the dust. Easier to manage than a flap if a man is in a hurry." Clayt handed back the field glass. "A Whitworth is a sniper's tool."

Mooney crimped his mouth and nodded. "Figured that."

Clayt watched the barn below. "Is the sher'ff still lookin' for me?"

"He in town, because the president there. But Grant leaves Laramie on the eastbound train later today. Cut his trip short." He turned to show Clayt the amusement in his eyes. "Too much Indian activity up north." Then Mooney's face sobered. "So far, nothing has happened to Grant. Sheriff thinks that because you are holed up in hills carrying a load of birdshot in your brisket."

Clayt frowned at him. "You didn' tell 'im 'bout us bein' up in Chatka's camp?"

Mooney huffed a dry laugh. "Sheriff not need to hear everything I know."

Clayt watched the tracker's eyes pan across the ranch below. "I reckon that means Teague don't know you found me?" Clayt said.

Mooney lifted his eyebrows. "Way I see it, wasn't me doing the finding. Same as you. I

499

got found." One corner of his mouth curled into a grin. He eased out a long breath and checked the sun. "I only deputy not in Laramie right now making big show of guarding great white chief." He shook his head. "Nothing going on in town but drinking, until Grant make speech and train take him away." He turned to Clayt. "Sheriff pay me half of what other deputies make . . . and I only one does any damn work."

Clayt nodded and adjusted the position of his leg. "What time's the train leave?"

"Four o'clock."

"So why are you out here at Shannonhaus's?"

Mooney kept his eyes on the barn below. "Guess I wanted to see things for myself." He shrugged. "Besides . . . I owe you." He chuckled quietly. "That damn Chatka ready to cut off my privates and feed them to coyotes."

Mooney left the field glass with Clayt and got to his knees. "I go down there."

"What're you gonna do?" Clayt whispered.

Mooney hesitated. "Pretend to see Shannonhaus about a tax assessment." He nodded toward Clayt's rifle. "You set up here with that Henry and keep your eyes open. I ride in. I want to see what tall man is doing in barn."

Mooney started to back away but stopped again, looking at the tattered orange blanket beneath Clayt. "Something I not tell you in mountains." He touched a corner of the alder-dyed wool. "Chatka . . . he say you have nothing to worry about from his people. You just show blanket. They know you." The deputy laughed deep in his chest and stroked the blanket. "Maybe I get one of these for myself." He gathered his legs under him and in a low crouch moved silently away through the pines.

Five minutes passed before Mooney appeared at the gate, his bay gelding clopping up the road in a slow shuffle of hooves. At the windmill the deputy dismounted, stretched his back and walked his horse to the paddock fence, where he tied the bay to the top rail. Passing up the barn he ambled to the main house and knocked on the door. After waiting a long minute he returned to the paddock. Reaching through the fence he filled a bucket from the trough and held it up to the bay's muzzle.

Then Mooney carried the bucket to the open door of the barn and faced the dark interior. Clayt could hear him call out a greeting, but no reply could be heard. When Mooney stepped inside, he was lost in shadow. Several minutes passed with no movement other than the horses nosing at the hay in the paddock.

The tall man came into the yard and looked around the bowl of land. In his slow, economical walk he untied Mooney's bay and walked it into the barn and out of view. Clayt picked up his rifle and waited. After a minute had passed, he cursed under his breath and began crawling back up the hill. By the time he reached the pines his leg was throbbing, and the wounds felt like fire, but he could see no fresh blood soaking through the legging. He rolled the blanket and stood looking back at the ranch.

Had he not gained this higher ground he would have missed seeing the activity behind the barn. The tall man was walking down the ravine that ran from the bluff past the back of the barn. He led two horses, one saddled and the other loaded with some kind of freight trussed up in a tarpaulin and draped over the animal's back. Moving through heavy shadow, the horses could not be identified by breed or color.

Clayt moved as quickly as his wound allowed — a stiff-legged stride on the bad leg followed by two hops on the good one. Skitter shied at his approach, and he had to talk to her for a time before he could jam the Henry into its scabbard and tie down the blanket. When mounted, he saw fresh blood seeping through the buckskin legging.

Hearing Skitter's labored breathing, Clayt let the dapple-gray ease down the slope at her own pace. They rounded the base of the hill, passed under Shannonhaus's gate, and entered the barn. There he found neither Mooney nor his bay. At the back outlet of the barn, he picked up the tracks of the two horses and the tall man's long, narrow-booted stride. Around the turn in the ravine the horses had stood briefly, and the boots milled about then disappeared, showing where the man had mounted. His horse, Clayt noted, showed a protruding nail trying to pry itself loose from the left fore shoe.

For the better part of a mile Clayt followed the tracks. A few hundred yards short of the main road he came upon a saddled horse, its reins hanging loose in the grass. It was Mooney's bay. Next to the horse lay a body sprawled out on a flat shelf of stone, and in the brush next to it was a canteen, its cap unplugged. Even from his saddle, Clayt could see that the deputy was dead, his skull crushed flat on the right side and seeping its contents like a raw egg dropped on a hardwood floor. There was no sign of the tarpaulin.

Mooney's saddle reflected the sun

brightly, and water beaded on the stirrup and fender. Clayt could imagine the scene as if he had been hiding here just moments ago, seeing the tall man wash blood off the saddle with Mooney's canteen, wanting it to appear as if an accident had happened here.

Clayt considered getting down, but with his leg throbbing from hip to knee, he knew that giving Mooney a decent burial would take more time and effort than he had to give. "If I can pull through this day without gittin' my own self kilt," Clayt whispered to the corpse, "I'll git back here and give you a proper burial. You got my word on it."

He laid over the reins on Skitter's neck and broke out of the brush onto the open road. There the roan's tracks stretched out into a familiar galloping pattern of four hoof marks defining a long crescent, followed by a clean leap, and then another crescent. Clayt pulled his hat low and urged Skitter into a lope. Anything more, he feared, would kill her.

At the old Pender windmill he spied a cloud of dust rising from behind a boulder field to the south. Soon a growing rumble of hooves reached his ears. Then they were upon him, mustangs parting around the rocks, charging across the road like a flash flood. Their backs were slick and shining with sweat, and their mouths frothed as they streamed past him, panicked and walleyed.

Skitter crow-hopped and tried to rear but could not manage it. Before Clayt could react, three half-naked warriors appeared on horseback — they just as surprised as he. The wiry riders swung wide of him, shouldering their rifles on the gallop. Their guns fired almost in unison. It was Skitter's stumbling that saved Clayt. Bullets cut the air, whining around him like angry hornets.

Half turned in the saddle, Clayt pulled the leather tie behind the cantle and jerked the bright blanket free. Clutching one edge, he unfurled it like a flag and held it high, where the wind caught it and opened it to the sun in a sudden flash of orange. The mustangs veered wider from him, and the shots stopped.

Not twenty yards away, a thin, bare-chested man with a long scar running diagonally across his knobby ribs held his pony in place and locked eyes with Clayt. Lowering his rifle the warrior relaxed his face from its fierce scowl to a countenance of curiosity. His loose, raven hair whipped in the wind as his horse snorted and fought the man's hold on the braided reins. He stretched his arm high, the rifle barrel pointing to the sky, and called out to the two men closest to him. Glaring at the white man, these three passed him by, their hostility held in check, their horses trembling with a pent-up energy. Following in the tracks of the wild mustangs, the horse-catchers took their mounts at a walk across Clayt's intended path. Suddenly, one man screeched a raspy cry, and the trio raced off into the dust storm left by the wild-eyed horses.

Clayt's heart pounded in his chest. He watched the herd head north, winding up the grassy bowl of the valley, the horsemen whipping their mounts to regain their flanking positions. Clayt wadded the blanket beneath his arm and took his horse at a walk along the road. Beyond the trampled dirt of the stampede, the tracks of the tall man's horse stretched out in the pattern of an animal pushed to its limits.

Up ahead was the low dip in the trail where Grassy Creek ran south to hook up with Shin Bone. The small stream was lined with cottonwoods; and so Clayt, following his instincts, approached it on a diagonal some distance from the road.

In the shade of the trees he waited, listened. Gathering his blanket under one arm he eased across the stream and scaled the rise beyond. As soon as he urged Skitter out of the shadows, there was an instant of inexplicable regret. He had made an error. The silence waiting on that side of the creek raised the hairs on the back of his neck, the warning as clear as a word spoken at his ear. Then he saw a puff of smoke suddenly blossom up ahead from a rock outcrop, and the air around him sang out the note of prophecy that he had heard talked about in the war. *The sniper's whisper,* they had called it. Like the sound of paper tearing. A ripping of the air. The impact of the bullet knocked him off the horse, turning the world aslant. He fell through a vacuum — this much he remembered — and in falling he heard the distant report of the gun from somewhere in another world that would go on without him.

The pain in his leg was now only a half-forgotten reminder of a former life as he gasped for breath in an airless space of deprived senses. A fog spread through his brain. His limbs lay useless beside him as nausea spread from his gut to engulf him with its cool flame. Sweat popped out on his brow.

Looking up into the sky he saw its emptiness for what it was — the vacuous grin of an unearthly demon who had patiently been waiting for him all this time. A reckoning had arrived to balance out all the sins of his past. His savage cruelties in the war had earned him this accounting. As he lay there feeling the shock of the bullet vibrate in his deflated chest, a single strident note rang in his ears, and that sound seemed to be an anthem for eternity, a sound he had only known before by its generic name — death.

Then came a surprise from the very center of him. Like a bubble rising from the depths of a dark lake to break at its surface, he gasped and sucked in a full breath of air. The coolness of the prairie entered his lungs as a redemptive blessing. He could taste its nourishing parts like a man separating the flavors of some new food on his tongue. The smell of the water churning in the creek. The sweet aroma of crushed grass. The sweat-soaked tang of saddle leather. The musky scent of freshly broken earth. And the faint stench of burned hair. All of this washed over him . . . into him.

His eyes cleared, and he raised his head. The blanket was still wadded into a thick mass beneath his left arm, the arm pressing tightly, trying to stanch the wound. Out in that other world to which he was returning, beneath the burning hum of the bullet that still buzzed in his ears, he made out the clatter of distant hooves moving away. He sat up, surprised to be oriented to the world again. A second dawning of this day. A resurrection.

Letting the blanket drop, he examined his chest and could make no sense of the mere dent in the smooth fabric of his coat. A dull pain abided in the flesh and bone beneath. He opened the coat and shirt and found a welt high up on the ribs next to his old scar. He touched it, and his hand came away clean.

Examining the blanket, he found the bullet's entry. The wool smelled burnt. As he unrolled the blanket, each layer revealed tear after ragged tear, each perforation larger than the last, until finally the bullet rolled into his lap. He picked it up and fingered the hexagonal base.

While examining the blanket, he had been holding his breath. Now the air eased out of him like a prayer as he stroked the wool, its soft, hairy nap now seeming mystical, even god-like. It had been a long time since he had thought about the old weaver woman in Tennessee. She had told him the blanket would protect him. She had told him.

Skitter approached from the trees, and Clayt grabbed the stirrup to pull himself up. The horse stood for it, even as blood ran from one of the old neck wounds, painting a thin line of red down a foreleg to the fetlock.

"Let's git you some water, girl." The dapple-gray followed as he limped back into the shade by the branch, where they both drank their fill. "We got a ways to go," Clayt said. "I hate askin' you, but we gotta do it." The horse stood in the creek head down, a chain of water dribbling from her chin. The nicker deep in her throat was answer enough. Clutching the horn and cantle, Clayt gritted his teeth, pulled himself up, and swung into the saddle.

CHAPTER 32

As he neared the river, the tracks were lost among a parade of hoof marks, all funneling to and from the bridge. Up ahead he saw ranchers and cowhands converging on the depot, all come to see the president. Clayt let Skitter clatter across the bridge at a walk, and then he cut behind the short spur of rail at the holding pens where cattle were counted before being shipped east to the slaughter houses.

A mass of people had crowded around the depot, and the mood was festive. The inner circle was dominated by a throng of dark suits — businessmen, merchants, and ranch owners. Interspersed as a minority throughout were women in fancy dresses, a layer of equally colorful parasols floating above them, bursting with high sheens of satiny blue, yellow, and red where the sun reflected off their tilted canopies.

Scattered throughout that elite core of

citizenry, Clayt saw the flashy shirts that cowboys usually reserved for dances and infrequent social events. In contrast to these were the muted work clothes that made up the fringe of the gathering. These were the farmers, the stockyard laborers, and the workers from the mills and brickyard. Everyone seemed to be talking, and the collective conversations were like the sustained roar of a waterfall. It looked like the Fourth of July had arrived a month early.

For Clayt, it was all a distraction. The momentum of the occasion seemed to have lulled the town into a false sense of security. He knew that this scenario was a perfect shield for a man planning to kill another. And he knew what a Whitworth could do in the right hands . . . and how far off a man could lie in wait and expect success.

The crowd moved in a slow current, tightening itself, closing in on the rear platform of the caboose, where the handrails were festooned in ribbons of red, white, and blue crepe. The peripheral streets were nearly empty, with only an occasional clerk or bar sweep running to join the audience at the rear of the train. Isolated gunshots built until the extended fusillade of weapons and the rowdy cheers that accompanied them rivaled the pitch of a battlefield. The air filled with sound.

Clayt felt the old rusted cogs of wartime reconnaissance begin to loosen inside him. He scanned the rooftops, considering the elements of trajectory and cover, looking for that vantage needed for an unobstructed shot and a swift escape. To see what he needed to see . . . to find the shooter . . . he had to think like the assassin.

Skirting the crowd he crossed the tracks at the water tank and spotted Frank Maschinot standing under the awning in front of the hotel. The deputy leaned his back into the building, his arms crossed over his chest, as his eyes panned across the mass of humanity. When the crowd worked up a vocal rhythm and began calling for the president, the reports of guns tapered off. Clayt urged his horse at a slow walk toward the deputy and reined up at the corner.

When Maschinot turned his head and saw Clayt, the deputy appeared to levitate from the wall. His arms unlocked but remained hovering at chest level. When he was able to wipe the surprise from his face, what remained was uncertainty. His tongue darted around his lips as he eyed the pistol butt jutting from Clayt's holster. Then his eyes flicked toward the crowd, and Clayt knew that the sheriff would be standing near the

513

back of the train with the other town dignitaries. Now close enough to be heard, Clayt sat his horse among the cluster of mounts tethered to the tie racks of First Street.

"Frank," Clayt said. "Just rest easy now." He opened his hands to show only his reins. "There ain't no time for trouble b'tween you and me." With the thumb of one hand he gestured toward the town. "We got a sniper here some'res."

Frank's brow pinched low over his eyes. "The sher'ff is sayin' that'd be you, Clayt." He cleared his throat. "You here to turn yourself in?" He took two steps toward Clayt, but his walk was relaxed, and his hand swung freely past his holstered revolver.

Clayt adjusted his weight in the saddle, taking pressure off his burning leg. "You see a tall fellow in a gray duster? Would'a rode in just now on a lathered-up roan."

Frowning, Maschinot looked out over the crowd. "Hell, Clayt, there's a helluva lotta people here." Then, when he turned back to Clayt, his gaze lowered to Skitter, and his eyes pinched with regret. "What the hell happened to your horse?"

"Listen to me, Frank. This fellow I'm talkin' 'bout . . . he's the one kilt Mr. Afton and Mr. Dunne. And now he's gone and kilt Mooney."

"Mooney!" Frank almost laughed. "Hell, Clayt, he's out trackin' you som'eres!"

Clayt shook his head. "Not no more, he ain't. He's lyin' dead out at the cutoff to the Shannonhaus place."

Maschinot stepped toward the edge of the boardwalk and checked up and down the street with birdlike motions of his head. Before he could reply, the crowd hushed for the sake of someone yelling from the caboose. The mayor's whiny, speech-giving voice began to expound on the honor of the town in hosting the president of the United States.

That was when Clayt saw Isabella in the crowd. A warmth ran through him and spread like needles across his throbbing left leg. She was dressed in the same outfit she had worn the day she had arrived in Laramie. Tom was by her side. In front of both of them, Henry Walsh was working his way toward the caboose, where the mayor was inviting him up on the platform. Rascher led the way for Walsh, parting the sea of bodies like the prow of a ship.

A short, robust, bearded man emerged from the rear door of the caboose and behind him a taller, thinner man, also bearded. Clayt recognized the stockier man

515

— General Grant — from the portrait that hung in the post office. The other man raised his arm to the crowd, and the people of Laramie raised their voices in a chorus befitting a congregation. Next through the door appeared the Pinkerton man, Hester, followed by two soldiers with rifles held diagonally at the ready.

Gunfire erupted again, and a great collective cheer rose with it. When the mayor reached down to lend a hand, Henry Walsh climbed the steps alone and took his place on the crowded coupling platform.

Everything was unfolding too fast. The eddying of the crowd. The swell of voices. The celebratory gunfire. By reflex, Clayt's senses tightened, and he turned painfully in his saddle, enough to eye the long, empty street extending west from the train. Amid the turmoil swirling around the caboose, he was already cataloguing every feature of the town as a breastwork or piece of strategy.

The water tank near the tracks stood high on its four posts, its vertical ladder reaching to a conical top with no less than two dozen rungs. Too cumbersome. Too exposed. No escape.

Next to the tower a grove of leafy cottonwoods dropped a pool of shadow that spilled out into the street. On both sides of the thoroughfare, the rows of stores showed "closed" signs in their windows. The false fronts that masked the roofs of the buildings offered no cover at this angle. Clayt considered and then dismissed each one as an impossible site from which to stage an ambush.

At the far end of the street, at least two hundred yards distant, the barn at the West End Livery closed the notch of visibility from points farther west. The interior of the barn was dark. Its loft above was more exposed, open in front and backlit by a matching hay window on the far side. Clayt's gaze returned to the ground floor of the barn, and in the deep shadow there he could just make out a horseless spring wagon sitting idle between the stalls. In that instant the old war instincts of his past coalesced deep in his gut, like a seed cracking its coat and taking root where all conditions were favorable to its mission.

Though he could see no one . . . no movement . . . this was the sniper's perch. Clayt knew it as clearly as if it had been handed to him on a map. The crowd in the street continued its mad pitch of oblivion.

Clayt kept his eyes fixed on the barn. "Frank?" he called out from the side of his mouth, just loud enough to be heard. When the deputy made no reply, Clayt turned to see him transfixed by the men standing on the back of the caboose. The mayor's arms were raised over his head, his fingers splayed, his hands waving down at the air in an attempt to quiet the unleashed roar of celebration. President Grant stood patiently, his face stoic as he endured the chaos of wild jubilation.

There was no separate, telltale report amid the staccato explosions of gunfire. There was only the dreamlike motion of a body falling backward, arms thrown outward to make a human crucifix, as though the victim expected to be caught by friendly hands. Hester and the soldiers reflexively sidestepped in the limited space, allowing the tumbling body to crash against the door. Henry Walsh slid to the platform, his head forced into an undignified angle by the door, his chin jammed into his ascot.

Silence fell over the closest spectators, and the stillness of shock began to spread outward into the crowd. The mayor and president turned as one, as if someone had called their names. Then Grant was surrounded by Hester and the soldiers as they huddled around him and escorted him through the door in quick, shuffling steps. Two more soldiers hurried up the platform steps and rushed the other bearded man inside with the president. Henry Walsh's body lay unattended in the doorway.

Clayt's attention shifted instinctively to Isabella and Tom, both staring wide eyed at the sight before them. She opened her mouth to speak, but now the spectators seemed to snap out of their momentary shock, and a chorus of protest erupted from the crowd, drowning out whatever she had tried to say. The scene broke into madness as those nearest the train pushed back into the throng and those farthest tried to advance closer.

Pulling his rifle from its scabbard, Clayt reined his horse into the street and began forcing a path through the frenzied mob toward the stables.

"Clayt!" Frank called to his back. "Where the hell're you goin'?"

Clayt turned his head as he pointed west with his rifle. "Look yonder, Frank," he yelled, "at the West End barn."

Squinting, Frank stepped down to the street. "What're you fixin' to do?" He gripped the butt of his holstered gun. "Damnit, Clayt, I'm *s'posed* to be arrestin' *you*."

Clayt *chick-chicked* from the side of his mouth and tapped his heels into Skitter's flanks. The ailing horse picked up its pace and pushed through the mass of onlookers. One man on his left turned, indignant at being shunted aside until he frowned at Clayt's bloodied leg and backed away.

"Clayton Jane!" a voice roared over the din of the crowd.

Clayt turned his head to see the sheriff standing ten yards behind him, a lane opening up between them as frightened spectators backed away from the potential of more violence. Like a duelist, Abel Teague had turned his ample body sideways, his feet spread and his gun outstretched. The barrel of the gun slowly bobbed up and down, matching the rhythm of the sheriff's labored breathing.

"Hand that rifle to Frank!" Teague ordered. "Stock first! Then git your hands up! Do like I'm tellin' you, Clayt, or I'll shoot you dead right here in the street!"

In the silence that fell over the standoff, the sheriff cocked the hammer of his revolver, the sound like the click of dice in a gambler's quick hand.

With a thrust of his rifle, Clayt pointed down the street toward the stables. "Abel, that shot had to 'a come from the barn."

Teague did not budge. "Or maybe from that rifle o' you'r'n."

Clayt looked to Maschinot for support. The deputy moved out into the street and stopped just shy of standing between the two men.

"It weren't Clayt, Sher'ff," he reported. "I been right here with 'im. Clayt ain't shot nobody."

Sheriff Teague glanced at Maschinot with a sour expression. "If you been with 'im, then why in hell ain't he arrested?"

While Frank struggled to come up with a reply, Clayt prodded his horse a step closer to the sheriff and reined up. "Abel, you known me for a long time. I think you know what Mr. Afton meant to me." He propped the Henry rifle over his shoulder and nodded back down the street. "I'm askin' you to come with me b'fore the man who done all this killin' can git away."

The sheriff glanced down at Clayt's leg and at Skitter's blood-streaked neck and chest. His eyes pinched with the first hint of doubt. Taking a deep breath he made a visible effort to exhume his authority.

"You can climb down or git shot down," Teague ordered.

Clayt wasted no more than a second in appraising the threat. "Then you'll have to shoot me in the back." Slowly, deliberately, he wheeled his horse around and began a steady trot toward the stables.

"Clayt!" Teague yelled. He stiffened his arm and took aim.

At the back of the caboose, Isabella Walsh stood beside the lifeless body of her husband, both her hands on the rail as if addressing the crowd. "Hasn't there been enough killing?" she called out in a shrill voice. Clayt reined up. The excited murmurs of the masses ceased, and all eyes turned to Isabella.

Her skin was as pale as sun-bleached bone, and her sagging body appeared numb with shock. Now her face filled with challenge as she glared at the sheriff.

"Can't you see Clayt's already been shot, for God's sake."

Below her on the tracks Tom stood beside Tessa. Looking up at his mother his teary eyes reflected light from the sky. Tessa's hand pressed lightly upon his shoulder.

Isabella descended the steps and made her way over the rail ties and tracks to where the sheriff stood. When she stopped before him, he lowered his gun. Her face shone with silvery tracks that streaked her cheeks, and her eyes burned with purpose.

"Wouldn't it make more sense to walk with him instead of shooting him," she said, her voice edged with reason. "He seems to know something about the man who killed my husband. Wouldn't that be your job, Sheriff . . . to help him?"

With a tap of his heels, Clayt nudged Skitter into a fast walk toward the barn. Isabella followed, her dress swishing with each stride and stirring dust from the street. Behind her, Abel Teague's face darkened like a ripe prickly pear.

Tessa leaned close to Tom's head and whispered in his ear. When the boy nodded, one of Tessa's girls took his hand, and Tessa crossed the tracks to follow Isabella.

"Well?" Tessa said as she passed the sheriff. "Are you coming, Abel? Or are you going to let two women and a wounded man do your job?"

When the sheriff began an angry march to follow the two females, Frank pulled out his pistol and hurried to join his boss. The crowd followed like water funneling through a breach in a dam.

CHAPTER 33

At the West End Stables Clayt veered and entered through the side livery gate, his rifle held level in one hand by the shank of the stock as he rounded the building to come at the barn from the rear. There in the back paddock he found Shannonhaus's team of Percherons nosing at the feed trough. The buckboard Clayt had seen leave the Shannonhaus ranch sat motionless inside the building, its tongue angled downward toward him in the soft dirt floor of the breezeway. The wagon bed was stacked with the wooden crates he had seen earlier. The boxes were stacked two high but for a two-foot-wide gap that ran the length of the center.

Clayt waited and listened. Nothing stirred inside the old building. He prodded Skitter forward until he could examine the freight in the wagon. Leaning, he opened the lid of the closest crate to find the box empty. He tried one more and found the same. On the far side of the bed, the three crates of the top tier had been attached end to end to form a single unit. Each long side of the conjoined structure was splinted by an eight-foot-long plank. The side facing Clayt was hinged at the top, making a long horizontal door that hung slightly ajar. The contraption was like a crude casket tipped on its side.

Coaxing his horse around the back of the wagon, he found the tailgate unlatched and hanging down. The jerry-rigged casket showed an uneven matching of the wood slats that capped off its end. With the muzzle of his rifle, Clayt tapped the bottom board, which resounded with a hollow rap. When he poked at the top board, it gave way a quarter inch, and only then did he notice the absence of nail heads in the board.

When he tapped a second time the board clattered into the dark cavity, leaving a rectangular hole almost the size of a woodstove's door. There was just enough light to show the space inside was empty, but Clayt now saw the contraption for what it was: a hiding place through which a prone man might sight a rifle. To check the alignment he reined Skitter around, but already he knew that the wagon had been parked on a perfect trajectory for the back of the train.

Isabella stood in the doorway of the barn, her forearms pressed across her midsection as if to warm herself. The wetness of her cheeks caught the light behind her in a fine, white line etched against deep shadow. Chiaroscuro. She was a living symbol of her own art.

Clayt removed his hat, took in a long breath, and let it ease out. "Is he dead?" he asked quietly.

"Yes," she answered, the word barely audible. Her eyes seemed to plead for a way to understand the chain of tragedies that the Wyoming Territory had thrown at her family. Then her brow knitted when her gaze moved down his leg.

"Clayt, you're hurt."

He fitted the hat to his head and looked down at the blood streaked legging. At least two of the wounds had torn open beneath the deerskin. When he looked up again, Tom was there, breathing hard, standing beside his mother, his fearful eyes fixed on Clayt's leg. Half a block away, Tessa, Sheriff Teague, and Frank Maschinot approached in a flank. Twenty yards behind them, a mob of citizens followed.

"The same man that kilt your brother kilt

your husband," Clayt said and tipped his head toward the wagon. "Today, he made that shot from right here."

When he looked up, the sheriff and his deputy were standing inside the doorway. The lawmen held their pistols before them as they peered into the dark of the barn.

Clayt sat his horse a little straighter. "We need to go after this man b'fore he can git too much a lead on us."

Teague brought his gun to bear on Clayt. "Nobody's goin' anywhere till I can figure out what the hell's goin' on here." He waggled the gun barrel toward the ground. "Git on down off your horse. Hell, Clayt . . . you're still under arrest . . . an' don' forget, damnit, you broke outta my jail."

Now the spectators who had come from the depot crowded the yard in front of the barn. Those who filled the doorway were quiet, their faces filled with expectation. Clayt lowered his rifle crosswise over the front of his saddle and gestured with his free hand toward his wounds. "I ain't too good on my feet right now, Abel."

The sheriff frowned at Clayt's leg and then at Skitter's bloodied chest. Lowering his gun, he seemed more angry than authoritarian.

"Well, would you tell me what it is we're

doin' down here at the livery?"

Clayt backed Skitter next to the side panel of the wagon. "Looks like this is where the shot came from that killed Mr. Walsh," he said. Leaning, he pried open the hinged door, revealing a wrinkled pallet of blankets running its length. Grunting against the pain in his leg, he hoisted the door up and over to slap on top of the connected crates.

"What the hell's that?" Frank Maschinot muttered.

Teague moved to the tailgate and studied the crates in the wagon bed. Frank stepped beside him, and both men peered into the long, makeshift box.

"This is Shannonhaus's wagon, ain't it?" Frank said.

Old Man Shannonhaus shouldered through the crowd and stood behind the two lawmen. Leland followed and took a place beside his father.

"Yeah, it's mine!" the elder Shannonhaus barked. "What of it?"

Keeping his eyes on the old man, Clayt casually gripped his rifle with both hands. "Abel, you and Frank might wanna keep your pistols trained on these two."

Leland's hand moved to his pistol grip but stopped when the sheriff's gun leveled on his chest. "Let's you just relax a little bit,

528

Leland, till we can sort this out."

Clayt looked into the hostile eyes of Old Man Shannonhaus. "How long were you plannin' on stayin' in town today, Mr. Shannonhaus?" The directness of the question seemed to take the old man off guard.

"We're not staying," he said gruffly. "We only have a few minutes. We just came to see the president off. We have to get back to our ranch."

Turning briefly, Clayt glanced toward the corral behind the barn, where the Shannonhaus Percherons mingled with the other horses. "I'm curious then," Clayt said friendly enough, "why you'd unhitch your team?" Clayt let his eyebrows float upward. "Seems like a lotta trouble for 'a few minutes,' don't it?"

Both Shannonhaus men glared at Clayt as he slowly swung his rifle in an arc to tap the muzzle against the nailed-together boxes. "You went to some trouble in hammerin' together this blind for that snake you hired to do your killin' for you."

Teague divided his attention between Clayt, the crates, and the Shannonhauses, but he kept his gun trained on Leland. Maschinot leveled his pistol at the old man.

"This here rig is set up for a sniper," Clayt announced to everyone within earshot. "It

529

wouldn' do to have those Percherons in the traces. They needed this wagon to sit still as a rock. A man can lay down in there completely hid and remove that top panel down at that end." Clayt pointed with the rifle. "T'other board serves as a rest for his weapon." He looked out the door. "A man would have a clean shot from here to the back o' the train."

Sheriff Teague's face hardened as he considered the trajectory. "What about that, Shannonhaus? What're these crates for?"

When the old man did not answer, Leland spat off to one side and tried for a gruff laugh. "There ain't no law 'bout carryin' 'round boxes in a wagon."

"We've been moving some fragiles," the father announced in his sandy voice, "from the main house out to some of the line shacks." He raised his good arm to point at Clayt and pivoted his head enough to let his voice carry behind him. "This man Jane is a murderer and a fugitive! We don't have to listen to him!" He scowled at Teague.

The sheriff cocked his head to one side and squinted. "And now here Jane is . . . come in of his own free will." Teague backed to the wagon and lifted the opened door atop the long box. It slammed shut with a rattling clatter that caused Maschinot to

530

jump. "You wanna try explainin' this contraption to me?"

The old man pointed at the sheriff. "You can keep your goddamn hands off our property." His hand went to the butt of his pistol. "We're leavin' right now!"

When Abel Teague stepped into Shannonhaus's path, the old man stopped. "Frank," the sheriff ordered, "go have a look up in the loft."

Clayt shook his head. "He won't be there, Abel."

Teague motioned with his gun. "Go on, Frank. Better to know than not know."

Clayt urged Skitter toward the front of the wagon, where he checked the soft dirt of the barn floor for tracks. Narrow boot prints showed where a man had jumped down from the side panel. The tracks led out the back of the barn into the paddock.

"Hold on, Clayt!" the sheriff called out. When he took a grip on the cheek strap of Skitter's bridle, the horse nickered and jerked its head. "Ain't nobody goin' anywhere."

Clayt shifted in his saddle, easing his weight off his throbbing leg. "He's aw-ready got a ten-minute start on us, Abel."

Teague reached up and eased Clayt's rifle from him. "Let's just sit tight here till I can sort this out." He frowned at the crates. "Just who is this man you say was in here?"

Clayt stared at the Shannonhauses as he answered. "Tall man, stands 'bout six-three, wears a gray duster, an' carries a British Whitworth with a scope. I seen 'im with Leland in the canyons . . . and I seen 'im at Shannonhaus's ranch." Clayt glanced at the sheriff. "Your man Mooney seen 'im practicin' his long shots out on the prairie."

Teague frowned at the report. "I reckon I'll let Mooney tell me 'bout that."

Clayt shook his head. "Same man kilt Mooney up at Shannonhaus's place this morning."

The sheriff's face hardened. He waggled his fingers for Clayt to return to the interior of the barn. Taking in a deep breath, Clayt looked out the back entrance of the barn and exhaled slowly. Across the street he spotted the young Negro who swept up at Ivinson's. The boy sat balled up atop one of the barrels lined up beside the front door, his feet drawn up close to his buttocks, and his thin forearms wrapped around his shins.

"Ezra!" Clayt called and raised a hand to summon him over.

The boy jumped down from the barrel and trotted across the street. As he got closer his large, soulful eyes fixed on Clayt's left leg.

"You bleedin', Mistah Clayt." His gaze shifted to the horse's chest, and his forehead creased with deep, horizontal lines. "An' Skittah, too."

Clayt nodded toward the store. "You been sittin' there long?"

Ezra nodded. "All mo'nin'. Mistah Iv's'n pay me to look aftah da goods out front whil'st he go to see da pres'dent." Ezra poked a thumb over his shoulder. "He did'n' wanna haff to haul eve'thin' inside." His brow tightened again as he looked at the sheriff. Then his eyes returned to Clayt's leg. "You aw-right, Mistah Clayt?"

"You see anybody at the livery a few minutes ago?" Clayt asked.

The boy pointed toward the horses behind the barn. "Seen a man in a long coat come out da barn an' climb ovah da fence." He swung his finger toward the post office. "He walk down dat alley. I seen 'im git on a hoss an' he head out fo' da river."

The sheriff broke into the conversation. "This man . . . what size was he, boy?"

"He big," Ezra said, his eyes wide. Then he nodded toward Clayt. "Taller'n you."

"What color was the coat?" the sheriff asked.

Ezra squinted both eyes as he thought. "Kind o' like da ashes in da woodstove."

"He carryin' anythin'?" Clayt asked.

The boy nodded with certainty. "Big ol' rolled-up blanket. I t'ought he part o' all da whoop-de-do at da depot."

"Why's that?" Teague asked.

" 'Cause dat blanket all blue an' red . . . like what dey put on da c'boose."

Clayt winked at the boy. "You're a good man, Ezra. Chalky'd be proud o' you." Clayt held out his hand to the sheriff. "Let me have my Henry, Abel. I'm goin' after 'im."

Teague lowered his brow and chewed on a lip. "Now just wait a damned minute!"

In the quiet that followed, Frank Maschinot began climbing down from the loft. "Ain't nobody up there, Sheriff."

"We've wasted enough time, Abel," Clayt said. "You keep Leland and his father here. And Rascher, too. He's in this somewhere."

Rascher pushed his way through the crowd and sidestepped to stand separate from the Shannonhauses. "Now hold on! I didn' know nothin' 'bout anybody tryin' to kill the president." He pointed at the wagon. "Or 'bout these crates here. I seen 'em out at the Shannonhaus ranch, but —"

"You been spying for 'em, ain't you!"

534

Clayt interrupted.

Rascher looked at the ground and shifted his weight. When he raised his eyes to the sheriff, the cowhand showed the same beaten expression he had worn after Clayt had knocked him down up on the Shin Bone flats.

Rascher pointed at Leland. "He was wantin' me to report on Afton's whereabouts anytime he weren't at the Rollin' F."

"Why?" Clayt said.

Rascher shrugged. "Didn' say. He just paid me to report."

Everyone stared at Rascher, waiting for more, but he said nothing else.

"And all this time you're drawing your pay from Mr. Aff," Clayt summed up. "How come you was to do that, Rascher?"

Letting his head sag, Rascher seemed to search for an answer in the soft, dark dirt of the barn. When he looked up, his face was flushed with color.

"They promised me a job as foreman once they expanded their holdings."

"He's a damned liar," Leland shouted. He lifted his chin toward Clayt. "Both of 'em are lyin'." He stretched out an arm to point at Rascher. "This saddle bum's been tryin' to work for us, but we got no use for 'im."

Rascher met Clayt's gaze and began shaking his head. "They said they were plannin' to take over the Rollin' F land. They never said how."

In the quiet of the barn, Clay began to nod. "This ain't never been 'bout the pres'dent. That was all a cover. This was about water . . . and pasturage. Shannonhaus planned to shoot Mr. Aff while he was with President Grant. Make it look like the assassin missed and hit the wrong man." Clayt looked at Isabella. "Then Mr. Walsh shows up, and now that he's the new owner, he's gotta be got rid of, too."

As Clayt reined Skitter around, he looked back at the sheriff and extended his hand. "I'm goin' after that man, Abel. You gonna give me that rifle?"

"No, by God!" Teague barked. "Nobody's leavin' here till —"

"Stop him!" Old Man Shannonhaus yelled and pulled his revolver. "He's getting away!"

When the gunshot went off inside the barn, the crowd flinched in unison. Clayt lurched in the saddle, almost falling as Skitter recoiled from the sound. Slumping low, he kept his seat by grabbing the pommel. He felt as though an axe had been swung into his midsection. It was all he could do to hang on as Skitter leapt into motion, galloping out the back into the street. Behind

536

him, Clayt heard four gunshots, two of the reports so close together they had to have come from different weapons. He reined Skitter into the alley beside the post office and pulled up to a stop.

The tracks were clear, made by the same horse he had followed into town. A loose nail in the front left shoe punched a shallow hole into the bottom of the print. The killer's horse had stood here, no doubt tethered to the old wagon axle lying in the alley.

When he heard footsteps behind him, Clay turned in the saddle to see Isabella rounding the alley corner in a rush, one hand lifting the front of her dress as she ran, the other gripping his Henry rifle. Stopping close to him, she fixed frightened eyes on the front of his coat. Clayt looked down at himself. A clean hole showed in the material. Pulling the jacket open he saw a stain of glistening red blood spreading across his shirt just above the waistband of his trousers.

"Oh, Clayt," she whispered, the words scraping dryly from her throat. Now her eyes brimmed with tears. "We've got to get you to a doctor."

Trying not to grimace, he leaned, took the Henry, and pushed it deep into his saddle scabbard. "What about all the shootin' back there?" he managed to say.

She wiped at her eyes with the backs of her wrists. "The man who shot you . . . the sheriff's deputy shot him. Then the man's son began shooting, and some of our employees used their guns." She shook her head in a quick trembling motion. "It all happened so fast. I could not tell who shot whom."

"Any o' our boys hurt?"

She wrinkled her face. "I'm not sure. I just grabbed your rifle and ran."

Clayt closed his eyes and waited out a sharp pain stabbing at his gut. She came closer and gently laid a hand below the wounds on his leg.

"Clayt, we have to get you to a hospital. Surely the fort has a surgeon who —"

"Isabella," he said, quieting her by the earnestness in his voice. He glanced down at his gut wound. "This here is a bad place to git shot." He smiled as if offering an apology. "There ain't nothin' for it."

Her face compressed with misery. "What do you mean?"

Clayt filled his lungs and let his breath seep out in a sigh. When he covered her hand with his, she met his grip palm to palm, and each squeezed tightly to the other. Gazing deep into her amber eyes, he hitched his head with regret.

"It was always gonna come to this, Isabella. I reckon I earned it a long time ago."

Her brow creased with lines. "What do you mean?"

He leaned closer to her and dropped his voice to a whisper. The pain in his gut was like a hot branding iron pushed into the wound.

"I tol' you I was in the war. I done some bad things then. The kind o' things no man wants to live with." The pain forced him to straighten and close his eyes. In this sudden dark, a scene of his past materialized. The details were so crisp and full of color, the memory brought back to him the smell of cannon smoke and the shrieks of the dying.

"We swept across this field in a flank. A cavalry charge. Seemed like the air itself was tearin' apart at the seams, bullets flyin' ever'where. I figured to be kilt any moment. I saw this one soldier up ahead, running away from me. I weren't gonna leave no enemy at my back."

Clayt looked down at their clasped hands, joined both by the strength of their grips and the smear of his blood. He swallowed dryly, determined to get out the words.

"He was just a boy, no older'n me when I

run off from home. His eyes were green, same as mine, an' his cheeks were soft and pink. Prob'ly never know'd the scrape of a razor."

Isabella tightened her grip. "Clayt, please, let's go to the fort and find a —"

"Listen to me!" he said firmly, making a plea with his eyes. When she closed her mouth, he continued. "I stared at that blue-coat boy . . . and him at me . . . and a cold-ness run down my spine. Like standin' under a snow-melt waterfall." He shook his head. "I'll never forget that boy, Isabella. It was 'bout like lookin' into a dusty mirror."

He could see a question forming on her lips, but she asked nothing.

"Didn' none o' that seem to matter. My arm came down, and my saber hacked into him. It was a terrible blow."

Tears streamed down her cheeks as she stared up at him. "Clayt, don't do this."

He seemed not to hear her. "I walked my mount back to the boy and looked down at the shameful work I'd done. I wanted to disappear, to be shed of the war, but I couldn't desert."

Isabella began to sob. "Clayt, why are you telling me this?"

His eyes held on her with a fierce desperation. "I don' want you thinkin' I'm any better'n I am."

She pressed closer to his leg and stifled her crying. "I know who you are, Clayt. It doesn't matter about your past. I know who you are now." She pulled the knot of their bloody hands to her lips and kissed the skin over his knuckles. When she looked up again, a smear of blood painted her lower lip.

He reached behind the cantle and pulled out the old orange blanket he had hastily stuffed under his saddlebags. Gripping the material at one edge with both hands, he tried to tear it, but he hadn't the strength.

From his trouser pocket he produced a folding knife and flipped it open with a thumbnail. After cutting a few inches into the edge, he closed the knife and pocketed it.

"Take a hold o' this end an' help me rip it."

Together they pulled, and the blanket tore with a sound like a darting bee. He folded the smaller piece and forced it under his waistband to press against the wound. She put her hand on his and helped push against the flow of blood.

"Please, Clayt," she pleaded. "A doctor could help you."

He shook his head. "It's no good, Isabella.

Cain't no doctor fix this. Only thing I know to do is go after the man who done all this killin'."

When she started to argue, he leaned down through the pain and kissed her, tasting his own blood on her lip. At first she remained as stiff as a mannequin in a store window. Then she hooked one hand on the back of his neck and pressed so hard, her teeth clicked against his own. When he straightened, the pain eased off.

"I'm sorry this place brung you so much misery, Isabella. But I'm proud you came. I learnt some things from you."

From the street a horse and rider came on fast and slowed for the turn into the alley. "Clayt!" Nestor began as he reined up. "Whatta you wanna do?"

Clayt sat erect in the saddle and dredged up his foreman's voice. "I want you to git Lou and a few o' the boys to join me. We're gonna track this fellow." He pointed to the tracks leading past the post office.

Nestor winced and hitched his head back toward the livery. "Lou got shot, Clayt." He raised one boot and patted his calf. "Right here." He toed back into the stirrup. "It ain't too bad." He frowned at Clayt's midsection. "What 'bout you? You aw-right?"

"I'm fine," Clayt said and began backing

away his horse. "Go an' find that Pinkerton man — Hester. He'll wanna be in on this. An' Johnny Waites, too. Just follow my tracks. Can you do that?"

When Nestor gathered his reins, his face was set with purpose, and he looked half again his age. "Damn right I can. We'll catch up to you, Clayt." He turned his horse but hesitated as his worried eyes checked the spread of blood at Clayt's midsection.

"Go on now!" Clayt said.

Nestor's cow pony leapt into a gallop and hurried back toward the livery. Clayt paused to look at Isabella one last time. The silent exchange lasted no longer than three heartbeats, but it seemed that time had stopped for them.

"I reckon now you know who I am," he said. "But I can tell you I'm a better man for knowin' you."

Despite the tears flowing from her amber eyes, she managed to smile. "I know you," she whispered. "I feel as if I've always known you." She sniffed wetly and wiped her cheeks with her fingertips. "I always will."

He leaned again, holding his face expressionless as the pain cut through his abdomen with a searing burn. When they kissed this time, the touch of their lips was like a snowflake alighting on an upturned face. Then he reined around in a sharp pivot and tapped the heel of his good leg into Skitter's flank.

"Let's go, girl," he whispered as he leaned low over the withers. "We got some time to make up."

CHAPTER 34

The tracks led him due west over the bridge and then turned south along the river past the railroad trestle. After only fifty yards the trail turned abruptly down the riverbank and disappeared into the water. On the far side of the stream, the smooth sandy bank was undisturbed. Clayt looked upstream and down, seeing no signs on either side of the river. He adjusted his cartridge belt to apply constant pressure to the compress over his gut wound. Beneath him Skitter blew and shifted her weight.

"How're you holdin' up, girl?" he said and stroked the dapple-gray's neck. Skitter nickered and turned her head enough for him to see one lackluster eye. She blew again and walked down to the water where she drank. He, too, was dry. His mouth tasted of bile and felt as parched as the arid land around him. Unscrewing his canteen he rinsed his mouth and spat off to the side.

Then he drank what was left of his supply.

Considering the kind of man he was trailing, Clayt returned to high ground and backtracked upstream past the trestle, following the unexpected turn. At the bridge the pilings sunk into the river bed showed clinging beads of water creeping down the post from two feet above the surface of the river. The roan had splashed its way upstream past the piling.

At the next grove of cottonwoods he reined up to study the shady bank below him. The mud along the shoreline was churned up like a buffalo wallow. A horse had mired there and struggled to free itself. He spotted where the man had gone afoot and tugged on the animal. Both sets of tracks gouged deep holes into the slope and climbed at an angle to the floodplain on which he now sat his horse.

Fighting the pain that was trying to distract his senses, Clayt picked up the assassin's tracks and headed northwest. When he crested the low summit that marked the edge of the Laramies, he caught sight of a rider a quarter mile distant on the long, open prairie that separated these hills from the Medicine Bows. Clayt eased his horse down into a coulee to watch.

The man sat tall in the saddle, pushing

his mount, but the horse fought him, jerking its head against the pull of the reins, crow-hopping, and breaching gaits. When the animal settled, Clayt saw that it limped with every push off its left rear leg.

"There you are, you son of a bitch," Clayt mumbled. "And your horse is lame."

As he watched, the tall man lashed at the roan's flank with the tail of the reins. The ailing horse dug in and slid with a spray of dust. Sidestepping into the brush, it pivoted a full circle before the man could regain control, and in that turn the white blaze on the roan's muzzle had shone like a bright blink of light.

When the rider's back was turned to him again, Clayt urged Skitter forward onto level ground, the horse settling into a lope, though wheezing and a little stiff legged as though the muscles in her legs were trying to freeze up. But Clayt could feel her heart in it. She had set a fair pace, and he knew it was all she could do. Bracing on the pommel he kept himself anchored in the saddle, occasionally posting in the stirrups when the jarring ride brought a bright bolt of pain to his midsection.

The two horsemen settled into a common rhythm, the distance between them slowly shortening on the otherwise empty plain.

Expecting Skitter to collapse at any moment, Clayt slid free the Henry rifle and balanced it across his blood-soaked lap. Sliding his left boot from the stirrup, he resigned himself to killing the man. If that meant taking a tumble and sighting on the man's back at two hundred yards, then so be it.

When the tall man rounded a low dome-shaped hill and went out of sight, Clayt turned up a cattle track that cut a corner on the roan's course. Emerging from a shallow coulee, Clayt found that he and Skitter had closed the distance by a third.

When the assassin-rider veered north from the coming bluffs, he chanced to twist around, his face flashing in the sun. Even at that distance, Clayt could see the anger in his eyes. The tall man tried to force the roan off the trail, but the horse resisted and plunged into an apron of shrubs bristling at the base of a rocky knoll.

When the man reined up on the other side of the knoll and pulled his rifle from its scabbard, Clayt kicked his heels into Skitter's ribs and charged the hill from seventy yards out. Sitting in the saddle the tall man fared poorly in settling his horse, but he pulled off a shot anyway. The bullet flew wide. Clayt sheathed his rifle and pulled his pistol, extending it before him just as he had done with Nathan Forrest and his men when they crossed open ground to meet the enemy.

The tall man jumped down from the roan to set up for a freestanding shot, the reins still held in one hand. The roan bucked and tried to pull away from him, limping through the scrub brush and towing its human cargo. This time when he sighted through his scope he aimed low, and Clayt knew that Skitter was the target. But the roan tried to bolt and spoiled the aim, and this shot kicked up dirt beside Clayt. The man pulled on the reins, digging in with his boots, applying all his weight to drag the horse to a halt. Then the horse spun to face him and tugged backward with neck and muzzle stretched forward, braying like a mule.

When the reins slipped from the man's hands, he turned to Clayt, dropped to one knee, and took aim, this time his arms locked into a steady brace. Thirty yards away Clayt laid the reins over and at full gallop coaxed Skitter to the right of the knoll. The shot cut the air so close that Skitter shook her head and whinnied, her mane whipping and flowing like hair gone weightless under water. When they rounded the knoll and slowed to a walk, Clayt saw the tall man running, having already covered most of the distance to a jumble of boulders at the base of the bluffs. There the assassin could take cover and lay down carefully aimed fire.

Clayt urged Skitter forward, but she balked. Wheezing and coughing, she stabbed her legs stiffly at the ground, but soon she stopped. He leaned down over her neck, stroking her, pressing the side of his face into her mane.

"You done good, girl," he said hoarsely. "Can you just walk it? 'Cause I cain't."

The horse staggered forward, her breaths labored and congestive. Each step jarred and threatened to be the last. But she pushed on. When the tall man reached the boulders, Clayt lost sight of him. Then the man was in the open, scrambling up an embankment toward a dark fissure in the bluff. If he made it to that recess — if it was deep enough — this duel would become a waiting game, and Clayt knew that he had no time for such a contest. Holstering his Colt's, Clayt snatched up the Henry, levered a round, and took a bead on the man crawling toward the dark asylum above.

When he squeezed off the shot, the man yelped and slid back down several feet. He remained there balled up for several seconds. When he began climbing again, his motions were frantic, one leg trailing uselessly behind him.

When Clayt fired off another shot, the bullet plucked at the man's gray duster, kicked up rock dust, and whined away. The desperate man became more animated and slithered into the crevice like a snake. Now he was gone from sight.

Knowing his Henry could never outmatch the man's Whitworth, Clayt sagged over Skitter's neck and urged her closer to the bluff. Progress was slow, dreamlike. Together man and horse breathed a ragged cadence. Looking at the bluff before him, Clayt didn't know how he would scale that slope — just that he would.

When Skitter's front leg folded, Clayt was almost unseated by the jolt, but she caught herself. He lay all his body weight forward, the pommel digging into his gut, keeping him aboard. Pain spread from the center of him to every part of his body. His arm hung limp, but his grip on the Henry was eternal.

"Little farther, girl," he coaxed.

When they were a dozen yards from the base of the bluff, the long barrel of the scoped rifle emerged from the cave. Growling against the pain, Clayt pushed himself upright, seated the rifle stock into his shoulder, aimed, and fired. A spray of white dust jumped across the shadow of the narrow cave, and right away the Whitworth's report echoed his. When the sounds faded, nothing was changed. There was only wind. And sun. And the rise of the bluff and the broad prairie that rolled away behind him. The whole of the land seemed too expansive, too carefully integrated by God's own hand to mark the passing of these two men and their folly.

Skitter stumbled and fell, the front legs folding first, then the rear collapsing so heavily that Clayt was thrown backward. The swiftness of the fall brought a swirl of dark spots to the back of his eyes — like a distant flock of crows swirling inside his head. His body arched backward against the horse's rump, and from there he slid to the ground.

When his vision cleared, all he saw was the great slate of blue sky. He tried to assess his body. Every part of him seemed loose and disconnected from the whole. With his back pressed against the earth, he turned his head to see Skitter lying on her side, her back to him, her breathing coming in deep, labored gasps. She had fallen on his dropped rifle, and all her weight was on it, only the rear of the stock showing. It was just inches from his reach, but it may as well have been a mile. He needed the Henry to finish this job, and so he fought to remain a part of this world a little longer.

Gripping his left hand on the saddle horn he pulled himself closer to Skitter, her great barrel chest like a protective wall shielding him. His view of the cave was partially obstructed by the boulders, which meant the man would have to stand in the entrance to get off a shot.

Turning his head, Clayt looked east at the empty prairie. He wondered how long it would take for Nestor and the others to track him. He hoped someone might spot the roan loose on the prairie, but he could not see in what direction it had wandered off.

Turning back to Skitter he laid his hand upon the mare's neck and stroked the warm, silky coat and spoke to her with quiet, reassuring words, simply letting her know that he was near. She tried to lift her head, but the big, flat cheekbone fell heavily back to the dirt.

"Easy, girl. You done all you could. Just rest easy now."

Between the heaving spasms of her breathing, she nickered weakly, and the effort seemed to come at a price. Now as she sucked in air, she moaned with each exhalation, the sound so full of misery that Clayt's heart tightened in his chest. Grabbing a fistful of mane, he drew closer and pressed his face into the back of Skitter's neck. Tears filled his eyes, and his throat hardened. It was as if a smooth stone had lodged there, blocking any words he might wish to speak.

Reaching to his hip he felt for the Colt's, slid it free, and positioned it before him. Taking it in both hands, he tried to steady the barrel. Lying on his side he cocked the gun and brought it to bear on the horse's skull. Through his blurred vision, he fixed his eyes on the fine hairs at the base of her ears, but he saw a parade of images run through his mind: stealing the young mare from a Yankee corral at night in Chattanooga; clutching her tail as the two swam across the Mississippi; crossing the broad swath of plains that had led to Wyoming; patrolling the Rolling F to look for signs of rustlers or renegade Sioux; riding nightherd with the cattle.

Skitter's breathing worsened, and Clayt forced resolve into the steadiness of his hands. A sudden calm came over him, and he fired off the shot. The report traveled along the face of the bluff like thunder rippling across the prairie.

Skitter made no response but to settle into permanent repose. She seemed to lie heavier on the ground, as if the certainty and finality of this resting place had given her the ballast of eternity.

We had a good go, he tried to say, but his throat was tighter still, and his voice emerged as a broken whisper of air.

The rifle discharged from above, not the crisp sound of a gun going off in open country, but hollow, echoing from the interior of the cave. The yowling screech of a cat issued from deep in the fissure, and Clayt raised his head to see the tall man backing out of the entrance, desperately working the breech on the Whitworth.

Clayt's head collapsed to the dirt, the pistol still clutched in his hands. When he raised his head again, he caught sight of a blurred movement of tawny fur at the entrance to the cave. The feline scream that followed was like the shriek of a crazed woman, rising in pitch and then dropping into a wet and guttural growl — a deep, muffled sound that eventually drowned out the hoarse cries of the tall man.

Clayt let his head rest on the ground. He didn't know how much time had passed before the painter stepped into his line of vision. The cat approached and lowered its head, its amber eyes locked on him with an intensity he had not seen since the war. But the color was familiar. They were Isabella's eyes.

Didn' reckon I'd be seein' you ag'in. Clayt closed his eyes, not sure if he had thought the words or spoken them. When he opened his eyes, he watched the painter back away, moving toward the bluff.

Clayt released the Colt's and let his head roll so that he looked up into the endless blue of the sky. He felt himself go light, as though already he were relinquishing any claim on his body. He knew that he was no longer involved with this world. He was turned outward from it, facing some other-worldly direction that could not be measured by any means known to him.

When he heard a scraping sound from the bluff, he turned his head enough to see the big cat pulling the tall man's body into the cave. The last movement he saw was the man's boots rocking from side to side as they disappeared into darkness.

The pain in Clayt's body seemed to leach out of him and sink into the earth, leaving him in a free state of comfort he had never before experienced. His hands went cold. Then his arms. His feet and legs were next.

With numbed fingers, he pulled what was left of the alder-dyed blanket from his saddle and tried to cover himself, but he realized there was no suffering in this coldness. He was simply fading. Comfort no longer figured into his story. He lay there, content to look up into the stunning blue of the sky.

He had heard others speculate about death . . . about a life flashing before a dying man's eyes. What came to Clayt was the sum of those little things that made up the chain of events in a working day at the Rolling F. Herding the cattle. Telling Mr. Aff what his crew could do and then keeping his word on it. Riding all night to get into town and back to spend a sweet night with Tessa. The feel of the morning when he lifted up the saddle and fitted it to Skitter's strong back. Lou. Chalky.

And Isabella.

He remembered the sanctity of choosing the words he spoke to her. The pure music of listening to her talk. The airy flame of indigo that rose from the prairie at twilight and gathered all things into one common meaning inside its transitory color.

When he opened his eyes, he lay inside the long band of shadow cast by the bluff. The sun had sunk below the ridge this one last time. He turned his head to look east toward town, but of course all he could see was prairie, now infused with its twilight indigo. The color spread all around him, extending as far as his eye could see. As it always did, the soft hue of blue seemed to rise from the earth itself, but this time he knew that he was more than an observer. Skitter, too. They were both a part of this light . . . and would be forever.

He closed his eyes, and, when he did, the color stayed with him. The indigo had waited for him, he knew. It had always waited for him.

EPILOGUE

The sun had not been long over the Laramies. For most of the early morning service the eastern sky had been burnished with burnt orange and streaks of crimson. Lou had set the time for the ceremony, because he knew that Clayt had favored this hour. It was the time he had spent with the horses.

Isabella and Tom stood on the knoll of grass between the two stones, the boy with both arms wrapped around his mother's waist and looking at the fresh grave positioned parallel to the other one. It was her fourth funeral in the span of a few weeks — Chalky, her brother, her husband, and now Clayt.

The woman gazed out over the valley, seeing nothing in particular but sensing the whole of the land. The boy's raw eyes were clamped shut. The wind carved around their solitary form, marking mother and son as one. That wind seemed to whisper from the vastness of the territory of the transient lives that passed through the land.

The stone markers were nearly identical, only their chiseled letters setting them apart. This difference mattered little, for neither man could have read them.

No one had remembered Chalky Sullens's birth date or the place of his origin. Chalky had never talked of himself unless asked, and few had asked. His was a simple epitaph — just a name and the year of his passing. Lou had said, if you had known the man, it was enough. Chalk would have wanted nothing more.

Everyone knew Clayt had hailed from Georgia, but no man better fit the Wyoming Territory than he, so Grady had hammered into the native stone words to that effect. That and the two dates defining his time in the world.

Clayton Jane–A Wyoming man–1849-1876.

Nestor stood alone and watched the changes of color in the sky. Johnny Waites sat in the wagon with Short-Stuff on the seat next to him. Harry, Whit, and G.T. stood under the lone gnarled oak and quietly talked.

At the grave, Lou leaned on his crutches with Clayt's rolled blanket draped over his shoulder. Then he swung around and started for the wagon but stopped after only a few yards. He turned to Mrs. Walsh's back and the boy who clung to her. Lou removed his hat and thought to say something to both of them, but all he could do was stare.

She had been wearing her hair loose on her shoulders the last few days. Lou had noticed earlier how it had caught some of the fiery colors of the morning sky. As if she had heard his thoughts, she turned to him.

"He had an eye for color," she said and smiled. "Did you know that?"

"Ma'am?" Lou said and swung a step closer. Leaning on the crutches, he held his hat over his chest as if he were making a pledge. When she said no more and turned back to the grave, he worked his way beside the mother and son and waited.

"Do you know the indigo that comes at twilight?" she said. She looked at Lou, at the doubt that spread into his eyes. "Clayt said it rises from the prairie like a last breath before the sun goes down."

Holding a frown on his face, Lou looked down at the freshly turned earth and wondered how it was that he felt like a stranger here by this grave. He and Clayt had ridden together through every season and against every hardship that this land could throw at them. The two of them had learned from

561

Chalky everything a man needed to know if he was to make a go of it in this country, but at some point along the way, Lou knew, he had started learning from Clayt. And now it was time to take these lessons as his own and pass them along just as Clayt had. Maybe to this young English boy.

When Clayt made foreman, they had still been like brothers — Clayt the older, even though he was, by count, a year younger than Lou. Lou smiled, realizing that his time with Clayt had been more than learning. It was trying to be like him. The same as Nestor did. But standing here with Isabella Walsh, he suspected that a woman could know more things about a man than anyone, if that woman was the right one.

"Some o' us wanted to bury him in this old blanket o' his." Lou patted the tattered roll of wool draped over his torso. "He wouldn' sleep under nothin' else. Even in the bunkhouse." Lou shrugged. "But a few o' the boys figured it oughta go to you. So we struck a bargain." He pulled the remnant of blanket from his shoulder. "It was awready tore up some, so I cut it into halves." He nodded toward the grave. "One part we spread over Clayt." He held out the gift like a formal presentation. "This'n's for you."

It was the first time she had smiled in the

two days that had passed since the shootings. She took the gift, unrolled it, and pressed it to her breast. Her eyes closed, and she looked like the dawn incarnate. The boy reached up and stroked the blanket as if it were a living creature cradled in the mother's arms.

"We'd best head back, ma'am. We need to see to the cattle in the south pasture."

Her head pivoted only enough to show that she had heard him. The boy kept a grip on the blanket and gazed back at the grave. Lou looked down at his hat as he turned it slowly in his hands. He studied the grave marker and the words he had helped choose.

"Don't hardly seem enough," he said. He pointed with his hat toward the marker. "He was as good a man as I ever met." Lou waited to see if she would say something. After a long half minute he turned to go.

"Even with those demons that lived inside him," she said quietly.

Lou stopped and cocked his head. "Ma'am?"

Isabella faced him, turning the boy with her, though Tom lowered his gaze to the ground. "Did he talk to you about the war?" she asked. Absently, she combed the errant locks of her son's hair and smiled. "He was not much older than Tom," she mused. "It must have been a horrible time for him."

Lou let his hat hang down by the bandages on his leg, and he stared at the engraved stone. "I know'd him goin' on nine years and didn' have the first notion he'd fought in that war. Not till just recent, anyway."

She disengaged from the boy and turned to look out over the prairie, and this gave Lou a chance to study her profile. When she had announced to the men that she would stay to run the ranch, he had felt the uncertain plans for his future grow muddier with his doubts about her. He had leaned toward moving on. Now he was not so sure. Something in the lift of her chin . . . the solemn acceptance in her face as she paid tribute to this land that had shaped them all. It was hard to see in her any resemblance to her brother, but this burn in her eye might have rivaled Afton's first look at this valley.

She kept gazing out over the land. The dawn smolder of the grass and the scrub brush among the rocks were losing their muted tones and sharpening with definition. Far across the valley, a cloud of dust rose between two low hills, and the mustangs poured through the gap and charged out onto the plain. The woman saw them first, and then Lou and Tom followed her line of sight. There was no sound of hooves from that distance, which gave the animals a dreamlike presence as they streamed down the valley.

"Like water," she said quietly. "A river of horses."

No one spoke again as the herd raced across the landscape, angling for the Shin Bone. The horses disappeared into shadow beneath the bluff that marked the boundary of the Afton property.

Lou cleared his throat quietly. "You want I should take the boy now? You 'bout ready, Tom?"

The boy sagged against his mother and moaned. Straight away she bent and took the boy by his shoulders to better see his face.

"Thomas, stand up straight. Whenever you stand here next to Clayt, you show him how tall you are. Do you hear?"

The boy looked up at her with bleary eyes and sniffed. "Can't I stay with you?"

"Not this time." She pushed a lock of hair off his forehead. "Come help me unload before you go back with Mr. Breakenridge."

She walked to the wagon, and the boy followed. There they unloaded the easel and her boxes of paints and jars. She lifted the last item alone — the painting of Chalky's grave — and carried it to the easel.

Lou watched her on the knoll — the woman standing beside her easel, Clayt's blanket wrapped around her shoulders. As she looked around at the setting, Lou figured she was soaking up whatever it was artists could glean from a place. Wearing the orange blanket, she stood out like a lone flame on the prairie, probably visible for miles. It flew against all reason, leaving her out here alone, but somehow he felt she was safe. It was as if Clayt were there with her, telling her to keep that blanket close, and she would be all right. Lou climbed up on the seat next to Tom.

"Can I come, too?" Tom said. "When you come back for her tonight?"

"Sure can, pard," Lou said. And he found himself thinking about that indigo she had mentioned — that breath coming off the prairie at twilight. Maybe the boy and he could look for it together.

ABOUT THE AUTHOR

Mark Warren is a teacher of Native American survival skills in the Appalachian Mountains of north Georgia, where he lives with his wife, Susan. He is a lifelong student/historian of the Old West, a musician, and an archer.

Warren's published books include a memoir, *Two Winters in a Tipi* (2012), which chronicles the years he spent living in the primitive abode of the plains Indians; a historical fiction trilogy titled *Wyatt Earp, an American Odyssey,* which includes *Adobe Moon* (2017), *Born to the Badge* (2018), and *Promised Land* (2019); and *Secrets of the Forest* (2020), a four-volume comprehensive guide to primitive survival skills and plant lore.

The employees of Thorndike Press hope you have enjoyed this Large Print book. All our Thorndike, Wheeler, and Kennebec Large Print titles are designed for easy reading, and all our books are made to last. Other Thorndike Press Large Print books are available at your library, through selected bookstores, or directly from us.

For information about titles, please call:
  (800) 223-1244

or visit our Web site at:
  http://gale.cengage.com/thorndike

To share your comments, please write:
  Publisher
  Thorndike Press
  10 Water St., Suite 310
  Waterville, ME 04901